SO-DQY-967

FEAR*less*

This novel provides a harrowing account of how fear creeps into the lives of whole nations, taking over so gradually that it taints government policies and infects their citizens before they even realize it is there. Only the powerful drive to live and thrive can dispel it. But is the compelling all-win principle sufficient to stop the epidemic of fear that has most of the world in its grip?

The story opens in Maurice's sumptuous mansion on the idyllic Costa Rican shore where we meet Bertram, author and business consultant, recovering from a burnout. In his wallet, he carries a newspaper clipping about the elusive Eliza. He longs to meet her. Little does he suspect how many lives will eventually depend on their ability to work closely together.

Here, we also meet Pim, a prominent systems scientist who, with his peers at the U.N.'s University of Peace, seeks ways to halt the epidemic of fear.

Already fear is causing wholesale slaughter in the nation of Kukundu, gaining momentum in more than 100 dictatorships, and has almost imperceptibly secured a stranglehold on the "free" world. In the background lurk the Masters of Fear themselves, the Holy Order of the Snake, close to gaining control of our world.

When Mary with her crew of young people arrive at Maurice's mansion, it becomes clear that there is still a chance to stop the fear epidemic, if they each mobilize their extensive connections with young people and activists worldwide.

As we experience the heights to which the human spirit can soar, we recognize the amount of power that is available to "ordinary" people to heal the wounds that fear has caused. The narrative leads us to people at every level of society, ranging from Heads of State to kids living in the slums, from representatives of NGOs working at the U.N. to people camping in the jungles fighting in the underground resistance; and we become acquainted with the tools that we, too, can use to break through the confines of fear. For there are frightening parallels between the fear epidemic set in 2010 and conditions we are living in today.

This novel has valuable insights for businesspeople, educators, statesmen and women and all people confronted with the challenges of living in to-day's world. It provides an anatomy of fear and its resolution--both profoundly complex and yet compellingly simple once you know where to begin.

FEAR*less*

*Ordinary people doing extraordinary
things in a world gripped by fear.*

*For Virginia,
Thank you for the beautiful
intuitive way you lead the
group,
Love, Lisinka Ulatowska 10 Dec '05*

Lisinka Ulatowska

authorHOUSE™

*1663 LIBERTY DRIVE, SUITE 200
BLOOMINGTON, INDIANA 47403
(800) 839-8640
WWW.AUTHORHOUSE.COM*

This book is a work of fiction. People, places, events, and situations are the product of the author's imagination. Any resemblance to actual persons, living or dead, or historical events, is purely coincidental unless expressly mentioned.

© 2005 Lisinka Ulatowska. All Rights Reserved.

No part of this book may be reproduced, stored in a retrieval system, or transmitted by any means without the written permission of the author.

First published by AuthorHouse 08/29/05

ISBN: 1-4208-7858-1 (sc)

Library of Congress Control Number: 2005907879

Printed in the United States of America
Bloomington, Indiana

This book is printed on acid-free paper.

To my sister, Pamela Graham, for her sixtieth birthday

Where there are no roads,
we will open roads,
Where there is no light,
we will shine our light,
Where there is no love,
we will fiercely love,
Where there is no peace,
we will be that peace.

My brother and my sister,
the torch has been passed to us.
There is no more time for doubting:
we must live what we believe.
Take up your sword of truth
that others might be free.
And live every moment,
aware that we choose
for all that is to be.

And where there are no roads,
we will open roads.
Where there is no light,
we will shine our light.
Where there is no love,
we will fiercely love.
Where there is no peace,
we will be that peace.

(Song composed for the Rainbow Bird Duo by Terry Burke[1])

If you like this book, pass it along to a friend…

For information on how to order the book and request talks and workshops on related topics, see the end of this book: ADDENDUM III "Contact with Author".

List Of Contents

Introduction and Acknowledgements ix

FEAR*less:*
Ordinary people doing extraordinary things in a world gripped by fear. 1

ADDENDUM I
The Universal Declaration of Human Rights 309

ADDENDUM II
A Self-financing World Marshall Plan. A Supplementary Income For Each Woman, Man And Child 317

ADDENDUM III
Contact With The Author 325

Other Useful Contacts And Organizations 327

ENDNOTES 331

INTRODUCTION and ACKNOWLEDGEMENTS

Fear is rampant around me, as I sit down to write. I want to fly away to a world of adventure and take you, my readers, with me. Our trip is to be like a good vacation: one that breaks with our everyday patterns, stimulates our creative juices, and returns us with a fresh zest for life, the desire to roll up our sleeves, get on with the business of living, and enjoy every minute.

I want our vacation to take us to a world where science serves the wellbeing of people, where psychological and spiritual expertise is applied to everyday life; and where the joys of being connected to people from every corner of the globe outweigh what now seem to be overwhelming challenges. In other words, I want to whisk you away to a place where the human heart can soar, even when it is confronted with fear. This fantasy world is not unlike our own. In fact, it already exists. It is that aspect of our lives where we, instead of running away, face our fears and thrive in the process. We all have the potential.

Wherever we look, we can find people who dare to face what they fear most and in so doing are able to achieve the extraordinary. This book was inspired by such people who overcame limitations, not unlike our own.

Fear has many faces. It can be a healthy reaction to danger, which evaporates when the danger is past.

Fear can also be connected to how we see ourselves in comparison to other people. Such fears of failure, of rejection, of living a life without meaning can undermine our relationships with those around us. These "psychological" fears have often been with us from such an early age that we barely know they are there. Such feelings affect how we live our lives and what we do and do not achieve. They can lead to withdrawal from friendships, burnouts at work or violent behavior.

When these fears *unconsciously* rule our behavior, they can prevent us from living life to the full. When we allow them to rule us, our behavior can infect our families, organizations, businesses, and even the well-being of humanity as a whole. For with fear in the driver's seat, it is hard to make the most of life and help others to thrive, too.

Fear can also be used as a tool and a weapon to control other people. It fuels power struggles, conflicts, wars and dictatorships. It lies at the root of our raping of the environment and is responsible for myriad global problems. Just now, fear has led to a preoccupation with terrorism as a means to assert self and as a justification to usurp power. In our world, where boundaries are fast disappearing, individuals and groups are grasping for control.

In this novel, all these fears are seen as interconnected. They must be dealt with as a whole or else random chaos will take over.

In this novel, set in the year 2010, the fear epidemic is rampant in dictatorships and formerly democratic nations alike. I have mentioned those with a long democratic tradition by name to make the point that even these are not immune to a fear epidemic. Those countries portrayed with sweeping problems have been given fictitious names. It is not my intention to demonize any nation. Yet the atrocities described are daily occurrences in the year 2005.

It is also not my intention to demonize any people, whether political leaders, delegates at the U.N. or 'ordinary' citizens, no matter what the policies of their governments. At the United Nations, I have met so many brave men and women who have risked their lives by either leaving a government whose policies they could no longer support, or else continuing to work within repressive structures to try to change them from the inside.

The Holy Order of the Snake is wholly fictitious and so is everything mentioned in connection with the Snake. I stress: everyone and everything. I do believe that everyone contains the seeds of the full range of human potential.

The characters, which are described in this book, each struggle with fears of their own. Together, they face the challenge of disabling the fear epidemic, which has reached global proportions. These are people like you and I. In fact, although this book is fiction, both the characters and their actions are inspired by real people. Some I should like to mention here, for they are the rich fertile soil in which this novel could unfurl.

First, my thanks to Pamela and Buz Graham and Tomek Ulatowski whose generosity made it possible to take time off to write this book. They have accompanied me for most of my life's journey. Each contributes to the well being of large numbers of people. In addition, Buz helped me with many of the medical details. Many thanks also to Ruth and Robert Motz, my adopted parents, and my friends Lung and Wayne Ogle for their generosity. Lung also painstakingly proofread the whole manuscript with, in the latter stages, Wayne's input. I am extremely grateful to Terry Burke who meticulously and tirelessly toothcombed the manuscript, spending hours brainstorming with me to find the most accurate wording or concept and making a host of wonderful suggestions regarding themes and style.

Among the scientists, the political leaders, and the NGOs which have specifically inspired the substance of this novel ("how to" bring about constructive global change) a number of them have proofed various aspects of the novel for accuracy. Among them are first and foremost: Professor Dr. Ralph Abraham, expert in the field of chaos theory, who has deeply influenced my thinking and Prof. Dr. Ervin Laszlo, founder and President of the *Club of Budapest*. Dr. Laszlo proofed the whole of *Fearless* for accuracy from a scientific perspective. He also generously allowed me to quote passages from his most recent book[2], which further clarify how an epidemic of fear can both come about and then be transformed into all-win relationships.

Then my thanks to my friends and colleagues who have inspired the characters I write about. This work of fiction is spiced with true stories. Among the many, I should like to mention Pim van Monsjou, Secretary General of the All-Win Network, trusted friend and colleague. In consultation with Pim, I set out to develop the all-win principle in such detail that it could more easily be used as a tool by people in a wide range of fields.

Before I started to write, I phoned Mary Duffield to clarify some themes for my novel. When I hung up (was it several hours later?), Mary had become a central character.

Mary also read and commented on the manuscript. Her skills as an English teacher, her knowledge of ham radio and experiences with young people were invaluable. So, too, were the comments of my dear friends, Tony Earl, formerly of the Education Department (Afdeling Ontwikkeling van Onderwijs) at the University of Utrecht, and Henk de Boer, writer. Henk supplied the theme of the *reptilian brain*, has a vast store of ideas and insights at his disposal—and endless patience! He is always ready to brainstorm, think through a concept and help with matters relating to my computer.

Then there are my many NGO friends and colleagues, most of whom I know through the U.N. They embody the all-win principles in their personal lives and in the actions of their organizations. They exemplify values and practices emerging in civil society today. Their characters have been worked out in more detail in the sequel to this novel, published in Dutch under the title, *Samenzwering Samenspel*. Many thanks also to the readers of that novel who became students of the all-win principle, and members of all-win think tanks, education and action groups. Together, they have deepened my understanding of how the all-win principle can be applied. Of these, I shall mention only Terry Burke and Luci Narewski of the *Rainbow Bird* duo by name. They, too, play a part in the narrative. Moreover Terry supplied the words to the songs, sung in this novel.

Finally, I should like to thank all those whose teachings have made this novel possible. First my personal teachers: the late David Bohm and Jidu Krishnamurti, Vimala Thakar, Michael Exeter, the teaching staff of the International Emissaries, and the members of my doctoral Committee at what was then the Union Graduate School, now the Union Institute and

University, and of course, to the United Nation's, which I consider my political home and in whose Department of Public Information (then OPI) in 1969, I started my professional career.

For their contribution to the substance of this book, I should also like to thank: Dr. Rupert Sheldrake, Dr. Elisabet Sahtouris, Lynne McTaggart's book, *The Field*[3], Elissavet Stamatopoulou-Robbins of the U.N.'s Human Rights Department; and Organizations, including The World Women's Summit Foundation (WWSF), Global Education Motivators, the Social Venture Network and businesses which are taking steps to become more sustainable and are participating in Kofi Annan's Global Compact.

Last but not least, I should like to thank my parents, the late Tiny and Boy Wolsey, to whom I owe my life. They nurtured me and still inspire my thinking.

FEAR*less*

1. Mary Arrives

This Novel Is Set In The Year 2010.

"They're here!" The words wafted in through the large open windows.

Bertram craned his neck. He was just in time to glimpse Count Maurice Le Sage's back. He was pulling on a robe, worming his toes into his thongs, while half hopping, half running down toward the dock.

With a grin, Bertram saved the chapter he had been writing, sent it to his printer, and leaned back in his chair. "Done!" he said aloud with satisfaction.

Something had shifted. After his discussion with Maurice's nephew the night before, a young man whose life was so riddled by fear that it dominated every aspect of his being, Bertram now realized that fear was a huge social issue. In the world he lived in, fear ruled, he now realized. It was no longer his problem alone. He saw that just belonging to human society made you vulnerable to fear. If he did not deal with his own fear, it would keep running his life. Getting a handle on fear had now become his quest.

Was fear an accidental by-product of modern life? Or was something much larger, more sinister going on behind the scenes? For a second, he savored his renewed zest for life. Then he jumped up and hurried out through the terrace doors, curious as to the Count's impetuous behavior.

Maurice Le Sage was the oddball youngest son of a fabulously wealthy family, which, it was rumored, controlled the arms and pharmaceutical industries from behind the scenes via the highest echelons of a variety of secret societies. Maurice was the only one of the four brothers who did not shun publicity. He was committed to improving the lives of people in general and was known to open his home to anyone who had anything of value to contribute. For several days now, he had been eagerly awaiting the arrival of Mary Duffield who happened to be both his and Bertram's friend.

Now a sailing boat was just pulling in, white sails billowing in the wind. A flock of young people were on board, at the helm a frail little lady, thick, brilliant white ponytail blowing from under her cap.

"Mary Duffield!? She made it!"

Bertram sprinted after Maurice. As he ran, his thick, black hair ruffled in abandon. A lithe six foot two, but slightly out of shape, he still managed to catch up with the older man just as he arrived at the dock.

Immediately, they were surrounded by a dozen scantily clothed young people who looked as if, for months, they'd been living at sea. All different shades of tan, a colorful bunch, they were laughing, joking and horsing around, excited to have firm land under their feet.

"Hey, you guys, these are my friends Maurice and Bertram!" Mary called, her indomitable earthy self. Half a century ago, she had been suddenly widowed. Surviving a hurricane with only her newly born son, she had pledged she would devote her life to young people. *"Now 50 years later, she is still keeping that promise,"* Bertram reflected, still trying to catch his breath.

"Welcome to Costa Rica!" Maurice said jovially, the hint of French giving an exotic lilt to his voice.

The group flocked around.

"So, Skipper Mary, these must be your star performers -- all ham radio operators who have won a vacation at sea?"

"Vacation?!" A long legged 18-year-old laughed, blue eyes shining as she brushed sun-bleached strands of golden hair out of her eyes. " We sail the Peace Warrior 8 full hours a day -- weather permitting, of course. And when we're not needed to crew the boat, we are communicating with kids by ham radio who we plan to meet along the way!"

Suddenly all were laughing again and speaking at once:

"Mary and vacation, you must be kidding!"

"You should see how many schools we have visited! Every night a different one!"

"Mary actually has us practicing our Spanish when we have time to relax!"

"And when you're not pushing each other over board!" Mary bantered back.

"Not *what?*" Maurice exclaimed with mock surprise.

"Oh yes! You get these energy balls out to sea and soon the boat's too small. The only way to deal with them is to show them that the boat is like the world: too many people and too little room. Then we discover ways to respect one another's space."

"Mary lets us make our own rules!" A slender 15-year-old said, her dark, almond-shaped eyes wide to emphasize the importance of her statement.

"This is my friend. He's a writer and gives lectures all over the world!" Maurice gestured toward Bertram.

"Really?" a youngster of no more than 14 years old with large coal-black eyes asked, impressed, "What do you write about?"

Maurice looked at Bertram. "Business relationships mostly, would you say?" he asked.

"Actually, anything is grist for my mill. I'm an author suffering from writer's block and a speaker with little to say, enjoying a wonderful vacation, lazing on the beach."

"That bad?" Maurice chuckled. Seeing Bertram's dancing eyes, he added. "Something in you has lightened up, though."

"Well actually, I talked all night with your nephew," Bertram added, addressing the group. "When he left this morning early, I had the first chapter of my new book! Unfortunately, the hero's on the verge of suicide already. I need to prolong his life. So all ideas are welcome." Bertram tried to deliver his reply with a dead pan face, but failed. His mischievous smile, which irresistibly played his lips and his eyes, refused to be suppressed.

"Perhaps you'd like to see the play we've been performing while we've been on this trip?" one of the younger boys, a Scottish lad, suggested.

"Play!?" Maurice exclaimed. "Sure, I'll get Edward to prepare the theatre and make sure the stage lighting is working!"

"Told you, you were in for a first rate time, you guys! A real stage! Usually we perform in classrooms." Mary laughed at the exclamations of the group.

"Sounds like perfect timing as far as I'm concerned," Bertram smiled. "I'm looking for new ideas!

"Mary!!!" he changed the subject, "We were afraid they'd hold you up at the border.

They're refusing to let anyone out of the US who smacks of goodwill missions. They must have been blind to let guys like you out of the country who 'fraternize' with 'foreigners'." He smiled at the circle of eager young faces.

"It's the Un-American Activities witch hunt all over again!" Mary was suddenly serious, "Except now it's terrorists, instead of 'commies'."

"It happened so suddenly!" Maurice agreed. "Barely did your President scrape into office or every one's seeing a terrorist behind every bush! Never seen a series of governments do an about turn that fast: the US, the UK, Australia, now other Western nations, Russia --- so-called 'defending democracy' by hostaging our rights as citizens!"

"But it's wonderful you made it!" Maurice reached out and, in French fashion, kissed Mary on each cheek and then began shaking hands with each of the young people in turn.

Mary grinned. "Thank God, we're considered harmless if we're young or very old. What do you say, you guys?" But the young people were talking excitedly among themselves. So she continued, "It worked out well for us. We managed to get out of California and sailed all the way here without anyone giving us a hard time!"

"That's Mary for you," Bertram smiled, reaching out affectionately and giving her a hug. How tiny she felt under her bulky shirt and jeans. She looked sixty at most. Bertram knew she was in her eighties.

Where did this slim little lady find the energy to keep going? She taught classes, organized conversations among young people from every corner of the earth via ham radio, video and e-mail-conferences. And to top it all in the vacations, she sailed around with her students to visit schools in foreign countries![4] All this moved young people to foster relationships which "make the heart sing". This was her way of building world citizenship[5]. This took tremendous courage at times like these when so many were driven by fear. This so-called war on terrorism masked an even more sinister war by more and more governments on their own peoples. Associating freely and peacefully with whomever one wished and holding personal beliefs had become 'politically dangerous'. And Mary Duffield was championing personal freedom, which she called "I win, you win, we all win relationships". She encouraged each person to do and be whatever they themselves wished, as long as they didn't harm others. Bertram foresaw the day that this would be officially dubbed "treasonous".

"I'm sure you would all like to clean up and have a long, cool drink while Consuela prepares a buffet for you all," Maurice interrupted Bertram's thoughts and motioned the group toward his 'abode'.

The group needed no encouragement.

With excited exclamations they turned and hurried up the path toward the huge red tile mansion. Its stucco white walls peeked through a rich mantel of purple bougainvillea, the whole embraced by a generous ornate terrace.

"I love your garden. All these flowers!" a young lady hung back to talk to Maurice. With her fingers, she combed her short, ear-length, red hair back out of her face, disclosing merry blue eyes and a nose full of freckles.

"Yes, I have allowed this part to grow completely wild, Pat. Each of these plants was wafted here on the wind. I love to see how Nature brings so many different colors and shapes together and then transforms one masterpiece into another with each changing season!"

Bertram felt a rush of warmth for Maurice, Mary, and this group of rambunctious young people. He had been alone for too long, in fact most of his life, and, until this very moment, never wanted for more.

"The guest rooms are ready, Sir." A voice said, as they approached the terrace.

"Oh, thanks, Edward. Perhaps you can help to get our young friends settled in.

6

"Edward's been with my family as long as I can remember," he said as he introduced his butler to the group. "You'll meet Consuela later. She cooks famously and takes care of the house."

Bertram watched as the young people followed Edward, his ruler-straight back, his formal gait, his demeanor, carefully devoid of personal expression, a man who had spent his life honing his image and who prided himself on 'knowing his place'.

In hushed voices the young people commented on the period furnishings, the high ceilings and long burgundy-colored drapes. The long-legged blond was walking hand in hand with a well-built Japanese-looking 18 or 19 year-old. Although in coloring, they were opposites, in build and height they were similar.

The youngest were twins, a boy and a girl, with huge, coal black eyes. They were no older than fourteen years old, walking with them was a young boy with Native American features. Bertram looked at him more closely. He was walking with a stiff, slightly uncertain gait, unusual in one so young.

Mary walked up. Bertram hurriedly looked away, but Mary had seen him staring. "That's David with the twins, Jeff and Jan, he's one of our youngest crewmembers. He only just started as a ham radio operator and passed his exams with flying colors." She hesitated and then added quietly, "You are bound to notice, so I'd better tell you now: he's just been diagnosed with multiple sclerosis – really unusual in someone so young. Terribly debilitating disease. It can last for a lifetime; but very occasionally it's fatal and a person can die within a year..." For a moment a haggard looked crossed her face, then she continued, "He's terribly shy," she smiled fondly, "but he really wanted to come and we very much wanted him with us. Fortunately, the doctors said it would be alright. Being active and happy is the best possible medicine. He's a great sport and refuses to give in to the disease."

Mary was about to follow the youngsters when Maurice held her back.

"There was a message for you from a John St. Clair. Said it was extremely urgent."

Mary turned around, surprised. "Last time I heard from John he was on his way to Kukundu to lecture on peaceful conflict resolution. That was at least a year ago. Surely, he's not still there!"

"Yes, he actually called from there!"

"Is he in danger?" Mary asked, sharply drawing in her breath.

Maurice hesitated.

"He's in the country and in hiding and badly needs your help, Mary. From what I hear, the situation in Kukundu has become untenable since General Kundana came to power. The whole country's in danger of being slaughtered in a rampage of murder, and outside the country, nobody wants to be bothered."

"Oh no! How can we reach him?" Mary asked in alarm.

"He said he was heading out to a jungle village and would try to reach you when he could call without giving away his whereabouts.

"John's looking to reach as many people in Kukundu as possible. Apparently people are so divided against one another and afraid that they can't imagine that things can ever be turned around. Hopes your young people's network can help."

"If the rest of the world hasn't managed so far --sounds as if he's grasping at straws!" She looked anxious. Suddenly, she smiled, "No harm in trying! These young ones're constantly surprising me. Who knows what they are capable of?"

2. Frightened

Far from Costa Rica, in a tiny jungle village in the war-torn land of Kukundu, things had come to a head. Pierre was frightened. He could barely think. He was trapped. There was no way out that he could see.

As he cowered in the corner of their hut, the diatribe on the radio reverberated through his head, *"The Mandus are corrupting the Kukundu tribe. Kill them to prove that you are a patriot."*

Suddenly his wife and two children had become official enemies of the State. And he, Pierre, was implicated for consorting with them. All he had done was marry Augustina, a perfect match - bright, cheerful, tall, voluptuous, a perfect mother for his children. And she had born him a healthy boy and a year later a girl. How lucky he had felt!

In the distance, a drum began beating out the message, spreading it to those who lived deep in the jungle, *"The Mandus are corrupting the Kukundu tribe. Kill them to prove that you are a patriot."*

Outside the laughter, yapping, and the delighted shrieks of his children. Damn them for making so much noise! Now aged three and four, they were indomitable, driven by a need to explore. This morning it was that mangy puppy, which had come drifting into the village. But there was no way of hiding them. Every one knew where they lived.

Pierre was torn. Should he box their ears? Or should he take them in his arms? There was so little time left. In the end, he didn't move. He couldn't. He was paralyzed by fear.

The solo drum was joined by another. And then in the distance their refrain was picked up by yet other drums. *"The Mandus are corrupting the Kukundu tribe. Kill them to prove that you are a patriot."*

There was no way out.

If only he could have foreseen all this on that infernal night his neighbor had made his proposition!

"Fifty Kukundu dollars if you canvass for General Kundana!"

"Fifty Kukundu dollars? Where'd that kind of money come from?" Pierre had asked.

"Oh, I have my connections…"

"But what about Daddy M'Bwene? He's been our President for years. Every one loves him.

Why go for Kundana? Kundana can't possibly win!"

"Kundana has contacts with wealthy companies. They could help us become rich!

"Fifty Kukundu dollars!" his neighbor insisted, "That's a week's wages!"

Pierre was apolitical. Buffooning with his kids, helping Augustina with household chores, every now and again, interrupting her passionate study of philosophy for a very brief romp with himself and the children – these to Pierre had been the spice of life. Yes, his family was everything to Pierre. Augustina and he had always been close, dedicated to caring for one another and enlivening the humdrum with fun.

"No problem!" he gave in to his neighbor.

He'd earned the 50 Kukundu dollars all right. But Kundana had lost the election. The sitting President, M'Bwene, nicknamed Daddy and universally beloved by his people, won a landslide victory. But the very next day, there was an announcement, "M'Bwene has been ousted. He's ceded his power to General Kundana!"

Every one was shaken up, but there was nothing they could do. When finally they heard that M'Bwene was safely abroad and campaigning to become reinstated, Kundana was already in firm control, backed by the army and a number of generals. In fact, the very day Kundana had become President, things had changed unrecognizably.

First, the prominent Mandus were demoted for 'treason', one after another. Then, because so many Mandus were "caught plotting the regime's downfall", a national emergency was announced and all Mandus were stripped of their rights.

Then, one day a Mandu had been stopped and robbed in the streets. Every one knew who the robbers were: a band of thugs who were in and out of jail. But the judiciary ruled against the Mandu. The bandits were acquitted. They had 'acted in self-defense'.

Gradually, robbing Mandus became a national pass-time. Every time the Kukundus were acquitted and the Mandus got the blame.

At first, Pierre had been horrified. He was deeply afraid that people would attack him because he had a Mandu wife. And yet he loved Augustina and could not think of living without her. He realized that if he ever were accused, he would need a great deal of money to "talk his way out of the situation".

Rough voices, shouts, screams now penetrated his mental fog. Pierre was jolted back to the present. The militia were approaching, rooting out the remaining Mandus. There was no way out with the drums beating out their murderous refrain: *"Kill them to prove that you are a patriot!"*

Oh dear God, what can I do? Augustina was visiting her mother. *Please let her stay away.* He loved his family and yet, they were placing him in an impossible situation. Life with them was coming to an end.

Surely, he had proved himself. He had helped to weaken the Mandu tribe. He hadn't put up any resistance when his neighbor propositioned him again.

"We're planning a raid," his neighbor had said and mentioned a wealthy Mandu family who lived at the far side of their village.

"So far these people have always been able to buy their way out of any court proceedings. They've pots of cash. You've nothing to lose. The police are on our side. After all, we're Kukundus! It would prove that you still support President Kundana and I'm sure you can use the cash, in case they see you are married to ---"

That had cinched it.

Frantically, he now tried to banish the shouts and screams as the militia approached.

Perhaps the cash he had saved from that raid and all those that followed would make it possible for him to buy his way out of what now they wanted him to do. He had robbed the Mandus and physically hurt them whenever he could. It relieved his guilt and anger at Augustina and the children for placing him in danger. And the fact that he loved them only compounded his confusion and pain.

Surely the militia would excuse him, surely... surely they would realize... The panic clutched at his throat and sending his thoughts into a spin, furled his mind in a mental fog.

When the thumps on the door finally came, he got up. Like a zombie, he picked up his machete and went out into the yard.

3. In Trouble

The young people had washed and rested up. They'd had had a sumptuous lunch, prepared with that extra touch of caring, which was Consuela's hallmark.

Bertram was reveling in the sparkle and fun, which surrounded Mary and her crew.

He and Maurice were sitting at either side of Mary in the comfortable little theatre.

Mary turned to Maurice. "They're so enthusiastic, they can't think about anything else than showing their play. Usually they perform for kids their own age. It's a big thing for them to be performing for adults! In this play, they really open themselves up. Quite remarkable coming from kids this age!"

Behind the scenes, muted by the heavy burgundy and gold curtains, there was the sound of laughing and chatting and furniture being dragged off the stage.

Edward, with great deference, was showing a small group how the projector, the lights, the curtain, and the various backdrops worked. "You can't use the sound system, I'm afraid. That's wired up to the family's many business centers." His tone indicated that he had no views on the matter.

"In Costa Rica?" Takeshi asked.

"No, they're all over the world, sir! Voice and visual messages come in and are automatically relayed out. State of the art equipment, I'm told. I can't change the settings. Not my place. But you'll find that the acoustics are excellent, sir. It's only a small theatre."

Consuela hovered near the door

"Come and join us," Maurice called.

She came over. "No offense, sir. I have scones baking in the oven."

The lights went out in the auditorium.

Then, lit by a spot, the long legged blond appears.

"This play is a sort of a Morality Play like they had in the Middle Ages. It shows our philosophy of life. It also shows what we've been through.

"At the same time, it's not like a Morality Play at all. To put it in a nutshell: we believe that people have tremendous possibilities if only they can follow their own hearts. In fact, this saved our lives."

Bertram's heart sank a little. He didn't feel like being preached at. He was here to rest.

"This is a true story," Annette continued, "For the most part, every one portrays themselves. My name is Annette. I'm an exception. I am both the narrator and later I play the role of our teacher, Mrs. Gladstone.

"The first scene may shock you. Yet these incidents actually happened. Corps Elite High School has high academic standards, but as the play opens, human kindness is hard to find.

"May I first introduce you to Ian MacDonald?"

The lights go out. A desk light comes on, illuminating the face and hands of a 16 year-old Scottish lad. He's typing away at a laptop. On the backdrop, the hands of a clock are projected. It's midnight. The hands move around: one o'clock, two o'clock. As the hands reach three, his typing slows down; every now and again he dozes off. By four, he is slumped over, fast asleep. At six, a man's voice shouts from back stage. "Ian! Ian! Come downstairs immediately! You got an A-minus! You're grounded. Do you hear?"

Ian jumps to his feet. "Oh father, please, I have to go to the school dance! I have my very first date! Please... I promise I'll make it up. Please, let me go. Please, father!"

"No!"

Darkness.

Bertram heaved a big sigh. He'd give anything to be baking in the sun. The scene reminded him of his recent self. Working ever-longer hours as this "high-powered" business consultant. His job: to help top executives access their full personal power by helping them to overcome their fears: fear of failure, fear of success, fear of too much responsibility. *Fear of globalization* was his specialty. That had placed him in the spotlight and catapulted him to fame.

His profession until then had consisted of asking people *why-questions* -- "*Why* do you not enjoy your work any more?", "If you're so burnt out, *why* then don't you take a vacation?" "*Why* are you sure that Brown will take over your position when your back is turned?" *Why? Why? Why?* Until finally the top executives would have rationalized away any feelings they may have had.

Then at the height of his success, three executives had called him within the space of a few days. Two said their fears were back with a vengeance. One had no feelings at all. All three were taking extreme measures to change their emotional discomfort. One had taken up hair-raising sports: bungy jumping, cliff hanging, "Anything to regain some sort of feeling." The other two, to deaden their fears, resorted to booze, drugs, TV, barely aware of what they were seeing. Then other complaints started to come in. It was clear that his approach was nothing but a "quick fix". In the long run, his approach was breaking down.

Fear gripped him. He began working day and night to perfect his approach. But other failures followed. He now knew his approach was flawed, but could not see where. He was terrified he was about to lose everything he had dedicated most of his life to building. Finally, too tired to think straight and too numbed to feel, he resorted to the same extreme means used by his executive clients: First it was ballroom dancing, *every night.* Then booze, drugs and finally when neither helped, a series of sex-more-than-love relationships. Anything to *feel,* to get in touch with his power. Women had always been attracted to him, and now superficial liaisons became his thing. Day after day, he would stagger out of bed, put on his suit and tie and pretend everything was fine until he had had to ask himself: "Is this all life is about? Do I want to go on at all?" *Burnout,* the condition was called.

Just as he realized he could not continue, he had bumped into Maurice and accepted his invitation to stay at his mansion to rest and perhaps write another book.

Until this morning, he had felt powerless to turn his life around. He had never been gripped by such fear before. He had always loved challenge, taken life by the horns. Now he was cowering in an earthly paradise, not knowing where to turn. This morning it had hit him. He was suffering from a widespread human condition, one of the many faces of fear that was increasingly haunting humanity. There was no one but himself to turn to. And meet the challenge he would! But that would not be easy.

"That same morning, Sharifa enters the school yard," Annette's voice penetrated his thoughts.

The sound of the curtains opening in the background.

Just one spot. In it, Sharifa, her almond shaped eyes, wide, looks very small and vulnerable.

"Here I stand terribly afraid and alone and don't know where to go."

"Look, Sharifa," Annette comments from back stage, "Here come Pat, Molly and Antonia".

The stage lights go on. Pat and Molly, busily chatting and giggling, with Antonia, trying to keep up with the others, desperate to look as if she's "one of the group". Antonia is younger than the other two and at the awkward stage when young people seem at odds with their own arms and legs. Her dark hair and eyes give her a Latin American look. While Pat and Molly are budding young women, Antonia is still a child.

Sharifa asks, "Excuse me, could you tell me where I can find a teacher? I arrived from Malaysia yesterday."

Antonia looks away shyly allowing the others to speak.

"Malaysia? Ugh! Sounds like the boonies to me," Molly says. Pat and Molly snigger and Antonia giggles, looking as if she wished she were elsewhere.

"Get that outfit at a fancy dress party or does it come from Malaysia, too?" Pat asks. Bertram is surprised that this could be the same red-haired young lady with the cute freckled face who was so taken with Maurice's flowers. Pat and Molly snigger again. Antonia, still giggling, turns around and looks determinedly at something in the distance. Anything, so as not to have to see the discomfort of the young newcomer.

"Who are you anyway to barge in on us like that?" Pat asks belligerently. Antonia's giggles are like a spasm. "Oh, look here comes Nerd!" She blurts out, relieved, as Ian walks into the schoolyard.

Molly and Pat leave Sharifa standing there. Antonia tries to keep up with them as they walk away, giggling uproariously.

Ian's shoulders are hunched, his eyes fixed on the ground as if he wishes he could disappear.

Annette explains, "Until Pat, Molly and Antonia met one another, they were each teased for getting poor grades. Now they find strength in one another's company. Their motto: *Attack before others attack you and don't let anyone drive a wedge between you and your friends.*

"Like Sharifa, they are afraid."

Sharifa starts in Ian's direction but draws back as a macho teenager swaggers up. He wears hip-hugging jeans, shirt open to the waist, and a gold medallion dangling from his neck.

Annette explains, "This is Arturo. Every one's afraid of him. He pushes drugs and outside school, he leads a gang of thugs."

"Hey, how're you doin'," Arturo greets Ian.

Ian looks up, surprised at the friendly tone.

"Looking down in the mouth! Here!" He fishes in his pocket and takes out a small envelope. "Sniff it! You'll feel better," he says almost kindly.

"But I don't have any money!" Ian blurts out.

"It's a gift, okay? Next lot you get to pay for."

Ian turns to the audience. "That was the first time I ever took drugs. After that I became one of Arturo's regular customers. I continued to work hard at school, but when I wasn't working, I would speed up or else mellow out. I went through detox many months later."

"You can't do that!" Annette's tall Japanese friend runs up and grabs Arturo by the arm. "This is Takeshi," Annette introduces him.

14

Arturo laughs scornfully and says, "See if I can't!" with a sharp jolt he frees himself from Takeshi and swaggers off.

Takeshi turns to Ian and tries to argue with him, but shoving the package into his pocket, Ian flees.

Sharifa recoils from the scene and bumps into Winston who comes ambling up.

"With Sharifa, Winston is one of the heroes of this scene," Annette explains, "As you see, he is the school's token black. He is shunned by the others. He also has difficulty following classes because his elementary education was in one of the poor schools in an all black section of town."

"Alright?" Winston catches Sharifa gently.

"Watch out, Winston!" Annette warns over the microphone, "Here comes Hugh!"

A tall blond 17-year-old grabs Winston and kicks at his shins. "You don't ever beat me at tennis again, understood?" And he kicks him again and again!

With a cry, Winston sinks to the ground.

"You're breaking his leg!" Sharifa screams and begins battering Hugh with her fists. Hugh grabs her wrists and pushes her away. Sharifa stumbles over Winston and falls.

"Here come the twins, Jan and Jeff, and David," Annette introduces the three. The three of them enter the stage. They notice Winston and Sharifa lying on the ground and hurriedly leave the scene.

Annette summarizes, "All students are afraid, each in their own way - afraid of failure, afraid of success and afraid of being hurt by parents and teachers, as well as other students. In this situation, all are losers. The school churns out class after class of mediocre graduates who interpret everything as a cutthroat race or else are too cowed to achieve anything at all. They're robbed of their self-worth and unable to develop their creativity. They lack a zest for living. The teachers, unaware of the root of the problem, are unaware of the wall of fear that is stifling their students' potential."

Winston is moaning softly to himself.

Sharifa pulls herself up onto hands and knees, takes off her sweater and cushions his head.

"Wait, I'll get help," she says and leaves.

The lights go out.

Bertram looked around. Despite the resolution he had made that morning to deal with fear, he found this all rather heavy. No point becoming depressed again, but before he could slip away, a spotlight comes on.

Too late to escape!

In the center of the spot, Sharifa.

"That was the moment that I decided I would live life on my own terms even if it meant standing up for what I believe in and getting beaten down."

Annette's voice is heard, "Sharifa and Winston become inseparable friends in and outside of school."

The spot goes out briefly.

When it comes on again, Sharifa and Winston are sitting cross-legged opposite one another, studying.

"Pass me that book, would you?" Sharifa asks.

Winston reaches out.

"Ouch!" Winston exclaims, as he brushes against a lamp. "That bulb is hot!"

Sharifa reaches over, takes his hand, and tenderly kisses his burnt fingertip. With genuine feeling, she asks after a minute or so, "There, does it feel any better?"

She looks up and as their eyes meet, it is clear something has changed between them. He reaches out and draws her onto him. Her small form cradled in his arms, she lies on top of him, tenderly kissing his face his neck while he laughs delightedly.

"And so they became lovers!" Annette comments.

The lights go out and almost immediately come back on.

Sharifa is standing with Winston behind her, holding her tenderly in his arms.

"I realize I loved Sharifa from the moment we met. But after that first loving contact, we felt a passion for each other, which still exists today. Unfortunately, one thing led to another, and Sharifa became pregnant."

Sharifa took over. "My family was shocked and shamed. They forced us to put our baby up for adoption. Winston and I had nothing to say. We were sent to remedial class. There we met Mrs. Gladstone and the students you have just met.

The curtain falls.

"End of the first act!" Annette appears on the stage.

Bertram joined Maurice and Mary in a boisterous applause.

"It's that quality of caring, however slight, that makes life worthwhile," he said. What had made him so blind? Life consisted of more than just *being effective and increasing profits*. With a bit of caring in the work place, life for his top executives would change. And yet, allowing feeling to play an important role in business was too often treated as a taboo.

"The character in my short story could have been right up there with them. He's so desperate for a bit of genuine love that he is ready to commit suicide when he can't get it. I'm just putting two and two together. It's that quality of empathy, caring and concern which connects us to things that matter in our lives. I've always had it with my work and taken it for granted in my friendships and so it was never an issue. Now it's suddenly obvious to me that life without caring's not worth living."

A lone figure, sitting quietly near the door, got up and walked toward them. Maurice waved to him, "Pim! You're back early from your conference! Come over here and meet Mary."

"So they arrived after all!" Pim was tall, slender, and reserved. He could have been 58, but Maurice had told Bertram confidentially that he, like Mary, was an octogenarian. An engineer, specializing in designing bombs to protect the West against its enemies, his later years had been dedicated to exploring new paradigms[6]. His kind blue eyes gave away a caring, sensitive presence that seemed to be constantly scanning the situation for how to be of assistance.

"Yes!" Maurice got up to introduce his guests, "This is Pim. You may already know him as Secretary General of the All-Win Network. He arrived yesterday. He's staying with me while he attends a meeting near here at the United Nations University of Peace[7]!"

He turned to Pim.

"Mary will bring peace to our world if she has to do it in person!" His good-natured laugh echoed through the auditorium.

Mary and Pim greeted each other cordially. They knew of each other, but had never met in person.

"Are these your students?" Pim smiled, as, rather formally, he shook Mary's hand and motioned to the stage. "I'm impressed!" he said. "Gruesome portrayal of today's culture for which, I'm afraid, scientists like myself are largely responsible!"

"Scientists or our whole generation of adults?" Mary became suddenly serious. "We educate our kids to feel afraid and are surprised when they become aggressive or depressed.

"But given half a chance," she continued in a lighter tone, "You'd be amazed, how resilient they can be!"

"Excuse me, sir!" Edward approached Maurice, "Consuela asks if you'd like to take a tea break. I believe she has hot scones, freshly out of the oven, with strawberry jam and fresh clotted cream!"

There was a whoop and young Jeff and his twin Jan jumped off the stage, followed by the rest of the group.

"Clearly the answer is 'Yes!'" Maurice laughed.

"You guys really impressed Pim here," he raised his voice to make himself heard.

"Pim, you might as well tell them what you are doing here. The refreshments will take a minute or two to arrive."

Pim blinked as if slightly apprehensive that the wave of bubbling energy might sweep him off his feet.

"Well, I'm a scientist," he hesitated. "I used to develop bombs. When we developed the latest kind, aimed at vaporizing people and leaving their property standing, I realized where science was heading. Possessions were more important than people. I simply couldn't carry on. I had to find another direction.

"You see, scientists have become the 'High Priests' of Western culture. We preach 'objectivity'. Too often we see the world as a machine. Everything made up of separate, mechanical parts. All that counts is what we can measure and weigh. So much so that people are taught to measure their own worth in terms of what they *produce and how much money they make.* And this leaves each person alone and afraid in competition with every one else -- just as you portrayed at Corps Elite High School!"

"*Schools, like Corps Elite High School mould people for top positions in the rat race by first filling them with fear!*" Bertram realized with a jolt. This was important stuff. Before he could return to work or even finish his novel, he would have to understand how and why this was done and how this situation could be changed. Fear was the separator. It separated people from what they loved most. It pitted person against person, group against group.

Pim continued, "Western science discounts feelings and thereby leaves out an essential part of what makes the world tick."

And he, Bertram was trying to use reason (why?-questions) to understand the emotion of fear. Reason and emotion were two different ways of understanding the world, like trying to use English to understand what someone was saying in Chinese. No wonder, he failed.

Fancy meeting Pim at breakfast and not having any idea at all what he was into.

Bertram was now sitting bolt upright riveted by what Pim was saying.

"Beginning as students and later as adults, we clutch at straws. Anything to feel secure. Usually we scramble for status or wealth; or we give up the rat race altogether, drop out, or submit to some "higher" authority. That can be a belief, the latest fashion in clothes, the company we work for, or a government – anything but the reality of who we, ourselves, are, and what actually exists. This is a win/lose society, where all lose in the end."

"But..." Takeshi, puzzled, on the verge of a smile, left the word dangling in the air.

"Sounds grandiose, I know! As if scientists are all powerful!" Pim smiled ironically, "But as a result of what mainstream scientists say, our culture sweeps the world with ads, technology and values which focus on things that can be measured in money. From this perspective, people and their feelings are seen as useful to the degree that they can help to boost sales."

"We have lost sight of what each person values, loves to do and wants to be," Mary looked around the pensive faces as if speaking for the group.

Pim continued, "As a result, educators, business people, doctors, politicians, and so on, see their clients, customers and constituents as numbers, automatons which, like machines, can be used, fixed up or programmed to act a certain way. The tragedy is that they think that way about others, because that's how they see themselves."

"This has led to us depleting, poisoning and then drowning our Mother Earth in excess production, anything to make a dime," Mary agreed. "It has hatched 101 dictatorships ...people scrambling for or giving away power in a fear-filled world."

"One hundred and two!" Maurice corrected, "Another coup. Somewhere in South America. Heard it this morning on the BBC[8] World Service."

"Well, 102 then!"

"But if the whole world thinks that way, what can you, one scientist do about it?" Takeshi inquired, politely.

"Doesn't look promising, I must admit. That's why a few of us are meeting at the U.N.'s University for Peace -- physicists, mathematicians, biologists, chemists, psychologists, sociologists and so on.

"As scientists we simply can't afford to look only at a part of reality. It's like trying to cure a case of blood poisoning by treating the cut on someone's finger. This partial approach makes a mockery of science. And so, my colleagues and I are looking at theories which acknowledge that all-that-is consists of one glorious, interdependent whole. At present problems have assumed world proportions and are escalating daily. Unless we learn to embrace the totality, we might compartmentalize ourselves out of existence!"

The totality! Bertram took a deep breath. That meant embracing all of life, all feelings, allowing people in close, and yes! embracing whatever came his way. Pim was doing it and so were Mary and her crew. If others could, so could he.

Pim concluded, "I'll be here for a while yet. Judging by your impressive play, we might even be able to help one another..."

The smell of freshly baked scones filled the room, as Edward and Consuela entered, peeking out over fully laden trays.

"Thanks!" Pim smiled at Edward, as he scooped up a scone, placed it on a plate, and with an apologetic smile took a bite, delicately catching a blob of whipped cream in his napkin, as it threatened to ooze down his chin.

4. Reign Of Terror

Stumbling along at breakneck speed, Augustina jumped out of the way, almost knocked over by a stray puppy, tail between its legs. As if pursued by the Grand Butcher himself, it yapped hysterically as it fled.

Regaining her balance, she stumbled on.

"*Oh God, please let Pierre come with me. Let us face this together!*"

The whole world pulsed with the relentless, rhythmic beat of the drums. "*The Mandus are corrupting the Kukundu tribe. Kill them to prove that you are a patriot.*

Kill them! Kill them! Kill them!"

Augustina ran on in a daze.

This last move had happened so suddenly.

She was sitting with her mother in the neighboring, largely Mandu village, when a radio car had driven through the streets, on the back the local Mayor. Turned up to maximum, the distorted radio voice had howled:

> "*There's been an explosion in our government buildings. It's a plot by Mandu traitors to overthrow the rightful rulers of Kukundu. Mandus are corrupting the Kukundu tribe by intermarrying with them.*
>
> "*So if you're married to a Mandu. Beware! You are under suspicion. Execution is the only way to purify our land. Execution of Mandus and with them their devilish brood!*
>
> "*Kukundus who act now will be honored with a Medal of Patriotism.*
>
> "*Our Patriotic Army will be watching you.*
>
> "*Act now in the name of Kukundu!*"

Immediately the village crier had drummed out the message. Soon in village after village, drums joined the rhythmic beat until the message "*The Mandus are corrupting the Kukundu tribe. Kill them to prove that you are a patriot* reverberated in the farthest corners of the jungle.

Kundana had finally fully succeeded in creating an unbridgeable gulch of suspicion between the Kukundus and Mandus, two tribes, which were so closely related that most could barely tell the difference. The Mandus at their puberty rites received two facial scars on the right cheek, while the Kukundus received three.

At the sound of the loudspeaker, both her mother and she had run out of the hut. The Kukundu mayor, a large megaphone in his hand, had encouraged the village to gather in the market place.

Her head throbbing with anxiety, barely able to catch her breath, she had followed the truck and then, every nerve on end, waited in the market place for the mayor to speak.

"To protect the inhabitants of this village," the mayor bassooned, I have prepared the church. If you hide there, you will be protected from the rightful wrath of your rulers. Just one condition: you must swear an oath of blind obedience to President Kundana and your Kukundu rulers!"

Augustina's mum had hurried home to collect her most valuable belongings. Any Mandu hut left unguarded would be ransacked and burglarized by Kukundus.

Augustina took the shortcut through the jungle, running and stumbling all the way home. She must pick up the children and bring them to safety. *"Oh, dear Pierre, please come!"* she prayed under her breath. *"We were always so happy together. What difference can it possibly make that you are a Kukundu and I am a Mandu? That may never come between us!"*

Initially, Pierre had been horrified at his government's policies and had promised to protect Augustina and their children from any attack. Then, gradually, Augustina felt the foundation sink from under her feet. First there was her estrangement from people in the village, which she had known all her life, who now saw her through different eyes. When the first attack on a Mandu home occurred, people in their village felt outraged. Then another happened and another and people became used to the idea. Augustina remembered her fear when she noticed her neighbor wearing a dress that had been stolen from a Mandu friend.

Indignantly she told Pierre.

Pierre had shrugged his shoulders. "Let's face it," he said, "This is just the way things are. You should think of moving in with your mother--for your own safety," he had added.

Augustina was aghast. Pierre seemed to have accepted the situation. It was as if there were an epidemic going around, not a physical disease, but fear. It was as if fear was in the air and every one was being affected. She barely recognized Pierre. Was this the man she loved? The chasm had grown between them.

And now this. License to kill her and her people. The bottom had dropped out of her life.

Augustina realized there was nowhere to go. Her only hope was the church. But could she trust the Kukundu mayor? …She had begun to suspect every one. The world had gone completely mad. And oh! without Pierre, she didn't want to go on.

Before Kundana came to power, Kukundu had been a peaceful nation. Poor yes! People lived in what in comparison to some nations would be considered primitive conditions. But education was available to all, and the infrastructures worked. Okay, they didn't have a television in every home, but there was a central telephone in every settlement and even Internet. For the rest, radio had sufficed. Every one's basic needs were met and the nation was clambering out of poverty.

For long as she could remember, the Kukundus and Mandus had peacefully governed together. Never before had there been any enmity between the two tribes. And now this! She simply could not fathom it any more. The world had gone crazy! And she was going crazy with it.

Propelled forward by her terror, she reached the edge of the jungle.

Augustina stopped dead. A feeling of dread.

Still under cover of the trees, she peered into the clearing at the edge of the village. There was the hut where she lived with Pierre and their two children.

The drums were still beating. But something else had changed. Where were the voices of her children?

She heard the rough shouts of the militia and the softer voice of her husband.

"Well done, man! You have proved yourself a worthy Kukundu. Certainly, earned the Patriot Medal!"

Augustina, carefully staying within the cover of the trees, crept around to a place where, unseen, she could see the front of her house.

There on the mud-baked ground lay the bloody bodies of her two babies. With a foolish grin on his face, Pierre stood in his hand a machete, the blood still dripping off its blade.

Augustina's senses boggled. Merciful oblivion took over. She crumpled in a heap on the ground.

5. A Glimmer Of Hope

The group was settled back in the theatre, as the curtain rises, revealing Annette, as Mrs. Gladstone, sitting on a chair, her blond hair in a tight bun. On the floor, her students slouch, hang and lie around her.

"This is a remedial class," she starts, "Your task? To become a credit to the school. Succeed, and you get to stay on. If you don't, you can kiss Corps Elite goodbye. We have two hours each day immediately after school 'til the end of the school year."

Molly and Pat yawn loudly. Antonia giggles. Arturo stretches out on his back and places his hands under his head.

Mildly, Mrs. Gladstone asks, "Perhaps this school is such a pain in the neck that you consider it a waste of time?"

"What's the point?" Arturo mumbles without opening his eyes.

"I intend to stay on!" Winston speaks up. No one would suspect his lightning responses on the tennis court. He's a stocky five-foot seven with large owl-like glasses, his arm protectively around Sharifa lends him a fatherly air. "I've never been happier in my life." He looks straight ahead as if merely speaking for the record and does not care what others think.

"Yes --fucking around," says Hugh.

"I intend to stay on, too!" Sharifa agrees, quietly ignoring Hugh, "I met Winston here. We love each other and that makes everything worthwhile. I don't care what anyone thinks."

"Great! Making babies for others to bring up," Molly says bitterly, as if personally feeling the abandonment.

Mrs. Gladstone remains impassive.

"You're right." Winston turns to Molly. "That was wrong of us. When we have our next child, we'll be ready to offer it a home. That's why I intend to finish this school and go on to university."

"You - university!?"

With surprising composure, Winston turns to Pat, "Okay, I'm not as bright as Ian or Takeshi. And I might not make Harvard or Yale. But this school has placed me way ahead of other Black kids in my neighborhood and *some* university will accept me. Especially with your help, Sharifa."

His frankness opens him wide to attack. But no one speaks. Antonia, for a moment forgetting her shyness, stares at them, intrigued.

Sharifa is unperturbed by the aggression. Fearlessly, she looks around the group. "You know Elbert who just got into Corps Elite?" she asks quietly, "Well, Winston tutored him twice a week. That's how he made it!"

"We are so lucky at Corps Elite, you have no idea!" Winston pointed out, "Even with my low grades, I can really help the kids in my neighborhood! Most of them are latchkey kids they come from single parent homes. Their mothers often work three jobs to put food on the table. Kids like Elbert have no support at home and none at school. The classes in poor areas are too large, and their teachers are too stressed out to give any of them the attention they need."

"Their schools may not compare to Corps Elite," Sharifa looked respectfully at Winston as she spoke, "but you should see how proud Winston's students are when they get their first A!"

A long silence follows and then Mrs. Gladstone phrases what is on every one's mind.

"Just a bit of loving attention can give us strength in ways that grades alone can't."

She pauses.

"School can be such a very lonely place when everything depends on making it. We're always trying to become something, focussing on what we are *not*. So how can we possibly hope to feel anything but weak and afraid? We're always feeling inadequate. And only a few make the top. So how to deal with feeling a failure -- that's a challenge when grades are all that count?"

"You feel a failure in other ways when you get straight A's!" Takeshi says. Like the others, he had lain slouched on the floor, now he sits up straight. "People hate you for reminding them that they did not 'make the grade'. I don't have a single friend at *Corps Elite, a*nd people put me down, too. It really hurts to be called a nerd! After all these years at Corps Elite, I wonder whether that's all I am."

"That's right," Ian agrees.

"The focus," Mrs. Gladstone repeats, "is on what each is *not*! That gives us nothing to work with at all. You can't like, respect, love, work with aspects of people that don't exist. And so the focus on what you are *not* makes life a lonely and terrifying experience!"

"Who feels Mrs. Gladstone is right?" Hugh asks. He holds up his hand. One after another hesitantly follows suit.

"If I'm not top at tennis, my father brings out his belt." Hugh lifts his shirt and displays a huge red welt across his back. "Every time I lose a game, he threatens to take me out of school. 'What's the good of spending all this money on education if you don't come out on top?' he repeats over and over again. To him, being on top is all that counts!"

David, the Native American, speaks up quietly, "Money and status are important. I'm fed up with being poor!"

"Money helps! But status is much more important. It gets people off your back!" Arturo clambered up and arranged himself into a cross-legged position.

"And so you earn your money by selling drugs and dragging other people down?!" Takeshi accuses him. "You nearly did Ian in!"

"And yet, Takeshi," Ian says mildly, "when Arturo came up and gave me my first hit, I felt he was really being kind. He noticed I was feeling

24

particularly down that day. It was a relief to be seen for what I actually was. And drugs are a way to escape from the constant pressure from home!

"In a way, it was also a relief to goof up behind my parents' back. For a time, drugs made me secretly feel like every one else...until I got caught shooting up."

"Doesn't make sense really," Hugh says, "Corps Elite promises to give us a head start as long as we get top grades. Then it makes us feel such losers that we scramble up the ladder and lose all self-respect in the process. I'm sure that is why money and status have become so important to my dad. Without money and status, he believes we don't exist."

Mrs. Gladstone says gently, "Money and status promise a surrogate power to make up for the inner strength you have lost. The more you feel a loser in yourself, the more important status and power become."

There was silence, the students each locked into their own thoughts, hardly daring to believe that the feelings of inadequacy they had believed were theirs alone were shared by their fellow students.

Mrs. Gladstone sums up.

"And so each of you copes with the situation in your own way," she smiles, "Some find a friend or two who come to be so important that other people and other responsibilities are all but forgotten. Others turn to drug pushing or taking, yet others undermine others' ability to compete, using violence, psychological or gang warfare; and yet others walk away from the scene of a crime and refuse to admit what they have seen.

"I must admit, though, each of you has been creative in your own ways! And yet, every one loses when there's only one game in town and that one's a game without winners. This is an all-lose situation. It creates young people who, often unconsciously, are driven by fear.

"As I see it, we have two options. We can snuff out your creativity; or else we can put it to better use. What do you guys say, we look for ways to create a school environment in which you can feel good about yourselves and get good grades into the bargain?"

"Sounds better than just doing nothing!" Arturo agrees.

"Tomorrow, I'll invite some friends of mine, I'd like you guys to meet!" Mrs. Gladstone smiles.

"Okay, the two hours are up. Enjoy what's left of the day!"

Curtain falls the light goes out.

As the tiny audience clapped enthusiastically, Edward walked in.

"There was a telephone call for you, Mrs. Duffield -- a certain John St. Clair. I told him you were unavailable!" He gave the barest of nods, as if to say, "At your service, madam."

"You what!?" Mary exclaimed. "But … but … Surely you might have checked with me!?" She took a deep breath, realizing that Edward was her host's butler and that it was not her place to give him a hard time.

"Please, Edward, if there are any more calls or anything else for that matter which concerns me, please let me know so that I can make my own decisions!" she added more mildly.

"Been with us forever," or words to that effect, is how Maurice had described Edward's relationship to his family. *"Surely,"* Mary thought indignantly, *"that does not give him the right to take charge of other people's business!?"*

6. Augustina Flees

With an excruciating pain, as if her leg was about to explode, Augustina came to. She was lying on the forest floor. In a daze, she wondered where she was. Her leg was buckled under her. "Broken!" she moaned. She lay there, mustering the courage to move. The undergrowth that surrounded her spun around in dizzying circles. She closed her eyes to steady herself.

Then the grotesque images appeared: Her two little children, lying there, bleeding, their heads in unnatural contortions! And Pierre with the machete…

She jumped to her feet, only to fall back down with a cry as the searing pain ripped through her body.

For a while she lay on the ground, trembling helplessly, trying to cope with both her physical pain and the memories which flooded her mind: Her babies, lying on the mud- baked yard. That sheepish grin on Pierre's face. The militia with guns pointing at his head. Then the radio broadcasts! Oh yes, the radio broadcasts inciting men to kill their wives… How could she possibly continue to live amid such, such…?

She lay there, she knew not how long, when she was roused by shouts.

A rustling close at hand.

Instinctively, Augustina dragged herself farther into the undergrowth. A young family from her village headed for the path.

A group of militia appeared with guns. They laughed as they caught sight of the back of one of the children. One of the militia took aim.

"It's okay. Let them go. They're heading for the church!" the commander barked.

The militia, laughing and joking among themselves, turned around and headed back into the village.

"The church!!! I was to meet mum in the church. They say it's a safe haven!" Could she still make it?

Blocking the pain out, she desperately dragged herself to where she could reach a thick stick. She tested it as well as she could, still sprawled on the ground. It would probably take her weight.

What normally took 10 minutes now seemed an interminable journey. A couple of times, she had to hide in the bushes as she heard voices approaching from behind. The voices mainly belonged to Mandus making for the safe haven of the church. But she no longer trusted anyone now. They were all caught up in this rampage of fear.

Finally, hopping along using her stick to steady herself, she could make out the church standing serenely as ever in the middle of the village square.

She crept closer until from where she stood still protected by the trees she could look through the open doors. It was packed! Outside the mayor encouraging people to enter.

"Step back!" he called through a bullhorn, "Make place for your friends and relatives!" As a space opened up, others pushed their way in until every one was wedged inside.

She was about to cry out for the mayor to wait. She had to get in! Then suddenly her nostrils flared: An acrid smell...

On an impulse she drew back. Petroleum? Leaning on her stick, she painfully hobbled to where she had a better view. A man dragging a tank on a wagon was dousing the building with gasoline!

"Ready," he called.

She heard the sharp retort as bolts were thrown into place. No one would be able to leave. The mayor laughed, there was a roar, and the dry wood of the building went up in a purgatory of flames.

A brief moment, then a lone voice called, "Fire!" and the air was filled with screams.

7. An Opportunity

The curtain rises to the same scene.

In front of the group on chairs: Annette, sitting primly, as Mrs. Gladstone, with Molly dressed up as a teacher, and Jan, one of the twins, dressed as a little girl, hair hurriedly bunched up in a pony tail, sticking up straight on the top of her head. The rest of the group, listening attentively, is sitting in a semicircle around them.

Mrs. Gladstone addresses the class, "These are my friends, Lynne and little Phoebe.

"Lynne is the headmistress of St. Lawrence High School[9]. St Lawrence is much poorer than Corps Elite but they have many of the same problems."

"Thank you, Joyce," Lynne takes over. " When I became principal four years ago, our school was closing its doors -- Lots of tensions, special students, different cultures. It used to be a tough place, but we have managed to turn that around.

"This is how we did it.

"In 2001, we met Wayne Jacoby from an organization called Global Education Motivators[10]. We took part in one of his programs. It gave the kids a sense of being a part of something much bigger than themselves. It took them away from their daily worries. The kids love it! It brings students together from all over the world. All study a common topic. This year it's human rights. Global Education Motivators supplies students with materials.

"Look!" Jan, in the role of Phoebe, holds up a document with paragraphs in different colors, each one beginning with a huge ornate letter. "Wayne sent each of us one of these. It's the *Universal Declaration of Human Rights.* That's what we're studying this year."

Lynne, smiling at little Phoebe, continues, "This project really levels the playing field because it doesn't matter how bright you are or how you do in the classroom.

"You see, based on what subject they have all focussed on that year, each student group develops its own individual project."

"It was sooo exciting," Jan, as little Phoebe, jumps up. "Last time it was on the environment and we could choose…" Her ponytail comes untied. Part of her hair flops forward, covering her face. Hurriedly she tries to gather her hair and redo her coiffure, her lines, forgotten in the process.

Lynne laughs with unfeigned delight. Every one else joins in.

"Throughout the whole process, groups support one another's projects via e-mail, chat groups and videoconferencing," Lynne explains, "Literally, hundreds of schools participate."

"We made a U.N. garden!" Phoebe has her hairdo under control. "In it we planted one plant from each country that's a Member of the U.N. -- That's almost all the countries in the world!" little Phoebe is unstoppable, "It was so much fun joining the chat groups. The kids told us about plants they had in their countries. There was this one guy. He was so clever! He could tell us which of the plants could grow in New Jersey where we live."

Winston reaches over and places his arm over Sharifa's shoulder. As she looks up at him, he gives her a squeeze and a smile, as if to say, "This is really great!"

"Then about 30 or 40 'student leaders' are selected," Lynne takes over, "They get to go to the U.N. All they have to do is pay for the trip. Once there, all costs are covered."

Phoebe bounces up and down in her chair. "At the U.N. we sat and talked. We each had a mike. There are great big screens. And you see the students from schools all over the world up there when they speak. They look like the reporters, you know, the ones you see on TV!

"We write down ideas which governments at the U.N. can use! It's called a *Declaration.*

"And guess what!" Phoebe was radiant, "I got to read it to the President of the U.N.'s General Assembly!" Eyes shining, she looked around at the group as if heaven had just dropped into her lap.

The lights go out and Lynne appears in one single spotlight. "We have some children who don't have parents, others who don't have good homes and children who are medicated. Some of them live horrendous lives. School is all they have. But they have their successes.

"Phoebe comes from a tough home, a separated family. Her mother left her, her father was somewhere else. She came to our school and really liked it. So she wanted to stay on and lived with her godmother who was a little better with her.

"Phoebe has 'special needs'. For instance, she doesn't know how many eggs in a dozen, nor the months of the year, yet she is in Grade 8. Yes, she's really handicapped, maybe not to look at her. And she got up at the U.N. and read the report! She did a beautiful job. People called from all over to say how spectacular she was.

"She was almost crying when she came back--she couldn't believe it.

"For one shining moment she was on top of the world and she will always remember that."

The stage lights go on. All are standing in a row including Molly and Jan who are now dressed as themselves.

Annette as Mrs. Gladstone says, "And so we joined Global Education Motivators.

"This year's topic is Human Rights."

"Every child, woman and man has 30 human rights," Ian MacDonald announced.

"We chose Article 26, which deals with education. The part of that Article which turned us on was," he read, "'*that every one has the right to an education, ...directed to the **full development of the human personality** and to the strengthening of respect for human rights and fundamental freedoms. It* *shall promote understanding, tolerance and friendship among all nations, racial or religious groups, and shall further the activities of the United Nations for the maintenance of peace...'*

"We were *looking for ways to create a school environment in which we could each feel good about ourselves and get good grades into the bargain*, as Mrs. Gladstone had suggested."

Hugh added, "It was so good to hear that even young people have rights which our parents and even Corps Elite must honor. For the first time, I felt that there was some support for who I was as a person even though I doubt my father or Corps Elite High School had ever heard of the Universal Declaration of Human Rights or that these 30 'rights and fundamental freedoms', as they are called, apply to every child, woman, and man on the planet."

"I think at that point we all realized that there was no turning back. If Phoebe could make a break through, so would we!"

Curtain.

Amid clapping, Edward and Consuela passed out glasses of fresh lemonade.

8. An Idea Catches On

Annette as Mrs. Gladstone sets the scene: "That evening Pat, Molly and Antonia went driving around a poor area of San José, when...

The curtain goes up. On the backdrop of the stage, a vacant lot is projected. Pat, Molly and Antonia are standing off to the side as if looking over the fence.

"See what I see?" Pat exclaims, her freckled face gleaming.

The others look at the lot in silence.

"Looks like a garbage dump to me," Molly says.

"What else?" Pat continues, eyes sparkling.

"Pat, you would! " Molly cries, "You really are going too far! Every window sill in your house is filled with plants, and now you want to sprout a garden here in the slums!"

"You're not thinking of copying St. Lawrence's?" Antonia asks, and giggles.

Molly wrinkles her nose. "A slum school next door...?"

"That's just the point! A *school* garden!" Pat laughs.

"Pat, that's great!" Antonia exclaims, forgetting her usual shyness.

"We'd have to get it cleared," Molly muses.

"The kids might help!" Antonia suggests. The words slip out spontaneously.

The others look at her, surprised. Her eyes are shining. For an instant, Antonia seems to have changed.

Then the lights go out.

Just one spot on the three friends.

Pat says, "When we got back to our remedial class and told them what we had seen, they were as wild about the idea as we were. Winston agreed to help us. The next day at lunchtime, we went to see the Principle of Golden Haven School. Turned out, the lot was school property. He was only too happy to provide a garden program for the kids.

'Our kids come largely from broken homes, parents on welfare. Many are angry, depressed, defensive and have little hope in life. I suggest you open the program to those who are really interested first. And then allow the good news to travel.

'That'll keep them out of trouble!' he said, 'Two conditions: you, young people, do all the work, and you raise the funds!'

"We got to our remedial class early, and when Mrs. Gladstone arrived, ideas were flying back and forth!"[11]

The lights go back on. The students are laughing and talking excitedly while Mrs. Gladstone listens.

"But it will take time to get started," Mrs. Gladstone points out.

"Actually, we could start straight away!" David says enthusiastically. Every one turns to David. He so seldom gives an opinion. "We just clear the garbage from a small patch first. Then, I can show the kids how everything in Nature works together." David is radiant. He has every one's surprised attention.

When no one says anything, he becomes self-conscious and mumbles, "My grandfather knows everything about nature. I spend the summers with him out on the reservation in New Mexico."

The lights go out.

The video screen flickers. The backdrop lights up. The vacant lot appears. In it, David, surrounded by a host of Black and Mexican children, is eagerly looking at something which he is pointing out to the children. David comments, "First, mainly the younger ones, then, in drips and drabs, some of the older kids joined our project. In the end, kids were crowding to get into our garden program."

The scene on the screen changes: A close up of the ground. An army of leaf cutter ants are moving back and forth from a fallen branch to their anthill. Each ant carefully bites off a chunk of leaf, almost bigger than itself and with supreme strength and endurance hauls it back to its home. The kids squat around the moving carpet of ants, careful not to impede their progress. They laugh with delight as the tiny ants with their huge loads clamber across the most impossible hurdles, rocks, tin cans and dead wood, each hurdle more challenging than the last.

David's voice, "These leaf cutter ants gather food and take care of the baby ants. See how the tree is gradually disappearing. When they have finished with it, the tree will have turned into soil.

"Look ! Look!" One little boy reaches up and picks up a worm, which had peeked out from under a dead leaf. He holds it up triumphantly; it wriggles indignantly.

"Put it down, please, Lawrence! This worm burrows holes in the soil so that the seeds can take root. See?"

The kids push and shove to get a better view of the tiny green speck David's pointing out.

Larry, no longer the center of attention, allows the worm to flop on the ground where it burrows its way to safety.

"See! The worm makes little passageways through the soil. And the green speck of new life – See how tiny it is? —this tiny speck can grow roots, because the worm loosens the soil and fills it with air."

A jackdaw perches on a nearby bush.

"See that bird? It eats fruit and then, through its droppings, the seeds fall out of the air and land on the soil. And so, you get new little shoots like this.

"Now, what have we here?"

The kids look around. The lot is covered in weeds. The camera zooms in and you see how what, at a distance, looks like weeds have delicately shaped, colorful flowers.

"These have all grown up out of soil like this which has been prepared by the leaf-cutter ants, the worms and the birds.

"If we allow Nature to do its thing and don't meddle, there's no waste at all!"

Waste becomes food and homes for other animals and plants. Nothing is ever lost!"

"No waste?" Molly asks, "I wonder ...perhaps we could use the garbage to make works of art?"

The scene changes and you see the remedial class and their little students gathering waste and placing it on separate heaps: bricks and stones, pieces of wood, paper, old bottles and broken glass, and lots of aluminum cans.

"We recycled everything!" David explains.

In the next slide, Hugh is tilling, raking and smoothing the soil with a group of girls and boys. Others lace stones around separate round, square and heart shaped beds.

An 8-year-old boy, with the utmost concentration, moves one of the stones from the bottom of the heart, trying to convert it into a circle.

"No, Jason, what y'a doin'?" a 10-year old runs up, the countless pigtails each decorated with colored beads bobbing as she runs.

"It's all … all crooked!" Jason says, still concentrating on placing the stone closer to the middle.

"No, stoopid, it's a heart!" She tries to pick up the stone. Jason holds it down. A scuffle ensues.

"Hey, you guys," Hugh laughs, "why don't you come over here, Jason, I need someone to help me build a flowerbed that's perfectly round. I really need your help."

Mollified, Jason relinquishes his stone.

On the next slide, Winston with the help of the wood is building a large square planter. He explains, "We can cover this with plastic to grow seedlings for next year!"

Off to the corner, Molly and Sharifa are sitting surrounded by old paper shopping bags and large pots of glue. Children alone in one-pointed concentration and kids in small groups are alternately bantering and bickering among themselves all intent on fashioning collages and sculptures. The camera moves from one to another. The figure of a man, made from a heap of stones. A dolls' house made from scraps of wood. A jungle made from twigs, leaves and weeds, stuck onto a huge piece of cardboard.

The spotlight moves to Pat, "We had great plans," she says, "a vegetable garden and some fruit trees, cooking lessons to augment school dinners, a herb garden to sell produce to the local community and then it became clear that the kids needed help doing their homework. So each of us made ourselves available. We each took a couple of hours once every two weeks to tutor the kids," she laughs, "I'm a less than brilliant student! But I felt so good about myself! I was able to help other kids. It actually got me interested in class. Anything I learned at Corps Elite, I was able to pass along. And the kids were eager to learn!"

Molly adds, " I hated school. And here these bright little minds are so grateful for every crumb they receive!"

"For many, school is their only hope," Pat continues.

"And you learned quite a bit from them!" Arturo teases.

"Thanks to you and Antonia!" Pat quips back.

Antonia is looking from one to another with a smile. For the first time, Bertram notices, she looks as if she feels part of the group.

Turning to the audience, Pat says, "The kids were largely Spanish speaking. Arturo and Antonia helped us communicate. They actually taught us the basics. And then guess what? Our students became our teachers!"

"You're a pretty good student!" Arturo grins. A spark passes between them.

"The kids laughed their heads off when we first tried speaking their language! Their laughs were so infectious, I think we all had just as much fun as the kids. In the end, we were laughing at ourselves!" Pat grins. "I never knew that making mistakes can be so hilarious!"

The spotlight switches to Mrs. Gladstone peering through her glasses.

"In remedial class," she says, "we planned each aspect of what was to be done. We taught one another, and the wonderful thing was that every one contributed. No one was left out. We even learned how to raise funds and to apply to the City Council for permits. In the end, the whole class knew all about writing business plans and reports and how to present them to the appropriate officials. We managed to get plans accepted by the school bureaucracy and the City Council. The group even made presentations to the press."

Bertram's heart was beating a little faster. Careful not to disturb Pim, Mary or Maurice, he slipped out, hurried to the library, picked up pencil and paper and ran back as Mrs. Gladstone was saying, "Imperceptibly, schoolwork was transformed from a duty to a resource as the class discovered how to combine the different subjects they learned at school to solve problems in the school garden projects which they now felt so passionate about."

Bertram slipped into the nearest seat in the little theatre and tried to get every word down.

Mrs. Gladstone continues, "And there was another benefit.

"Because the problems we encounter in life are as diverse as there are people, each student found that her or his particular skills and passions could be put to good use. Each student grew to be respected in her or his own right and the classmates became close knit friends."

The lights go out.

When the lights go on, the whole class is holding hands, standing at the edge of the stage. Solemnly, Takeshi says, "And then the bombshell burst! Mrs. Gladstone was called before the Board of Directors and given a dressing down. She was to be sacked at the end of term for allowing the remedial class to 'run wild'."

9. John St. Clair

"Oh No! No! No!" Augustina screamed, as the church burst into flames. A hand was thrust over her mouth.

A voice said in English, "Quiet! You must keep quiet! In your own interest! I'll try and get you to safety!"

Augustina carefully eased herself around to look her captor in the face. Concerned gray eyes looked down at her, offset by a silver-gray, open-necked linen shirt.

His voice barely audible above the shrieks exploding from the church, the man spoke into her ear, "If anyone finds out what we've seen, we'll be executed immediately."

When he was sure she was not going to scream, he leaned her against the crook of his arm and, in Kukundu fashion, held up his hand in a salute, palm forward. With his lips close to her ear, he said, as clearly as he could, "My name is John St. Clair. I'm a peace worker. I've been living here in hiding ever since Kundana came to power."

Augustina, still in a daze, had no idea what he meant. A peace worker was too incongruous under the present circumstances. But, one way or another, she was in his hands. She had no alternative but to trust him. Hesitantly, she placed her palm against his, as a token of cooperation.

"I'll try and get you to safety," he repeated.

With concern he pointed to her leg. "One moment, and I'll take care of this. It looks as if it could be broken."

Easing Augustina against the trunk of a tree hidden from view of the path, he furtively looked around, picked up a lose branch from the ground, and wiped away any evidence of their presence.

He then picked up a mini video camera he had dropped by the side of the path and carefully hid it in a pouch he was carrying around his neck.

The persistent shrieks coming from the church were swelling to a roar, as the jungle now fully alive with squawking, chattering, shrieking of birds, insects and monkeys, drove the agitation toward a climax.

Augustina held her hands to her ears trying to banish the confusion. "Oh mummy! Oh mummy!" Augustina moaned, the ache in her heart competing with the searing pain in her leg. "My mother's in the church!" she cried.

John cast around for a suitable stick and, locating one, he eased his rucksack from his back, fished around inside and pulled out a first aid kit. Out of it, he took disinfectant and a large bandage. With his back to Augustina, he gently explored her leg with his fingertips until she cried out in pain.

"Yes! It's definitely broken!" he said, his voice barely audible above the clamor. He started to caress her calf some distance from the wound, as if trying to ease the pain and then, with his hands at either side of the breach, when she least expected it, he wrenched the bone apart and allowed the two parts to gently slip into place. Augustina screamed and then moaned loudly as he quickly disinfected and bandaged the leg, setting it firmly against the stick.

Finally he looked up.

Both he and Augustina listened, but the terrified shrieks from the village and the animal world, the raucous laugh of the mayor and the shouts from his deputies had drowned out Augustina's cries.

"It's okay now!" John moved aside, so that Augustina could see. For a while he tenderly held her leg.

"We need to move as soon as you can," he said. "Whenever you are ready to go!"

Very gradually, the pain began to ease.

Then with a sign from Augustina, he helped her up. With her leaning on him, they inched their way into the jungle. Moving so slowly, John was able to make out the barely visible track.

Augustina allowed herself to be led. John seemed to know where he was heading. "Eventually, this will take us to the river," John said during the first of their frequent rests.

After what seemed an eternity, Augustina found a clumsy rhythm and they began to make better time.

10. The Final Act

The curtain goes up. The backdrop: Golden Haven School, lit up by street lamps. In front, the remedial class, barely visible huddled in a circle. In the center, a glass jar with a single candle.

"The bottom's dropped out!" Hugh says somberly, holding up a letter.

"The schoolboard writes

> *To the remedial class:*
> *Our decision stands firm. Mrs. Gladstone is undermining Corps Elite's excellent academic tradition. Corps Elite High School prepares its students for top executive positions in society, not to work in the filth of the slums, nor with the dregs of society. It is not for nothing you find yourselves in a remedial class. We hope herewith to make it clear that our decision is irrevocable.*

"You guys, I hadn't realized how used to you all I've become, the feeling of being a part of a team, of…of caring, appreciating one another and the goodwill, that just … just flows …and…" he falters.

"The feeling of 'making it' together, where no one gets hurt…" Winston concludes softly.

"What really does it for me is what our project means to our Golden Haven students…," Pat pulls out a Kleenex and blows her nose. "I must admit, …"

The single candle plays on the circle of faces, alternately shrouding them in shadow and then, like MacBeth witches, distorting them into grotesque grimaces.

"The School Board doesn't even congratulate us that we were chosen to present our project at the U.N. in New York by Global Education Motivators!"

"It seems almost a betrayal to accept the invitation now, what with all that's important to Mrs. Gladstone going up in smoke!"

"It turns out what we thought we were building had no leg to stand on!" Pat's voice trembles and again she defiantly blows her nose.

"Did your parents come through, Ian?" Takeshi asked.

"My dad called the Board. They were polite, he said, but firmly turned his request down."

"Remedial class indeed! They've never had any class ever do what we are doing! We should … we should show them what we can achieve!" Arturo burst out

"Say we all get straight A's…?" Sharifa mused.

The spot goes out for a minute. There's bustling on the stage.

The stage lights come on.

The class is sitting in small groups. They are alternately asking questions, explaining things to one another and scribbling down notes. Mrs. Gladstone is circulating, answering questions, and explaining.

Pat looks up and addresses the audience. "After that, we spent our remedial class doing homework together. Takeshi and Ian were trumps. They did not stop until every one thoroughly knew their work. After class, we would all go to Golden Haven where we worked until after dark."

"Then came the exams," Jeff, one of the twins, took over. "I was so sure of myself, I wasn't even surprised when I got straight A's. Straight A's!!! For the very first time in my life! We were sure that this would prove to the whole school that Mrs. Gladstone was a first rate teacher. But the next day, we heard from Ian's father who was on the School Board that, after all, Mrs. Gladstone was to be sacked."

"We were shattered!" Takeshi exclaimed. "We agreed to meet at Golden Haven, work briefly on our projects and then decide what we would do."

The lights go out and the backdrop lights up. The projector whirrs: The Golden Haven school garden with kids busily at work. In the corner a group of kids gathered around, and on the stage in front of the screen, David is checking their mini ecosystem.

Hugh, dressed as a stranger in hat and coat, is watching from the side.

"Excuse me," he says, "I'm a journalist from the *San José Beacon*."

David looks up, sees the man is talking to him, and watches him with distrust.

"Could I have a word?"

David gets up reluctantly and walks over to the man.

" I'm a journalist. Impressive what you kids are doing here. Mind if I look around?"

David looks relieved.

"Be our guest. Let me call the others."

David hurries away.

Lights go out and the screen lights up:

"A series of slides show a beautiful garden with bright colored flower beds, rows of vegetables, a little 'sculptures and arts pavilion made of roughly hewn planks, David's 'wilderness' area and groups of young people busily at work.

The screen goes dark.

A spot comes on: the journalist chatting with the remedial class.

"I'd love to do a full spread article with photos of your Golden Haven project."

"That's our chance!" Jeff says excitedly.

Every one talks at once. The journalist looks from one to the other, as their story is told. "Perhaps I can help you get Mrs. Gladstone reinstated!" The journalist pauses.

The silence is electric.

"The *San Jose Beacon* is the most popular paper around these parts, but I'll call around, get some of the other papers interested, like the *San Francisco Chronicle*. I have some friends there," he said.

"Perhaps, you can organize a media day. Gather all the kids together and show the media exactly what you are doing."

The screen goes dark

When a dim light goes on, the remedial class is sitting comfortably together in Golden Haven School Garden. The heart shaped flowerbed visible behind them, candles carefully placed in glass jars, dotting the area around them.

By the light of a lantern, Pat is studying list and ticking off names.

Takeshi has a large pile of newspapers on his lap. "We made nearly all the local papers this side of San Francisco and all of Silicone Valley," he announces.

"Did any of the articles mention the quotes from the Universal Declaration of Human Rights?" Hugh asked.

"*The San Francisco Chronicle* did. Said that Mrs. Gladstone had reinstated our 'inalienable' rights."

"Wow! That's the most influential newspaper in the area!"

"Hey, you guys, I have this great idea!" Hugh jumps up, "Why not create a school environment at Corps Elite where *all students would enjoy learning and getting good grades into the bargain*? And get the students themselves to decide what that environment would look like?"

"But how could we do that?" Jeff asked, his coal-black eyes wide.

"We could create a Students' Council." Hugh sits down again and looks pensive. He continues, "You know, one kid from every class would be on the Students' Council. Their job: to gather ideas from their classmates and share them with other members of the Council! The Students' Council could then think along with the faculty and the Board!"

There were eager nods of approval. "We'd have to get the word out, because without pressure from the outside, the School Board would never agree."

Pat looks up from her list, her freckled nose wrinkles as she laughs. "Guess what! We made half of the radio and even TV shows in the Greater Bay Area!" Pat holds up the sheet of paper for the rest of the group to see. "And not only that, I was called by Kris Welch's Show, *The Saturday Morning*

Talkies on KPFA.[12] I have a sense that others are still coming in and…!" Pat looks around as if about to give the news of the Second Coming, "we have an invitation from the *Planet Today Show!*[13] National TV!"

The lights go out.

Then on the backdrop, a video of the TV screen with Hope Goodwin herself introducing the group, as the whole remedial class walks to the small stage surrounded by their students who are hanging on their arms, colored beads and ribbons in their hair, all spruced up in their very best clothes.

Hope's words resound through the theatre: "Corps Elite is no ivory tower, removed from every day life. It is actually preparing its students for a global world -- a world where problems can no longer be divided into separate boxes and where people from different cultures have no alternative but to work together.

In the audience, Bertram begins scribbling down notes.

Hope continues, "The students at Corps Elite School are motivated. They apply what they have learned at school to real life situations. They have mastered the art of working as a team and creating cross-cultural relationships. Corps Elite is a model of what modern education should be. None of this could have come about without the sensitive and intelligent guidance of Mrs. Joyce Gladstone!"

Mrs. Gladstone appears on the TV screen.

"It has been suggested by many of the students from Corps Elite High School that Mrs. Gladstone's approach be implemented throughout the school and that a Students' Council be formed so that all students can give the input, Mrs. Gladstone's approach requires. A majority of students are eager to participate and to help *create the environment in which all students will be motivated to learn and as a result get good grades.*"

Hugh comes forward and speaks: "Needless to say, we all gave credit to Corps Elite High School for the excellent project we have undertaken and to Mrs. Gladstone for her brilliance, great wisdom and guidance without which none of this could have taken place."

The School was flattered. It had made a splash on nothing less than the *Planet Today Show* on nationwide TV.

Mrs. Gladstone is still there, and a Students' Council is now up and running with the full permission and support of the Board," Hugh concludes.

11. Pierre

As the footsteps and the raucous laughter of the militia moved away, Pierre stood, machete in hand, smiling inanely. Totally numbed, his mind in a daze, not being able to absorb the scene at his feet: his children's bodies, bleeding, heads lying at strange angles-- his babies! Perhaps they were just sick.

Carefully, he lifted the mangled corpse of his little boy and gently holding his head in place, he walked into his hut and tenderly laid the small form on its bed. As he looked down at his little son who, just an hour ago, had been singing in the yard, he wondered where his daughter was and went out to check. Gently, he gathered up her little form and laid her next to her brother. The blood bothered him. So he tenderly washed it away, dabbing it with a towel to stem the flow. He grabbed a sheet and covered the hideous gashes so that only their faces were visible.

Then he closed their eyes and stood back. They looked as if they were sleeping.

"There! There! Sleep well. Tomorrow, you'll feel better," he whispered and sank down in a chair.

Softly, he began to sing a lullaby, which his mother used to sing to him. And when he had finished, he sang another, and then another. He sang to take their hurt away, he sang to still his fear, he sang to soothe the pain of the world which he could no longer bear, and he sang to ease the searing pain in his heart, which was radiating out through his body. He sang and he sang until finally, he sang himself to sleep.

12. The Police

Augustina was barely conscious. She had been walking in a haze of pain. Time had no more meaning. All she knew was that she had to keep going if she were going to survive. John supported her as she hobbled forward. Hop! Hop! Hop...

John stopped.

Holding Augustina up with his right arm, he put his left hand to his ear. "The river!" he whispered. "If all is well, the boat should be very close!"

Carefully, he eased Augustina down until she was resting against a tree. Then he inched forward on his own.

Carefully positioned behind a bush, he let out a low whistle, waited and then whistled again. He whistled three times in succession, waited for a minute and then repeated the process over again and again.

Finally an answering whistle. This time five staccato trills. These were also repeated several times.

John broke his cover and waved. There was a soft, "Chug! Chug!" as a boat engine softly came to life.

John moved toward the boat where Augustina could no longer see him.

Again an interminable wait and then the sound of footsteps. There were greetings in the Kukundu language.

Augustina waited, every nerve on end. She could trust no one. Not even John! Had she been betrayed? Betrayed by his ignorance?

John had been kind; he had witnessed the massacre in the church. But coming from one of those so-called democratic countries, he could never suspect the horror of what was befalling Kukundu – husbands killing their children and that by government decree!

Moreover, no one who had not been born and bred in Kukundu understood the language of the drums, which had carried the message to kill to each and every corner of the land. All this flashed through her mind. Then John, followed by a tall policeman carrying a gun, burst through the brush.

"He's a Kukundu!" Augustina cried.

Desperately, on all fours, she tried to scramble away, dragging her broken leg behind her.

13. Bertram's Vignette

On the terrace, the whole group lounged on chaises longues, too full of impressions to speak and too excited to go to bed. The dinner had been light and delicious. In the background, the tinkling of porcelain, crystal and silverware as Consuela set the tables for breakfast.

In preparation for nightfall, Edward had lit the torches. Their flames danced merrily in the slight breeze. The atmosphere was lulled by the hint of waves, caressing the beach in the distance.

Bertram had just spent a quiet half-hour staring into space, only to find his concerns mounting. The young people had made some good points in their play. Schools were making kids vulnerable to fear by forcing them to constantly compare themselves to others; their noses were constantly rubbed in what they were *not*, instead of their individual strengths. As a result, they doubted their own authority and gave away their personal power. Schools like Corps Elite were common in the West. They churned out top business executives who were run by competition and fear – executives whose life only too often came to a grinding halt and who then came seeking Bertram's help.

But weren't governments using competition and fear to keep their citizens in place?

Maurice's voice interrupted his thoughts, "Bertram, why don't you tell the group something about your novel?"

"Yes! Great idea, Maurice!" Mary entered the terrace through the library doors and sank down onto a chaise longue.

Bertram hesitated, then resolutely clicked the back of his lounger into an upright position, dragged it around, and surveyed the whole group relaxing wraggle taggle on the terrace with only Pim perched on a high backed chair. It struck him that there was something about these youngsters, which was different from others he knew– a poise, a self-assurance, he decided.

"Okay, confession time!" He smiled mischievously, as he felt himself rising to the challenge. "Let me begin with myself. I've been thinking a great deal about life today, largely thanks to you.

"I've been more fortunate than most: wealth, status, a successful career, even good, loving parents, and yet, once I had achieved everything I had set out to become, I realized I had lost something essential. It's a feeling of security, belonging, self-confidence, a zest for life, an ability to act from a deep inner conviction. After meeting you, I am getting a better sense of what that is."

He smiled at Annette. "Mrs. Gladstone told us we lose this sense when the emphasis is placed on what we are *not*. Ironically, we lose the feeling of belonging as soon as we let go of what makes our heart sing in order to gain the approval of others. You showed how young people lose it at home and at school. Then you showed how you found it back again when you followed your hearts. The hero in my book barely experienced a feeling of connection at all, and that makes his life feel meaningless.

"The hero has much in common with some of the business executives I get to deal with in my work."

"Actually, I am related to him," Maurice said, "He's the son of one of my brothers. Our whole family is big in the business world, but tend to steer clear of the media."

Bertram acknowledged Maurice and went on, "Your nephew was more than willing to share about himself, though. Yesterday, he joined me on the beach talking up a storm. Lucrative job offers, the fabulous riches in his family, and all the important people he knew. The more he talked, the more I sensed, something important was missing.

"Last night over a cup of hot chocolate, I prodded him, and he opened right up. I must say, I felt deeply touched and privileged. (You already know the story, Maurice, and had gone to bed early.)

"He told me how he lost all sense of connection.

"This morning, he gave me permission to use his story for my new book, providing I didn't mention any names. He said he was leaving this morning early to find something meaningful he could pour himself into."

"I could read you the last page I wrote," Bertram looked around the group. "Mind you, it's not upbeat!"

"Great!"

"Oh, yes!"

Bertram, delighted by the enthusiastic nods, jumped up, skipped into the library, swooped up the pages from his printer and was about to run back out to the terrace when, as an afterthought, he carefully picked up a slender book that lay open on his desk.

As he walked out of the large double doors, Edward, bearing a tray with large bowl- shaped crystal glasses, was doing his rounds of the group.

"Alcohol-free champagne?" Edward intoned and offered Bertram a glass.

"Wonderful!" Bertram exclaimed.

"Heresy to a Frenchman!" Maurice commented and smiled, "But I remember that in California it's forbidden to drink alcohol until you're 21!"

With great care, Bertram placed the slender book he had brought under his chaise longue.

He chose a sheet from among the pile of papers he held in his hand and respectfully holding the large crystal bowl of his glass between his finger and thumb, he sipped the aromatic alcohol free drink.

There was just enough sunlight left to read by.

"This vignette describes what can happen inside a young person who is brought up and educated in situations such as your play describes.

Bertram began,

The Hero, clad in designer pajamas, crept between the sensuous, satin sheets and with a sound that was somewhere between a sigh and a sob sunk back into the soft, oversized pillows. He was oblivious to the sumptuous textures, which were unable to soothe his pain.

Sensual enjoyment must have slipped out of his life when his nursemaid, Mag, was replaced by a governess, the grim faced Mrs. Finch.

He strained his memory.

What had it felt like to be cushioned in Mag's lap? He remembered the long straggling strands of hair, which hung over her shoulders. He'd loved to hold them and pull.

She'd let out a long "Ah!" and then gently, ever so gently, she would take his little fist, ease it open, kiss it and tickle his tummy until he crowed with delight. Surely he must have felt something then?

But the very strain of remembering ruptured the fragile thread of feeling that connected him to his earliest years: the memory wafted away and with it any hope of locating the sense of connection he yearned for so desperately. Immediately, fear raised its head - the fear that he would never succeed in finding something - anything! -that could give meaning to his life.

Was it possible that he had ever relaxed when physically close to another person?

How he longed for someone to say, "Come here," and to just listen to what he had done at school, how the teacher had acknowledged him when he gave a right answer, and how scared he was when Muscle, as the school bully was called, beat up his friend Merlin. Instead, his mother taught him not to touch her for fear of ruffling her appearance. Once he clambered on her lap and was almost brutally pushed away. All he got when he sidled up to his parents was, "Run along now, Johnny, be a good boy."

Bertram looked up at the group. "Earlier, I describe how he grows up with everything, except meaningful contact"

Bertram continued to read:

And then, Mable Smily entered his life, the daughter of his mother's personal maid. He made a pass at her, expecting her to feel flattered.

She looked at him for a long time, then reached out and drew him to her with an expression he could not place. It looked like pity, only that did not make sense. She was plain and poor and had little to recommend her.

"Come here," she had said with a warmth he had never experienced before. She cradled him in her arms and gradually began stroking his back, his torso, his buttocks, his legs. It was then that the memory of Mag tried to surface again. He sensed that something special was taking place, and yet his skin, which had lost all memory of the pleasure of being caressed, felt numb and here and there even painful as his inexperienced senses tried to respond.

45

He returned to Mable the next night and the one after that. They did not actually have sex. Then last night, in a desperate attempt to grasp the experience he sensed was close and which still eluded him, he had forced himself on Mable Smily.

She wrestled herself free.

White and shaken, she ran out of the room wrenching her skirt away from him as she ran.

This morning, when he went down to breakfast, he heard she had left for good. And no one, not even her mother -- the maid! -- would tell him where she was.

He ran up to his room and locked the door.

He had been encouraged to reach for something he had yearned for all his life and before he knew what it was, it had disintegrated and was irretrievably lost. This experience, he sensed, could have restored the thread of his life. He now knew that without that element - whatever it was - life was without value.

Again he strained his memory to feel what life with Mag had been like. But the experience was out of reach. He felt overwhelmed.

Mable knew what it was; she had conveyed it with her touch, with the expression in her eyes and her inner poise.

He must find her. He must force people to help him. But no one trusted him enough.

"What worries me," Bertram looked up, "is that this young man is so desperate for any sense of connection, there's no telling where he will end up!"

"I quite agree!" said Maurice gravely, "Actually, he's done remarkably well. People with his poor start in life fill our mental hospitals or become fanatics, fundamentalists and terrorists. And we're breeding them in our very best schools!"

Suddenly, Bertram had a sense of foreboding, it had something to do with Maurice's nephew, but he could not pinpoint what it could be.

14. The Police Boat

Wildly scrambling to escape, Augustina did not get far. The two men pinned her down, and a hand was clamped firmly over her mouth.

Augustina struggled. It was no good. She was wounded, weak, and powerless against their determined strength.

"What on Earth got into you, Augustina" John whispered urgently, "You'll get us all killed yet!"

With the help of the Kukundu policeman, John managed to turn her around so that he could look at her.

"Augustina, please! This is Jacques. He is a policeman, okay! But he is also part of the underground peace effort. He will be taking us over the border. There we'll both be safe!"

She was sobbing wildly out of control. Patiently, the two men waited. Finally, she looked up and nodded. Supported by the two men, Augustina half hobbled and was half carried to the boat. On board, she was introduced more formally to Jacques, the Kukundu policeman and captain, and Jean the only other member of the crew.

Jacques said, "I'm sorry to have given you such a scare!"

Augustina was too numbed to respond.

John explained, "This is a police patrol boat. Of course, practically nobody knows that Jacques and Jean are a part of the underground peace movement.

"I'm helping them. We've been in touch with the outside world to let them know what is happening. But people refuse to believe us. We'd be extremely grateful if you would help us. But first try and get some rest."

Then she was taken below board to a cabin with a single bunk, made comfortable and given painkillers.

"Please don't go to sleep, Augustina. We need your help urgently. Moreover, who knows what we will encounter on the way? If we are held up, you and I shall have to hide. That means clambering under the floor boards of the boat." He indicated her broken leg.

Augustina closed her eyes; her head was in a spin. In her mind appeared images of her children, lying helplessly there, Pierre with his foolish grin, in the background the screams coming from the church - the church where her mother had gone to meet her, expecting to find a safe haven.

She shuddered and tried to think clearly of the present situation, but the nightmare images kept churning away. It was almost a relief when 15 minutes later the door opened and John entered with Jacques bearing a tray with 3 steaming bowls of chicken soup.

"Jean thought we would like this," Jacques said.

Augustina declined.

"Perhaps you'll feel up to it later," Jacques suggested, "Here, let me put it next to your bed."

From where she was lying, she could see out of the portal. She noticed that the boat was on the move. They were still cruising through the jungle.

The luscious green, adorned with bright splashes of orchids, did little to soothe her churning thoughts.

John explained, "We have had to start the return journey to make the border in time. It is important that we cross in cover of darkness and that Jacques make it back before dawn."

In between sips, he told her how, at the University of Capital City, he had taught students how to find their inner strengths and how to help others to do so also. He was a part of the All-Win Network, which had an office at the U.N.

"Of course, when Kundana came to power, my position was terminated."

Augustina felt a little relief focussing on what he was saying. His gentle voice and large gray, kindly eyes had a soothing effect. As he spoke, he held her foot and his touch seemed to ease the pain.

John continued, "As soon as Kundana came to power, as you know only too well, a divide and rule policy was adopted, pitting Kukundus against Mandus. My friends begged me to stay on secretly and to use all-win principles to turn the policies around. But with Kundana firmly in control, we simply couldn't form the necessary alliances.

"So I've been trying to get help from the outside world. But so far, we have failed there, too."

Jacques could clearly follow the English without any problem. And he used English when he finally spoke to include John in the conversation.

"When we heard via police channels that that mayor in the village where you and John met intended to 'take extreme measures', we decided to come and find out what these were. We had no idea what they were planning."

John continued, "I was just video taping the scene. Then I noticed a movement to the side of the church. I had just aimed the camera in that direction when it dawned on me what that man had been doing. At that moment, the church burst into flames and I heard you scream."

There was a knock at the door. Jean entered. He looked shaken. "Messages flying back and forth that Mandus are being burned alive in churches all across the country!"

Nobody spoke.

Then Augustina broke down and sobbed. The others, deeply shaken, tried to absorb the news.

"It's going to take pictures like this to get people in the Wealthy Countries to pay attention," John said finally. "Augustina, you must help us!

"There's just a chance that if you tell people what you saw and how it came about, and if we combine it with what I filmed, someone might sit up and listen. It's going to take bombshells like this to shake people into looking beyond their personal lives.

"We can video tape you while you speak and then transmit it via this state-of-the-art phone; it transmits both sound and images to anywhere in the world. It's amazing how in the year 2010 new technology is being made available even in poor countries like Kukundu."

Jacques got up and looked out of the window. "What's our bearing?" He turned to Jean. Jean gave him their approximate location.

"But we must do it *now*!" Jacques exclaimed, "We're almost too close to the next settlement. We might get caught. The place is crawling with militia!"

Augustina was too despondent to feel the danger and too tired to resist, and so the filming began.

15. A Scrap Of Paper

Takeshi said hesitantly, "Your story, Bertram, describes some people who grow up in Wealthy Countries in the West.

"In Japan, young people are often torn between wanting economic security, duty to family, doing what is expected by society, and a fear of losing face. That way, doing what you yourself love to do also falls between the cracks. It's all the same thing really. Not being able to follow your heart. And not knowing how."

In the background, the sky looked as if it were on fire, kindled into bright yellow, dark red, and angry orange by the last rays of the setting sun.

"Yes," Bertram said, "in the course of today, it became really clear to me that connection is what it's all about: connection with what we love to do, with what we long to know, to other people, to the good of the Planet. Connection -- you can call it by lots of names: Love, friendship, respect! Pim, isn't that what you were saying? Being connected to the totality, nothing left out?"

Pim, from the heights of his straight backed chair, was following the conversation with his kindly gaze. Nodding, he was just about to reply when Winston said, "That *feeling* of connection ... well, you helped me to feel connected, Sharifa, -- more even than that, I felt cared for and appreciated for what I was and then I no longer needed to think about myself alone. You were by my side, helping to look out for me. I wanted to grow and develop not just for myself or for you but for other people, too. That's why, when Elbert came to me wanting to get into a good school, I tutored him and allowed him to feel the appreciation I feel from you!

"*Feeling* connection's sort of contagious!" he grinned. "I wish that every one could feel appreciated the way I do now."

"That must be it!" Bertram marveled, "Connection leads to a sense of belonging and joy as if your cup is flowing over. And with it comes a surge of desire to pass on this…this bounty to others."

"Yes," Winston agreed, "Bounty's the right word. And when it fills you to overflowing, all you want is to give back what you receive to everyone and everything that can receive it! But the very first step is the caring connection with yourself. That is where it all begins."

Daylight was now gradually losing strength. The light of the torches took over, their flames evidencing in an evening breeze, which was dissipating the blanket of still warm summer air which hung over the terrace.

"What's that book you brought out with you?" Maurice interrupted his thought.

"A man who falls in love with a married woman. Impossible love. Similar theme, written by the German Shakespeare, Wolfgang Goethe. I found this booklet in your bookcase, Maurice, *Die Leiden des jungen Werthers* (Passions of the Young Werther)," Bertram translated.

Delicately, between finger and thumb, he held up the slender volume.

"I can't believe it was there among all your other books, not under lock and key. It's a first edition! Printed in the 1770s -- just lying around in your bookcase!"

"I have little idea of what is kept here," Maurice shrugged. "This is just one of my family homes."

Noticing the puzzled expressions, he continued, "I get to live here, there and everywhere and often I have no idea what a particular home contains."

By now the group looked completely baffled.

Maurice smiled, "Actually, I was practically brought up in boarding schools. My parents traveled all over the world. They died just as I was finishing university and my three brothers inherited the family businesses.

"I was considered the dreamer of the family - a hopeless case--," he chuckled, "and so I get to dispose of my part of the family fortune, live in our family homes, which for the most part stand empty all over the world. The only proviso: 'don't meddle in family affairs.'

"I'm their barometer, they say, as to what's happening among the dreamers of the world!"

For a moment, he absorbed their expressions of awe with a mixture of gratefulness and affection. "You see, this way I get to spend my time with exciting people like you!" His fine crew-cut, like an uncertain halo, for a moment looked translucent, as a slight gust caught the fire of the torches.

"Love, connection…" Bertram turned back to the book in his hand while Maurice puffed away at his cigar.

"Goethe writes about a man who commits suicide because he can't have the woman he loves. Started an epidemic of suicides. Basically, the same theme-- the thread of feeling that connects us to essential parts of our lives snaps and the reason to go on living slips away."

He opened the book toward the end and was about to begin translating from the German when a jagged scrap of paper wafted away, swept along by the breeze.

Ian jumped up and tried to trap the scrap under his foot. For a moment, he seemed about to succeed but, just as he brought his foot down, it wafted up again with Ian in hot pursuit.

Every one burst out laughing, including Ian himself.

With grim determination, Ian made a last lunge and captured the illusive scrap.

Carefully, he picked it up.

"Thanks, Ian!" Bertram said, as Ian handed it to him. He squinted to discern the faint, childlike handwriting by the light of the flickering torches.

"Hssss!" Bertram let out his breath and continued staring at the paper. "It's written in the Old Gothic German script, which was outdated by the middle of the twentieth century."

"What does it say?" one of the twins asked shyly, eyes wide with wonder.

"This is intriguing!" Bertram spoke as if to himself, "Great theme for my next novel," he smiled, "There are some words written across the top, which I can't see very clearly… Half of the paper is missing…but there's a sort of poem." Slowly he translated,

> *To Govern the World*
> *Separate people from what they yearn for most,*
> *Kindle the flame of fear and*
> *The dominion of the planet*
> *Falls into our hands and remains there throughout the ages!*

There was a long silence.

"Sounds like a political strategy …one that's beginning to deliver even the democratic countries into the hands of their leaders!" Mary said gravely. "And the book dates from 17- so- much?"

"Could this scrap of paper also be that old…?" Bertram looked at Maurice.

Maurice puffed thoughtfully at his cigar for a while, then reflected, "It could be, I suppose. This mansion has been in the family forever. Built by one of my French ancestors who came to Costa Rica with the Spanish.

"Probably just one of the classical works they brought with them from Europe. The piece of paper probably found its way into the book by accident and has lain there forgotten since then."

There was a long silence.

"Could be that sinister plot to take over the world!" Ian MacDonald piped up, "Isn't that the story that was going around when he telephone lines were blocked and New York was thrown into chaos? You remember the old conspiracy theory of the Holy Order of the Snake?!"

That set off a couple of hours of speculation, wild imaginings about conspiracy theories.

Around 10 o'clock, exhausted by all the impressions and the long day's sail, one after another drooped off to bed until only Bertram remained.

16. Fewer Have A Say In World Policy

Long after every one had turned in for the night, Bertram remained on the terrace. As he allowed thoughts to come and go, his uneasiness increased.

That scrap of paper… He picked it up. By the flickering light of the torches, he was now just able to discern the words, which he translated from the German:

govern—separate—fear—yearn—kindle—dominion—remain

These words were written in a faint, adult handwriting across the top of the paper. Then underneath in a childish hand:

> To <u>govern</u> the World
> <u>Separate</u> people from what they <u>yearn</u> for most,
> <u>Kindle</u> the flame of <u>fear</u> and
> The <u>dominion</u> of the planet
> Falls into our hands and <u>remains</u> there throughout the ages!"

He shivered.

Pulling his long sleeved cotton shirt on, he got up and walked into the library. To his pleasure, he was greeted by a cozily lit room, thanks, no doubt, to Consuela.

He sank down into a voluptuous easy chair basking in the warm atmosphere.

But it was powerless to drive away the cold chill, which had lodged itself deep inside: *separate, fear, dominion...* the play they had seen that afternoon, the story he himself had written-- all that topped off with a large dose of conspiracy theories... he shuddered.

For a long time he sat with the uncomfortable feeling that there was something he wasn't seeing. In the background, the Tick! Tick! Tick! of the grandfather's clock. Time was seeping away. Had their imaginations been running wild as they had bantered on the terrace? Or was there really a Holy Order of the Snake? Could there possibly be a network of the wealthiest, most powerful men who secretly controlled the arms industry and were out for complete control of the Earth? Would ordinary citizens be forced to fight their governments to hold on to their fundamental rights? And were their governments nothing but mere puppets being manipulated by Snake? That very evening, young Ian MacDonald had mentioned how he, with his ham radio buddies, helped Eliza and her All-Win Network make contact with the outside world, when, a few years back, the telephone lines in the whole of New York City had been jammed during an important U.N. Conference. And that he had asserted had been the doing of the Snake!

"Eliza..."

Fleeing from the feeling of helplessness that was beginning to take over, his thoughts fled to a conversation between Maurice and Mary that morning.

"Strange John St. Clair would ask *my* help," Mary had said, "Surely, Eliza would be a better choice. After all, with Gaia, she heads the All-Win Network's office at the United Nations!"

With a rush of pleasure, he had turned to Mary. "Not the Eliza who was chased around the Middle East wearing a slinky red outfit?" he had asked.

Mary had laughed, "That's Eliza all right! She was forced to flee without her long black cape, just wearing a bright red outfit that, in a Moslem culture, was "unconventional". Just one of her exciting adventures, which sent us all into conniptions!"

"Can you believe it," Bertram had marveled, "Just a few days ago, I was cleaning out my wallet and in the lining I found this tiny yellow newspaper clipping with on it her photo. Must have been there for years! I remember cutting it out. I thought the incident hilarious and really liked her zest for life and that she had helped to found the All-Win Network – well, that did it for me."

Now alone in the library, he walked over to his desk, reached into his jacket pocket and pulled out the newspaper clipping. He found himself looking at the face of the woman with shoulder-length brown hair. She was smiling up at him as if to say, "I'm at the top of the world and loving it! You, too, can feel good!"

"Why not?" He said out loud and grinned to himself. With a thrill of anticipation, he sat down at his computer and checked the Internet. Yes, there was a web site, www.all-winterwork.org with a contact address. He felt an irresistible urge to write to her.

Hurriedly, he tapped out an e-mail.

> *Dear Eliza,*
>
> *I'm a writer/consultant /international speaker. My job? To help top executives cope with globalization and the feelings of fear which often surface as boundaries fall away. I'm noticing an atmosphere of fear is forming. It's affecting more and more people, not least myself. Now I've taken several months off to see what I can do about it. Sitting alone late at night, I find my thoughts dwelling on the Holy Order of the Snake. Could such a thing exist?*

It seemed to him that a powerful, wealthy minority was becoming more and more powerful at the expense of 'ordinary' citizens, and governments were somehow beholden to them. For, with terrorism as an excuse, governments breached or annulled their people's rights while blatantly ignoring the will of millions of demonstrators. In this respect, there was little difference between dictatorships and "so-called democracies!

He continued to write,

> *Actual political power is wielded by a handful of people. In the business world, small companies are being swallowed up by mammoth corporations where just a few people make all-important decisions.*
>
> *So, of the many we believe to be in positions of responsibility, just a few actually hold the reins. And whoever controls this dwindling number could conceivably control our world.*
>
> *If this is more than a figment of an overheated imagination, it lends a dimension of extra urgency to both your and my work.*

Bertram pondered this possibility for a while.

Of course, it is far-fetched ... But if the rumors were true, it would be just conceivable that the Holy Order of the Snake could gain total control. A close-knit family with the arms industry at its beck and call could well use an epidemic of fear to conquer those at the very top of the pyramid of power.

On an impulse, he signed it, hurriedly sent it away and with a sigh returned to his easy chair. For a moment, he sat quietly, trying to pinpoint what he felt. He had followed a feeling that was no more than a hunch and now he was feeling content.

He grinned. He suddenly felt more in control of his life. He must first learn how fear worked, for fear divided reality between what you did and did not want to confront. It impoverished your life. Transforming fear into a *yes!* to life would help him to embrace more without constantly wanting to flee. Just thinking about it gave him the sense that a burden was falling away.

A sweet longing stirred in him. He tried to pinpoint what it was about. In his mind's eye, he saw himself standing next to Eliza, surrounded by a whole network of friends. The yearning increased. After a long life on his own, he realized he was now finally ready for a deep friendship with someone like Eliza.

His reverie was interrupted by footsteps.

The door opened. Maurice walked in, draped in a red silk burgundy-colored robe, which perfectly matched the drapes in the library and in other parts of the house.

"Bertram!" he exclaimed, "You can't sleep either?" Maurice sank down opposite him into an easy chair.

17. Fear As A Conscious Policy

"So what's keeping you up so late?" Maurice asked, "It's past midnight!"

Bertram pursed his lips in a perfunctory smile and said hesitantly, "You have to admit the power is in the hands of less and less people... "

Maurice raised his eyebrows, encouraging him to continue.

Bertram poured out his concerns.

"Many people think that way, and they may well be right," Maurice fixed Bertram with a kindly gaze.

"On the other hand," Maurice teased, "When I think back to the time when every one was talking about the Holy Order of the Snake, their plot was clearly shrouded in so much secrecy that no-one ever saw any proof!" He laughed outright.

Bertram didn't smile.

For a while the two men sat staring in front of them. Then Maurice picked up the scrap of paper Bertram had dropped on the floor. For a long time, he mulled over the words. Sounds like phrases I hear quite a lot… in certain circles," he added. "My parents used words like *divide and rule* a lot and so do my brothers.

"I wonder what the rest of the paper said?" Maurice mused, staring into space.

On sudden impulse, Bertram got up, walked to the bookcase where he had first seen the *Passions of the Young Werther* and felt around in the empty space where the slender volume had stood. The space was just above his head, too high to be able to peer into. "There doesn't seem to be anything here…" his voice was constricted with the effort.

He was about to give up but Maurice jumped up and pulled the chair from behind the desk. With one hand leaning on his host's back, Bertram clambered up and reached all the way in.

"There's another scrap of paper, sticking out from under one of the books." He could just feel the edge.

"Careful!" Maurice cautioned, "The paper's so old, it might tear!"

Painstakingly Bertram removed, one by one, the books under which the paper was jammed. He moved excruciatingly slowly, careful not to tear the ancient piece of paper. Finally, he held it in his hand.

Gingerly, Maurice took it from him. Holding it up to the light, he placed it neatly against the other scrap. "Looks like the missing half to me!" He held the two scraps under the lamp.

"Here, Bertram!" He handed their new discovery to Bertram who was peering over his shoulder. "There's something in light red pencil. I can't read it - what does it say?

Bertram squinted and read slowly "G-u-t!"

"That's German for 'Good'. *A teacher must have graded the poem!*" Bertram exclaimed, aghast.

"Teaching a child how to rule, using fear --deeply disturbing! " Maurice shuddered

"Gruesome to think of a child even thinking these things let alone writing poems about shattering relationships, setting men against one another and enflaming fear, and …and"

"This is a completely different order of magnitude from a Corps Elite School. The school system is perpetuated by people who don't realize they are breeding fear. This is part of a conscious policy! A child, brought up with the idea of taking power over the world as a whole by … by breaking people's spirit…It's …it's…"

"Don't tell me you guys have been up all night!" Mary walked in.

Bertram drew his breath in sharply as he saw her face.

"My word, Mary, you look as if you had seen a ghost!"

"I wish it had been just that! No, much worse! This is reality!"

18. John Gets Through At Last

Bertram jumped up and pulled up an easy chair, as Mary launched into how she had woken up at 5 a.m. as usual and had turned on the BBC World Service. Without interrupting her story, Mary sat down.

"The US's picking up more and more people under the Anti-Terrorist Act according to the BBC. Only reason? They belong to a disenfranchised group. People're simply shoved into jail. No charges, no trial. Glaring breaches of their rights! The jails are overflowing, and they're putting people in camps, forcing them to work in hazardous conditions making vaporizing bombs and guns. And now, they are debating an Anti-Terrorist Act Two!" She seemed to choke on her words.

Bertram was sitting on the edge of his chair, barely daring to breathe.

"Act Two gives US authorities the right to incarcerate anyone, simply for 'consorting with' suspicious minorities. *That means us!*"

Maurice leaned back in his chair with a worried frown. "Surely!…"

"They were quite specific. There are two classes of citizens: the 'haves' and the 'have-nots'. Most have-nots have roots in other countries.

"And then, countries are divided into the same two categories: the Wealthy Countries and those that have 'not yet made it' – in economic terms that is! – This is another designation for what is officially referred to as the 'developing countries'. The idea of this legislation is to safeguard the wealthy (countries and people) from those who want what they have achieved. They say, 'It's their envy, which causes terrorism.'

"The only exceptions to this rule are those who help the powers that be in specific ways. Oil producing countries and others that supply the US with special products or expertise belong to a *Most Favored Nations List.* Then there is '*The President's Most Favored Person's List*', which is made up of people who benefit the US, or, more specifically, the present US Administration.

"Just talking about these things creates a chasm between the haves and the have-nots. It's been building for a long time: all the problems about taking in refugees, identifying certain minorities as 'terrorists', besmirching people and governments from poorer countries and, of course, the Anti-Terrorist Act One itself."

Maurice and Bertram looked at each other. The night's discussion seemed like a far off nightmare suddenly become reality.

"It's economic Apartheid now on a global scale," Maurice said. "Whatever the US does is soon picked up by its 'friends'. The *Most Favorite Nations List* will be an incentive for individual people and governments to do whatever the US requests! This has to be prevented."

"Did Anti-Terrorist Act Two pass?" Bertram asked. His voice trembling slightly. He realized that working with fears of globalization and how to feel comfortable with nationals from other cultures would place him bang smack right in the center of any list of "least desirable people.

"Not yet! But they interviewed a Member of Congress, a fervent supporter of the President's," Mary replied. "Said she'd been offered a large sum of money if she would vote for Terrorist Act Two. Apparently, they didn't think she'd squeal. Thank God, she did. Now, at least, we know what we're up against!"

"I wonder where the Administration gets all the money from? Could there be extremely wealthy backers working behind the scenes?" Bertram whispered. "We're going the same way as Kukundu!"

No one replied. They were each absorbed in their own fears.

After several minutes, Mary spoke, "We must get the exact text both of what the Congress Woman said and of Anti-Terrorist Act Two from the BBC's web site[14]. Then get it out to everyone attending our hook-up. We can suggest all those from the US write to their own Members of Congress for proof of their transparency. With their constituents clamoring for proof that they are honest, they will think twice before taking bribes. Even if they don't deliver proof, they'll be afraid their opponents discover any leanings toward misconduct and then use it against them at election time! After all, they're still elected by their constituents. That's one right, we still have in the US."

Again the three sat in silence.

Dawn was beginning to break. The cozy lights in the library were gradually replaced by the cold light of morning entering through the terrace doors. In the distance, a fragment of birdsong. Then an answering call, heralding the new day. Soon duets, trios, clucking, trills swelled into a symphony as if the whole of Creation were reverberating.

"Hmm!" It was Edward standing in the doorway, "There you are, madam."

"Good morning, Edward. You're up early!"

"Yes, madam.

"Um, it's the phone. The same gentleman who called yesterday is back on the line. You weren't in your room, and then I heard voices down here…"

Eagerly, Mary took the phone, "John? I'm sitting here with Maurice and Bertram, two old friends of mine. We're all working along the same lines. I'll put this on *speakerphone* so that they can listen in.

"Where are you?" She pressed the knob, and John's voice boomed into the room.

"Oh Mary, great to get you on the line at last! Listen. I must be quick. I'm in Kukundu on my way to the border. People in Kukundu have been fed a diet of fear for so long that they are willing to do anything to lessen the tension. Things are completely out of hand. Atrocities, you can't believe, and I can't get anyone outside of Kukundu to pay any attention at all!

"I've been in touch with the U.N. Secretary General's office. Couldn't get the SG himself– too many crank calls, I suppose. His office would not listen to my story, unless I had tangible proof.

"I've also been in touch with the U.N.'s Human Rights Committee -- same thing. They, too, need proof."

"What about Eliza and the rest of the All-Win Network? They are inside the U.N.[15]," Mary said.

Bertram pricked up his ears.

"I tried their office. Eliza was there," John's voice continued. "She did everything to rouse the groups. If anyone can persuade groups to act, it is she, but in the end she failed. Every one is too busy surviving. They're holding their heads low, afraid to attract attention to any of their activities. Even the Human Rights NGOs which have remained active say that they have 102 dictatorships to deal with and Kukundu is a lost cause."

There was a brief silence, then John's voice continued, "The new US President has it in for organizations affiliated with the U.N. Doesn't like the U.N. at all. Just fraternizing with disenfranchised groups can get you into trouble. And since the local All-Win Education Centers take in *anyone* local, including 'suspect' minorities, they are constantly courting danger. The last thing they want to do is to attract the authorities' attention. Eliza says the word is, 'We've too much on our own plates already. If we take on anything else, we'll botch everything we do.' She says that personally she will do anything in her power to help."

Bertram felt his heart sink. Even Eliza's hands were tied. Anti-Terrorist Act Two or not, the persecution was already in full swing.

"Eliza's spending time outside the office since Brian died several months back."

Bertram caught his breath.

"Is Eliza alright? This is Bertram speaking."

"I think she is having a rough time. But you know Eliza. She's a loner when it comes to her own feelings. Tends to withdraw and lick her wounds, instead of seeking support. The only thing we can do for her is to give her the space she wants!"

Bertram felt in his pocket. The newspaper clipping was still there. In the background, he heard John let out a long sigh, unaware that it was heard by his friends so many miles away.

Then in a small voice, John said, "Mary, I need your help! You're my last chance!

"Are you still holding your ham radio meetings with the network of kids around the world?"

"Well, yes. There'll be one next Thursday here, combined both with an email discussion and a video hook-up!" Mary answered.

"We're desperate to get the word out to people outside of Kukundu about the atrocities that are happening here," John said.

"You can be sure that if it grabs the young people, their parents, peers, anyone they can reach will soon know all about it," Mary smiled, "Actually your call is perfectly timed!" And she told him about the concentration camps in the US, the Anti-Terrorist Act Two, and the attempt to bribe the Congresswoman. "Perhaps hearing about what is happening in Kukundu will alert people to the dangers developing in the US."

John asked, "Would you also be able to reach people in Kukundu itself?"

"Yes, these hook-ups are geared to the young people's networks, but anyone can tune in," Mary pointed out.

"Well, we're trying to rally people inside Kukundu, as well as those who have fled the country to start a dialogue on how to reverse the situation.

"By the way, I have a film about the atrocities in Kukundu, but I warn you-- it's shocking. Could you show it to your young people's networks during the video hook-up?"

"When can you get the film to us, John?" Mary inquired.

"We're still in the middle of filming it. Augustina who we're interviewing is taking a break. But it's almost done. With a late model of the solar video phone, you can have it within a couple of hours."

Mary turned to Maurice. "Perhaps you could discuss the technical details with John?"

Maurice seemed at a loss.

"Perhaps I can help," Edward's voice spoke from the shadows behind the open door.

Edward, inconspicuous as ever, had been following the conversation without anyone noticing him.

As John outlined the technicalities, Edward responded, "No problem, sir... Okay. Just as soon as you send it, sir, we will be ready to show it!"

19. The Videotape

Still strapped into their regime at sea, the group was awake by six. Radiating her 'get up and go' energy, Mary was still pale and tense. To the tinkling of silverware and of bone-thin china, she told them about the Anti-Terrorist Act Two, the attempt at bribery, John's phone call and the Kukundu film, which had already arrived.

"I suggest we view that as soon as we can. John says it's a horrendous situation and we're his last chance. It's important. A Kukundu-type situation could happen to us."

Bertram allowed his thoughts to linger on where Eliza was and what had become of her now that her husband had passed away. Would she answer his e-mail, he wondered.

In the background, his friends were urgently exploring the new situation. Had Kukundu reached a point of no return? Were other countries following in its tracks? Could Kukundu's example motivate the rest of the world do an about-turn?

While Consuela cleared the dishes away, Edward accompanied Ian and Hugh to the little theatre where together they set up the video.

Bertram joined Mary as she strolled out through the library doors onto the majestic terrace. The afternoon breeze fanned his face and ruffled his hair while the tang of the salt in the air titillated his nostrils. Pim was perched on the top of the balustrade, looking out to sea. In the distance, the cliffs, jagged against the bright blue sky, were like so many teeth ready to devour a next victim.

"Pim, anyway you can stay and watch the film?" Mary asked.

He turned.

"Perhaps if I know what's happening in Kukundu, I can ask my colleagues' advice on what we can do. I'd better let them know I'll be late." Stiffly, he descended from his perch and disappeared into the library.

Fifteen minutes later, again with an air of awe, they were all filing back into the plush, yet cozy theatre auditorium where the day before they had performed their play. Above them rose three stories of balconies with private stalls like an earlobe from the stage. The room, seats, curtains, balconies -- all burgundy, decorated with gold, the trademark of this part of the house.

The screen was already set up, and the film was ready to go.

After a last minute check that everything was under control, Edward withdrew.

A few minutes later, two floors up, a door to a balcony stall opened, and a figure, not visible from where the group was sitting, silently positioned himself so that he had a perfect view of the screen.

With a crackling sound, Augustina's tear-stained face appeared on the screen. Her English was broken, and her words were alternately jumbled and halting. She told about the divisions which had been enflamed as soon as Kundana came to power, how bribes had been paid out to supporters of Kundana, and how Kundana's frequent media addresses had intensified the atmosphere of insecurity. Bertram felt nauseous. There could be no doubt that what Augustina reported was true. It was in line with BBC World Service Reports and he was a firm believer in the BBC.

"Perhaps it is best to stop the film here! I'm not sure watching this is a good idea," Mary interrupted. But, their dazed expressions intent on the screen, the young people remained glued to their seats.

Augustina described how fear began to color relations with her friends and neighbors whom she had known all her life; and how the fear then created a chasm between herself and her husband and led to the first atrocities between friends. She told how the Kukundus had been encouraged to rob and attack the Mandus until the President's final cry for blood. Then, with full sound intensity, came the scenes around the church and the final conflagration, accompanied by screams.

Then the video screen went black.

The group sat in stunned silence.

Edward, who had stood watching the video from the open doorway, turned on the lights.

Finally a tiny voice said, "How can they let something like that happen?" Jan's large dark eyes had a hollow, haunted look. She was too shocked to cry.

Her question was left hanging unanswered. No one trusted themselves to speak.

"Pim, can you help us cope with what we have just seen?" Mary whispered in his ear. Pim looked around at the stricken expressions.

"Let's go out and sit in the sun," he said on sudden impulse. "It has been a shock to every one's system."

"Silently, the group filed out of the room through the library and onto the terrace. They huddled together, in twos and threes, seeking solace in one another's proximity. The twins on one chaise long, Annette and Takeshi on another, Sharifa coiled against Winston's large frame and the others nestling on the couches.

Maurice sat bolt upright on his chaise longue, his crewcut glistening in the sun, but without his usual cigar.

Bertram wondered, "Would their physical closeness, warmth, friendship, and even love help them to come to grips with a world which defied understanding? He realized that he, as much as any of the others, needed time to integrate what he had experienced. He thought of how much warmth and love he even now received from his own mother, even though she was approaching 95. To think of anything happening to her at all gave him the shivers. He couldn't imagine the horror, if she were burning alive in a church like Augustina's mother, while he was forced to look on.

He looked over at Mary. She, like every one else, was clearly affected by the film. Her eyes darted from one to the other of her young crewmembers, her eyes registering the pain of each one there.

For several hours, they all ranted, cried and mulled over every possible angle of what they had seen. Pim allowed the disjointed comments, emotions and rationalizations to run their full course.

Bertram was still nauseous, overwhelmed by a sense of hopelessness. Such horrors could never be forgotten. How could anyone live with the memory of such atrocities, be it as witness, victim or perpetrator?

Finally, the group fell silent.

With a nod and an attempted smile from Mary, Pim asked, "So how does a situation like that make people do things they would otherwise never dream of doing? And is it possible to reverse such a situation?

"Ever heard the story of the Hundredth Monkey?"

There was a surprised giggle from Antonia. Then a few laughs: a welcome change of subject.

"I remember," Jan called out, disentangling herself from her twin, "One monkey started washing sweet potatoes before eating them. Then other monkeys copied its behavior. Then, when one hundred monkeys started washing their potatoes, monkeys on far away islands got the same idea. They somehow picked it up from the others without even meeting them!"

"That's right!" Pim smiled, "Ideas seem to hang in the air, forming a sort of atmosphere. The more people think and feel a certain way, the stronger that particular atmosphere becomes. Often without knowing it, people pick it up. In Kukundu the atmosphere of fear is so strong that no one can ignore it."

"Our dog picks up fear!" Jeff pointed out. "Toby's every one's friend! Just give him a tidbit and he'll follow you home. But as soon as someone's afraid, he senses it and, even if the person would never harm him, he growls threateningly!"

"Reminds me of a book I once read," Pat plunged into the lighthearted conversation. "About this dog who would know when his master would come home. I could just see this black and white longhaired ball of fur. No matter what time his master came, his dog'd be waiting in exactly the same place, around ten minutes ahead of time! He knew what his master was thinking.

Pim nodded. "The writer you are talking about is called Rupert Sheldrake -- a scientist I greatly respect. He documented around 5000 cases of animals that knew things about their masters that their ordinary senses could not have picked up. He developed a theory about what he calls *morphogenetic fields*."

Concerned whether they were able to follow him, he looked around.

"*Morphogenetic fields?*" Jeff prompted.

"These are fields of information which connect people, animals and things to others to whom the information is relevant. I picture it this way: everything and every one automatically emits information, like a radio transmitter, without necessarily realizing it. The information is picked up by who or whatsoever is open to receiving it. People are most sensitized to people and things they feel most connected with. So twins are often closely attuned to each another's information fields." He looked at Jeff and Jan. "All human cells are attuned to a field that informs each how to develop. All plants and animals of the same species have a common field. And so do those with similar experiences, those from the same culture, race, nationality, etc each has its own field. People, animals and places that share common experiences – Each phenomenon is connected to a number of morphogenetic or information fields. Churches pick up an atmosphere. Electrons that have shared a same locality are in touch with one another throughout the ages. The Universe is one huge information field, through which information is constantly being exchanged between individuals, species, and particles of matter[16].

Fear is an emotion, which many people are sensitized to; it is associated with survival. And so people tend to pick up fear from the field without knowing it. They feel afraid and their fear then heightens the atmosphere of fear. And so fear breeds fear without people realizing what is happening.

Bertram caught his breath. "*That's why I who am seldom afraid have been in the grip of fear! I was right to think that fear has become a generalized human condition, especially in the world of business*," he thought. His challenge was becoming clearer. He would have to find out how to free himself from this atmosphere of fear and stay clear of its influence!

"In Kukundu, fear has assumed epidemic proportions and may well be spilling over into the rest of the world. And when such an atmosphere is enflamed by, say, a government egging people on, people will do anything – anything at all! -- to rid themselves of the tension."

"The Governments in the Wealthy Countries are dangerously close to bringing this about. This new Anti-Terrorist Act Two would give people's darkest fears a boost."

Bertram wondered whether unconsciously the atmosphere of fear in the business world had been gnawing away at him. He had called it fear of globalization, but fear was in the air.

"Well, Kukundu is a poor country!"

"People simply don't know any better!"

"Nothing like that could happen here!"

"I wish it were as simple as that!" Pim interrupted the group's exclamations quietly.

Why don't we break for a swim and then lunch and meet back here at one?

During the break, Bertram checked his computer in the slim hope that Eliza would have answered his e-mail. And there it was: a short note.

> *Dear Bertram,*
>
> *I believe there is a Holy Order of the Snake. I have forwarded your e-mail to one of our co-workers who lives in hiding. He answers these types of questions. Also contact any of the World Citizen Centers if you would like help with your feelings. These specialize in helping people come to grips with the low-level anxiety which alienates us from ourselves.*
>
> *There are several organizations, which might help you to prepare top business executives to better handle the complex processes of globalization.*
>
> ➢ *The World Federalists are one of the oldest peace movements. Today, they are leaders of democratic global governance and international democracy. Their vision of the U.N. becoming a democracy of Nations and peoples was ignored for many years while leaders, like Everett Millard, crafted excellent proposals to strengthen the U.N. These are finally being taken seriously. Bill Pace, the World Federalist General Secretary, has played a leading role in the establishment of a new world court for war crimes and the acknowledgment by the UN that the ideas of nine 'major groups' maybe relevant to the work of the UN. Business is one of these 9 Major Groups. Representatives of the global business community therefore occasionally have an opportunity to attend U.N. conferences, to provide input into draft global agreements, and to occasionally take the floor. The World*

Federalists might be able to provide speakers to give corporations a better idea of how the U.N. works and where it is headed.

➤ *The Brahma Kumaris Spiritual University provides people with useful tools to calm their minds and get in touch with their creativity. This can help business people to more easily fashion their job descriptions to better capitalize on their unique strengths. The Brahma Kumaris is unique. It is run by women, although many members are men. They are known for their projects, which make huge masses of people aware of how each can contribute constructively, as we become an increasingly global world.*

One of their projects consists of a Guidebook, called Living Values, which can be used to help your business clients integrate specific all-win values into their daily lives. Among the 12 they mention are honesty, love, peace, respect, responsibility and tolerance.

These days, I tend to focus on helping people, organizations, governments, and the U.N. to see how the all-win principle can be used to deflate fear. The all-win principle is a useful tool for organizations which are moving into global markets. It can help them work more harmoniously with people from different cultural and religious backgrounds.

These are challenging times, I know. Sometimes it's tempting to give up, Bertram, but please continue with your research!

Eliza.

Bertram felt a rush of joy. She took his concerns seriously. The kinship he'd felt when he'd cut out her photo was growing and all because he'd followed a hunch and written to her. Had the strength of his feelings communicated itself to her via the morphogenetic field? He smiled: he must be careful not to get carried away, neither with his growing feelings for Eliza, nor with any theories however "cutting edge" they might be.

20. Meanwhile Eliza Is In New York

Eliza hurried along First Avenue, while on her left, the row of flags of the U.N.'s 200 –odd Members gaily snaked along for the full five city blocks occupied by the United Nations. Flashing her badge at the guard, she skirted the Dag Hammarskjöld Library with its thousands of official U.N. documents and then again showing her badge, she entered the 50-story Secretariat.

Juan, the slender guard from Peru, greeted her with a "How are you, this morning?" Eliza smiled, allowing herself to absorb the atmosphere of peace. Past the elevator blocks, she turned left down the large hall with the black and white marble floor. Walking past the row of paintings of the U.N.'s Secretary-Generals, she silently greeted Trygve Lee and Dag Hammarskjöld with whom she had a special bond.

Since the death of her husband, Brian, she had kept her feelings of grief at arm's length, by plunging herself into her work. Today, she had awoken with a gnawing sensation of sadness and knew the time had come to stop running away from her feelings. Gaia, her friend and colleague at the office, was organizing a lunch time concert. They had decided to close down the office so that both of them could attend.

Eliza entered the Conference Building and took the lift to the fourth floor where she was ushered into a private dining room, just as lunch was being served.

A seat near the door was vacant. A cool gazpacho soup was gently placed before her as she sat down. Before her, bowls of white and whole-wheat rolls and large pats of sweet butter stood invitingly on the table.

The event was being sponsored by the All India Spiritual University. Gaia was opening the meeting.

"Before we start, I'd like to invite Terry and Luci of the Rainbow Bird to give us a taste of their after dinner concert." Gaia tossed her long pigtail over her shoulder. Then, with her characteristically mischievous smile, she drew her white sari around her, and ceded the stage to the singers.

The duo looked familiar, but Eliza couldn't place them...

The petite brunette with soft, curly hair and eyes which at one moment were earnest and intense and the next were bubbling with humor stood with one foot resting on a low stool. Her almost childlike frame was dwarfed by her 12-string guitar. Though small in stature, it was her inner charisma that reached out to everyone in every corner of the room. Next to her, her companion Luci, a tall, attractive blond, complimented her fiery companion with her warm womanliness. Both hummed a melancholy tune, and then the words engulfed Eliza, carried by the tender longing tones of Terry's voice. Luci's full, high soprano sometimes danced above the melody. At other times it sank down below it to provide a warm bedding for the haunting tune.

> *You...you are the morning star*
> *First light, companion to the sunrise*
> *You shine on the world,*
> *you bring so much beauty*
> *it touches me to the core.*
> *You are the sunrise and so much more,*
> *Beloved morning star*[17]

The words clutched at Eliza's heart until she felt as if her heart were being squeezed into a tight ball. The sense of connection with something so much larger than herself had been a part of her life as long as she could remember. It had been a part she had later shared so intimately with Brian. Yet this lifeline had been savagely ruptured, when Brian had been killed. Now, engulfed by the music, she allowed herself, for the first time since he had passed away, to feel the full impact of being alone.

Tears welled up inside of her. She struggled to hold them back, but the surge was too strong and her tears began to stream down her cheeks. Eliza got up hastily, stumbled out of the room, passed the elevators and ran into the ladies room. She pushed the door of the bathroom closed, locked herself in the stall and, with a sense of great relief, allowed her feelings full flow.

She must have sat there for a good half-hour, head in hands. Her pain and acute loneliness gradually ebbed away, her sobs became less explosive and finally she just sat there, weak and numbed. Carefully, she opened the door of the stall and looked at her face in the mirror.

No, she looked too ravaged to return to the dinner. Her friends would feel concerned. She didn't feel like attracting attention just now. She wanted to be alone. She had better go back to the office.

She managed to find an empty elevator and hurried out of the Visitor's Entrance, across First Avenue and into the DC 1 building. Holding her head down as she greeted the guard, she took the elevator up, entered her office and hurriedly closed the door. She hoped that no one would disturb her. She needed time to herself.

Again she allowed her tears to flow, grateful for the relief it brought. Then she lay down on the couch and gave herself permission to numbly stare into space.

21. The Defunct Reptilian Brain

A cool swim, a short bake in the hot sun followed by a break for lunch took the edge off the Kukundu experience.

Pim was waiting for them on the terrace in the shadow of the balustrade. His long-sleeved, olive colored dress shirt, top button daringly undone, matched his olive colored pants from which protruded incongruously his two bare feet, toes nonchalantly covered with sand from his walk along the beach.

Edward was plying every one with tall glasses of cool, fresh lemonade. A feeling of peace had descended, except for Arturo and Pat. Bertram smiled:

Arturo was sitting comfortably on the sofa, his arm draped over the back, while Pat, next to him, sat bolt upright. Her bearing shouted for every one to hear: *"I'm avoiding physical contact. I'm not reaching out to him."*

Pim began.

"What is happening to Kukundu is intimately connected to each of our own lives.

"Look at your experience at Corps Elite. You were all acting from fear. Not the practical, helpful sort of fear that prompts you to steer clear of a fire. It is an existential anxiety. One created by your thoughts -- those that tend to bug you over and over again for large parts of your life: *Can I succeed? Will others respect me?* – we each have our own combination. These fears color our experience during the day and dominate our dreams when we sleep. These fear-thoughts go on year after year. They're like a chronic pain. We're so used to them, we're not even conscious they are there. These fears meld into an existential anxiety."

Pat unthinkingly leaned back with a sigh. Then feeling the crook of Arturo's arm, she violently jerked away, looking up at him as if to say, "How dare you make a pass at me!"

He grinned, enjoying his own ability to create such a reaction in her.

Bertram watched the growing intimacy with a smile.

"So," Pim continued, "cut a *person* off from what makes his heart sing and you are creating a fearful person.

"Create a *system*, which cuts people off from themselves -- be it a school, a family, a place of work or a whole country like Kukundu, then the fears of all the people in that system feed off one another and you get a whole atmosphere of fear."

Jan extricated herself from her twin. "But I don't feel that sort of fear!"

Pat, bolt up right again, shifted uncomfortably to relieve the ache in her back.

"Quite. Because when we live in an atmosphere of fear," Pim continued, "we each translate the feelings into our own terms. You mentioned the fear of getting bad grades, another is afraid of people with a different color skin. And most of us are afraid of being rejected by others, not living up to expectations, not looking good, not keeping up with the Jones's etc., which ultimately translate into fears for our own survival if we don't fit into our communities."

"In business, we're afraid of not being able to perform on the job, not making it in a global world, having people take over our positions, not getting our next pay-raise," Bertram thought.

Pim continued, "We're each driven by our personal versions of the fear. We believe our *individual* survival is at stake. We think that it's our personal problem and don't realize to what extent we are being driven by fear that is, as it were, 'hanging in the air.'"

"Problems exist," Pim went on, "Don't get me wrong. But the atmosphere of fear blows them out of all proportion. And so, we have no eyes or ears for anything beside our own travails. The result? While we're involved with our personal versions of fear, governments pass anti-terrorist legislation and spirit away our rights. And we allow them to do it because we're too distracted to notice. Or we and they both are unable to distinguish psychological fear from real danger."

Mary rubbed her thighs. Deciding they had had enough sun, she covered them with her towel. She was now visibly more relaxed. "More and more government policies play on our fears of terrorism, foreigners, minorities, the 'have-nots', power hungry wealthy people," Mary remarked, "These fears are used to justify laws, like the Anti-Terrorist Act. These give governments a stranglehold on us, their citizens.

"The Anti-Terrorist Act allows the FBI to monitor everything from e-mail, to medical records, to library accounts—really scary," Mary continued. "They can now legally wiretap phones, break into homes and offices, and access financial records without probable cause.[18]"

"In direct violation of Article 12 of the *Universal Declaration of Human Rights*, which gives each person the right to privacy," Hugh said.

"And so, while we look the other way, the fear epidemic increases," Bertram thought. Too restless to remain seated, he got up and leaned against the balustrade from where he could see the golden beach, the turquoise sea and the bright white waves lapping the shore. How he wished that he didn't have to face what was being said. He took a deep breath and forced himself to focus on what Pim was saying.

"A Kukundu situation can come about when a country's in the hands of people who believe money, status or power is where it's at," Pim continued.

"In other words, in the hands of people like us might have become," Hugh said, "if we had not met Mrs. Gladstone and Mary."

"You, or Bertram's hero," Pim agreed. "Kukundu is no different from any other society, where people are sensitized to fear. It's a matter of degree. The situation in the US, even with the present Anti-Terrorist Act, is like a tinderbox. Just one incident, fuelled by the powers that be, can inflame fear to such a fever pitch that people's behavior changes unrecognizably."

Pat's fidgeting increased.

Arturo took his arm off the backrest and softly eased her back.

Struggling briefly, she turned to look at him. He smiled gently and with a "come hither!" nod of his head, he coaxed her to relax until she settled in the crook of his arm.

Pim continued, "In a heightened state of fear, the more humane human qualities tend to be bypassed – specifically those qualities which urge us to pause, reason and assess. And with these qualities gone, we lose our natural sense of right and wrong.

Without these human qualities, we revert to a more primitive state in which fear and aggression, flight or fight dominate what we feel, think and do. This fight or flight state of mind has much in common with what is sometimes called the *reptilian brain*[19].

All eyes were now riveted on Pim.

"With an important difference," he continued, not giving them time to relax. "And that's where the problem comes in. You see, reptilian and other animal behavior is instinctually kept in check. Animals kill in moderation. Instead of massacring, they tend to use threatening body language and sounds to ward off competitors.

"Human beings have *lost their moderating animal instincts.* Their animal instincts made way for free will, accompanied by a natural sense of right and wrong, an inborn conscience.

But when we by-pass our inborn conscious, revert to our reptilian brain, we no longer have the instincts that moderate animal behavior. So both our human conscience and our animal instincts no longer function. In effect, our reptilian brain is defunct! Gone all sense of moderation!

There was a "Pooooof!" as Bertram, who had stood listening to Pim sank back into the soft pillows of his lounger.

"Compounded by existential anxiety, our behavior knows no bounds. We see everything through fear colored glasses. In this state, we are capable of bending or breaking the law and committing the most heinous crimes, going on rampages of killing, justified because we believe we stand alone, under attack in a dangerous world."

"That's how my people almost became extinct!" David said softly, "My ancestors, the first American inhabitants, were slaughtered just like the buffalo."

"Yes, David. When we are acting from our defunct reptilian brain, fear turns into greed and violence. We believe that money or power will save us from what we fear. Yours is one example among many where an atmosphere of fear, greed and lust for power took hold in countries. It was mainly the British, French and Spanish who conquered the Americas. They purposely gave the Native Americans blankets infested with small pox and wiped out whole villages. The British discovered the concentration camps. The culture, which produced Goethe, Mozart, Beethoven and Bach, further refined these death camps. And the Israelis, many of whom were brought up in the shadow of the holocaust, have themselves reduced Arab settlements to rubble, leaving people like themselves with nowhere to turn. In Africa, the Blacks captured their own kind and sold them into slavery and treat the Pygmies and Bushmen like second-class citizens. The atrocities perpetrated by a Djenghis Khan, Stalin and so on are examples of the defunct reptilian brain."

22. Orange-tinted Glasses

"But surely, people don't have to act from their reptilian brain!" Jan exclaimed.

"It's not as easy as all that." Pim clambered up off his high-backed chair and looked around the group. It was essential that they understand this point, "When every one is infected with fear, you sense it wherever you go. And worst of all: the atmosphere is so part of you that you're not conscious that it's there![20]

"You see, even when we're constantly a little anxious, we don't realize what's happening, until it's too late. It's like seeing the world through dark orange-tinted glasses. We can't see anything clearly and some things we don't see at all. And this creates a whole slew of problems." He began pacing to and fro.

"You mean this is what makes us feel unsure of ourselves?" Jan frowned.

"That's right. To start with, we don't trust ourselves sufficiently to know who is trustworthy or not, and so we either don't trust anyone, or trust the wrong people. This makes us feel defensive and terribly insecure. It also makes it impossible to work closely with anyone at all. And so our loneliness increases and so does our fear together with the greed, lust for power and other emotions that we are tempted to use increasingly to cope with a hostile world.

Bertram allowed himself to smell the tang in the air, to be engulfed by the swishing sound of the waves, softly lapping at the beach. It did him good to be so acutely aware of the beauty that also existed, besides these threatening sides of life.

Pim continued, "This way of life causes stampedes for resources, brings us the nuclear threat, global warming, the population explosion and has led us to contaminate chickens, pigs and cows with diseases contagious to humans." As he spoke in his quiet unassuming way, Pim's eyes moved around the group, stressing, as he looked down at his new friends with the mixture of intensity and concern, what he seldom did with his voice.

He continued, "And each of the problems we are creating increases the level of fear in the air. So when a person comes along with a strong-armed approach, we're only too happy to have a father figure that takes responsibility for our lives.

"Eventually, such a person gets so much power that he can order people to do the most terrible crimes."

Arturo carefully freed his arm, easing Pat gently until she leaned comfortably against the back of the sofa. His golden necklace flashed against his dark tan, as he sat up straight. "You know, as a gang leader, I literally was given the power over life and death of the members of my gang! Gang members would in some cases give their lives for the gang."

Pim nodded, "Yes, I'm sure you're right, because once we have given ourselves over to a strong leader, there seems to be no way out. By the very act of capitulating, we're saying to ourselves *'I'm weak and the leader is so strong that he (and it's usually a he) is better able than me to take charge of my life.'* And so, we turn a blind eye to any failings the leader may have. And together, we create a Kukundu, Nazi Germany, Stalin's Russia, but because of our orange-tinted glasses, we don't realize the situations, we, ourselves, are creating."

Arturo gently eased Pat's head against his shoulder again. With a smile, she looked up at him and relaxed.

Pim continued gravely, "It's as if the world is divided into two groups of people. There are those whose fear glasses, most of the time, lead them to focus on a strong leader, someone who interprets reality for her or him; and then there are those who, more often than not, are aware that they are intuitively connected with and therefore feel a part of the world around them. This last group tends to be less easily manipulated than the first. Of course, each of us has both sides in us. That's what makes life such a challenge."

Bertram felt too restless to lie down. He hoisted himself up out of his lounger again and paced to and fro.

"Remember that scrap of paper?" he burst out, "Well, last night Maurice and I located the missing half. Turned out it was a ghoulish exercise some child had been exposed to. His British phlegmatism now irretrievably lost, he told them about his recent e-mail from Eliza about the Holy Order of the Snake.

"The atmosphere of fear is intensifying. Just imagine if a tiny group of people would want supreme power, then creating a terrorist scare can frighten people into giving dictatorial powers to their governments. It is happening in democracies, such as the US, the UK, and Australia. So why not everywhere else? What with our present leaders dividing us, their citizens, into "good guys" and "bad guys", I wonder how much is necessary before people start attacking one another? And if then the government turns a blind eye, (or even fuels the conflicts), the US, the UK, and Australia or other previously democratic countries will each turn into their own versions of Kukundu."

Jeff exclaimed, "You mean that if people become scared enough, a network like the Holy Order of the Snake could actually rule the whole world by stirring us up against one another?"

"That is certainly possible," Pim agreed, "The fear epidemic threatens our survival, no matter where we are."

Completing Pim's thought, Maurice said, "And to reverse this situation, we must reclaim the power over our own lives and inspire 7 billion-odd others to do the same – and that without increasing people's fears. And we have to succeed, otherwise a group of people like Bertram's Hero or President Kundana with a ruthless group of supporters could take control of our world!"

Pim chuckled, "You are right, Maurice! To be frank, neither I, nor my scientist colleagues have the answer. And yet the Universe is full of marvels…!"

Bertram suddenly grinned. How wonderful to be with such friends! Without them, it would be easy to continue to feel overwhelmed. There had to be a way of tackling this. He would not give up now! He would face this fear of being overwhelmed, of not being able to cope. He was no different from Eliza, Pim. Mary, these courageous young people. His only option was to deal with his fears and then he would find ways of helping others to each take control of their own lives.

"Let's take a ten minute break," Pim suggested, and Edward who had been standing out of sight just inside the library door hurried away to the kitchen.

23. Bertram Follows His Heart

Bertram hurried into the library and sat down at his computer. Leaning his chin on his cupped hands, he sat for a while conjuring up the image of the face on the yellowed newspaper photo. He had liked her instantly, her bright smile, that quality of not being beaten, of saying "Yes!" to life and encouraging others to do the same. How he would like to be like that and have someone like her by his side. His loner days were over. For a moment, he stared into space, allowing the words to emerge. He started to write,

> *Dear Eliza,*
> *Thank you for your e-mail. Today, I heard of the death of your husband. This must be a difficult time.*

He hesitated. *"Aren't I being too personal?"* He decided to take the plunge and say whatever his heart dictated.

He continued,

> *It means a great deal to me that you took the time to respond to my e-mail.*

An image flashed across his mind of his high-school girlfriend, brown curly hair, sparkling eyes, full of a zest for living he had never encountered in quite that way until he had seen Eliza's photo in the paper. She was telling him excitedly that she had been accepted as a U.N. Volunteer to go to Africa for a year. Then came the phone call from her parents... *"How can life snatch someone away who was so full of the love for living?"* He swallowed, trying to get rid of the lump in his throat, but it refused to dissolve. He had never allowed himself to experience the pain surrounding her death. Now it had surfaced. He continued to write:

> *My high school girlfriend died in an earthquake in Africa, as we were about to turn twenty. And as I write to you, I realize, I have never allowed myself to grieve: I plunged myself into my work and have been working ever since. My relationships with women have been more sexual than a man/woman type of intimacy. What have I missed out on, I wonder? Never having had the guts to grieve has made me leery of my feelings.*
>
> *And now, I realize, I have no alternative but to face my fears.*
>
> *Eliza, thank you so much for taking the time to reply. As I write this e-mail, and after the last one, too, I realize that our correspondence is causing me to look inwards and to learn about aspects of myself, I never knew were there.*
>
> *I wish you courage and wisdom in dealing with your loss.*
>
> *With warm support,*
>
> *Bertram*

Bertram felt moved, as he thought of Eliza, as if her loss were his own. What was she going through? He felt deeply connected to her and that made him uncomfortably vulnerable. How would she react to his confession? Would she feel put off? Would she answer at all?

He had never acknowledged to others how afraid he had been of allowing his feelings free flow. Until now, he hadn't even acknowledged it to himself. For a moment, he allowed himself to sense how he felt about this huge step he had taken in opening himself up to another woman. It felt good, he decided, and somehow safe to be opening up to Eliza.

24. Eliza and Gaia

Unbeknown to Bertram, as he had been typing his letter, Eliza had been going through her own grieving process. Now, finally in the office, Eliza locked her office door, threw herself onto the couch, and allowed her feelings full rein. She had held them in far too long.

A quiet tap at the door.

A gentle voice, "Eliza, it's Gaia!" And Gaia entered.

"I'm probably up for a vacation," Eliza smiled as she hurriedly wiped away her tears. "You looked so tense," Gaia said, "when you entered the Dining Room. Then as Terry and Luci started singing, you looked … you looked overcome." Her large, dark eyes were gently scanning Eliza's face. Tossing her long, thick pigtail over her shoulder and drawing her white sari around her, she sank down opposite Eliza.

There was something about Gaia's gentle voice … Eliza felt touched. While up there on the stage, Gaia had taken the trouble to notice how she, Eliza, was feeling. Without wanting to, Eliza started crying softly, while Gaia sat quietly, her presence exuding a warm haven, until, finally, Eliza wiped her tears away again with the back of her hand.

"It's about Brian, isn't it?" Gaia asked gently. "It's taken you such a long time to come to terms with your grief. I've watched you work so very hard and I suspected that it was all pent up inside, perhaps too excruciating for you to dare to let it out. It's been painful watching you, always up beat, yet deep down you were so sad. And I had the feeling that the last thing you wanted for anyone to touch was this raw nerve. And I'm one of your very best friends who you see almost every day. Would you believe that I didn't feel free to ask how you were really feeling? I'm so glad you are allowing me to be here while you grieve!" Gaia said, "If you'd like to tell me all about it, there's nothing I should rather do than listen deeply."

Eliza felt a wave of gratitude. Until she had heard Terry and Luci sing, her memories of Brian had lain buried under a layer of fear, fear that made her flinch when it confronted her with anything that might remind her of their love.

Grieving consisted of facing and penetrating the fear and allowing herself to experience the pain, so that there was no longer anything to flinch from. Once she was no longer afraid of the pain, she would be able to consciously embrace all her memories of Brian and build on what they had shared.

Gaia's warmth nourished Eliza. Gaia neither tried to comfort her and thereby cover up her grief, nor did she infringe on her privacy by touching her or moving in closer. Gaia was extending her the gift of her loving acceptance of anything Eliza might say.

"Thank you, Gaia. You're such a very good friend!"

Eliza told of how she had waited so long to finally be together with Brian. With Brian at her side, her life had seemed transformed. She felt she intuitively knew him, understood and loved his quirks, like bellowing out a sneeze when he thought no one was around and singing in the bath."

Eliza burst out laughing, wiping the tears from her face again with the back of her hand and Gaia, laughing with her, jumped up, slipped into the bathroom and came out with a wad of tissue that she handed to Eliza.

Eliza blew her nose and then began to share her feelings of relief and expansiveness, as she opened herself to Brian until she had held nothing back, and how, when they were together, he had also dared to face his own darkest fears. She told how this had only brought them closer and their relationship had thrived! Secure in the love they shared, they had each known the bliss of encouraging the other to flourish. Perhaps because they had waited so long to finally become close, they made the most of every minute. Then, there had been their respective jobs, hers with the All-Win Network, his at the U.N. Both revolved around the growing unity among human beings. Each had grown in wisdom and stature as they had shared each other's worlds: Brian's Native American heritage and her ancestors who, for several generations, had lived and worked internationally as civil engineers.

"We shared everything together!" Eliza looked away.

After a while, Gaia asked softly, "I remember how long you and Brian had been together before you shared your relationship with us. Of course, it was all happening during the last strike by the Holy Order of the Snake. But once you guys let the world know. You always seemed to be together.

"What are you most afraid of now?" She asked and waited.

Slowly, Eliza responded, "Of feeling the pain of being without him! Of not having his wisdom and love. Of never again feeling what I allowed myself to feel for him. You know, I have always had men friends but seldom allowed them in close. Brian, on the other hand, became an integral part of my life. Oh!..." Her tears flowed more easily now.

"You're doing very well, experiencing your pain!" The warmth of Gaia's smile turned her words into a boost of confidence, encouraging her to let her feelings flow freely.

"Thank you, Gaia, it feels safe here with you. Already, I feel less afraid, now I am facing my fears!" Eliza wiped her eyes at last and blew her nose in the tissue.

"Is there anything else you are afraid of?" Gaia probed.

Eliza pulled a wry face. "Afraid that I shall give in to my old patterns and deluge myself with work. Afraid that I shall avoid loving and sensuality and die without fully tasting all of life. Afraid of becoming old before my time without giving in to my femininity. Fear of shutting myself away and not taking another partner. It took Brian so long to penetrate my defenses. Who else could summons such patience?"

Gaia burst out laughing, a long, melodious, loving laugh that told Eliza that Gaia believed she was mistaken and that her fears were a passing phase. Her laugh boosted Eliza's confidence in her self without the limitation of words.

For a long time, Eliza was silent.

"And what other feelings do you feel?" Gaia asked.

"I'm angry that by dying he deserted me..." Eliza suddenly grinned. "I feel pleasure at being alone!"

Gaia laughed again. "Feelings never make sense!" she said, "Well, there's nothing wrong with wanting everything: Brian's company, and plenty of space."

For a while, the conversation lingered on until Eliza had expressed all the painful feelings she had been too afraid to face alone.

When the two went back to work, Eliza was feeling comfortably relaxed, if rather vulnerable, yet ready to embrace the future.

25. An All-encompassing, All-pervasive *Field*

Bertram hurriedly checked his watch. The ten minutes were up. He walked out onto the terrace.

The group had reassembled – all except Arturo and Pat.

Bertram positioned himself on his chaise longue.

Takeshi, sharing a lounger with Annette, hoisted himself into a sitting position and asked the question that had unconsciously been preying on everyone's mind, "Pim, if most people living in society feel some form of low level fear, how can we change the atmosphere which is being reinforced by more than 7 billion people?"

For a moment, Pim looked at the empty seats then decided to begin.

"You, young people, are well on the way," he answered.

"Remember when, in the remedial class, each of you followed your hearts, you found yourselves working as a team? Well, while fear energy separates people, heart energy builds bridges. So on the one hand, we have *a large number of people* radiating fear energy, which pulls relationships apart so that every one's on their own, swimming upstream, as it were, in conflict with everyone and all else.

"On the other hand, there is *a whole Universe of energy and information fields,* which are reinforcing one another (with exceptions, we shall look at later). If you are in harmony with these *fields,* you are as it were going with the flow. You are supported both by your own energy and consciousness and by that of almost everything around you, whether alive or inanimate. Without knowing it, you were using these *'fields'* in your Golden Haven project.

"The art is to know how these *'fields'* work and consciously tap their power."

Bertram felt a thrill of excitement: if he knew more about how this universal energy worked, he would feel less overwhelmed. Who knows, he might even encourage his business clients to use the tremendous vibrancy and resources available through commerce to resolve, rather than, sometimes quite unconsciously, to increase world problems.

Just then, Pat and Arturo came hurrying in, flushed, hand in hand. Hurriedly, they sank down close together in the deep pillows of the couch. Pat snuggled against Arturo; Arturo had his arm protectively around Pat's shoulders.

Pim summarized what he had discussed.

"Do these fields include the morphogenetic field you mentioned earlier?" Takeshi inquired.

"I personally assume they do," Pim answered, "You see, each scientist in our group has approached the universe as a whole from the perspective of her or his own area of expertise.

"So Sheldrake, as a biologist, posits that there are fields of information which connect *living* things and which he calls morphogenetic fields. Others posit that there is *a field of low-level energy,* which *permeates the whole universe,* which they call the Zero Point Field. In fact, we have known about this phenomenon for thousands of years. Then it was called the Akasha. Later in the 1600s, it was discovered in the West. Now Erwin Laszlo, the founder and president of the Club of Budapest, has coined the term *Akasha Field (A-Field* for short). At the U.N.'s University of Peace, we agree that *we and our thoughts can be seen as parts of this all-encompassing, all pervasive system of fields.* We find that our theories reinforce one another and together produce a more complete understanding of how the universe works as a whole. We agree that both the information[21] and energy fields pervade all that is. We can model them mathematically[22]. Their existence allows us to explain phenomena we could not explain without them. We know they are connected, but we don't know how, nor how they work.[23] And so we have agreed to call the energy and information fields together, *the field*

Bertram watched as Arturo whisked a tiny cluster of bougainvillea from his pocket and gently wedged it in the buttonhole of Pat's blouse. Again a vague feeling of longing stirred in him for the intimacy he had avoided for so long, an intimacy which clearly connected the Universe as a whole and which he had not yet learned to consciously tap.

Pim was continuing, "The *field* allows us to explain things like the Holy Spirit, psychic phenomena, why right now we are particularly susceptible to chaos and fear, and what we can do about it.[24]

"And this combination of energy and information fields guides the growth of our bodies, permeates our consciousness and influences what we think. This field is the motor of our being. It determines every aspect of our existence. It is our brain, our feelings, our memory. It permeates every electron, molecule and cell. It is a record of the whole evolution of our world and contains all that has ever happened and everything we have ever thought. What's more, we are in constant interaction with the field. We are being created by it and adding to its content every second, day and night."[25]

"At the U.N.'s University of Peace, we are attempting to make sense of all the scientific studies that deal with the totality. Now that we are beginning to understand the field, it is becoming possible to work consciously with the powers which make our world tick. And we can draw both information and energy from this field because it permeates both our consciousness and every cell in our bodies and connects us to all that is.

"I don't feel connected to all that is!" Jan said indignantly. "I feel I am me!"

"And so you are, Jan. You are separate and connected at the same time.

You see, just looking at each of us from an energetic point of view, we are each electrical charges; and we exist within a field of energy."

"Like people swimming in the sea, only it's a field of energy?" Takeshi asked.

"More than that," Pim explained, "we are made of the same energy that the sea of energy consists of. You see, from this perspective there is no "me" or "no me" when it comes to our relations with the cosmos.

"As Einstein once put it, 'The field is the only reality,'" he concluded.

"So this field transmits the fear that we are all responding to, and it, too, permeates every cell of our bodies?" Hugh looked overwhelmed.

"Exactly," Pim smiled, "And that is like a double edged sword. On the one hand, it can mean that we are at effect of the field. On the other hand, all that is changing. You see, we are discovering that there is a central organizing principle. And the better we understand this central organizing principle, the more easily, we can become co-creators consciously working with the field."

"And influence 7 billion people?" Hugh asked, grasping at a straw.

"Quite," Pim agreed.

"But how do we do that?" Takeshi asked.

The sense of listening was almost tangible on the terrace, as every one strained to hear and understand what Pim was about to say.

"It's both enormously complex and simplicity itself – all at the same time," Pim smiled. "In fact, my colleagues and I are just scratching the surface, but we have had some extremely revealing insights.

"For instance, *intuition is our umbilical chord to the field*. Knowing how to follow our intuition allows us to consciously tap into both the information and the energy of the field. Now, when you decided the Golden Haven Project and while you were developing it, you were following your hearts, your hunches, your intuition. Each of you was centered in your power, you found you were more creative than you had ever been before. You were tapping into the field.

"So, a first challenge is to consciously learn how to follow our hearts, at the same time, we must learn to remove our orange-tinted glasses, because these distort our intuition. It is our orange-tinted glasses, which give intuition a bad name.

The less polluted our intuitive connection to the field, the greater our influence on it.

Mary was sitting on the edge of her chaise longue. Excitedly, she exclaimed, "So then we don't have to convert, or psychologize 7 billion-odd people individually. We can use this energy/information/communication field to dissipate fear. We change the atmosphere, as it were, and people become less susceptible to fear."

"Yes, but there is a great deal more to this then meets the eye," Pim continued, "because in fact we are each both individual energetic charges and an integral part of humankind—cells in the body of humanity. We are each a part of a superorganism, a super energetic charge, as it were.[26] And so, working with the field requires two things: to learn simply and purely to follow our own hearts; and to harmoniously work with those forces in the field, which are propelling humanity as a whole.

To maximize our personal power, we must improve our connection with the field, cooperate with others doing the same and together act in sync with evolutionary forces, which determine how humanity can evolve.

Working together is, in fact, the challenge of our times. In fact, with every person working intimately with others who are in harmony with the field, our influence on the field grows by leaps and bounds. Once a critical mass of people are consciously in sync with one another and the field, the fear epidemic will cease."

"How long will that take?" Jan asked eagerly.

Pim laughed.

"My colleagues and I are still learning to remove our fear-colored glasses. To practice we have formed what we call an *all-win think tank* in which we practice solving a wide variety of conflicts. This forces us to master the process of removing our orange-tinted glasses. I hope that in several months we shall be so proficient that I can pass on our experience to you.

"But this afternoon, I want to give you some keys, so that you can consciously work with the forces which are both impacting your personal lives and propelling humanity as a whole. Once you learn to apply these in your everyday living, you will be able to take some first steps to consciously influence the field!" His smile lit up his whole face as he watched their eyes open wide, a gleam of hope fighting to break through, even though they hardly dared to believe him.

"What do you say, we meet in the auditorium at 4 p.m.? I'll have a film to show you, I hope."

26. Pierre Looks For Augustina

Pierre woke to a steady buzzing. Something landed on his nose. How long had he been out? A day? More?

In front of him lay his children, barely visible through a swarm of flies. Aghast he saw the blood drenched sheets, and memories flooded his mind.

"No!" he screeched at the top of his lungs and jumped out of his chair. At the same time, he felt as if his foot was on fire. While he was wracked with pain and intent on his children, the snake slithered away without Pierre realizing it had bitten him.

He hobbled out to the tool shed, grabbed a pick and shovel. Then, as if driven by the devil himself, he hacked away at the hard mud floor in a corner of the hut. His foot burned and throbbed, he was so tired he almost threw up but if only he suffered enough, this nightmare might go away.

Finally, when the hole was large enough, he smoothed the sides and the bottom. Taking the new sheets that Augustina had bought, he lined the grave and laid his babies inside, his little daughter, nestled in her brother's arms. Tenderly he covered them with another sheet and then, spade full after slow spade full, he closed the grave.

He stood back.

Before him, the grave, an ugly pockmark, as if the Earth had been wounded. Hurriedly he snatched the beautifully embroidered cloth off Augustina's altar and draped it across the little mound.

They were her babies, too, he thought, Augustina wouldn't mind.

"Augustina? Augustina!" He must let her know! She would know what to do!

He turned to run out of the hut, stumbling over his swollen foot.

Picking himself up, he staggered out of the door, across the clearing and along the jungle path. Augustina must be at her mother's. She would set things right!

Calling her name at the top of his lungs, he entered the next village.

There was no one there. Pierre staggered through the streets, still calling his wife's name. But no one answered his calls. Everything was deserted.

At the Village Square, he pulled up short. The church had disappeared. Half crazed, half in a daze, he stopped dead in his tracks. Only a smoldering heap where the church had once stood.

"All gone! All burned! That's the end of the Mandus." A man, shocked beyond his senses, kept mumbling as he wandered through the rubble.

"Augustina!" Pierre roared as if, through the power of his voice, he could force the world to undo the atrocities that he was unable to fathom.

"She's dead. They all burned. All the Mandus are dead. They were bad people, bad people!" And he stumbled away.

Pierre staggered into the jungle, shouting at the top of his lungs. Gradually, as the poison from the snakebite got the better of him, his cries lost their strength until he fell to the ground, unconscious.

27. Eight Thousand Computers

Every one filed into the darkened auditorium, blinking, as their eyes adjusted from the bright sunlight outside.

Hugh was preparing an old-fashioned projector to show the ancient film.

"Okay, Hugh?" Pim stood up, slightly flushed from bending over fiddling with the screen.

As Hugh signaled, Pim began, "Okay, so we're all different densities of a field. And this energy field is so fluid, it penetrates all cells, all atoms, even electrons and intermingles with an information field which also pervade all that is. We're calling these *the field*.

"How does this *field* operate? And how can we apply what we learn about these universal processes to our own individual lives?

"Let's see what this film can tell us. It was made decades ago. So this knowledge has been with us for a long time.[27]"

There was a whirring sound.

"Now, there are many ways in which evolution proceeds. One way is through a series of leaps.

"Lights please, Hugh."

As the lights went out, a curtain moved on one of the balconies and a figure crept forward, intent on seeing the screen. Only Bertram, hurrying in from the library, noticed the movement but could not see the figure. It was hidden behind a pillar. This was the second time he had had the impression they were being watched. Could it be that Maurice, without knowing it, had a visitor? Or was a family member checking Maurice's activities? After all, he had said he was his brothers' 'barometer', as to what was happening among the dreamers of the world! Or was he, Bertram, seeing things through fear-tinged glasses? he pondered.

Suddenly all worries were swept away, as the image of a Japanese flag appeared on the screen.

Pim explains "This image is produced by 8000 computers linked in groups of four. For the rest, they are not connected other than that each is emitting waves which project dots onto the screen! Now just imagine that each of you is one of the 8000 colored dots being inspired to follow your hearts by your individual relationship to the *field*. This information field connects you all to one another like a giant sea flowing through each electron in each of your bodies. The scientists who did this experiment then deregulated the 8000 computers so that the computers all started emitting *chaotic* signals. [28]

"Now watch what happens!"

As soon as the energy changes, a chaotic jumble of dots appears.

Pim points out, "This chaos can be likened to the fear-infused situation in which we are living today.

"Now watch how order proceeds out of chaos."

Suddenly in one corner of the screen, an intricate pattern emerges.

"See that pattern in the corner?" Pim asks, "We find that random information waves influence one another in such a way that the computers come into sync and in this new part of the field, a beautiful pattern appears. Now each dot in that pattern has organized itself – *each of its own accord*! -- so that each brings out the beauty of all others and it's own beauty is highlighted at the same time."

"It's like a pattern in my kaleidoscope!" Jan exclaimed.

"Yes!" Pim smiled, "All dots benefit from the association with all the others. They are in *all-win relationship* with one another.

"You experienced this leap from chaos to an all-win pattern of relationships when you *opened yourselves* to your own creativity, and out of your communication evolved the Golden Haven School Garden.

84

"Now watch what happens.

"This pattern is still being bombarded by the chaotic impact of the remaining computers, much like your Golden Haven project was affected by the win/lose atmosphere which still ruled Corps Elite High School and their threat to sack Mrs. Gladstone."

The chaotic information changes the environment and the pattern disintegrates.

The group oo's and ah's as another quite different pattern emerges. Then another appears.

Pim explains, "Again the same process, this time simultaneously on two separate parts of the screen."

"Notice how in each different combination, the computer signals organize themselves into quite different patterns."

Bertram watches as these also disintegrate under the chaotic barrage of the remaining computers.

Then larger patterns come and go until a huge, highly complex pattern appears, taking up most of the screen.

"See, now almost all of the computers are in sync," Pim points out, "but there is still a small corner of chaos. And the chaos influences the pattern until it, too, falls apart." The chaotic jumble of dots then makes way for a beautiful white cross with a multicolored background pattern. It fills the screen and remains stable.

"All 8000 computers are now in sync," Pim explains. "This is an example of how chaos seeks order. Your Golden Haven Garden Project could not become stable until the all-win pattern was allowed to embrace the whole, both schools, Golden Haven and Corps Elite. Your Student Council together with the School Board together form the governing pattern which allows all-win relationships at Corps Elite to be maintained."

Wows! and laughter.

"Lights, please, Hugh!"

A slight sound caught Bertram's attention. He quickly looked up. Again the curtain was moving. He turned to tell Maurice but thought better of it as Pim continued, "So lets just summarize the essence of what you have seen:

"First the environment changes and chaos appears. Then out of the chaos emerges a series of all-win patterns, until *all elements have been united in all-win relationships.* This final pattern is stable. So the Evolutionary Leap[29] can be said to consist of three steps:

1.a change in the atmosphere or energy of the environment,
2. chaos, and then
3.a stable all-win pattern.

85

These three steps have repeated themselves over and over again throughout time. The final pattern can be stable for billions of years. Examples of stable and durable all-win patterns: the atom, the cell, millions of plant and animal species, the human body, solar systems."

"So chaos is a natural phase in an evolutionary leap?" Ian asked.

"Yes. The evolutionary leap may not succeed immediately, mind you! Remember how patterns kept falling apart and coming together until *all* parts were in one all-win pattern? But chaos heralds an attempt to move into a new all-win constellation," Pim replied.

"So chaos is not negative. It's working with us!" Hugh exclaimed, still sitting at the projector.

"Yes!" Pim said, "It comes about naturally. But if we would not have allowed the computers to 'do their own thing', if, say, we had exposed them to an erratic electromagnetic field (which would serve the same function as an atmosphere of fear) sweeping through the computers, the resulting pattern would have been disharmonious. Fear over time produces diseased patterns, be they physical or mental. And that is why it is so important to understand how we can practically affect *the field*, using *all-win relationships*, and thus dissolve fear."

Pim turned to Hugh who was still sitting at the projector, "Thank you, Hugh, for your help."

Switching off the equipment, Hugh joined the group.

"But how can you stop being afraid when you're scared?" Jan asked, eyes wide.

"You did it when you started the Golden Haven School Garden – remember?" Pim replied, "You allowed your heart to lead the way, doing what made you and others most happy. The heart's a powerful guide to what to do and what not to. When we follow our hearts we want to do well by ourselves and others, too. And that gives us an inner strength and makes people want to work with us. We, like the rest of 'all that is', have an ongoing, intuitive heart connection to the *field*. The choice is ours. We can allow ourselves to be victims of the fear field and add to the problem, or we can do whatever we can, so that both we, ourselves, and all others become integrated in a human community in which each person can flourish in her or his own way."

Bertram caught his breath. A new world had opened up.

"It's a tall order. Well nigh impossible, if you ask me!" he exclaimed, "And yet, I'd rather die exploring how to live in all-win relationship than be a victim of my own and everyone else's fears!" Despite what seemed an insurmountable challenge, he laughed a deep, spontaneous belly laugh for the first time in many months.

28. The Kukundu Resistance

A raucous cry from a bird in the jungle. Pierre stirred. Finally consciousness was dawning. He was lying in a roughly hewn hut. In the background, the quiet hum of relaxed conversation. Outside, squawks, trills, the chattering of monkeys, all to the chirping accompaniment of crickets.

"He's come to!" A woman's voice said, rich and low. Pierre found himself looking into the kind eyes of a Mandu with silver gray hair.

"A Mandu!" With a cry, Pierre struggled to get up.

He was gently restrained.

"It's okay!" It was a Kukundu speaking, "We're not going to hurt you.

"We heard you shouting. When we arrived, we found you passed out on the jungle path. You had been bitten by a snake," the Mandu woman said, "Judging by the swelling of your foot, it had to have happened several hours before. But we had no idea what type of snake we were dealing with and so all we could do was nurse you until now you have come to of your own accord."

"Welcome back!" She laid the palm of her hand on his; and gave him a soft squeeze in traditional Kukundu greeting. Her hand was gnarled, the hand of an older person, used to physical labor.

"You've been through the mill!" she said.

"How do you know?" Pierre said, alarmed, "What do you know about me?"

"You have been delirious for several days," she laughed. "A regular story teller you are!" Suddenly grave she added, "You told us about your wife. We think Augustina was one of the Mandus burned alive in the church. You also told us about how you had executed and buried your two children..."

"But you're in good company!" the Kukundu reassured him, "Each one of us has committed similar atrocities either directly, or by looking on, while others committed crimes."

Pierre looked around the rough walls of the hut. Light barely penetrated through the small window. They were surrounded by dense jungle.

"So how did you get here?" he asked.

"Each came in a different way. But we all have one thing in common: we could no longer bear to stand by and watch ...we felt we just had to take action. But that's not possible – yet," he added, "not the way the situation is right now in Kukundu itself!"

There were others in the room, Pierre sensed, whom he could not see.

"How many of you are there?" Pierre asked, weakly.

"We'll get to that later, perhaps. But first things first. You are welcome to stay here until you have recovered enough to go back home." Said the woman with the gentle eyes.

"But I can't return!" Pierre pleaded, suddenly desperate, as he remembered the little grave in his hut."

"We won't make you leave immediately, but if you decide to stay, there are a number of conditions. They all involve an almost super human effort.

"Anything!" Pierre pleaded, "Anything is better than going home and facing what I left behind!"

"I mean mental and emotional strength! In fact, it involves *taking full responsibility* for every thing you, yourself, have done, and for everything that you have condoned by not intervening.

"But this is a later decision. It is time for you to rest up and perhaps have something to eat. We have a delicious squash stew!"

"Josette, can I have a word?" A young man stood in the doorway. "Privately, please?"

Jules was the communications officer of this jungle community, Pierre would later find out.

29. The All-win Waltz

Still laughing, Bertram said, "So globalization --fears, conflict, atrocities and all-- are parts of a natural process; and its main aim is to move through the destruction phase to a global community in which *everyone* can live a full life?"

"Quite right, Bertram," Pim agreed. "Each of us has the choice, fight the process or join the dance of evolution."

"And I burned out fighting evolution itself!" A tone of awe crept into Bertram's voice.

Bertram was suddenly serious.

"Nothing less!" Pim smiled.

"But how can we dance the dance of evolution?" Jeff asked.

"Yes, how?" Jan chimed in.

"By learning the *All-Win Waltz*!" Pim replied.

"All win waltz!" Jan and Jeff giggled.

"Yes, it's the dance of life itself. Actually, we are following the same principle as the dots on the screen. Only, because humans are always developing, it's like a dance." Pim took a couple of steps back toward the stage and leaned against the edge. Just out of sight, a figure recoiled, remaining just outside of Pim's line of vision.

"It goes like this: each person moves, following her or his own heart, mingling with others along the way. All move in larger and larger constellations (call it globalization if you like). Finally, when all are included in the same dance, a new dance has been created. This dance can be danced over and over again, because it enables all dancers to dance to their heart's content while they're supported by all others. Such a final dance pattern remains stable, because all needs are fully met."

This must be applied to the business world, Bertram realized, *but before I can teach the all-win waltz, I must master it myself. And that means being less of a loner.* His thoughts started drifting toward Eliza, but snapped back as Pim went on, "The all-win waltz has three steps."

Bertram reached down under his chair, located his notepad and pen and hurriedly began taking notes.

"Firstly, like the dots on the screen, we follow our hearts.

"Secondly, we empower others to follow their own hearts in such a way that no one is harmed.

"Finally, a governing structure takes hold."

Next door in the dining room, Consuela was busy setting the tables. The tinkling of crystal accompanied the cheerful tune she hummed as she moved through the room.

"A governing pattern, what's that?" Jeff asked.

Pim answered, "It's anything that guards the all-win process. It could be a set of values, standards or a well-run organizational structure that allows its members and employees to each come into their own as they participate and develop the organization's activities and, at the same time ensures that the activities of the organization don't harm anything or anyone. It can be a set of agreements, like a constitution or a deeply rooted tradition.

"The all-win waltz must be danced over and over again before we become proficient at it: in chance meetings throughout the day; in all sorts of long term relationships -- in our families, schools, organizations, local communities, political parties and, of course, the U.N.

"Finally, the smaller groupings become the building blocks of the global community itself."

"So that means that each of us must go on looking out for ourselves and all other people, *all the time?*" It was clear from Jan's tone that she thought that that was pushing "being good" much too far.

Everyone laughed.

"The process grows on you, I suppose," Hugh grinned at her. "It gets easier with practice." He turned to Pim, "And all these all-win units, families, organizations are straining to become harmonious parts of the same all-win Universe, which already consists of species of plants and animals, natural systems of water and air, solar systems and galaxies? Is that what you meant, Pim, with 'there is *a whole Universe of influences,* which are pulling in similar directions'?"

"Yes. If we allow our hearts to guide us, we will know how to act and where to go. And we shall be helping the process to move via an energy change and chaos to a new all-win constellation. Then whatever we do will be supported by Universal forces."

"Wow! The whole Universe?!" Jan exclaimed.

There was a stunned silence.

"The urge to live fully and flourish at every phase of your life cycle is more than just 'wanting to have a good time'. It is a fundamental need of 'all that is' whether it is an electron, a human being or a whole ecosystem. And when a group makes it possible for all its members to realize themselves, it is building on this powerful urge. It makes sense that things remain stable when everyone is doing and being whatever they love most."

"But, ..." Arturo began.

There was the sound of the kitchen door swinging to and fro, and a lid being placed over a large dish. Then the smell of savory pie seeped into the auditorium.

Bertram's stomach growled. There were a few giggles.

Pim laughed, "And when any needs are not met, it's time for the next all-win quest to begin. I think that's what Bertram's stomach is telling us."

"But, the U.N...." Arturo insisted.

"One moment, Arturo," Pim interrupted quickly, not sure how to meet the challenge he knew he could not avoid. "How about we have supper now and then meet again on the terrace?"

30. Eliza Has A Dream

Eliza decided not to go home. She would sleep on the couch. In the office, they kept a sleeping bag and toiletries for the occasional emergency.

That night, she dreamed she was in Brian's arms. She felt completely engulfed by his body, his warmth, and somehow she sensed everything he was feeling. Then gradually, the firmness of his body softened and all she felt was his presence wrapped around her and gradually entering into her through the pores of her skin until she and he had merged into one.

At that moment, she saw a specter of Brian standing by the door. He waved to her and simultaneously she knew what he was thinking. He was, after all, incongruously, still a part of her.

She absorbed his words, "I shall always be a part of you and now you are free to lead your life as you please. Just one thing, if you want to honor what we had together, please do not isolate yourself. Lead your life to the full!"

31. United Nations And Our Evolutionary Leap

The friends took their tea and iced coffee out onto the terrace. Pim was the last one to arrive. Stretched out on his chaise longue, Hugh was leafing through a little booklet.

"This Universal Declaration of Human Rights -- it's amazing! All three steps of the all-win principle are right there. The people who developed these rights must have known all about the all-win waltz,"[30] he mused, "Take Article 26, the *right to develop our whole personality:* It's *not* saying education must trot out clones, or that our parents may decide our futures. It's saying that education must help us become who we really are—unique people. And that means each following our own hearts, because no one but each of us individually knows what deeply turns us on.

"Then there are a whole slew of rights which are necessary for each of us to grow strong, like – of course-- the right to life (he grinned), education..." he continued to leaf through the booklet, "the right to leisure, ...work, ... privacy, ...freedom of movement, ...security, etc., etc." He looked around the group. Everyone was looking at him impressed.

Only Jan was fidgeting. She burst out, "So what about the governing structure then? If we don't want anymore people burned alive, must we accept a governing pattern?" She obviously didn't take to the idea. Suspiciously, she asked, "so what *is* a governing pattern anyway? "

Hugh grinned, "It's something that *we choose. 'Everyone has the right to take part in the government of his country,'* it says, Like *we* helped to elect our Student Council at Corps Elite High School."

"Article 21, remember?" Ian turned to Jan. "We learned it in Mrs. Gladstone's class? It also says, *'The will of the people shall be the basis of the authority of government,'*" Ian quoted by heart.

"Oh, I remember that part! It was printed in yellow!" Jan crowed. The group laughed.

Everyone was genuinely fond of Jan. She had the knack of asking those basic questions that others overlooked.

Still smiling at Jan's exuberance, Mary asked Pim, "Don't you think the United Nations itself is a governing structure? It allows *countries* to meet their individual needs."

With a nod, Pim urged her to continue.

"Think of the U.N.'s Universal Postal Union," Mary went on. "It makes it possible for the citizens of each country to send and receive letters from abroad. Or the U.N.'s International Telecommunications Union without which the Internet couldn't exist; the World Meteorological Organization which allows each country to forecast the weather; then there's the U.N.'s World Health Organization which helps us to deal with epidemics that move from country to country. There are now around 30 U.N. Specialized Agencies. In each case, each Nation helps to design the structures and laws that each believes will give it the access it needs to worldwide networks, information and resources.

"On the other hand, no country would have access to these worldwide services, if it did not contribute its share. We seldom give credit to governments for the degree to which they participate harmoniously in dancing the all-win waltz. For instance, when it comes to dealing with the AIDS pandemic, Uganda has a leading role: As one of the nations which was hardest hit, it has a great deal of expertise and know-how that it contributes to the rest of the world. Each country builds its individual sections of the necessary infrastructures, like telephone lines, airports, postal systems and provides information only they can give, such as statistics, experience, discoveries, etc. in exchange for having well-functioning international networks. They help to hammer out agreements until each serves all individual needs – agreements all nations keep to because it is in their self-interest to do so."

"All win agreements!" Hugh nodded, as if to himself, still leafing through the Universal Declaration.

"These U.N. Specialized Agencies are communications processes between governments. They're always in flux and facing new challenges. But they do work and mostly they work well!"

"And that's no coincidence!" Pim interjected, as Mary paused for breath, "because all humanity does is subject to natural laws. It's striking how much humanity as a whole parallels the natural world. For instance, it's as if all these U.N. Specialized Agencies together are weaving a cocoon of communications systems and international agreements. These have sped up communications and changed the atmosphere: everyone is busy, busy, busy! That's the *energy change:* the first step of the Evolutionary Leap.

"Now we're all in that cocoon, being influenced by the *field* and the energy change is producing *chaos.* The communications systems are breaking down boundaries. The Internet, tourism, migrant labor, exchange students, and world problems are throwing people from different cultures and religions together. As boundaries fall away, conflicts and chaos increase so that now human survival is threatened. Our traditional social structures, like segments of a caterpillar, are disintegrating within the cocoon and the very chaos we produce is forcing us to move from step two to the final step of the Evolutionary Leap: all-win collaboration.

"Now, the all-win phase, step number three, is clearly in view to some. Humanity is transforming itself into a butterfly! Some of us are already following our hearts and discovering our positioning in the all-win waltz. People are switching careers, women are claiming their rights, churches are adopting new forms and the U.N., which is actually a organization for *governments* is embracing the views and advice of more and more *citizens'* groups."

Looking at Jan he added, "And the U.N. with all of its Specialized Agencies is a governance structure *in the making.* Even though it is far from perfect it is already coordinating our evolution and propelling it forward."

"But isn't the U.N. also a part of the problem?" Arturo frowned.

Pat looked up at him in surprise.

"In the film with the 8000 computers, remember that the process kept falling apart? It wasn't until every last bit of chaos had become integrated that the new form became stable. Well, what about the U.N.'s Security Council then? That's like that one bit of chaos!" As he spoke, Pat beamed at him in admiration. Then she snuggled back into his arms.

Pim got up awkwardly trying to formulate his response when Hugh chimed in, "That's right! How can the Security Council ever become an all-win structure? China, France, the UK, the US and Russia are the only Permanent Members and they rule the roost. On top of that, they are the only nations which have the right to veto any Security Council decision, including to change the U.N.'s Charter. Can you see any of them giving up their privileges and allowing the Charter to be changed? And the Charter *must* be changed if all nations are to become equal. The Permanent Five have the power to block evolution and nothing stands in their way!"

All eyes were now on Pim.

Pim seemed at a loss for words. Finally, he said, "Quite right, I wish I had an answer. I'm afraid I do not.

"An all-win global community requires a fully democratic humanity. Until that happens, global democracy is a passing whim and we're all doomed to spiraling chaos and conflict and increasing destruction. The Security Council is a particularly hard nut to crack…but we have no alternative but to trust the process. Don't forget that we are working with the field and the more people live the all-win process, the more easily others will pick it up. Never have large worldwide networks of human beings consciously attempted to work with the forces that help the Universe to evolve and to consciously together take an evolutionary leap. What we are about to do is totally new!"

"So what is needed is an all-win solution…" Hugh reflected.

"There you go!" Pim grinned, "Humanity still has a chance! Don't forget, the self-interest of even the five most powerful nations is minute when pitted against all other nations together, backed by the natural systems of the whole Universe. I don't yet see how we can win through, I must admit, but I'm positive that in the end we still can!"

Antonia giggled nervously. There was a buzz of conversation, everyone letting off steam. Jeff punched Jan and she hit him back, Arturo kissed Pat on the ear lobe and she grinned up at him. Takeshi whispered something to Annette and then raising his voice, he suggested,

"What do you guys say, we rewrite our play and include the all-win principle? That way, we can spread the word through all the schools we visit in Central and South America. The play can illustrate the all-win principle and the incredible power it has. Then we can ask the students we meet how they can apply it to their lives. Perhaps they can get their parents interested and all their friends and relations."

"What would happen if kids used it in their homework to educate their teachers…?" Annette's eyes were shining. "I'm thinking when we write essays for history class, we could concentrate on all the misery caused by win/lose battles, or on all-win discoveries and in how far these survive."

"Yes, and in geography, we can ask our teachers how a country's industry and technology dealt with their natural resources and what happened when they were used up," Ian agreed.

"In social studies, it's really powerful to point out that in the Universal Declaration of Human Rights, natural and human laws converge!" Hugh pointed out.

Pat added enthusiastically, "And in our biology classes we can bring up how brilliant and creative animals and plants can be. And how many of our discoveries were inspired by ways they use to survive. I bet Velcro was inspired by those burrs that stick to your clothes when you take a walk through the woods."

"Some of our parents might get ideas from us that they can use in their work," Takeshi added, "You know, office politics and how the all-win principle can help, how to use it to assess what our government is doing, and the advantages of modeling nature!"

"I think that we should learn how to be quiet at school!" David almost whispered. There was a sudden silence, "I mean quiet inside," he added, shyly.

Everyone stared at David. Embarrassed, he forced himself to explain, "On the reservation where my grandfather lives, there are long pauses when the Elders discuss anything…" When no one said anything, he continued,

"It's like everything that is said is really taken seriously and people don't jump to conclusions. Also, people don't speak at these Council meetings if they don't have anything to say—anything, anything that really matters... I always feel more sure of myself when silence is the...the...*earth* from which words grow!" Totally embarrassed he looked away.

"Inner quiet, as I understand, is indeed the place from which you can hear your heart speak!" Pim said, impressed.

"Wow!" Mary exclaimed, after a few moments, "You kids can begin a new trend among the adults simply by getting friends and relations excited about the discoveries you are all making yourselves!"

"That's the right spirit!" Pim beamed, "The more people are seriously applying the all-win principle to everyday situations, using it to solve conflicts, to assess achievements, *really living the all-win principle,* the more easily the all-win field will dissipate the fear epidemic!"

Only too happy to be back on an upbeat track, the others agreed. There was much laughing and joking around. Doing anything was better than feeling overwhelmed.

"But," Annette cautioned, "tomorrow we're leaving early for our day trip to visit our next school. We won't have time to write the all-win principle into the script of our play and learn our lines before we go."

"Perhaps you can just tell that school what we've been talking about and see how it goes," Pim suggested, "They might give you some more ideas! Just remember, even talking and brainstorming like we're doing now is deflating the fear epidemic."

Mary's face lit up, as an idea hit her, "Modern communications – amazing how many people we can reach!" Looking at Takeshi, she said, "Why don't we open this Thursday's hook-up to the families, friends and relations you just mentioned, Takeshi, --anyone who is interested, not just young people?"

"That reminds me!" she added, "There's still stuff to do. This week it'll be a really big deal: by e-mail, ham radio and videophone – all at the same time. We must decide the topic... what do you guys say, we show how ...the planned Anti Terrorist Act Two is ...heading us down a path, dangerously similar to Kukundu's, and how ...the all-win principle can help us change course?" she said, thinking up the title as she spoke.

There were enthusiastic nods of agreement.

Ian volunteered, "I'll get the announcements out over the airwaves, if Edward can help me operate the equipment. Mary, can you write down that title?"

"Perhaps, I and my scientist friends can participate from the U.N.'s University of Peace then?" Pim asked. "You see, there are two things I know *we* would be eager to learn from you guys."

There was a surprised silence.

"Firstly, how to help people take the step from being fear-driven to following their hearts. In other words, how to take off our orange-colored glasses. And secondly, how to use hook-ups like these to mobilize large numbers of people.

32. Contact!

"We're about to make contact with the outside world!" Jules said excitedly to Josette, as they left the hut where Pierre was still lying on his makeshift bed. As they headed toward the communications hut, Jule's thick glasses gleaming in the sunlight, there was a sharp rat-a-tat sound high in the trees. For a split second each was all ears, until, with sighs of relief, they recognized it was a woodpecker scaring insects out of hiding.

Jules, continued, " I was scanning the airwaves. There's a group of scientists meeting at the United Nations University for Peace and it looks like there'll be a network of young people organizing a meeting by e-mail, ham radio and video-hookup! Actually mentioned Kukundu! First time, anyone thinks of us!"

"Did you speak to anyone personally?"

"No, I was searching the various radio bands and this message came in: "There will be a meeting next Thursday morning at --- (I still have to work out what time that will be here). Subject: *the planned Anti-Terrorist Act Two to keep us from fraternizing with minorities, how, outside of Kukundu, we are following in its tracks, a joint search for solutions and the role of the all-win principle. Please pass this on to anyone you know, especially in Kukundu.*"

"Anyone at all!?" Josette was shocked.

"Yes! They say that it is vital that we *all* face what is going on. Only then can we make informed decisions and develop a strategy for action. They also want our help. They say Kukundu is spearheading the fear epidemic, and that the rest of the world is rapidly heading that way. I have the ways to connect.

Josette looked doubtful. "There's not much we can contribute..."

"Oh yes there is!" Jules was adamant. "You have helped around 80 people come to grips with their crimes. You have the knack of doing it so thoroughly that all those you have taught have dedicated their lives to making up for what they have done.

"Do you think we dare risk sending a resonant message by drum?" he asked.

"Let's call a group meeting and see..."

33. Bertram Takes Over Mary's Correspondence

Bright and early, the group got ready to visit a neighboring school. As the crew prepared the *Peace Warrior,* Bertram walked Mary out onto the terrace.

"You're sure you don't mind?" Mary asked.

"No, I'll monitor your messages as they come in and let people know about Thursday's hook-up."

With a quick wave, Mary hurried down the steps and down the path to the dock. The *Peace Warrior's* sails were flapping in the wind. She jumped on board and the *Peace Warrior* took off.

Bertram watched it, as it veered past the devil's teeth and finally was nothing more than a speck. Then he turned back to the library. For a long time he gazed out of the window. Should he work on his novel? As a novelist, he knew better, than to wait for inspiration. Nevertheless, he hesitated. Today he would follow his heart.

How he'd love to help people learn about the all-win principle and the Evolutionary Leap. He worked only with the upper echelons of the world business community. Could he help them to connect with inspiring groups like those he was hearing about from Mary, Pim and Maurice?

He found himself looking over at Mary's computer. An e-mail had just arrived. He read,

> *Dear Mary,*
>
> *I got your address from some young people where I live. I am a Pygmy woman. As Pygmies, we are considered second class citizens by many. Even subhuman by some. Nothing we say or do is taken seriously. It is as if we are invisible.*
>
> *"The legal system doesn't treat us as equals. We are rejected and marginalized and are often used as cheap labor. The wisdom we have built up over the centuries is discounted and the values of the modern consumer are threatening to deluge our people.*
>
> *We are losing our traditional way of making a living. We are torn between preserving our traditional culture, including our deep connection to the forest, and adapting to the values of a modern consumer society. Have you any suggestions which could help us?*
>
> *(Patricia, South Cameroon Province)*

How different Patricia's world was from anything he, Bertram knew. He wandered out onto the terrace. The wind had risen and the sea was dashing up against the devil's teeth in huge fountains of white water. He hoped Mary and her crew would be safe. Already this beautiful paradise seemed empty without them. Perhaps that's how the Pygmies felt, alone, left to their own devices.

What was it like living deep in a forest? The rains pelting the leaves, the drip, drip, drip after a torrent; the animals who lived in the forests, small feet scurrying around at night, the plants vying for rays from the sun, each with their own unique flowers and leaves. Such a forest harbored different types of insects and plants, together creating a delicate balance from which Patricia and her people could live. It was a part of a much greater womb of Nature on which all life depended.

Patricia and her people were so closely attuned to nature, if only they could follow their hearts and could contribute to the outside world, which was taking over their habitat, so that each could benefit from the other.

Hurrying back into the library, he sat down and tapped out a message,

> *Dear Patricia,*
> *Mary has left for the day and has charged me with answering her mail. Your way of life has so much to teach the "dominant culture". We've lost contact with our natural roots.*
> *If you were able to follow your heart, what activities would you and your fellow Pygmies pursue? Is there any way that you can pull together? After all, there is strength in numbers. The challenge is to make yourselves heard.*

Remembering a wonderful organization in Geneva, the *Women's World Summit Foundation*, which gave awards to rural women worldwide, he suggested that they might be able to help. He added the information on the hook-up and signed and sent the e-mail.

Thinking of Patricia fighting to follow her heart and help her people to do the same filled Bertram with warmth. How much easier his life was than hers. He had the feeling as if a strong woman at the other end of the world had reached out and touched his heart. He no longer felt alone.

Then he checked his own computer for mail.

A note from a man called Recluse. That was the man Eliza had mentioned! Bertram's interest quickened. He read:

> *Dear Bertram,*
> *The Holy Order of the Snake[31] is alive and well and has been for several centuries. It consists of a wealthy family, which sprouted from*

one man whose visions to gain full hegemony of the world are being carried out today.

This dynasty by now has become spread out and meets in secret sessions. Each branch of the family has one heir (it's always a he), groomed to attend their secret sessions. Their heirs secretly train their heirs-to-be from birth to be emotionally untouched by other people. Snake now has spread as the dynasty has grown. It is ruled by just three men. These oversee all operations.

The family has, by now, spread out geographically throughout the world. They make their money in many ways. From the beginning, the arms industry has been a fount for their fabulous wealth. They have perfected the art of 'divide and rule'. They fuel conflicts worldwide. Conflicts require the arms they provide and arms sales in turn provide them with vast wealth.

They seldom take prominent positions, preferring to work through stooges in key positions. If you are alert, you will notice their influence wherever you look. People unwittingly play into their hands. No longer do Heads of State or large corporations rule our world. These are mostly in the pockets of the Snake, which uses fear, their sense of duty, greed and/or lust for power to ensure blind obedience, as they rule them from behind the scenes.

Beware of meddling in this. They have eyes and ears everywhere. They use you without you knowing it. With globalization, their Plan to Take Over the World is rapidly becoming reality.

Our only weapon is the all-win principle. That's why we founded and now foster the All-Win Network. Eliza says you are studying the principles. Use them wherever you can. They are the only means we have to undermine their divide and rule policies without increasing conflict and playing into their hands.

Above all be alert!
Recluse

Bertram wrote a thank you and sat quietly, as the harrowing information fell into place. The poem on the scrap of paper, the intricate communications center in the auditorium, the moving curtain – was all this connected to Snake?

With a shudder, he opened his next e-mail. It was from Geoffrey, Maurice's nephew, who had inspired his fictional Hero, thanking him for allowing him to unburden his heart and wondering how the novel was progressing. He said he had not yet found anything to give himself to, heart and soul, but his Uncle Percy had promised to help.

Bertram pondered Geoffrey's connection to the whole. Was he without knowing it being groomed by Snake? He remembered how eager Geoffrey had been to learn to *feel*. He was probably not yet aware that he could be one of Snake's heirs. Carefully Bertram formulated an e-mail, strongly urging him to follow his heart. He added the tip he had received from Eliza about the All-Win Education Centers. *Perhaps these can give you the support you need to connect with other people.* Snake probably knew all about them, he would not be placing them in danger.

Finally, there was a note from Eliza.

> *Dear Bertram,*
>
> *I feel we are like ships passing in the night. As I sit down to write, I realize it is easier to share things with you than with those dear friends in my immediate surroundings whose concern would color our daily dealings.*
>
> *Thank you for your caring message about my husband's death. Recently, several loved ones have passed away, one after another. So grieving has been uppermost in my mind.*
>
> *I find that grieving has a rhythm all its own. Memories surface bit by bit. Sometimes, when I feel strong, a whole lot can surface all in one go. It's as if every memory wants to be transformed in the light of the new situation of no longer being together with Brian. So, things I loved about being with my husband become sad in the light of his passing. On the other hand, being completely free is a pleasant feeling. Yesterday, with the support of my dear friend Gaia with whom I run the All-Win Network Office, I, for the first time, had the guts to experience my loss without running away. Then last night I had a wonderful dream, in which my husband and I entered a new phase of being together. On the one hand, I felt him become a part of me; on the other, he left my life as a physical being.*
>
> *I feel so light all at once, filled with a sense that a new life is waiting. At the same time, I feel a little vulnerable and want to inch into this new phase.*
>
> *Thanks again for your kind concern. Facing fear is not easy. Yet, the alternative is worse: a life, which becomes more and more anemic until it is devoid of all meaning.*
>
> *With warmest best wishes,*
> *Eliza.*

34. The Resonant Drums

They were gathered in the jungle clearing, all 95: the whole community of resistance fighters, including Josette and Jules. Only five brave drummers were missing. They had left the camp two days before; and Pierre was still inside the hut, too weak to get up.

The task of the drummers was to go to the outposts of the land and to broadcast the hook-up to the whole of Kukundu.

The sky was red; the jungle was alive with a symphony of sounds. The freedom fighters were wrapped in a restless silence. Precisely at sundown, the message would go out. Would other drums take up the beat and pass the message along? Or would their own lone drummers be hounded down as traitors, and hanged?

"Yes!" a voice whispered. In the far distance, the rhythmic beat of a drum.

Drum language was universally understood in Kukundu. The message began: "There will be a meeting by ham radio, video phone and Internet to discuss relations between Kukundu and the outside world and it gave an Internet site for further information.

Over and over the lonely drum spoke.

No others joined in.

Josette wondered how the other 4 were faring. Had they been discovered and arrested before they could begin drumming?

Then all of sudden the beat was picked up. For minute after minute, the duo continued. The beat suddenly became louder. A third drum!

With baited breath, Josette listened.

A sigh of relief went up in the crowd, as the rhythmic message began to swell. Now other drummers from around Kukundu were joining in until the whole world was throbbing. The group let out a soft cheer and every one started laughing and chatting.

Will we be able to attract enough people? Josette felt a thrill of excitement. *"Once a large enough group is in complete agreement, there is little a government can do,"* she thought. Thinking of how Gandhi freed India, she felt a surge of hope.

35. The Hook Up

"Contact!"

The light flickered on the screen. Static filled the room. Several days had passed since the messages of the drums had spread the news. Now all were waiting in hushed silence for the hook-up to begin.

Josette looked around the darkened hut. Tense, dark expectant faces, torn between hope and fear. These were the English speakers among their resistance community. Next to her, lying restlessly on a makeshift cot was Pierre with awkwardly bandaged foot, the last victim to arrive.

Was there a way out of this grinding existence, the daily struggles to keep hope alive, day and night in their jungle hideout, trying desperately to come to terms with the atrocities, scarring their lives?

The tension grew in the room, as the static increased, followed by a murmur, as the face of a young Japanese man, gentle, composed, appeared on the screen.

"My name is Takeshi. Welcome to the Young People's Hook-up. This time, we have opened this broadcast to whoever we could reach."

Next door, Josette heard a voice translating for the rest of the community.

"We are a network of young people from all over the world. We meet regularly to work on world peace. Most participating in this hook-up represent whole networks of other people, young and old. The Young People's Network spans the globe. Whatever comes up by ham radio, email or video will be available for whoever is interested." He listed a number of ways in which others could tune in in the future and get an update.

In the background, Josette heard the tap tapping of Morse code. Jules was in the communications hut transcribing the abbreviated ham radio messages.

As Takeshi spoke, a summary appeared on the screen:

"A few days ago, the BBC World Service announced the US Administration's attempt to pass a second Anti-Terrorist Act. This would pit the haves against the have-nots and create an explosive situation much like that in Kukundu. Today, the BBC World Service[32] informs us that the US Attorney General wants the right to dub citizens who he considers disloyal to the present Administration 'enemy combatants,' This would allow him to order the indefinite incarceration of those of us who fraternize with minorities and summarily strip us of our constitutional rights and access to the courts. Such steps will heighten the fear epidemic and poise the US to follow in Kukundu's footsteps. Given the leading position of the US, this policy is likely to be followed in other, formerly democratic countries.

Today's program:
➢*Actions we can take both in Kukundu and outside to dissipate fear and reclaim our human rights.*
➢*The all-win principle as a tool*

"My name is Annette!" A young longhaired blond appeared. "We have received a video which we shall show at the end of the broadcast. But before we discuss the fear epidemic, here are a few scenes.

A crackling sound. The screen flickered. Then the tear-stained face of a Mandu woman.

A scream!

Josette jumped up, as Pierre, hysterically shouting, struggled to get up out of his cot, "Augustina! Oh, Augustina!"

He thrashed around.

Afraid he would hurt himself, Josette tried to calm him. Finally, she saw no alternative but to roll on top of him with her full 250-pounds. Trying not to smother him, she pinned him in place until two strong men could drag Pierre, cot and all, outside. One stayed with Pierre to gently help him come to terms with what he had seen.

Josette watched the door close behind Pierre's stretcher being carried out, when it was pushed open again and a figure hurried to where she was sitting. It was Jules, the communications officer.

"They want you to speak!" he whispered. "Come with me and then I can get you hooked up!"

"But…" Josette protested.

"It's okay! You won't appear on video. It's only your voice. Moreover, no one, outside of our own freedom fighters, knows where we are hiding out!"

With difficulty, Josette hoisted herself up and followed Jules outside.

36. Fighting For Fundamental Human Rights

The first three rows of burgundy and gold fauteuils now lined the walls of the auditorium, embracing a hub of activity. As he walked in, Bertram saw Arturo, Pat, and Hugh in front of him, in charge of the technical side. They were orchestrating the computers, video filming and screens. Pat was talking to people who were waiting in line to participate.

In the other corner, Ian with the twin's assistance was manning the ham radio and busily transcribing incoming messages.

Annette and Takeshi were on the stage, in front of the cameras. They were facilitating the videoconference. Pim would be appearing on video from the campus of the U.N.'s University of Peace.

Bertram turned and noticed another large screen, under the balcony opposite the stage. Here, Molly was in charge of the e-mail discussion. The rest stood by, anxiously watching, ready to lend a hand.

Bertram tingled with expectation. This was a global network of activists. Would the young people just be talking to themselves or would others participate? He hoped that his young friends would succeed in contacting people in Kukundu. So much depended on being able to learn from one another.

"Here's John St. Clair! He'll be suggesting action in Kukundu!" Arturo whispered and all eyes turned to the video screen. At the same time, there was another scurry of activity. The first e-mail message was appearing on a second screen, where Molly was sitting.

While he was straining to watch both screens at once, a movement caught Bertram's eye, just above the screen on the first-floor balcony. His heart started pounding.

Since Recluse's e-mail about the Holy Order of the Snake, Bertram had been feeling ill at ease at the thought of this secret visitor. This time, he intended to find out who this person was. The hook-up would be going on for an hour.

Bertram slipped through a side door, up one flight of steps, two at a time. This led him to a red carpeted foyer. He sniffed: an unusual aromatic blend of cigarette smoke!

Four doors to choose from!

He chose the door to his right.

He tried the handle, the door opened, and he slipped inside. A large, heavy curtain blocked his view. Carefully brushing it aside, in a flash, he took in the scene.

A flight of steps led downwards, with rows of fauteuils on either side. The whole area was empty. Below him, the stage. On the stage, in the wings stood Edward, gesticulating, but not at him. It was to someone to his left.

Bertram swung around. The sound of a door closing, muffled by the heavy curtain!

Wrestling with the curtain in his booth, he finally reached the door, wrenched it open and ran back into the foyer.

The smell of cigarette smoke was stronger. He looked to the left and the right. At the end of the hall, a tiny pile of cigarette ashes stood out against the red carpet just in front of a heavy door.

In a few steps, Bertram was there. Grabbing the door handle, he rattled the door. It was locked. The door was massive and did not budge. Impatiently he knocked, but the dense oak did not carry the sound. Suddenly, he felt sheepish. What if someone were watching? There was no response at all.

He slunk back downstairs. Brushing by Edward, who was now heading toward the kitchen, he kept his head down, walked briskly through the library and out onto the terrace. There he sank into one of the loungers, trying to organize his thoughts.

Edward had ignored him. Perhaps, he hadn't noticed him, or even heard him banging on the door. But Bertram knew this was wishful thinking. Edward knew Bertram had been snooping around. He felt embarrassed. Maurice's relationship with his butler, or his brother's visitors, for that matter, were not Bertram's to worry about. He couldn't very well tell his host his own brothers were spying on him. He must forget the whole incident.

For a few moments, he sat in the sun, trying to compose himself.

The hook-up! He suddenly remembered. It had totally slipped his mind! He hurried back inside.

On the screen, a summary of the proceedings so far.

With a sense of satisfaction, Bertram read:

> *Suggested action to counter Anti-Terrorist Act Two and "Enemy Combatant Legislation, which is being considered in the US and will probably be copied by nations hoping to make the US's 'Most Favored Nation' List.*
>
> *Write to your Government Representative, mentioning the following points:*
> - *The human rights enumerated in the Universal Declaration of Human Rights are inalienable. That means that it is against international law to breach them.*
> - *Some Government Representatives are nevertheless being pressured to vote for the Enemy Combatant Legislation.*
> - *The World Corruption Watch[33], consisting of accountants and lawyers, is on hand to challenge those suspected of taking bribes or giving in to pressure; and to defend those falsely accused.*

"Great action!" Bertram thought, *"No one will want to risk being accused of bribery, falsely, or otherwise! Representatives are still chosen by their constituents.*

The threat that the powerful Corruption Watch is breathing down their necks is likely to keep them on the straight and narrow."

Nevertheless, the success of the action would depend on how many people participated.

He walked over to Pat who was now typing a list of names. Behind each name was a number: 50, 500, 6 million ….

Feeling his presence, she looked up and smiled. For a moment, her red hair looked as if it were catching fire as it was lit up by a ray of sunlight piercing through a chink in the curtain.

She explained, "This is the estimated number of participants. Each person, when they come on line, is asked whether they represent themselves or a group; and if a group, how many members the group has.

"After the hook-up, each is asked to download a summary of the proceedings, and pass it on to their networks with the request that they carry out the recommendations.

"To give an example, the World Corruption Watch has accountants and lawyers worldwide. Their Board was on line. They will be dividing up the task they have taken upon themselves among their members in each country. The Women's World Summit Foundation told us it awards 35 rural women a prize every year and many of these women lead groups of tens, even hundreds of others. Many can't read or write but the news travels through word of mouth. The Baha'is[34], who are always very active in youth and family projects have 5 million members in 204 nations and territories, and so, you see that the ideas of just one hook up reach millions of people.

"And as young people, we're pretty ingenious. Each of us tells our parents about what has been discussed. Most are pretty impressed that their kids talk with young people worldwide. For instance, at Corps Elite, many of our parents got hold of a copy of the Universal Declaration of Human Rights and passed it on to their friends. No telling after a hook-up what types of actions adults run with."

As Pat turned back to her typing, Bertram glanced over at the video screen; Pim was outlining the all-win principle. A summary appeared of the three aspects appeared on the screen.

At the opposite side of the room, the discussion by e-mail was also projected on a screen.

Bertram wandered over and, standing behind Molly's chair, he read:

> ➤*I am 35 and have only just discovered that I have fundamental, inalienable human rights. How can we stand up for ourselves, if we don't know our rights? How can I help to make the Universal Declaration better known?*

Molly had hurriedly attached the Universal Declaration in English with a note that translations were available from the U.N.[35]

There was a brief lull in the responses, as people downloaded the Declaration. Then a number of e-mails followed. As they came in, Molly placed them in order.

> ➤*I facilitate an e-mail discussion on human rights. If you would like to share your ideas there, they will reach hundreds of people. We also take action with respect to governments which breach their people's rights. We choose one country at a time and then boycott their most essential products and, where not too dangerous, we organize go-slow actions within the country itself. One country is all we can manage to target. Yet this does have an effect, because other countries see the boycott at work and hurriedly adjust their Human Rights policies. Anything to avoid the full wrath of world public opinion. A country at a time, we have managed to get thousands of people involved. (Mat, Columbus, Ohio, USA)*

Molly wrote:

> *Thanks, Mat!*
> *The Universal Declaration of Human Rights has become a part of the Constitution of most Nations. That means that when human rights are violated, it is possible to take the violators to court. Unfortunately, this does not work in most dictatorships and, even in democratic countries, governments are illegally withdrawing our rights.*
> *We're always looking for other peaceful ways to bring pressure to bear on violators.*
> (Molly, Costa Rica)[36]

A whole slew of ideas followed. Molly placed them in order for easy reading."

> ➤*Becoming members of all sorts of boards gives us a say in how our communities are run. Library, school, and municipal boards often consider young people. Many governments have a place for at least one young person on their delegation to the U.N. Let's see how many of us, young people, can get a say in the future of our world!*
> (Ragnar, the Young People's Network in Iceland.)

Then there were suggestions from women who lived in dictatorships whose husbands were part of the hierarchy.

> ➤*My husband is a high official in our village. I refuse to sleep with him when I feel he's being unjust. His response: to beat me so badly that sometimes I can barely walk. In the past, I hid my bruises; I was so ashamed. Now when people ask about my wounds, I tell them quite openly what happened and also why I was beaten.*
> (Zamira, Chuma Republic)

> ➤*Recently, a battered women's support group was started here to bring both public and legal pressures to bear on such violent domestic situations.*
> (Polly, Canada)

> ➤*Thanks, Polly, but I think I would be terrified of such a group. I know it doesn't make sense, but I would be lost without my husband. I find it very helpful to have a group of women friends who support me, no matter what.*
> (Susan, Chika Republic)

> ➤*My husband is a torturer. Last night he came home with human blood on his shirt. I am afraid, I can't stand living with him any longer – not if he continues, even though at home he is kind and gentle. If I could find a group to support me, I would be willing to try to persuade him to change his job. If I don't succeed, I might have to leave him and take the children with me.*
> (Anita, San Leon)

Molly added a quick addition

> ➤*I'm just checking your actions against the all-win principle and notice that we should add that, beside following our hearts, it is up to us to categorically withdraw our support from win/lose or all-lose situations. Thank you for that lesson.*

Barely had Molly finished arranging the messages, or a different subject was broached,

> ➤ *"We are a group of Pygmy women, gathering in an Internet Cafe in Cameroon.*

Bertram let out an exclamation and moved in closer.

> ➤*We greet you all. As Pygmy women, we are in danger of losing our traditional way of living. I wish to thank Bertram for inviting us to join your meeting. On his recommendation, I contacted the Women's World Summit Foundation (WWSF) and was referred to Eugenie Nouale Nkoro, a Bakola Pygmy woman[37], who has awarded a prize for women's creativity in rural life. Eugenie believes in lobbying the political party in power. She encourages us, Pygmy women, to obtain identity cards. These allow us to vote. We shall all be placing our names on the voting lists and go to the polls as a group. At our very first meeting, Eugenie encouraged me to run for local office! I'm still looking at how best to follow my heart. Even after a few days, I'm feeling much stronger just working alongside of Eugenie! Sharing the same goals with other women is really empowering! Of course, problems don't just disappear. Some time ago, I hear, the neighboring Bantu tribe decided to take over land which traditionally had been inhabited by Pygmies. Instead of allowing hostilities to erupt, Eugenie negotiated sufficient land for our use, so that we can continue to make a living. Eugenie is a true leader! We don't presume to compare ourselves to our brothers and sisters in Kukundu. But we urge you not to give up. I am finding out that together with others, we in the Cameroon are achieving things beyond my wildest dreams only a few days ago. You can, too! Our best wishes are with you!"*
> *We greet you from the Cameroon.*
> *(Patricia, South Cameroon Province).*

Molly whispered, "Talk about dredging up powerful energy!"

"But no firm all-win relationship yet with the Bantus," Bertram pointed out, "The governance pattern is missing to hold all-win relations in place. How to deal with people when they have so much power over us?

"I can't believe that she actually tuned in! I wrote to her just a few days ago!

"Molly, scoot over for a sec."
Bertram hurriedly wrote a response:

> *Dear Patricia,*
> *Thanks for tuning in! I must say, I was personally feeling rather overwhelmed when you contacted me the other day. Just hearing about the sort of problems you so courageously are dealing with gave me the courage to follow my own advice. It is new for me, too, to be following my heart.*
> *You inspired me, Patricia, and hearing what you have done in just a few days inspires me further!*
> *Any way of creating a more solid all-win relationship with your Bantu neighbors? I'm thinking of the governance pattern, Pim just mentioned.*
> *Thank you so much!*
> *Warmest greetings,*
> *(Bertram, Costa Rica)*

Bertram made place for Molly and walked over to watch the video screen. He didn't notice that the next e-mail was from Eliza.

> *Dear Friends,*
> *I'm writing from the office of the All-Win Network, which has All-Win Centers all over the world. You can use these Centers to learn to apply the all-win principle to your everyday living.*[38] *Our clients are largely people who have time and money. We have two main needs:*
> *1. to reach more of you, including the very poor, street children, the homeless; and*
> *2. to promote environmental projects. After all, all-win relationships with Nature are the foundation of all-win living.*
> *All help is welcome.*
> *Eliza*

Molly sat down and responded.

> *Dear Eliza,*
> *Great to hear from you in person. The Young People's Network will be mentioning your concerns wherever we go.*
> *Best wishes,*
> *(Molly, Costa Rica)*

110

This message elicited a spate of others, asking for more information about the All-Win Network and the location of All-Win Education Centers in various countries.

"No need to fear that the Young People's Network is talking to themselves," Bertram thought with satisfaction. He wondered how the discussions via ham radio and videophone were progressing.

37. Fuelling The Fear Epidemic

Many miles away, at the other side of the world, three powerful, elderly gentlemen relaxed in earnest conversation.

They were cousins, descendents of Ahab the First, Founder of the Holy Order of the Snake. Ahab the First had become fabulously rich, fuelling wars worldwide. Driven by his lust for power, he had fine-tuned the policy of *divide and rule*. Aided by the dark forces, he then developed an Illustrious Plan, which, far ahead of its time, would capitalize on globalization. This Plan had been passed on from eldest son to eldest son, generation after generation. Bit by bit, the Plan had moved toward full fruition.

Throughout the ages, their stranglehold on the world had increased. They worked with a few highly effective tools: a field of fear that could be intensified to destabilize the global situation whenever they felt they could tighten their grip; and stooges in key leadership positions.

These stooges in key leadership positions, without realizing it, were carrying out Snake's commands. All they knew was that there were some seemingly very powerful people in the background giving them good advice. These powerful people would point out the dangers if they did not take certain actions, sometimes appeal to their sense of duty and often reward them one way or another for following their advice. Pleasure, pain and duty were tools Snake used to "persuade" people to do their bidding.

Snake worked almost exclusively through stooges. Some were from the dynasty of Ahab itself, others had been carefully molded through Snake trainings and yet others were simply kept in line through manipulation and intimidation.

The eldest who seemed to be in charge clapped his hands. A butler appeared, served refreshments, and then left again immediately.

For a while, the three men were silent.

And then, the eldest cleared his throat, "We have increased the intensity of the fear people are living in to fever pitch. It is now officially referred to as a fear epidemic. It is time to make the adjustments to the existing global leadership. Some people in top positions must be eliminated; and pockets of resistance brought under our control. Today, I wish to hear your reports on the status quo. And then we can discuss our next steps."

"Well, everything's sliding along nicely," the middle cousin sighed with satisfaction. The large heart-shaped purple birthmark on the right side of his head, partly covered by a shock of Einstein type white hair.

"Much better than we had dared to hope!" agreed the youngest of the three, looking at his long, elegantly manicured hands, "It looks as if we finally have what were once the democratic countries in our control. With a few neat tricks in the elections, our stooges are now mostly in place. Now just for the last few pockets of resistance.

"We can start with your report on the political situations in the Wealthy Countries then," the leader said, addressing his youngest cousin.

The youngest steepled his elegant hands and began, "Most countries and most large corporations are indeed ruled by our stooges. Together with these, we have been destabilizing the areas under their jurisdiction to screw up the level of fear. A couple of well-staged 'terrorist attacks' prepared the way for the 'Anti-Terrorist Act' through which all human rights have been annulled. Our stooges can now arrest anyone without a warrant, hold them indefinitely, bring them to trial without a jury, and execute them without the intrusion of world public opinion."

"Can you guarantee blind obedience from those in industry and finance?" the leader asked.

"Greed's the key!" the man with the elegant hands replied, "They all excel in their leadership abilities—and ambitions!" he added with a wicked smile. "These will do anything to maintain their Membership in our 'Alliance to Rule the World!' For one, they feel safe because they know that whenever they follow our advice, they are immune from the ambitions of their competitors and they are richly rewarded. They realize that as soon as they do not obey that there are others to take their places. Of course, it helps to know that if they ever decided to leave that they would not get far—*alive!*

The three laughed heartily.

The cousin with the elegant hands contemplated his fingernails and continued.

"Recently, I got one of our stooges to push for an Anti-Terrorist Act Two and 'Enemy Combatants' Legislation. Once this is adopted, we'd just have to point at anyone who is a nuisance factor to have him thrown into jail!"

"Brilliant!" the leader agreed.

Screened from the house and the outside world by a thick hedge twice as high as a tall human being, the three gentlemen sat on a plush lawn at the edge of the beach.

The waves lapped good-naturedly in the distance.

All three were casually dressed in elegant, expensive simplicity. All three were between 75 and 80 years old. Their energy and power was seldom found in men half their age. These men were old hands at wielding the scepter. The influence of their army of stooges, after years of subtle adjustments, now reached into human hearts and minds.

"And how about the herd itself?" the bald one asked, turning to his cousin with the purple birthmark who settled comfortably in his chair and answered, "I'm quite pleased with what we have achieved.

"In business, we have forced little companies to sell out to a few large firms. The collapse of the Internet boom scared the living daylights out of the herd. The large companies are getting too big for their boots and alienating foreign markets. They are now being forced to cut back and reward cutthroat practices.

"Now, the stress factor in almost all businesses is so high that workers are at one another's throats, vying for the most prized positions. And thanks to the reliable Peter Principle, most firms have promoted Chief Executive Officers to positions where they are inept. These defend their jobs against more creative and energetic climbers or anyone who shows up their inefficiency. Such firms are riddled by fear, while *we* pull the strings.

"What about the media?" The baldheaded man inquired.

"The media is now in the hands of 4 or 5 magnates, with *us* dictating what they say.

"They sprinkle people's lives with a good dose of life threatening problems. Fear of hunger; polluted air, water and soil; rising sea levels; dwindling fish stocks; desertification; climate change; and terrorism, of course. You name it; we use it to whip up the fear level.

"Fear is taking over so gradually that most people don't even notice. They experience fear as a slight unease, not realizing that their heart disease, bowel problems, trouble sleeping at night, and addictions are all fear symptoms. Addiction's a wonderful tool and so easy to use!

"Ha!" he laughed, animated by the scenario he was evoking, " The beauty of it all is that every one of these symptoms blossoms into fresh fears: fear of disease, not being able to cope, losing one's job, being overwhelmed by others, fear of natural phenomena and after a time, a generalized screen of fear that colors whatever they encounter. Warms my heart to think how the fear transforms dreams into nightmares. Yes, I'd say we are well on our way! And no one's picking up on what's happening!"

"It constantly amazes me," the bald-headed eldest rejoined, "that we tighten the thumb screws and nobody turns a hair, at least, no one who makes any difference. It is wonderful how skilled (he made the sign of the

Snake in the air) has become over the ages at holding the reins of power. As long as our changes are gradual enough, people can cry out for all they are worth, but no one sees the urgency to do anything about it."

He clapped his hands and through the hedge his butler reappeared and topped up the glasses. Again, the three cousins sat in silence until the butler had disappeared.

Finally, the bald cousin looked at his watch and said, "Now—what's happening with the leaders we are grooming for key positions in finance and industry?"

The cousin with the elegant hands reached for his folder, pulled out some lists, and handed one to each of his companions.

He then said, "You asked me to make a selection from the list we compiled together. I thank Satan daily for how easily our tactics work. These leaders are eating out of our hands, lapping up our divide and rule teachings, applying them to their fields and fuelling the fear epidemic.

"Now they have got to the final phase of their education. They are drawing up two plans each: one on how they will keep their opposition under control; and the other one on how they will rule their own domain. This last plan covers how, while the herd is in desperate panic, they will convince them to surrender to *their* leadership, rather than to that of another. Of course, this latter plan has to be drawn up in conjunction with all others so that all our stooges in leadership positions are simply doing our bidding.

"Have you told them the price for admission?" the cousin with the purple birthmark smirked.

"This will be broached with each privately, closer to the launch," his younger cousin retorted. "Now we are grooming them for the simultaneous launch when we shall sow panic without any one of them suspecting that any one, let alone we, are choreographing the situation."

"Do we have plenty of contenders for key leadership positions in industry, finance and government for *all* nations?" the bald one inquired.

"Yes, all countries are well covered. In fact, we have enough contenders so that we shall be able to eliminate some if they turn out not to be fully controllable. Even so, we shall probably have a surplus which we shall need to eliminate in time."

The youngest took a slice of quiche and, for a few minutes, he savored its delicate flavor. A soft sea breeze was blowing. In the background, the sea softly winked in the bright sun light as if to say, "Hey, enjoy life. That's why you're here. But none of them noticed.

The bald cousin prompted him, "And now last but certainly not least: the selection and training of our *lapdogs!*" His cousins chuckled, as with an uncharacteristically broad smile, he continued, "Our ultimate goal: our lapdogs in each nation in positions of supreme power, controlling the total herd!"

His youngest cousin reached into his folder and handed each cousin another list.

He began, "Well, training started some time ago without anyone suspecting who calls the shots.

"I screened all participants on this list on two main points: Does each have an air of integrity about them and the charisma to win over whole nations? And does each have a distinct moral flaw so that we can turn the screws?

"I have marked down some of the fatal flaws I noticed during the training. I have been watching each one closely via videos, of course. Where I do not sense obedience, I have the candidate eliminated.

"Yes, I had noticed a few cases in the papers!" the cousin with the birthmark chuckled.

The eldest cousin said sternly, "We shall need to be kept informed of your progress at every step. If anything goes wrong with the grooming of our lapdogs, the Plan will be in jeopardy and I shall insist that it be postponed. The key powers at the heads of nations need to be our puppets. If not, the Final Launch of the Illustrious Plan will have to be postponed."

"You can rely on me to proceed with due caution," his cousin said with dignity, "Like you, I feel honored to be at the helm after all these centuries when the Final Phase of the Illustrious Plan goes into fulfillment. Nothing, I repeat nothing at all, may jeopardize our sacred quest."

"Good luck then!" The bald headed man rose and his cousins, in turn, bent over his ring and brushed it with their lips.

As they turned, the bald one asked, "And what about Maurice?"

"He's holed up with an ancient school ma'am, a burnt out writer, a lame duck scientist and a handful of kids. Nothing much worth reporting on that front. Slug's on the premises. He keeps us regularly updated on what goes on, using our global telecommunications network in the theatre auditorium," the Einstein look-alike replied.

"Slug?" The bald one asked.

"Don't worry," his cousin rejoined. He has strict orders – no violence! He might be a brute but he has been programmed to repeat to us flawlessly whatever he hears."

38. **Reconciliation**

"I'd like to welcome one of our friends from Kukundu," Pim introduced Josette.

Josette had instantly liked the slender, retiring Dutchman on the screen. He was modest, quiet-spoken and caring. Now she was talking to him by phone."

"Thank you, Pim," Josette answered, her anxiety ebbing away, "We're not switching to video and I won't say my name. You see, we're in hiding. Yet, we're hoping that others who live in Kukundu will be interested in what we are doing and that one day we can work more openly together."

Pim interjected, "By the way, I hear from my young friend here that there are a number of groups from Kukundu online. You are the only one who is willing to speak. Thank you for your courage!

"You're working with the reconciliation process?" Pim prompted.

"Yes," Josette answered, "reconciliation is different from working with crimes, punishment, incarceration and execution. In Kukundu, every one of us without exception is guilty. Each of us has been involved in the crimes either directly or else by standing by and letting them happen. Reconciliation assumes that all are one and that every person is important. It's a form of communication that comes from the heart and seeks to speak to the heart of all others. All people in Kukundu require healing and forgiveness. Each must come to grips with her or his own pain and guilt.

"I work with the fears that flare up, as we face our pain. For instance, I blew up our local village hall with the whole all-Kukundu City Council in session. My husband and son were among the dead. Of course, I can never bring them back. But before I can even think of making up for what I have done, I must first face the *fear* of my own painful feelings. You see, fear propels our attention away from what we fear. Once we allow ourselves to *experience* our fear, it dissipates because we are no longer running away. With fear out of the way, our feelings change. We can see our experiences for what they are. And only then can we fully make amends.

"Unfortunately, in our jungle hide-out, we are separated from those we have wronged. And so, we have to empathize from a distance by in imagination creeping inside their skins."

"How do you do that?" Pim asked.

"I sit quietly and then I imagine that my body takes on the form of the person whose experience I want to empathize with!"

A good-natured laugh could be heard, rumbling over the phone. Josette joined in. A deep infectious belly laugh.

"My friends here are having difficulty visualizing what I mean!" She was still laughing. "You see, I am sort of bulky: I weigh some 250 pounds!"

Pim's face relaxed into a good-natured smile. "I have the opposite problem," he said, "My friends tease me because I'm too skinny!

"But it is interesting that you would talk about adopting the *form of another person.*

Remember the morphogenetic field I mentioned just now? Well this *inform*ation field tends to connect and *form* things or people with similar shapes. So when in imagination you creep into the skin or *form* of another, you are accessing the information fields that most directly permeate that person --the reality, which she or he personally inhabits.

"And so you relive the process from the other's perspective?" he asked.

"Exactly!" Josette replied, "And when you are done, the orange-tinted glasses you mentioned just now have turned into clear, clean glass. In other words, you are back in reality and the reality is no longer distorted by fear. You see and feel everything as it is. And if by chance you interpret things wrongly, you can easily correct your interpretation, because fear is no longer urging you to look the other way."

"Once we have fully experienced the pain, there is a renewed will to live. Some of us feel even more alive than we felt before the atrocities took place. It is as if inner debris has been cleared away. Once we face life fully – splendor, complexity, atrocities, and all—we are profoundly moved and find ourselves following our hearts."

"This is most useful," Pim admitted, "What you describe is how to transform fear into love and in the process resolve conflicts, clear up misunderstandings, and heal rifts between cultures, religions, and nations."

"Once fear no longer is in control and the heart can take over, the next steps tend to emerge," Josette continued, "For us in Kukundu, this means rebuilding our beloved country. Most who have been through a course of mine return to their villages and help others to heal or prepare for future change. Reconciliation or Ubuntu, as we call it, is an ancient African approach. It can only take place when all Kukundu citizens realize that all of us are one and reconciliation is our only choice."

"But what if they don't?" Pim inquired.

"That's where things become dangerous.

"So usually those who have returned to their villages wait until a neighbor or friend reaches out for help. Only then do they lend a hand."

"Do you see any steps Kukundu, as a whole, can take to transform this black page in its history?" Pim asked.

"First persuade President Kundana to hold a referendum and give our dear 'Daddy' M'Bwene an opportunity to come back and continue running the country.

"Then we shall have to have local tribunals in which people, like myself, take full responsibility for what we have done. And hear what we can do to make amends. Our fellow citizens will have to decide.

"At the same time, we shall have to have citizens' councils and public hook-ups like these with Mandus and Kukundu refugees so that we can develop a new Kukundu along the all-win lines you suggested, Pim.

"Before signing off," Josette added, "I should like to say to all my fellow Mandu and Kukundu citizens: the road we have taken is a dead-end. None of us can build a life on robbery and murder. There is, therefore, only one alternative. We must choose the road which has been suggested here: all-win relationships!"

With Josette's impassioned plea, the meeting came to an end.

Back in the Costa Rica auditorium in consultation with her crew, times were arranged for following hook-ups with the general public and passed on via e-mail, ham radio and videophone.

Everyone was tired and excited. There was a general consensus that never before had they ever reached as many people as they had reached that day.

Walking out onto the terrace, Bertram mused, *"And this is just the beginning. All will be taking what they have heard back into their everyday lives. The insights and the contacts will spread in all directions indefinitely into the future!"*

39. The Message Of The Drums

Five drummers gathered hurriedly in the clearing, and moved into the forest, each in a different direction. Each was blindfolded and escorted part of the way by a resident Mandu. An hour later, the first drum roll was heard, **"Claim your life back, go all-win. A conscious policy of all-win for every man, woman and child!** Then it gave the ways of tuning into the ham radio, Internet chat groups, and video broadcasts to read up on what had been discussed. Each drum was joined by a second, a third and then others picked up the beat.

Soon, Josette knew, their message would be heard all over the country and Kukundu would be resounding with people curious what was meant. And nothing the authorities could do about it.

Some would inevitably act.

And so, bit by bit the messages of hope would reach the general population. One day, the freedom fighters now in separate enclaves would meet and be able to work together.

40. The Young People Sail Away

The hook up was considered a great success. In the days that followed, e-mails poured in. Mary had decided to organize one extra hook-up a week to include the general public, beside the Thursday morning one, which was limited to young people.

"Mind you, it's just a first step!" Mary cautioned. "The challenge will be to work together!" She smiled at Pim. "After all, cooperation's where it's at!"

Then the day of departure arrived.

Bertram with Maurice and Pim accompanied Mary to the dock where their young friends were waiting.

Then, sails billowing in the wind, the *Peace Warrior* moved away, bucking on the waves as she went.

Cries of "Bye! See you in the South of France!" wafted toward them as they waved. Soon even Mary's white cap was the merest dot, as she steered the boat out of the bay past the devil's teeth.

The air was heavy with humidity. The waves lapped at the dock with a hollow blop! blop! sploosh! Even the pungent salty smell of the beach barely registered. Bertram felt sad and empty. The bustle and laughter and the burgeoning struggle to come to grips with fear had collapsed into a single date in his diary, when in just under a year's time, they would gather with other movers and shakers in Maurice's Castle in the South of France.

Maurice chuckled, "Well, before you know it the *all-win principle* will be advertised all up and down the South American coast! Not to mention via the airwaves every Thursday morning!

"I almost saw you sailing off with them, as 'playwright in residence', Bertram! You could have been one of Mary's students!"

"Except for my graying temples!" Bertram grinned. "Anyway, they were helping me as much as I helped them. My novel is progressing nicely."

"Oh?" Maurice inquired.

Bertram's zest for life was back again. " The Hero of my book is brought up on a diet of divide and rule, hammered in by private tutors. But through Mable Smily, he is going to discover the all-win principle and take a leading role applying it to business, politics and education -- perfect theme for a new series of lectures and workshops.

"Eventually, I hope to use our Kukundu friend's method of creeping into people's skin with my Chief Executive clients. Heal the rifts caused by cutthroat competition. Removing my own fear-tinged glasses is my first challenge, though!" Bertram chuckled."

Bertram meandered with Maurice and Pim back up to the terrace.

"When do you start back on tour?" Pim asked.

Bertram responded, "Well, Maurice has been so good as to invite me to stay as long as I like. It will take me another three months, I should think, to complete my novel and then I must find a publisher. Hope you can stand me for so long!" Bertram smiled at Maurice.

"And after that?" Pim asked.

"My first lecture tour will be in the States, if I can find a publisher there, possibly with a few side steps to Europe!

"And how about you?" he asked Pim.

"I shall be staying another month or so; then my colleagues and I will have progressed far enough to continue communications by e-mail," Pim turned to Maurice. "Fancy! A castle in the South of France! Thanks for your generous invitation. By next year, we should be ready to pool our findings with our young friends."

"The conference will be a perfect opportunity to learn from one another. Yes, thanks, Maurice!" Bertram agreed.

"Pure self-interest!" Maurice smiled, "I'd love to participate! As long as you fellows organize the proceedings and I don't have to get up on the stage."

Edward met them on the terrace with iced coffee topped generously with a blop of freshly whipped cream flavored with a soupcon of vanilla.

Grateful for the cool drink, Bertram tried to recapture the feeling of levity, which had characterized the past days.

Yet, how divested of life, the terrace felt—like an empty shell from a bygone era, abandoned and without heart. Edward had cleared away the extra sofas and lounge chairs – all but three. With Mary and her crew, the atmosphere of warmth and caring had gone that had nurtured Bertram back to health.

"I contributed to that atmosphere," he suddenly realized. Now it was up to him to generate this warm caring atmosphere for others.

"Thank you, Edward," Maurice smiled as he took a drink. Careful not to spill it, he undid his robe, kicked off his thongs and sank down on one of the chaises longues.

"Hmm!" Edward waited, as Maurice looked up.

"I couldn't help overhearing you mention your plan to meet in the South of France. If it is to be a scientific meeting with so many organizations, wouldn't it be an idea to invite Professor Perspicio?"

"Percy?" Maurice looked surprised. "Well, I suppose we could. He's always eager to stay in touch with what I and my 'blissed out' circles are up to.

"Asked me only the other day when he could come to one of my friendly meetings. He'd probably feel left out if he knew that I was dabbling in science and he wasn't invited to the conference."

"He's my elder brother," he explained, "As a scientist, rather conventional, I believe. But he would probably be only too willing to play host. Of course, Pim, you would be in charge of the conference's content."

"Uncle Percy--wasn't that where your nephew went?" Bertram asked.

"That's right," Maurice replied.

41. Quiet Changes In Kukundu

Setting foot outside the hut for the first time, Pierre felt he was entering a foreign land. He had lived at the edge of the jungle for most of his life. Now he felt as if he were seeing it for the very first time. The drip, drip of moisture, gently prodding the dank soil to release its musty odor, the prolific thrust of greens and browns, reaching for the light. Pierre was following the one jungle path that led through the encampment. On both sides, huts peeked from behind the lush undergrowth, as if each were in hiding.

Holding on to Josette's arm for support, Pierre walked very slowly.

"One hundred people at any one time live in this secret settlement," Josette explained, "The Mandus are, of course, permanent. But the Kukundus come and go.

"But how do you ensure that they don't give you away?" Pierre asked.

"They are blindfolded whenever they move back and forth and led via circuitous routes. That way, even under torture, they can't give us away," Josette replied.

"But how do they get back here?" Pierre asked.

"We arrange to meet them in places which we hold under observation, to make sure they are not followed," Josette answered. "There is a constant coming and going. You see, we are creating a quiet revolution."

"But how can you do that? At the first signs of rebellion, people are put to death."

"The all-win principle has, from the beginning, been an integral part of our strategy."

"But how?"

"Well, the Kukundus that go back to their villages and towns, of course, visit their friends and neighbors to inquire how they are. That way, they discover their concerns. If they are missing Mandu family members who have fled as refugees, they might wonder whether in the long run they will be reunited again. As soon as my trainees feel a genuine openness, they very carefully broach the subject of change."

"But isn't that seen as treason?" Pierre asked.

"No, because we are extremely careful. Each of us has learned to follow the all-win principle all the way through. We have trained ourselves to creep into the skin of all parties and talk from their perspectives. Also, when we discuss these matters, we are sure to show our concern for the safety and well being of every one concerned, including those in power.

"For instance, if Kukundu friends and neighbors mention any misgivings at all, we share our personal misgivings about our own complicity. We talk about systems that bring people like ourselves to trial, such as the Neurenburg Trials, the various U.N. Tribunals, its Human Rights Committee, and its International Criminal Court. We show how systems like ours, based on win/lose situations, inevitably produce such strong resistance and how many have failed in the end. Then, when they see the dangers of the situation they are helping to create, we mention in an off-hand sort of way, that there might be a way out for every one concerned.

"More often than not, if we do this carefully enough without any pressure whatever, people will return to the subject themselves often discreetly seeking our help."

"And what *can be done*?" Pierre asked Josette, indignantly. "You can't possibly hope to wrestle power from the powers that be?"

"Did any of your friends join the militia?" Josette seemed to evade the question.

"Well, yes! Once Kundana took power, more and more joined him."

"Yes, seeking security, just like you," Josette agreed. "To some, it was the security of being on the winning side. To others, the power to loot and rape at will. And to yet others, it is the security of being true to your government."

"But ..."

"Win-lose situations generate resistance. Eventually, they fall apart. Deep down people know this. It makes them uneasy and in the long run, ready to change. But we have allowed President Kundana to gain too much power. We can't tackle him directly. The most we can do now is to prepare ourselves and others for whenever the change happens."

Wandering along the jungle path, Pierre thought of the tape of the video meeting, which he had seen over and over again, and how Pim had stated that chaos could be seen as a step toward a new stable all-win system.

A bird's trill echoed through the jungle. It was repeated three times. After a moment, the signal was repeated three times again.

It was the signal that dinner was being served. They turned back.

42. Breaking The Spell Of Kukundu

(Four Months Later)

After four months of individual and group sessions with Josette, Pierre was reclaiming his own life.

"Everything is so beautiful," Pierre greeted her, "But it feels so unreal to me!"

"That's what happens when the fear is still there," She replied, as they sat down on the bench in the clearing where she conducted her sessions.

"I'm so sick of going over my experiences again and again! My home, my village, my first petty crime. In each group session, we each confront one another, then I go over the whole thing again in private sessions with you. Robbery and assault are beginning to feel as if they are a natural part of everyday!"

"Well, that was the state of mind you were in, before you murdered your children!" Josette was purposefully blunt, "Until you can fully face what you have done, you won't be able to take responsibility, make amends, or reclaim your life!"

Pierre and Josette headed toward a small bench in the jungle where they had recently held their sessions.

"So let's go back over your experiences again," Josette proposed.

Pierre allowed himself to be swallowed up by the drip, drip, dripping sounds as rain from the recent deluge slid from the leaves to the jungle floor. Gradually, the soothing sounds eroded his resistance.

"I can remember feeling deeply shocked when the first Mandus were assaulted and the Kukundu criminals were never brought to justice," he began.

"Then it happened a second time and my outrage became less fierce. And finally, as it happened over and over again the outrage wore off. Others were going through the same process!" Pierre looked at Josette defiantly, "It was as if we all together just glided into seeing it as normal, until even I began to distrust the Mandus."

"But what about your wife? How did you feel about her?"

Pierre sighed. "I have always loved Augustina. She is terribly bright, and has a great sense of humor. She's tall and slender and ..." Suddenly he laughed. "She has huge feet! I love that about her. On the one hand, she's feminine. On the other she's powerful like a man. She was always a wonderful mother..." Pierre's voice trailed off. His eyes filled with tears. "Here I go again," he thought helplessly as sobs wracked his body.

Josette let him cry without interrupting.

"That helps to wash away the pain," she said tenderly, when he finally looked up.

Pierre wiped his tears away with a sweaty hand and stared unseeingly into the jungle.

"What interests me," Josette mused eventually, "is how did you get from being outraged to assaulting your wife's people?"

Pierre was silent for a long time.

For the umpteenth time, he repeated, "All I can say is that the atmosphere changed and that made it okay...."

"See if you can go deeper!" Josette coaxed.

Pierre sat quietly taking in the peaceful jungle clearing. Children playing ... a voice singing in the kitchen hut...people sitting around in groups discussing strategies: how to mend relationships, how to develop structures of government, and other scenarios for when Kukundu would be freed. That quiet trust in one another, the loving teamwork here in the middle of the jungle ... Yes, that was it! It was that atmosphere which had characterized his marriage with Augustina. It was the feeling that they were losing the most precious thing they shared -- that had kept nagging in the back of his mind, all the time that the change was occurring.

"There was always that feeling of guilt in the back of my mind," he said finally, "I was terrified that Augustina would find out...Yes there were two things, which stand out. On the one hand, that terrible fear. I was married to a Mandu and that placed me in danger. I was also terrified that something would take her away from me...and then there were the kids too; they were at the center of our lives. To think that something from the outside could break us apart. I hoped with enough money I could buy my way out.

"Fear was one reason that I started to rob and steal. But there was another thing which was less clear." He paused. His lips moved slightly as if about to say something and then stopped.

Again a long hesitation.

Finally, he looked at Josette squarely, " It had to do with revenge. Let me see, how shall I put it..... a feeling of spite. You see, unconsciously I was blaming her for being a Mandu. I know this sounds absurd. But her being a Mandu was the cause of my fear, because it endangered our family.

"Oh, I know she couldn't help it, but a part of me hated her for it and wanted to get back at her. I chose to do a combination of things that would have really hurt her terribly. My stealing would have totally horrified her, but if she had found out that I had robbed and even assaulted Mandus, because they belonged to her tribe, she would have been completely devastated. And to compound it all, I did it behind her back!" He burst out sobbing, "That last part topped it all," he cried, adding between sobs, "You see, since we had been together, we had had a pact never to keep secrets from the other. To do all this behind her back – well, I had to, in order to keep our marriage in tact and at the same time, it was my revenge."

His sobs eased and he sat numbly staring into the jungle.

Finally he said with surprising calm: "Yes, there was the atmosphere that made it okay and next to that the feelings of fear, guilt, spite and revenge..."

"Thank you, Pierre! That was a brave thing to admit.

"Now the ultimate question: What led you to behead your children?"

43. Bertram

Immediately after Mary and her crew had left, Bertram found a publisher for his book. Three months later, his book was completed and he spent another month, while it was being printed and distributed, relaxing with Maurice and expanding their network of friends.

"It looks as if anyone in the NGO world who is into global community building will be joining us in the South of France," Maurice beamed, "I'm amazed at what our small group has been able to achieve in just a few months!" They had just returned from a late afternoon swim and were lounging on the terrace.

"All except Eliza!" Bertram thought.

The two friends were by now so attuned to each other that small talk no longer was necessary. They enjoyed their long, warm evenings together on the terrace without the need for conversation, each wrapped in his own reverie, now and again making a passing comment.

Now Bertram's thoughts drifted to Eliza. She had written,

> *I sense that toward that time, I shall be ready to relax by myself. My work is so filled with people – wonderful people, mind you!—that every*

> *now and again, I feel the need to be alone. I am thinking of going back to Europe.*

He treasured his regular correspondence with her, sharing his personal hopes and dreams, and how he was learning to trust his feelings and learning to follow his intuition. He had written about the joys and travails he experienced while writing his book and his excitement as he saw how the principles of evolution provided a handle on globalization.

He loved the way she embraced life and felt privileged that although she tended to keep her innermost feelings to herself, she had shared so much of her grieving process with him.

Eliza had given him a number of all-win ideas, which he could use in his work. For instance, she had written:

> *I appreciate how you try and apply everything Pim told you about the "field" to practical every day challenges. I have much the same inclination. To me, theory is useful to the extent it can be applied to enhance life. Besides providing a sense of mastery over our own destinies, I find that living experience of these principles lends both immediacy and credibility to what I teach. The International Emissaries[39] are very helpful in this respect. They teach the practical skills necessary to apply the "field" to everyday situations.*

Bertram had liked what the Emissaries had to offer so much that he had taken two courses in succession. He had learned to speak in public under stress and without notes, to "draw from the field" as he spoke and to be more finely attuned to his audiences. He also learned from the Emissaries how groups of people can work in sync with high quality results even when under time constraints. He had noticed that many Emissaries were consciously able to strengthen the energy aspect of the *"field"* in their surroundings using a process they called *attunement.* This centered them in their personal power and made them more sensitive to the needs of others and, in some cases, it enabled them to speed up healing processes.[40]

Every day he would sit quietly, allowing his thoughts to slow down, so as to be more in touch with the *field.* Every night, he would also go over his day and pay attention to any aspects, which might need some caring attention, and then he would consciously feel grateful for everything that had come his way. This helped him to connect more deeply with every aspect of his life, to feel more anchored in what mattered deeply to himself and less at the effect of other people. He realized that the added sense of inner poise would be helpful in a high-pressured business environment.

Eliza had also put him in touch with the Baha'is[41].
She had written,

> *Their organization is growing by leaps and bounds all over the world. They form a group wherever there are 9 or more in an area. They are bridge builders par excellence. They believe that each major religion has something of essential value to offer. They themselves specialize in unity. At present, they have a worldwide network of trainings which embraces the globe to help individuals to consciously apply their spiritual strengths to the challenges of everyday life; and classes on meditation. The trainings are geared to all age groups, including babies and young children.*
>
> *They do not believe in imposing anything on anyone else. So individual Baha'is are able to follow their hearts.*
>
> *They have developed a form of problem solving process through consultation that can be used for peaceful conflict resolution.*
>
> *This is how it works: participants come together. Each speaks when she or he feels the right moment has come. The challenge is to express ones views honestly and courteously in an atmosphere of openness and selflessness. Hereby the thought expressed by anyone is offered as the property of the group as a whole and can be examined dispassionately and the clash of opinion is anticipated and accepted as a means of producing the spark of truth. As the conversation proceeds, all points of view are eventually heard. Each point of view can be appreciated because it is seen in connection to others, rather than opposing and invalidating them. And in the end the opposing views, like black and white in a painting, instead of detracting from one another, are ordered in such a way that they each contribute to a harmonious understanding of the over all picture.*
>
> *Finally, they believe in a world governed by international law under a strengthened U.N., inspired by natural law, the ultimate all-win governing pattern. So all three levels of the all-win waltz are fostered by their organization. Perhaps therefore, it has become the fastest growing religion with around 6 million members worldwide.*

Encouraged by what he had learned from the Emissaries, he attended some of the activities organized by the Baha'is and was now planning to use their conflict resolution and problem solving approach in his business seminars.

In a later letter, Eliza wrote:

> *There's a 'zero waste' movement. Everything that businesses are now throwing away is put to good use. Hundred per cent recycling! That's how nature works! Can you imagine what that means? It's good for business: they can capitalize on all their resources and throw nothing away. It is good for the customer because the increased efficiency allows companies to keep their costs down and their prices low and it is oh! so necessary for Mother Earth.*
>
> *Oh yes, and then there's the U.N. Secretary General's "Global Compact[42]". Here's how it works: businesses openly pledge to uphold human rights in all their dealings and abide by specific international laws. In exchange, the anti-globalization movement tends to leave them alone. Finally, there is All-Win Business, International[43].*

He would use this fount of useful information in the seminars he was now developing.

He hardly dared to admit to himself that his feelings for Eliza were increasing. Secretly, he hoped that one day their paths would cross.

Maurice and he had a regular correspondence with Mary and members of her crew.

In her last letter, Mary had written:

> *Every school year, I open my classes to beginners. The older students stay on. David and Antonia are in the same class this year. Even though most of this class is younger than they, they each tend to keep to themselves. David's multiple sclerosis is much worse. I don't know how he makes it to school. So far, he has never missed a ham radio hook-up. Other than that, things are moving along smoothly.*

More and more groups were attending her hook ups, Mary had written. Where before, she had had one, she now had three hookups a week. One was open to the general public – adults as well as young people.

As a spin off from the hook-up they had organized while with Maurice, a number of actions had taken off. The Universal Declaration of Human Rights was regularly mentioned by the media and there were a growing number of lawsuits dealing with breaches of human rights. All this publicity, of course, strengthened the *field*, informed people of their rights, and made it easier to uphold them.

And the e-mail discussion group on how to get governments to implement their citizens rights was exploring the use of boycotts. The question they were considering was which products of a country where human rights were seriously being breached could best be boycotted to have most effect. Such boycotts were based on the premise that supporting the all-win principle went hand in hand with withdrawing ones support from win/lose and all-lose situations.

The woman who had threatened to leave her torturer husband had carried out her threat and had made headlines in the world press. Now others were following suit.

And an increasing number of young people were gaining seats on local and national civic boards where they actively stressed the importance of the Universal Declaration of Human Rights and the all-win principle which lay at its heart.

44. How Did You Come To Behead Your Children?

"How did I come to behead my children? It's hard to explain, Josette."

Pierre thought for a few minutes, "It reminds me of when I was in the military. I was practicing how to shoot people, slit their throats. And it felt okay. While you're in that atmosphere, it's just the ordinary thing to do, but as soon as you're back in your village, you would never consider such acts. Yes, ...it was a bit like that...

His thoughts went back to that fateful day. It had taken him many sessions to be able to recall it clearly, now it was vividly present. "Before I killed my children," he began, "I heard the militia approach, banging on door after door, getting closer every minute. There was a feeling of inevitability. I knew what was expected of me. Yes, it *was* as if I were infected by the atmosphere of '*this is the way things are and there is no escaping them.*' Part of me just wanted to get it over with..."

He paused for a long time and then said softly, "Part of me was terribly angry... Just like with Augustina..." His voice sounded strangled.

"I felt a little like a zombie who was programmed and had to obey – Ah!!!!!!" His scream seemed to be wrenched from his gut. "I *wanted* to kill my babies. Anything to get away from the tension!"

He started dry retching.

Josette sank down on the ground and supported his head in her hands.

But nothing came. Spasm followed spasm. Gradually these eased. Pierre slumped onto the ground and cried.

Awkwardly, Josette let her large bulk down beside him, took him in her arms and cuddled him like a child, until he fell asleep.

Every now and again, he would sob, moan or sigh in his sleep while Josette was rocking him gently, gently ....

Finally, he opened his eyes.

Disoriented, he softly extricated himself from Josette's large bulk and then gingerly hoisted himself up.

"Can you remember what you told me just now?" she asked softly.

Pierre nodded.

As Josette hoisted her large body into a standing position and joined him on the bench, he quietly summarized what he had said.

He ended, "The horror of it all! It just didn't sink in. Otherwise, why would I put them to bed? Even when I had buried them, I was still in a crazed world. To think that I would run to Augustina for comfort!"

"The mind's like the body that way," Josette explained, "When you are badly hurt, you feel numb, or sometimes even lose consciousness. The full pain doesn't hit you 'til later. That's what grieving is: the slow realization that you've lost someone irretrievably. By going over your experiences again and again, we're accelerating the grieving process so that you can reclaim all the thoughts and feelings that were too painful to feel. You have no idea how much energy it takes to avoid a whole slew of experiences. Once you are no longer afraid of anything you have done, you find you have all that energy at your disposal!"

"How do you feel now?" Josette asked gently.

The moist musty humidity, the frantic greens of the jungle, the chirping of the crickets, and in the distance the odor of cooking and hushed melody of voices...

"I feel calm inside...calm and...and...surprisingly strong.

"Oh God, Josette, this place is beautiful!"

Josette's laugh, tinged with delight, rocked her large body.

"I do believe that you are fast reclaiming your full personal power! Once you're not afraid, it's difficult for people to manipulate you."

"Josette!" a voice called from the communications hut, "Your input is needed."

As Jules approached, he said in a conversational tone, "Command's making a film on how to free ourselves from the fear with which Kundana and his henchmen hold us in their power! They ask whether you would demonstrate how you do it.

"Be right there," Josette called back.

She hesitated, looking speculatively at Pierre.

"Pierre, why don't you come along, too! I think what you have just been through is a valuable example of how we work.

"I know you are still feeling vulnerable, but that is exactly what people need to see. "

45. Bertram In Full Swing

(Eight Months Later)

Bertram's lecture tour had started with many smaller meetings. Now the large Fortune Five Hundred conference had just begun. Today he had given his keynote speech. It had been warmly received. There had been many questions. Now he had the afternoon off and was lying on his bed.

Bertram liked Luxor best of all the hotel casinos in Las Vegas. Its quiet marble corridors, the elevators, which sped guests at – was it a 60-degree angle? -- from the main floor to the bedrooms, right in the heart of the pyramid. The inner pyramid temperatures were a welcome relief from the 100-degree Fahrenheit furnace outside. And to think that the laser beam of light that issued from its uppermost point could be seen from Outer Space!

His old self again, he was back to work and loving every minute.

Yet today, he felt weary--weary of talking heads, weary of the all-male cast, weary of the token females clothed in male mannerisms, thought structures and costumes. How strange! He had lived in these surroundings for so long and it had never bothered him before.

Then it struck him. He was missing Eliza. He had come to count on his correspondence with her about everything that was important to him.

Only that morning, he had mentioned in his talk two approaches, which were based on how Nature herself worked. Both came from Eliza. They had discussed the *zero-waste* concept and the financial advantages for business if they could turn all their wastes to profits.

He had also mentioned the approach to taxes Eliza was discussing with Governments at the U.N.; whereby, only those people and businesses pay taxes that harm the environment or extract non-renewable resources, such as oil, coal and other minerals, or make products which can not be fully recycled.

"And these are zapped by taxes," Bertram had explained, "and people are moreover required to return the Earth, as far as possible, to her natural state!"

"But this would be the end of business!" One man commented, aghast.

"It would bring about drastic change," Bertram had smiled. "It would force the economy to move from a product centered waste economy with products being transported half-way across the world to a more service centered one, which is oriented toward community, life and health.

"In the long run, every one would benefit. We would stop poisoning the air, water and land, and *ourselves*. We would stop clear-cutting our forests, depleting fish stocks, over-breeding and making our natural home unfit for human life. It would force us to become respectful of Mother Earth who is the source of our livelihoods, and also to respect ourselves, because such a tax approach will ensure we don't mortgage our own futures. It's an all-win approach to living. The economy benefits, because only unsustainable practices are taxed. And all people, instead of blindly consuming, learn to respect all that is. Once such a tax system turns the economy around, a new tax system can be devised. But a sustainable economy requires far less taxes, because zillion problems will have been resolved!

"Just imagine if you are one of the businesses which voluntarily makes such changes how far you would be ahead of everyone else! And with what savings! It's an all-win approach," he had stressed again, "Once one large company has made the switch, the benefits are so great that others can not help but follow.

"What would it take for each of you to begin to make such changes in your companies?" he had asked and given them all time to answer that question on paper provided for the purpose. Then, in the discussion that followed, he had allowed them to inspire one another with their ideas.

Many businesses had become intrigued by the U.N. and had invited World Federalist speakers. As a result, a growing number of large businesses were beginning to see the U.N. as the powerful tool that it is.

The tools from the Brahma Kumaris and the International Emissaries had been embraced. Businesses found where their employees loved what they were doing and were able to work under stress as a team, business flourished.

And so, Eliza was never far from Bertram's thoughts, even while at work.

A sweet melancholy engulfed him. His life had become so inextricably bound up with hers. And yet, opening himself to feelings of intimacy had extracted a price. Gone was his peace of mind. Why hadn't she written? If something were wrong, he would hear about it. They had so many friends in common. He had already written her three e-mails since hearing from her last. Was he overwhelming her with his e-mails?

The phone rang.

He could almost smell the Rive Gauche, which had inundated him as, every few minutes at the conference opening, Helga had leant over to whisper comments in his ear, in the process sweeping his shoulders with her platinum blond hair.

"Bertram, how nice to meet you this morning. What d'ya say, we order room service in my suite and spend a quiet siesta together?" "Thanks, Helga!" he laughed. "When I'm on tour, I keep to a strict bachelor/ loner regime in my spare time. Nothing personal! Frankly, I'm tired and feel a need for space."

He promised he would see her at the conference the next morning and hung up with a grin.

How his life had changed! Instead of relaxing in the company of other people, he was spending more time alone. He enjoyed living in an atmosphere of quiet where his hunches and intuitive insights flowed. Coming out of these periods of quiet, he felt both peaceful and powerful. He tended to know what he wanted and could assert what was important to him peacefully, and yet firmly. He was learning to follow his heart and not give his power away.

Taking time to himself, he felt more attuned to his audience. The inner quiet he felt in himself communicated itself to them. Gone was the restlessness that came with having to out-perform others. Those who had known mostly competition, now saw advantages in relaxing, just by looking at him. The numbers requesting private consultations and workshops was therefore increasing.

His mind drifted away from his work.

Costa Rica, Maurice, Pim, Mary and her young people seemed a long way away. Also the sinister scraps of paper, the feeling of being watched, moving curtains, the man on the balcony – all seemed to evaporate once the young people had left.

Here on tour, he was back on the stage where he felt he could personally bring about change. His talk at this Fortune Five Hundred conference had made quite a stir. His thinking was novel. He had managed to present his thoughts so convincingly that firms were eager to know more.

The Global Compact businesses could enter into with the United Nations was catching on fast. Businesses operating internationally were concerned about their growing unpopularity. The Global Compact could be seen as a self-imposed seal of approval to help restore positive understanding between businesses and the anti-globalists.

Members of the Global Compact would state publicly that they agreed to observe human rights and a number of other international agreements. In this way, they would imply the intention not to exploit the poor and unprotected and were helping to build a foundation for an all-win global community. Every year members of the Global Compact would provide an audit, open to public scrutiny, summarizing their successes and failures as they had tried to abide by their agreements. The Global Compact was, in fact, a process of ongoing learning.[44]

British Petroleum was already a *Global Compact Member.* And so was Shell. BP had even had an action it had named *Beyond Petroleum,* and were now participating in the experiment with London buses running on hydrogen. But activists were still suspicious of all giant companies. These activists constituted the "stick behind the door", which kept Global Compact Members busy refining their compliance with the nine Global Compact[45] principles. The more such large companies came on board, becoming more transparent in the process, the more other companies would follow suit, Bertram was convinced.

"But businesses need support if they are to make the switch," Bertram reflected. He therefore made a point of helping them to join like-minded groups like Social Venture Network. This consisted of firms, which "see business as a catalyst for change towards a socially and environmentally sustainable future"[46]. He also introduced them to All-Win Business, International, founded by Eliza's ex-husband, Macek. He had been in touch with Macek to find out more about the Zero-Waste approach.

That brought his thoughts right back to Eliza again with a sense of sweet longing.

The phone jolted him out of his reverie.

"You know that Global Compact you mentioned?" it was Helga's husky voice, "Guaranteed, you get the U.N. breathing down your neck!"

"You mean, the U.N. plays watchdog?" Bertram asked, "No, actually the U.N. doesn't have the funds. The NGOs do it for them. Some are set up specially to monitor companies' compliance. But don't join the Global Compact unless you intend to uphold your end. Integrity's the name of the game. Do your best and the anti globalization movement will probably leave you alone. Don't, and you'll feel sorry you ever stuck out your neck."

From where he lay, air conditioning going full blast, gold Egyptian columns with traces of green and red were reflected back at him in the large mirrors.

His computer light was flashing. Messages. Would there be one from Eliza?

"Any place I can find out more about it? Sorry, I left my conference folder downstairs," Helga's voice penetrated his thoughts.

"The Global Compact is mentioned on the U.N.'s web site, www.un.org. They also have a web site of their own."[47] He gave Helga the web address and hung up.

He reached for the white terry cloth bathrobe and striding over to the computer, recovered his messages.

A name he didn't recognize. "Juanita? … Juanita?" He opened it.

It was a student he had known at Oxford, who had participated in a few of his tutorials. She had been half dating a man from San Leon, the son of some dictator, or was he a prince? What was his name…?

He read:

> *Dear Bertram,*
>
> *Read your bestseller! Congratulations. I'm in San Leon for a series of articles on social conditions in emerging dictatorships.*
>
> *Remember Joaquim? He became king when his father died. It's strange being so close to Joaquim and not being able to pop in for a natter. Married Esmeralda, a real prima donna.*
>
> *Anyway, congratulations with your success!*
>
> *Juanita.*
>
> *(Journalist, Magazine: Global Trends)*

There was one from Geoffrey, Maurice's nephew who had inspired the Hero in his book. He mentioned that his Uncle Percy had invited him to the meeting in the South of France and that he had arranged to come. Bertram smiled. He was in good hands, if his Uncle Percy was anything like Maurice.

Then an e-mail from the Cameroon from Patricia, his Pygmy friend! Eagerly, he read:

> *Dear Bertram,*
>
> *Soon after the hook-up, one of our Bantu neighbors came down with a serious disease, and we were able to cure him, using our medicinal plants. After that, more and more Bantus started coming to us whenever they were sick. We told them that without access to the forests, we could not continue to help. With Eugenie's assistance, we brokered a legal agreement under which they would leave the forests to us. In return, we would treat them for a fee when they got ill. They would also market our plants for a share of the profits.*
>
> *It has taken 8 months but now all three elements of the all-win agreement are present: our needs are met, so are the Bantu's and we have an official agreement which all parties uphold because it is in their direct interest to do so.*
>
> *By the way, I am now following my heart: making use of my computer skills, I am logging native plants and describing their medicinal properties!*
>
> *With many thanks for your help!*
>
> *Patricia from the Cameroon.*

With a rush of warmth, Bertram wrote back to say how delighted he was. He suggested she send a copy of this e-mail to the All-Win Network, which, in their newsletters and web site logged such all-win examples.

One last e-mail from Mary.

With a flush of pleasure he opened it.

> *Three hook-ups every week are physically challenging, but I am enjoying them immensely. One hook-up is limited to kids from 14-16, the one with David and Antonia. David's multiple sclerosis suddenly took a turn for the worse. He is almost completely crippled now, walks with a drunken gait. His condition is deteriorating so rapidly, I fear he belongs to the few who actually die from the disease. It breaks my heart. He is so courageous and attends class religiously.*

Bertram felt a pang of sorrow as he remembered David with the kids admiring the beauty of the tiny insects and the weeds. He brought such love to everything he did. That such a beautiful life should be cut so short…

Mary's e-mail continued:

> *Kids worldwide are taking part in governance: library, school and municipal boards, some on their governments' U.N. delegations. They give updates every hook-up! It's catching on like wild fire. The kids are learning to incorporate what we learned about the "field" in their work. Thank you for putting me in touch with the Brahma Kumaris, the International Emissaries and the Baha'is. The beauty of each of these organizations is that they have members worldwide and are set up to help people apply the all-win principle to their everyday lives. In fact, all three are associates of the All-Win Network and run All-Win Education Centers where people are taught to apply the all-win principle to each of their relationships. In this way, each is helping to dissipate the atmosphere of fear.* [48]
>
> *The Human Rights movement is rapidly gathering steam. The Universal Declaration is being discussed at home; parents introduce it at work.*
>
> *One group is working on an international boycott of governments which breach their citizen's rights. They began by making a list of offending countries, and are researching which of their products are to be targeted. Yes, withholding support from harmful activities is central to the all-win approach.*

> *In the Mandu refugee camps, John St. Clair is introducing Josette's reconciliation techniques.*
>
> *The bad news: At the U.N., Eliza's lobby for all-win governance is being blocked by the Five Permanent Member Nations of the Security Council. As Arturo and Hugh pointed out when we were with Maurice, with their veto, they can block any changes to the U.N.'s Charter and if this basic inequality between nations is not changed in the U.N., there can be no all-win governance and all our efforts may collapse. What with the more and more frequent arrests of people like us for consorting with foreigners, chaos and destruction are always lurking, ready to take over.*

It was unusual for Mary to end on a downbeat note.

Bertram dashed off a full update of his activities, ending with the words:

> *"My next challenge is to develop a workshop for businesses for all-win conflict resolution to be used in "think-tanks". Any idea where I can learn the Ubuntu approach mentioned by Josette?"*

On a sudden impulse, he copied the text to Eliza.

At the end he added to Eliza:

> *I'm in Luxor, the Las Vegas Hotel Casino. Back in my exciting work life, I'm taking more and more time to myself to make sure I can stay in touch with my subtler feelings. I can't help anyone else to change if I don't take care of myself.*
>
> *I wonder do you get your ration of alone time? Or does it feel better to keep busy?*
>
> *I find myself looking out for your e-mails. I enjoy the contact we have. I only hope I have not overwhelmed you with my spate of recent letters.*
>
> *I do so hope that one day we shall meet.*
>
> *Take care!*
>
> *Bertram*

46. David Comes Through

David staggered into Mary's class, unable to hide his pain. That morning Mary had been told confidentially that his multiple sclerosis was in its final stage. The doctor had given him just a few more weeks to live.

David had never missed any of Mary's classes, despite the great effort it took him to get there. His disease had progressed so far that his walk had become a stagger and people, thinking he was drunk, laughed and hurled insults at him in the streets.

The class David and Antonia had joined had learned to use the ham radio the year before. With great zest, the students had learned to take the ham radio apart, put it back together, work with antennas, and tap out messages in Morse code. When it was early morning in Santa Cruz, it was suppertime in Australia and the kids loved to ask their Aussie friends what they were having for supper. The whole class had passed their exams with flying colors!

With a heavy heart, Mary greeted David at the door. With a lump in her throat, she asked, "David, would you like to preside over the next project?"

"Me?" His eyes opened wide with surprise. Mary noticed that his eyes had a vague expression. His sight had also been affected.

If she had wondered whether she was doing the right thing, whether this timid young man who, on all fronts, was battling his disease could possibly handle the job, her doubts were instantly removed. His whole countenance lit up. Head held high, he staggered toward her desk at the front of the class, holding on to whatever he could as he went. Mary walked behind him, wondering whether she could hold him if he fell. Yet he exuded a dignity, which she had not held possible. He hoisted himself onto her chair and with great reverence, he took the little handheld telephone-like ham radio out of her hands.

Mary walked to the back of the class and sat down at an empty desk. The atmosphere in the class was instantly transformed. The rumbustiousness made way for a hushed silence - all eyes on David. All awed by the air of leadership which he suddenly radiated.

"Okay, you guys, it's time to start," David said, his extreme shyness gone. He sat firmly planted in the teacher's chair, facing the rest of the class.

He hesitated, then as if deciding to take the plunge, he said with complete self-assurance. "Today, I'd like to begin with a few minutes of silence." Mary was reminded of David's suggestion on Maurice's terrace in Costa Rica when he talked about the periods of silence during the Council of Elders on his grandfather's reservation.

To Mary's surprise, no one protested. At first, his classmates fidgeted. Then they quieted down and the room became tranquil.

When David finally roused them with the words, "Okay, lets start with our usual brain storming before making contact with the others," the class roused itself so slowly, it was as if they were returning from a very deep sleep.

Then Mary clicked on the tape recorder and the class bandied around ideas.

"We could collect money for the kids who are homeless. Even in New York City, there are 10,000 kids our own age…Just think of how many there are in places like Rio De Janeiro."

"Yes, but even if we all gave all our pocket money, how much could we raise?"

"Well I could ask my parents for money," a little boy volunteered. His glasses were so large they covered half of his face.

The ideas kept coming, each one discussed. To these bright-eyed kids, this class was a reprieve from tensions and break-ups at home due to joblessness, poor social services and a downward plunge of the markets, acerbated by globalization and a dark cloud of fear. Yet the shadow of this cloud completely disappeared for the hour they were together. If anything today, they were more focussed than ever. Mary wondered whether this was due to David's period of silence.

A sound just behind her.

Mary turned.

To her surprise there stood Freddy.

Freddy was an 18-year-old with Down's Syndrome who barely ever talked. His mother, worked at the corner store. Three mornings a week, she dropped Freddy off in front of the television in the hall. There he would sit passively, eating popcorn until around one o'clock when his mother would fetch him for lunch.

No one ever bothered with Freddy.

Now he stood in the doorframe, listening intently to what was being said.

"*I wonder*," Mary thought, "*can he understand after all?*" She had never heard him utter a word. "Freddy," she heard herself say, "what would you like to do for the rest of the world?"

There were suppressed giggles.

Mary focussed her full warmth on Freddy and waited patiently, not wishing to hurry him in any way.

The giggling made way for an awed silence as Freddy began to speak.

"I want to help make a world where people don't make fun of you if you don't look like them or talk like them!" He spoke as loudly and clearly as any of the other kids. And what he said touched each one to the core.

"I'd like to see what we can do about that!" Everyone turned surprised, Antonia so seldom spoke.

There were nods of agreement.

With confidence and authority, as if he had been born to lead, David looked around the class. "Would you be able to see what you can come up with, Antonia, please?" he asked, "Perhaps that can be one of our next projects."

"I'll try," Antonia said quietly.

Mary pulled up a chair beside her, and Freddy sat down.

David looked at his watch. "Okay, it's time to make contact!" he announced and tapped out the Morse code:

"CQ! CQ! Come in! This is World Citizens." Mary noticed with relief that despite the progression of his disease, he still had the necessary dexterity.

After introducing himself to groups that participated from all over the world, David suggested, "Let's first make a list of young people who this week have been given leadership positions. Then, we'll decide our next project."

Mary was amazed each week again at the number of young people who thrived in positions of leadership, both in the democratic world, and – to her amazement—even in dictatorships. In San Leon, for instance, ham radio had become all the rage. Here youth participation was treated seriously. And many were on school boards. A couple on County Councils.

"Perhaps they feel that young people don't really carry much weight," Mary caught herself thinking and smiled. "Little do they know what young people can do! For a moment, she was transported back to Costa Rica.

Around her, the young people were into their brain storming session now.

Let's make a list," David suggested.

The communications came in first in dribs and drabs and then with increasing intensity.

Soon there were messages coming from all over the world. Then the brain storming for a common project was suddenly in full swing. Young people spoke diverse languages with teachers doing the translations. At least, half of all the children participating came from India, encouraged by a campaign by former Head of State Rajiv Gandhi and his wife who both were ham radio operators[49].

The ideas which came over the radio waves were a dismal enumeration of problems children should never have to face but which had become the common currency of most of their lives: How to live in the shadow of nuclear war now that both India and Pakistan had the bomb? What to do about victims from landmines in Cambodia and other former and present war zones? The victims were for the most part totally dependent on families too poor to provide for their own. How to survive on the streets, find food, reach out to children less fortunate than themselves? How to deal with parents when they lashed out under stress? How to help their single mothers or fathers, who should be caring for their children, when they were down and out or suffering from alcoholism or drug addictions?

The poor lacked the basic necessities of life but often lived in more loving, closely-knit communities than those in the Wealthy Countries. While those in the Wealthy Countries, many of whom were not rich either, often lived lonely, desolate lives even when they were materially better off.

Eliza's brief e-mail during the hook-up in Costa Rica flashed through Mary's mind and she thought of the street children who were even worse off. The huge group of street kids had no where to go. They were the victims of poverty, broken homes and the Aids epidemic. They were having to make a living pilfering, looting, anyway they could and at very early ages already showed amazing problem solving skills, usually outside of the law. Mary wished that there would be some way that their creativity could be harnessed and that they could be given the support they deserved.

The grim list of ideas was continuing. Mary thrilled as she saw the kids at work and realized that the mere opportunity to participate in a ham radio hook-up with their peers from around the world was enough for these young people to rise above their constraints and to do whatever they could to make the planet a better place.

"It's Earth Day in one month!" came over the radio. "Our Earth needs help..."

Mary held her breath. Hadn't Eliza mentioned street children and the environment in the same e-mail? She smiled, were Eliza and the All-Win Network's concerns being communicated via the morphogenetic fields?

It was Mary's policy not to intrude and to allow the young people to conduct their own meetings. So she did not interrupt the flow of enthusiastic suggestions entering the classroom.

"We could each plant a tree. This is Colin in Barbados," came the response.

Sudden silence.

"We could each plant a tree..." David repeated under his breath, "If we could each get friends to join in ...!" He looked jubilant. Hurriedly, he tapped out the message over the airwaves. There was a silence as the teachers translated what had been said in their various languages. Then a chorus of responses: "Let's do that!" "Yes!" "Da!" "Si!", "Tak!" "I'd like that!!!" A clamor of sounds.

"Jacek here suggests that he could ask other kids at his school to join in!" That must be one of the teachers, tapping out a message she had translated from Polish into English.

"So could I!"

"Coralita says she could ask kids at her sister's school!" This message from South America.

"Aisha from Lahore, Pakistan, suggests that we ask all schools in our town!" probably another teacher.

"If each of us gets one or two schools involved, who knows how many trees we can plant!" David sent the message.

It was as if the children had been inspired by a breath of fresh air: instead of getting bogged down in the fear and misery of every day life, they were going to each give a gift to Mother Earth, a gesture that lifted them above both their own misery and the misery of other human beings.

"That is an all-win situation," David tapped out, emphasizing the main theme of their discussions. Trees hold water, give us oxygen to breathe and stop the soil from eroding so that the farmers can grow food and animals can eat and sleep and have plenty of shelter. We feel good about giving a gift. People and other living things benefit, and Mother Nature is strengthened. And she helps everything on Earth to survive. Mother Nature is the governance principle?" He looked questioningly at Mary.

She nodded warmly. "You certainly have the hang of it, David," she said.

Thus with David in the chair, their next project was decided.

47. Freddy

Mary took Freddy home after school with the feeling that something very unusual had happened.

"Listen to this," she played back Freddy's voice on the tape recorder for Freddy and his mother to hear.

"I want to help make a world where people don't make fun of you if you don't look like them or talk like them!" Freddy's voice came loudly and clearly.

Freddy was standing beside her, his hand in hers.

"That's the real me!" he said, again totally coherently. His mother burst into tears and took her son in her arms. "You are so wise, Freddy, my love, so wise. And to think that I never ever suspected!"

Later, 20 tape recorders were donated to the center where Freddy spent his other two days a week. The teacher found that allowing students with Down's Syndrome to talk into a tape recorder and have their voices played back gave each one a sense of importance they had never felt before. The focus on them as a unique person in their own right inspired a clarity of speech and thought that was not there when they were seen merely as someone, "suffering from Down's Syndrome".[50]

142

48. The Human Rights Committee

Augustina hesitated at the large glass doors of the U.N. cafeteria. She could scarcely believe that she was actually inside the U.N. in New York City after her escape from Kukundu. At the far side, she located Eliza. Eliza was sitting at the large windows overlooking the East River wearing a bright red suit, which stood out against the bright blue waters. Staring into space, Eliza made occasional notes. Her talks to New York City High Schools, Augustina knew. "The U.N. as Motor in International Relations and How Young People Can Become Involved."

"Always working," Augustina thought and paused, but already Eliza had sensed her friend's arrival and had jumped to her feet, waving.

"How did it go?" she asked as Augustina hurried toward her.

The two women had been introduced to each other by John St. Clair and had instantly become friends. Both tended to be warm and welcoming in their relations with other people and both had a private side that demanded space. Instinctively, the two women had understood each other from the first day they had met.

"The Human Rights Committee had already seen my film and even heard a tape of my interview on the BBC World Service – the one John organized for me in London," Augustina answered, slightly out of breath.

The women hugged and Augustina slipped the strap of her bag off her shoulder, took off her jacket, hung both on the back of a chair and sat down opposite Eliza.

"So what's next?" Eliza asked keenly searching her face.

"They will review all my evidence and then call in the U.N. Ambassador for Kukundu and present my case to him. The Ambassador will get time to discuss it with the Kukundu Government; and then there will be another meeting!"

"So they are taking your case seriously!" Eliza felt suddenly lighter. If only a beginning could be made with Augustina's case, then there might be some hope for both Kukundu, and the rest of the world. "What a relief! Celebration time! The chef has made a delicious fruit tart with freshly whipped cream. My treat! And what about some tea. Mint tea, okay? Whipped cream, mmmm delicious!!!" Eliza was already up and away.

"No whipped cream for me," Augustina called after her.

"But you looked as if you could eat an elephant!" Eliza turned.

"You're right!" Augustina grinned impishly, "I'm famished! How about two tarts?"

"Two tarts for you then!" Eliza called over her shoulder and laughed, "You could do with some extra weight! The time for worrying is over!"

Augustina looked out of the window. The East River winked at her as through a zillion eyes, as for the first time in months she began to relax.

The warm pungent steam of the mint tea made Augusta's nostrils tingle when a few minutes later, Eliza placed two cups on the table in front of her with two plates with fresh fruit pie for Augustina, her own plate smothered in a huge mound of fluffy whipped cream.

"Thanks!" Augustina grinned and tucked in.

"For my wedding breakfast I had four helpings of freshly whipped cream!" Eliza grinned, "I was too modest to ask for a fifth!" She laughed.

For a while the friends ate in silence. Then Augustina said, "If only the Human Rights Committee can persuade President Kundana to either call a referendum or to cede the Presidency to M'Bwene. You know, it's not just that M'Bwene was democratically elected, but we all loved him so, he was Daddy M'Bwene to us."

"Well, I just heard from John this morning," Eliza pushed her empty plate aside.

Out of her briefcase, she pulled a page of notes and read, "The resistance in Kukundu is growing, the various hubs have made contact and they are beginning to work together. And John is still moving between Mandu refugee camps teaching reconciliation. Apparently, he has trained a number of teachers now with the help of Josette." Eliza skimmed her notes to see whether there was anything she had missed.

Augustina's eyes were suddenly moist. "Kukundu! Oh, Eliza, it's such a gorgeous place. The torrents of rain."

Eliza could not help laughing. "Can't imagine longing for rain!"

Augustina laughed with her. The sheer joy that one day she might return to her country. "Sounds crazy, I know. But did you know that rain actually awakens the perfume of the earth, trees and flowers? It's so different from the blanket of humidity in New York where, raining or not in summer, you feel you're taking a hot shower."

Augustina took a sip of her tea.

Eliza watched her and held her breath. *Should she ask Augustina now? Or was it too close to her ordeal with the Human Rights Committee?* Then the question came tumbling out.

"Augustina, you mentioned that in Kukundu each person allowed the power to slip out of their hands?"

"Yes." Augustina looked at Eliza for a full minute, hesitant to think back to that time.

Eliza held back, suddenly uncertain.

Augustina nodded for her friend to go on.

Eliza surged ahead, "A similar situation is developing here and yet few people see the urgency to act. Your experiences could jolt people out of their inertia.

"Would you help us to see the dangers we in the US are allowing ourselves to slip into?

"The reason I'm asking – a lot of us NGOs[51] at the U.N. have been treading water. We have not undertaken any actions, afraid of being harassed by the US Government and of being accused of supporting terrorists. Right now, no one is safe. Anyone can be accused of consorting with the enemy by a disgruntled neighbor. Sticking our heads out as NGOs we're likely targets. You might be able to shake us awake. It's crazy that the Governments should withhold our rights, be able to disregard huge demonstrations, and do as they please, while we stand by and wait until it's too late."

Augustina turned to her. Her dark eyes a mixture of sadness and anger.

"I'm sorry. I didn't mean to put you on the spot!" Eliza said quickly, searching her friend's face.

"It's okay. To think I let things slide that far and lost everything in the process. It will be hard, but perhaps it will help me to see things more clearly myself!"

For a moment, she looked at Eliza, deep in thought. "Perhaps this will help me make amends for allowing my world to slip out of control. At least, I shall be able to use my experience to help others avoid my mistakes. Thank you, Eliza, for the opportunity!"

49. The Security Council Has A Stranglehold On Evolution

The next day, Eliza woke early and arrived at the U.N. in time for a leisurely breakfast. She ordered a scrumptious portion of yogurt, fresh fruit salad and a large steaming cup of mint tea. Then, eager to get going, she hurried back to the office. Last night, after her meeting with Augustina, she'd received an e-mail from Hugh. "How to ease the Five Permanent Members' stranglehold on the Security Council, and with it their stranglehold on evolution." he had asked. Then came his brilliant idea. Hard to believe that he was still in his teens. Eliza was excited and impressed. For so long, she had been lobbying without any success. Now, Hugh had found an all-win approach.

First she would answer her e-mails and, upon Hugh's request, send Hugh's idea around to as many as possible people for their review. In between, she would set up appointments for Augustina to speak with her fellow NGOs.

The first e-mail was from Bertram. Her heart did a little skip.

"I'm lying here in Luxor, the Las Vegas Hotel Casino…"

She enjoyed hearing about his work, his growth and the tender tone that Bertram and her e-mails were assuming. She skimmed the e-mail, then read it again, her eyes pausing uneasily at the last sentence.

"I do so hope that one day we shall meet…"

Some time ago, he had mentioned a conference in the South of France. *"I'd love to be there with you!"* he had written." Hurriedly, she had refused. She needed her space and didn't want to tie herself down too far ahead of time, she had said. In her heart, she sensed a confusion of feelings, which she had yet to unravel.

Again she read through his e-mail.

He was becoming interested in her personally. For a long time, she had suspected it and had not written back, unsure of how she herself felt. And yet, their correspondence had already assumed an unusual degree of intimacy. What was she running away from? Then she remembered Brian's words, *"If you want to honor what we had together, never go back to your old isolation. Always lead your life to the full!"*

"Okay, Brian!" she said aloud and grinned, "I really like that feeling I get whenever he writes. I feel… I feel…" She thought for a while. "I feel all warm, fuzzy, and excited… the woman in me comes alive. No harm in going with the flow… "

She wrote:

> *Dear Bertram,*
> *I very much enjoy receiving your e-mails. Please do keep them coming!*
> *There's plenty of exciting news at this end.*

She brought him up to date on Augustina's Human Rights Committee meeting, her agreement to help persuade Eliza's NGO colleagues to act, and the problems she, Eliza, had had introducing the all-win standard.

> *"The Security Council is a constant stumbling block. No one dares to question the five Permanent Members—not for anything they consider such a back-burner issue as all-win values and norms.*
> *Now Hugh whom you know from Costa Rica has thought of a way to gradually break the impasse. After I introduced him to the World*

Federalists (which I mentioned to you in an earlier e-mail), he came up with the following ideas. I'd be grateful for your response.

Hugh writes:

'We must now find some way of undoing the weighted Security Council decision making process. If humanity is to complete its next evolutionary leap, the Security Council must become fully democratic. And that is impossible, for at present it has 15 Members Nations of which 10 represent the regions of the world and are elected for two year periods; and 5 are Permanent Members. These five have a veto; they can therefore block any important decision, including Charter reform. Without Charter reform there can be no democracy of Nations within the U.N. And these Five won't give up their power to veto unless it is to their advantage.

How, as an interim step, to involve more Nations in Security Council decisions?

Here are some hopeful developments.

The last few Security Council resolutions were bulldozed through by one of the most influential Permanent Members against the will of many. The other four Permanent Members simply abstained. These resolutions met with passive resistance among all nations and in the end, each time again, that Permanent Member lost face. It's ironic that the more a Permanent Member throws its weight around, the more ineffectual it becomes. This is an all-lose situation. This Member's very ineffectualness might be a motive for the Permanent Members to consider building a broad base of agreement before the Security Council votes on their motions.

Strong support, according to the World Federalists[52], might involve a wholehearted 'Yes!' from a combination of countries which together

➤*represent 2/3 of the people of the world,*
➤*own 2/3 of the wealth (GDP) of the world economy; and*
➤*fund 2/3 of the U.N. budget.*

Before putting any motions to a vote, the Permanent Five could invite all U.N. Member Nations (even those without a seat on the Security Council) to provide unofficial input. They could then fairly quickly incorporate anything that would, in their own eyes, strengthen their motion, while building a strong support base. This would ensure that if their motion were adopted it would be wholeheartedly carried out. With this procedure in place they would be appreciated rather than resented and, instead of losing face, their prestige would grow because their fellow nations would appreciate their inclusiveness and wisdom.

Mind you, the communication process must be speeded up. After all, the Security Council handles emergencies. So, those nations that want to be consulted must have decision-makers on standby day and night within easy reach of the U.N. and so must the Permanent Five. With modern technology this could be arranged without too much extra expense or inconvenience for the officials concerned.

Once this new, more comprehensive process has become automatic and more and more nations give their input, all will experience the advantages of all-win relationships. Eventually, Charter reform will be welcomed.

Can you imagine how an all-win democracy among nations would affect the political climate?! An all-win governance structure for our global community will then evolve easily and naturally.

Eliza added:

After finishing Corps Elite High School, Hugh is planning to go to University in New York, to be near the U.N. He plans to join Gaia and myself lobbying for all-win values and norms and working on Security Council reform.

Fortunately, the all-win principle and human rights are increasingly mentioned in the same breath. So if Hugh's idea can be introduced, things will once more be on the move!

For a long time, Eliza stared out of the window. Then she wrote:

I am about to go on vacation: I've rather overdone the work thing and sometimes I feel quite overwhelmed. As you suggest, I need time to myself.

Please don't worry if I don't reply. But do keep writing! I so enjoy our friendship!

50. How Many Trees Did We Plant?

Meanwhile on the West Coast of the USA, Mary's ham radio classes had met weekly. For two months now, David had presided over her youngest group. Every week, he would start with a brief silence in class; and then, once connected by ham radio worldwide, he did a count both of how many young people had assumed public office; and how many trees his network had planted.

Then Earth Day rolled around and it was time for the final tally. Mary sat at the back, calculator poised, carefully adding each number, as it came over the radio waves. With every result, a cheer broke out.

Finally all eyes were on Mary.

"How many trees have we planted?" David asked, his voice broke with excitement. "I bet you there must be nearly one million!"

Mary pushed the button for the grand total. There was complete silence. Every one held their breath.

"How much? Mrs. Duffield?" "How much?" "How many?" voices suddenly clamored around her while a wild clicking came over the air waves, "How many? We aren't hearing anything from your side!"

Mary stared at the total, then carefully counted the number of locations. Yes, that sounded right. Then she looked at the numbers of trees and counted them under her breath.

"Yes!" she said, eyes shining, a huge smile lighting up her face, "Two million trees! One million planted in India alone!"

There was a hushed silence, as the full impact of the amount tried to sink in, followed by teachers translating for their classes. Loud gasps all around and suddenly a loud cheer broke out in her class and excited Morse code messages started coming in as all young people joined in at once." Tears of joy and pride streamed over David's face.

David was whisked off the teacher's chair and carried around the class in triumph.

"Good for David!"

"You never let up!"

"Every week you made us listen to how many trees had been planted!"

"Yes and that made us all work all the harder!"

"We just could not help getting turned on after the first two weeks!"

Finally David was deposited back on his chair. Tears of joy still staining his cheeks. The class resumed their seats and waited for him to speak. The airwaves, also, had quieted down. Then David tapped out his message.

"Perhaps, as a next step in this project, each person can adopt the tree they planted. Everything we do must be nurtured otherwise it will shrivel up and die. Can we all solemnly promise to take care of our own trees?"

"What a wonderful idea!" Mary exclaimed.

"David, I wonder whether each school can tell their local town council about this project and what they have achieved. They can mention young people in their town are supporting the work of the United Nations. The

U.N. is concerned that the world plants new trees to replace those that are being chopped down."

"David tapped the message out over the airwaves and clicks echoed back. All waited patiently as each station agreed both to approach their town councils and to see to it that each tree was given regular care.

Finally, he took a deep breath and tapped out. "This is the end of this phase of the project and with it, my chairmanship. I want to thank each and every one of you for what you have done. I feel so proud to have been your chairperson for this project."

For a moment, he seemed to struggle with himself. Then he continued tapping, " My whole life will have been worthwhile if I die tomorrow."

Two weeks later, David passed away.[53]

51. Snake Gets A Stranglehold On The Dictatorships

The helicopter hovered, sending the high hedge into paroxysms.

Shielded from the disturbance, the bald man stared out to sea.

Then, once the helicopter's engines were switched off, he leaned forward and filled three glasses with vodka and fresh orange juice from a crystal carafe.

The hedge opened and his two cousins appeared. The three greeted one another with the sign of the Snake. Then the two younger cousins bent over their eldest cousin's signet ring and brushed it with their lips.

"How is the next phase coming along?" the bald one queried after they were settled.

The youngest took a sip of his drink and responded, "We have a delightfully sad bunch of weaklings in the last batch—all nestled in the dictatorships, lapping up tidbits we throw at them. They love the course I developed and they're all keeping pace. Some are already in positions of leadership and just need a refresher course so that they can develop their aspects of the Final Plan. All of them, old lapdogs or lapdogs-to-be—they all go into contortions to please my instructors—anything to have access to power."

"Are all being trained at the same speed?"

"All groups have their own pace. All those individuals being groomed to take over the dictatorships have been going for the same length of time. Just one from San Leon is about to start. He's the one I requested to oversee in person. I can put his genius to good use."

"This group of 101 dictators and this chap from San Leon—I want regular updates on these. This batch of lapdogs are central to our plan. We can't afford to have anything go wrong with any of them. Without them under our control, there would be no point in proceeding.

"So all stooges in all countries will be able to meet the deadline of our simultaneous launch?" the eldest cousin persisted.

"No problem that I can see," his younger cousin said evenly.

The bald cousin turned to the Einstein look-alike and asked, "And what about the herd?" "The fear epidemic is now fuelling itself nicely. There's just one group I should like to milk, before our launch takes place. This conference Maurice is organizing is presenting a welcome opportunity."

52. Joaquim And Juanita

King Joaquim suppressed a smile as Juanita entered in her disguise. With her pencil-shaped moustache and jagged street-urchin haircut -- all the latest rage!-- she passed for an attractive youth.

"Thank you, Carlos," he said to his personal assistant, "No disturbances, please."

Barely had Carlos closed the door, or Joaquim strode across the room and took Juanita's hands in his. With a brilliant smile, he held her gaze as he pressed her fingertips to his lips.

"You sent for me, Joaquim! Or should I say 'Your Majesty?" Juanita made a mock courtesy.

"'Joaquim' to you as always, Juanita," he said seriously. His eyes softened as he held her gaze. "Our friendship remains, even if our positions – and, of course, my marriage to Esmerelda-- don't permit us to meet as friends. But I badly wanted to speak with you. I so miss our daily chats at Oxford, our classes together and the moments when we could slip away unnoticed."

She pulled a wry face. "For so long you were the center of my day; then you shriveled into some hastily scribbled words." Her nostrils flared whenever she became agitated, like a horse, sensing danger, smells the wind. For a moment he was back at Oxford with her next to him, both sitting on his bed, her legs nonchalantly thrown over his, half-sitting on his lap. With each penetrating discussion on world politics, with each sharing about their own hopes and fears and then as they grew physically close, with each caress, each knew their inevitable parting was being made more difficult. How often he had seen that skittish expression on her face.

Without resentment, she now quoted the note he had written her so long ago, "*Off to become King. You'll always be in my heart, although no one may know. I'll always love you, Joaquim.'* I know the words backwards. I was away for the day and when I returned, you had been ferreted away!"

Sadness clouded her gaze for a moment. He realized he had not even stopped to wonder how his departure was affecting her. He was too busy being groomed in whirlwind tempo to become Head of State.

"Of course, we both knew that as soon as my father would pass away, the army would expect me to take over…" he said lamely. "But who could guess he'd have a heart attack? And that so young? And then things happened so quickly: General Sanchez appeared, informed me of my father's passing and took me back for the funeral and accession to the throne.

"That note to you? I wrote it in the bathroom, smuggled it to Carlos, and he managed to get it to you."

"How are you, Joaquim?" She searched his face. Her large dark eyes warm and gentle. "Are you happy?"

How he loved the intensity with which her eyes sought to read what he could not find the words to say. How he had longed for that quality of caring.

He led her to the hearth. The nights got quite chilly in his summer abode in the mountains. The warm glow enveloped them. For a moment they were back in Oxford, sharing their challenges and ideals.

"Did you know I covered both your accession to the throne and your marriage to Esmerelda?"

"Did I ever! *The enlightened dictator with a golden heart!* You catapulted me into stardom."

Juanita, as feature writer for *Global Trends,* the glossy magazine aimed at top decision makers, had outlined his ideals to develop a democracy based fully on the Universal Declaration of Human Rights[54]. She remembered how he had just read the whole Declaration through once and had been able to recite it by heart. Of course, she had not mentioned his photographic memory, nor anything else she had found out. No one must know of the long hours they spent studying together in his room.

As he spoke, Juanita's gaze watched his familiar face. Dark sparkling eyes in a surprisingly fair complexion, raven black, immaculately combed hair, a dark shadow of a beard and moustache, despite regular close shaves. Here and there his skin was pitted from when he had had acne as a teenager. She remembered caressing the little grooves and telling him how much she loved every part of him. Her physical attraction to him had never ceased, yet it was his warm heart and love for his people, which had made him so dear to her. But how could he have permitted himself to be married off to a spoiled diva, who would stop at nothing, even shaming him in public, in order to get her way? Was it a marriage of convenience? Or did he really love her?

"Where's Esmerelda?" she asked.

"On one of her shopping sprees in Paris." Joaquim looked away. Juanita knew the expression: "Stop! No farther!"

He urged her to sit down in one of the easy chairs and took a seat opposite her at the other side of the hearth.

Reaching over to a table behind him, he said, "Look, guess what I managed to get! He held out a dish with digestive biscuits covered in dark chocolate. Then he poured her a cup of coffee from a silver coffeepot. "This is real San Leon coffee! Beats the nightly Nescafé we brewed ourselves at Oxford!" He grinned.

For a while each munched at their biscuits. Then, taking a sip of the dark sweet coffee, Juanita asked, "And what's it like being Head of State? Do you feel prepared?"

"Are you ever for such a job? My father's death was so sudden. Never knew he was no more than a puppet in the hands of the generals. All the pomp surrounding everything he did was just show. He was Head of State in name only. Convenient for them to keep the popular Monarchy in place, which people had believed lived to serve their best interests. It must have been my grandfather who allowed the generals to take over. I still haven't found out what he got in return. Perhaps it was money... Certainly, I see little advantages to having the generals in power. "

A look of anxiety flashed across his face.

'That's why I asked you to come here ...I feel like a fly in a web. I am forced to dance to a tune and don't know who the fiddler is. The Wealthy Countries with their thriving weapon's industry keep the generals in place. In return, they haul away our resources at rock bottom prices. My signature's forged under arms deals and when I protest, I find myself a prisoner in my own palace. All the things we talked about at Oxford--well here I am, king of a nation, and my hands are tied behind my back."

As he spoke, his shoulders slumped. He took a few sips of his coffee and stared off into the distance. She suspected that he'd experienced more than house arrest since she had seen him last.

"Even dictatorships need their people's support!" she said gently. "So what is their position in all this?"

"Many groups back the generals in exchange for getting their way here or there. Most are desperately poor. And the trade unions are under close army supervision and have very little power. "

The fire crackled in the hearth, the flames threw strange shadows around the room.

He smiled suddenly. "One thing I am allowed to do! In fact, it's one of my regular duties: I visit schools and good causes. Here I can speak informally with people - mainly children, women, the destitute, those without a voice.

"At least, I get to make a real difference to the lives of one or two people."

"Like what?" Juanita asked. She so wanted to draw forth the confident Joaquim, she had once known so well.

"For instance, I have managed to connect a number of schools with the young people's Ham Radio Network and have supplied a number of schools with ham radios, confidentially, of course.

"Paid them from my Swiss Bank Account. One of the few things which the generals can't get at."

His or Esmerelda's? Juanita thought and immediately felt ashamed.

"You're taking quite a risk, aren't you?" Juanita asked, wondering again what price Joaquim was paying to further his ideals. "Dictators don't normally like to have their citizens talking too freely, especially not with people outside of their country."

"I know a number of the Headmasters from my own school days, these and the young people themselves are careful. Never known anything else but dictatorship. But desperate for freedom. So those who had to know the radios came from me are careful to honor my trust. "

"What's the human rights situation like?" Juanita asked.

"Dismal. Although I don't have positive proof, I am pretty sure people are tortured, that they do not get fair trials, and that people's privacy is interfered with. Not even I am allowed to leave or enter the country without permission from the generals, or to publicly state my opinions.

"Some kids don't even enter elementary school. Health care is sparse except for a few programs run by the United Nations. And according to the U.N. Development Report (I was lucky enough to have someone smuggle one in for me), one out of every 5 children is malnourished and lives below the poverty line. Hordes of street children, wherever you go!"

He grimaced.

"But I help wherever I get a chance. UNESCO, the U.N.'s Food and Agricultural Organization and NGOs, like the Grameen Bank and the Trickle Up Program are wonderful[55]. For instance, Trickle Up gives the very poor conditional grants to start their own businesses, such as keeping pigs, or planting crops, tailoring, or arts and crafts. The Grameen Bank gives small loans. Once a business is running, they return the money. This is then made available to someone else. So there is a tremendous community pressure on each person to repay the loan on time. And more than 90% of the loans are repaid."

As he spoke, Juanita was taken back to the long evenings spent together, his gentle voice, the silky feel of his skin, the smell of his aftershave designed by Christian Dior especially for him, and always his concern for his people.

"Oh Juanita, my people are so terribly poor." The desperate edge in his voice wrenched at her heart.

Esmerelda would not be much of a support, Juanita decided, but didn't trust herself to comment.

"Is there anything at all I can do?" she asked finally.

"Well, that's why I called you! Just listen to the offer I just received! There's no one else I dare to tell!"

"Yesterday I spoke at the opening of a branch of one of those large international firms. You know the thing. Low labor costs, etc. Sort of win/ win deal for those with pots of money, and an all-lose for everyone else, 'cause all these deals are financed by the blood and sweat of my people.

"Anyway, the president of the company introduced me to a gentleman, one of those immaculately dressed and heeled elderly types who never seems to retire.

"He coached world leaders on *how to wield power.*'

"The coach asked if he could meet me in private.

"Well, I was just feeling desperate about my situation when this happened. All my plans to develop a well-run country -- I despaired I would ever get to first base."

"Were you able to meet him?" Juanita asked.

"He was given a slot on my meeting schedule the very next day, no questions asked, rubberstamped by the generals and all!

"Strange man with long fingers, perfectly manicured. Always inspecting his nails. For the rest an air of simple elegant wealth, sort of wiry and athletic with his elderly boyish looks -- a cultured man, instantly recognized my van Gogh, Pisarro and the Ming Dynasty lions. Was surprised at how I was able to combine such different works of art in the same space and rather liked how I had done it. He was pretty impressed with my Oxford background. Had obviously boned up on everything I had done."

As he described his teacher to her, Joachim was struggling to fathom what made this elderly gentleman tick.

"He walked in and took charge. The funniest thing. He walked me all through my suite, admiring my art and then out onto the balcony to 'look at the view'.

"'Nobody can hear us here, ' he whispered, 'In your position, you never know. Inferiors love to spy. My course focuses on keeping your inferiors in their place. Mind if we check your suite, in case it is bugged? The course I want to discuss with you is, of course, top secret."

"The man had no idea what a puppet I am. I'm guarded day and night. I was only able to smuggle you in, Juanita, thanks to dear old Carlos, who distracted the guards with a couple of hits of dope. I doubt anyone would bother to eavesdrop on me. I'm a complete prisoner in my own palace.

"Anyway, he had a special gadget, and we checked every nook and cranny. No bug to be found. In the process, I have become quite an expert. They can be tiny, apparently.

"When our search was complete, the man said, 'I have a very important and private proposition to make, you have distinguished yourself in so many ways, while others, your inferiors, wield the power and dispose of the resources, which are rightfully yours.'

Juanita felt a rush of apprehension. Those words were not Joaquim's own. Nor was this way of thinking. This was not the old Joaquim she knew, that quiet unassuming idealist.

Joaquim continued, "In the past, he said, his organization had been a secret finishing school for royalty. Now it accepts other world leaders, who are exceptionally gifted, but through the political situation were not able to come fully into their own power. I was both royalty and a world leader, according to him. He was offering me a private course in Wielding Power without Fear.

"'I doubt that I shall be able to take time off …' I said, a little disappointed.

"Please don't worry. We have such a good name. We never have a problem arranging an afternoon here and there. With you, we shall have students in similar positions to your own from 102 countries. While you are busy with our course, the generals believe they can consolidate their power. Of course, they have no idea that you are developing tools against which they have no defenses. That's the irony of the situation.'

"'How much does all this cost?' I asked, 'You see all my official expenditures are controlled by the generals.'

"'For centuries, our finishing school has been in the employ of the fabulously rich. We have no shortage of resources. We help only those with exceptional potential. Later, we shall show you how together with others like yourself, you can take over leadership of the Earth! There's plenty of time to pay us back!'

"Can you believe that, Juanita, *leadership of the Earth*?"

"Joaquim," Juanita exclaimed, suddenly scared, "This is not what it seems!"

"What do you mean? They can give me the tools I need to lead my own country and make the world a better place!"

"Students from one hundred and two countries?" she asked, her voice suddenly shrill.

"Working with 102 countries, using the same methodology. Just think what together we can do!"

"What is their methodology? Did he say?"

"He said, 'We shall teach you to manage the opposition by mobilizing the divisions in their own ranks. A little fear here and there does wonders. A dash of terror spread throughout the population is even better still. Once people are terrified, they're no problem!'"

"Divide and rule!" Juanita breathed. "No! Joaquim," she cried. "This is… this is extremely dangerous. It's the Holy Order of the Snake! They're busy with a take-over of the 102 dictatorships!"

"Nonsense. Surely, Juanita, you don't believe childish rumors."

"Joaquim, no! You mustn't!"

"I know! I know! Sounds bad. But if I want to get to first base, I have to act!"

"But not this, Joaquim! It's the opposite of what you believed in at Oxford!"

"But he has me convinced, Juanita! Look at the Super Powers: how the threat of terrorism brings people together, cowering behind their leaders. 'The vaguer the threat, the more terrifying,' the man said, 'So you don't even have to act. The threat grows with the amount of imagination your enemies bring to it! And while they imagine all the terrible things that can happen to them, you hold the reins.'"

Joaquim continued more urgently, "'Look also at countries like Kukundu. The people themselves slaughtered those who gave their government a hard time. President Kundana is a master at divide and rule. He now has supreme control, a standard of living he deserves, and the population is like putty in his hands.' The man makes sense!"

"But. Kukundu!" Juanita gasped, "Haven't you been following the news? Do you realize how many people were killed?! The population is still divided and broken. After such massacres, how is reconciliation possible? The genocide in Kukundu exceeded the death toll in both World Wars combined!"

"Of course, Juanita, don't you think I pointed this out to him? But the massacre's not necessary. All that's needed is the threat. Once people are a little scared, I can carry out my duties."

"But Joaquim, there are laws!"

"No one, least of all governments of the Wealthy Countries, pays any attention to world law!" There was an edge of exasperation in Joaquim's voice, "The strategy's a way to become a country in which human rights are respected!"

"The Wealthy Countries are into power politics – agreed!" Juanita spoke urgently, "And so are the 102 dictatorships! But it's your job, a Head of State to see that laws are upheld. That way, *every one*, (not just you!) can come into their own. If you, as Head of State, don't enforce the law, who else will?

"The Universal Declaration states that the will of the people shall be the basis of the authority of government. How can the people express their will if they live in fear? People will become docile, suppress their passion—until, all of a sudden, violence and aggression explode.

"You're condoning a reign of terror in a world governed by fear! All lose in such a situation, including you and the generals!

"Oh! Joaquim, I don't have to tell you all this. You have a photographic mind. You know all the laws backwards and forwards I know!"

"But it's only for a short time!"

"Joaquim, it is your job to see to it that all people know their rights and how to stand up for themselves. They need to know that governments are afraid of world public opinion that can damage their international standing. Once people know this, two things happen: they will no longer tolerate dictatorships and they become more cooperative with whoever stands up for their rights.

"Anyway, who's to say that you are the only one in San Leon that they are grooming to rule the world and that once you join that unholy Alliance there won't be a whole host of others contending to wield power in San Leon?"

"But don't you see, Juanita, my hands are tied. I have no power at all! This management consultant can help me get at least some of the power that is mine by rights of my position. And then, only then, will I be able to make the changes that you suggest! I have no alternative! Don't you see!? " Joaquim felt bitterly disappointed.

He added, "Okay, you might not see my point of view - yet! But will you promise me one thing? Please no word about any of this to anyone. Promise?"

Juanita hesitated. "As a journalist, you have my word. I promise that I won't publicize anything you say without your express permission. But... " She chose her words carefully, assessing his every expression as she spoke. " ... I have a feeling that this teacher will either use you for his own ends or else put you out of commission.

"Joaquim, I can't let anything happen to you. I might have to turn to my friends. You must understand, Joaquim. Alone, I would be helpless!"

"Not a word, Juanita, do you hear? Or I shall stop you, come what may!"

Juanita was suddenly desperate, "Joachim, please listen! Don't let yourself in with this sinister gentleman. He is no good. I am concerned for you!"

"If you can't promise me to keep quiet about this, you force my hand, Juanita, hate it as I may!"

"Don't you see, I can't!" Juanita was nearly in tears, "Joaquim, I beg you!"

"I have warned you, Juanita, you leave me no alternative."

Joaquim, flushed with exasperation, rang the bell and Carlos appeared.

"See the lady--- I mean the gentleman out!" he said and see he gets home safely. You take him home personally and come straight back!" Thank God for Carlos, his secretary and aid, the man who had practically brought him up. This was the one man he could trust to do exactly as he bade. Juanita was totally out of hand!

53. The President Laughs

From the glass booth, Augustina peered down onto the floor of the U.N.'s Economic and Social Council. The Chair of the U.N. Human Rights Committee was speaking. He was introducing her case. Augustina listened, heart pounding.

As he spoke, her eyes roamed the horseshoe-shaped table below where each of the 54 Members represented a separate Nation. Each had a different history with Kukundu and each was intent on playing it safe, lest their own human right's skeletons were hauled out of the closet and hurled to the vengeance of world public opinion.

The Chairman spoke, "I now give the floor to the Ambassador of Kukundu."

Next to her, Wim, the sound technician, punched a switch on his panel.

A small red light flashed on at the end of the horseshoe table. Pushing the lighted button, the Ambassador of Kukundu said, "Thank you, Mr. Chairman,

"I have reported to President Kundana the evidence Your Excellency gave me. I'm afraid he was unable to give it more than a cursory glance. He did, however, establish that the regrettable case in question must have been an exception.

"Thank you, Mr. Chairman." With a look of finality, he looked fixedly at the red light on

his mike, willing it to be switched off.

"The evidence we provided is based on numerous cases," the Chair insisted, "The situation you are referring to was not an isolated incident. In fact, similar scenes were

taking place simultaneously all over Kukundu."

Wim switched on the Ambassador's mike and the red light flashed back on.

"I did mention that to our President, Mr. Chairman." The Ambassador pulled at his collar as if trying to breathe..

"Of course, you're aware that Kukundu is a sovereign nation and that, according to the U.N. Charter, unless we commit aggression outside our borders, no one may intrude in our internal affairs."

"That was indeed true until the Genocide Convention was adopted. Now, whenever genocide is established, national borders no longer provide a shield!"

"I did point that out to the President!" The Ambassador tugged at his collar again.

Wim was watching the hall, ready to immediately switch on the right mike, as soon as the next speaker took the floor.

There was an uncomfortable silence.

Finally, the Ambassador spoke, "President Kundana pointed out that the days are over when Kukundu has to ask for outside help. We have powerful allies and all the resources we require."

A mystified silence followed.

"We're talking not about power but about *international law*," the Chair of the Human Rights Committee pointed out.

Another long uncomfortable silence.

Finally, the Ambassador leaned forward as Wim pounced to switch on his mike. "The President laughed!" he blurted out.

Augustina let out a sob. "This is a farce!" she cried.

Wim reached out and grabbed her arm. "Shsh!" he hissed, " I'll lose my job! No one may know you are here! This is a closed meeting!"

But Augustina was sobbing beyond control. Wrenching herself free, she jumped up and hurtled headlong out of the booth, padded up the stairs two, three at a time her large feet twice slipping off the steps and almost sending her back down to the bottom.

On the landing, she threw open the doors, falling into the large public corridor. There, almost knocking Eliza over.

Getting her balance, Eliza exclaimed, "Augustina, I've been waiting for you. Are you alright?

"Augustina! How was ..."

As Augustina dashed off along the hall, Eliza made a lunge and was just in time to catch the seam of her jacket and just as she was sure she was about to be jerked off her feet, Augustina was brought to a stop.

"Hey, Augustina, calm down!" Eliza said, addressing her back, "The guards'll wonder what is wrong and you'll have to tell them where you've been. Wim'll be thrown out of his job. Those proceedings are top secret!"

Augustina whirled around, eyes flashing, nostrils flaring. For the first time seeing Eliza, she stopped and gulped, trying to catch her breath.

"The President laughed!" she said, almost choking on the words.

Calmer now, Eliza was able to lead her out of the Conference Building and through the Public Entrance to the DC Building across the street where the All-Win Office was housed.

As they walked, Augustina's story came out, punctuated with sobs, "There's no hope for Kukundu, no justice'll get done. The U.N.'s too weak!"

With growing apprehension, Eliza listened.

Finally, when Augustina paused for breath, she said, "President Kundana had to be talking about the Holy Order of the Snake. That's all I can see. How else could a poor nation, like Kukundu, thumb its nose at the rest of the world?

"The All-Win Network was founded to show up Snake's policies of divide and rule. We know something of how they function," Eliza pointed out.

"How do you know about this Holy Order of the Snake?" Augustina asked suspiciously.

"One of their members confessed just before he died in Viet Nam. A friend of ours was with him. At first, he thought it was the gibberish of a dying man, 'til he researched what he heard. Since then, we've been finding out more and more."

"Well, will the Security Council want to hear the case? Or are Governments too scared?" Augustina asked defiantly.

"Oh!" her voice broke like the string of a violin snapping under tension. "What's the point. I wish Pierre were here and we were facing this together."

Eliza unlocked her office and eased her down into an easy chair.

"It's not the end!" she said softly, sitting down, "It's the beginning.

"Yesterday, we received a request from John St. Clair to help the peace effort in Kukundu. I was waiting 'til after the Human Rights Committee hearing to tell you. Thought you might be ready then to consider your next steps." Eliza searched Augustina's face not wishing to put her in an awkward position.

Augustina nodded for her to carry on.

Eliza said, "Since the Young People's public hook-ups small discussion groups are forming in people's houses in Kukundu. They are exploring how to use the all-win principle to rebuild Kukundu. They're looking to involve as many refugees living outside the country as they can.

" John St. Clair has asked us to help to locate people like yourself."

Eliza paused to give Augustina time to think.

Augustina replied softly, "I'd like to participate. At least I'd be doing something!"

Eliza hesitated and then took the plunge. "John sent us a film by video phone about reconciliation and how it is being practiced in Kukundu – like a speeded up grieving process. Once it is completed, the people are generally ready to make amends. They return to their villages if they can (of course the Mandus have to stay in hiding) and then join the discussion groups. John believes that inside Kukundu people increasingly agree that the path of murder and violence is a dead-end.

"You can see the film, if you like."

"I'd like to!" Augustina managed a wan smile.

"Just one thing. The person speaking—it's your husband, Pierre!"

54. Juanita Acts As Quickly As She Can

Carlos dropped Juanita at her door.

Hurriedly, Juanita entered her apartment, closed and bolted the door, and shoved the police lock in place. Throwing her coat on a chair, she dashed into her study, snapped on her computer, and long pink nails woodpecking the desk, she watched, as her computer slowly and methodically loaded its software. Finally an e-mail blank appeared on the screen. She rapped out an SOS to Bertram:

> *Urgent, Bertram!*
> *Snake is rearing its head. This time roping in Heads of State -- 102 countries were mentioned. Isn't that the number of dictatorships today? They're teaching them divide and rule skills. Same policies as in Kukundu. Can not mention names to protect friend.*

Outside her apartment, she heard the lift doors open. Military footsteps: two or three men approaching.

> *Police outside -- to arrest me?*
> *Help!*

Juanita.
Reporter Global Trends (student from Oxford)

Fists banged on her door.

Juanita hammered 'send', deleted the message, switched off her laptop computer, ran to her walk-in closet and with a surge of strength, moved a heavy chest of drawers away from the wall.

More banging. This time louder.

"Quick! The air vent! She removed the grid, shoved her laptop through the opening, replaced the grid, and with another surge of strength, heaved the chest back into place.

"Open up immediately! We know you're there!" Someone rammed the door.

Juanita looked around frantically. No escape. Bluff – her only hope!

She ran to the door, and opened it.

"Please gather together some basic clothes and toiletries. We are placing you under arrest!" the military policeman cried.

"What am I being charged with!?" Her calm self-confident tone belied the wild pounding of her heart. "I'm a foreign journalist. If I'm arrested without due process, there'll be an international stink!"

"You're under arrest for masquerading as a man!" His tone rocklike.

Juanita looked in the hall mirror. The pencil shaped moustache was still in place.

"There's no law against that!" she cried exasperated.

"There is, if you try to gain access to a royal abode!"

Joaquim had kept his promise. Now it was her word against his. With a feeling of deep betrayal, she realized she had no choice but to do as they said.

Being thrown into a San Leoni jail was one thing, getting out was quite something else. She might well be there for years!

55. Mary Is Up Early

Mary was up early as usual. Five a.m. Her coffee was already percolating on the stove. Leisurely, she switched on her computer. How she loved her life – the enthusiasm of the young people and the way they gave their all to the peace work they were doing together. Very occasionally, she wondered how things would change when she was no longer there. How much initiative would there be to carry on? Or would all they had built up together crumble and all go their own separate ways?

An e-mail from Bertram. Yes, he was putting his finger on precisely the point both her students from Corps Elite and Pim had been making: The need to learn all-win conflict resolution.

She responded,

> *Dear Bertram,*
>
> *Good news! Pim is coming to the Santa Cruz, California, to teach us about Ubuntu. Apparently, it is both a tool to help us remove our fear-colored glasses and to solve conflicts peacefully. Remember, Pim promised to teach us, once he and his colleagues had, themselves, mastered the process?*
>
> *He will by then also have met Erwin Laszlo. Remember the child-prodigy pianist from Hungary, who became the president (and, also the founder) of the prestigious Club of Budapest? Laszlo suggests we create grass roots think tanks to solve conflicts and to come to grips with global issues.*
>
> *So the plan is for all of us who were at Maurice's last summer to meet to practice three things: to remove our fear-colored glasses, practice peaceful conflict resolution; and learn how to function as a think tank. It looks as if these are precisely the skills you were looking to teach to business. Of course, we are all looking forward to seeing you there!*
>
> *Maurice will unfortunately not be able to attend. He will be with Percy, his brother, working on logistics for our conference in the South of France.*

Her only other e-mail was from Antonia. Mary was surprised: Antonia who still barely dared to speak up in class, even after the summer she had spent sailing the Peace Warrior with Mary, David and the others.

Mary eagerly read on:

> *Dear Mary,*
>
> *I miss David. So many attended his funeral. All of us who were staying with Maurice were there—all except Bertram and Maurice, but then they are so busy! So like David--his last wish: no flowers, but money for trees!*
>
> *David was sort of my idol. I often joined his nature walks with the kids at Golden Haven School. I never dared to talk to him and he was the only other person who was as shy as me. And then he got 2 million kids to plant trees!*
>
> *I want to be like David, do things that are really good.*

Really funny, as soon as I got the idea, I thought something I'd never thought before. Sounds silly, but I realized that I'm not the center of the world. People aren't thinking about me. Often they don't even know I'm there. So why am I so scared of what others think about me? And the funny thing is that as soon as I started thinking that way, I stopped being so shy. It just seemed to go away.

Remember, David asked me to get information on how to stop teasing? I found a great program and am sending you the information. Friend of my brother's told me about it. He used to belong to a local gang and quit after taking the program. It's called Challenge Day[56]. What counts now is what I can do for other people. I feel all of a sudden, as if David is right there, cheering me along.

Mary smiled to herself: here she had been worrying what would happen when she was gone and now Antonia, one of her most timid students, was taking the initiative to introduce a new project! Eagerly, she read on:

Reading about the program made me realize that being a bully and being chicken like me are both the same. Both bullies and chickens do what we do, 'cause we're scared. Imagine if after such a Challenge Day, students, both bullies and chickens could get together to help one another to change. We could talk about how to deal with scary situations. We would have to do it straight after the Challenge Day, though, before everyone forgot what they'd learned.

What a wise little lady! Mary mused as she popped some bread into the toaster.

How Antonia had changed. If only others could see the new Antonia! If only there was something she could do to nurture this brave little person who was trying to emerge. She placed Antonia's e-mail on the Young People's web site for all to read. Then she had an idea … Yes! Why shouldn't Antonia follow in David's footsteps and chair the next project?

56. Augustina And Pierre

"Pierre!" Augustina breathed, as he appeared on the screen. There she was, back in Kukundu, the little hut where they had lived. The sweet smell of yam cooking on the stove wafted through Augustina's mind. She saw the birds flitting in and out of the trees, the bright splashes of the orchids against the frantic green of the jungle, and heard the voices of her children, singing and playing. These were images from their last evening together. Her heart ached for what even then she sensed might have been.

She reached out to touch his image. How old he had become. His skin wrinkled.

Pierre's tender, sorrowful voice described how he saw himself disintegrate into a monster, driven by fear, anger and revenge, how he had cruelly held her, Augustina, at bay. "His mainstay," he called her, "the only woman he had ever loved," and then he told how, "like a butcher", he had slaughtered their children.

His openness! His pain, as he acknowledged his shame! So clear, the way he outlined his feelings! The only thing that mattered now was to make amends, to use his mistakes as grist for the mill, and to nurture Kukundu back to health.

"This message is to all those of you who had to flee. Please help us to build a Kukundu in which you would want to live. Help us to decide how we can best make amends. Please let us together rebuild Kukundu into an 'All-Win Nation'. We can do this, if we all work together."

Long after Pierre had stopped speaking, Augustina sat, barely breathing, a rough and tumble of emotions crowding her mind. The ache of her separation from Kukundu, the fierce longing for her babies, her mother, and, permeating the inner chaos, the tender longing to be back with Pierre. His rich voice singing as he pottered around the yard, always slightly off key – how familiar, how endearing, how comforting this had been.

Finally, she got up and went next door.

Eliza was on the phone.

"Thanks, Hercule, for phoning back. You guys must be busy at the NGO Resource Center with so many new NGOs in town…

" I needed around 60 copies of the *U.N. Charter* and the *Universal Declaration of Human Rights* in Chinese – I'll be speaking at the Presbyterian Church in China Town--and about 100 in Spanish for talks in High Schools in Spanish Harlem…"

Intently, her gaze fixed on Augustina as she stood in the doorway. She signaled that the call would not take long and that Augustina should take a seat in the lounge next door.

"No, I'll be speaking in English, but I'm hoping that the members of the audience will take the documents home to their families and friends in their respective communities where many don't speak or read English well. The ripple effect, you know!

"Great! I'll be by later this morning then. Thanks for your trouble!" Eliza hung up and hurried next door where Augustina was sitting bent over in an easy chair, head in hands, staring straight ahead. Sitting down opposite her, she felt her friend's intense sadness, but refrained from interfering with her feelings.

"His hair's turned white…!" Augustina's voice broke.

She took a deep breath and steadying herself, she continued, "He looks like an old man. And yet the man I married, his tenderness, and the loyalty he reserved for me and the children… it's all still there. Only now it's bigger. It's for Kukundu.

Her lip quivered. "I still love him," Augustina said quietly.

Eliza did not speak, not wishing to interrupt Augustina's feelings. They needed to be expressed at their own pace.

"You know the way he slid, step by step, into this other side of himself? I was doing exactly the same thing. I created scenes, but never really rebelled. We were both guilty. He for what he did, and me for allowing it to happen. He slid faster and deeper. What's that people say? *The road to hell is paved with small steps?*

"If only we'd dared to face what was taking place!"

Augustina's eyes welled over and she allowed the tears to flow over her face without making any effort to wipe them away. Eliza slipped over and sitting on the armrest of her friend's chair, she cradled her friend's head against her chest and allowed her to cry gently.

When she was finished, the friends sat quietly, Eliza's arm around Augustina's shoulders, allowing the experience to fade away.

"Would you like to reconnect with Kukundu, Augustina?" she inquired quietly.

"Yes, if I can send a video message via John to Pierre. Perhaps we can set up regular meetings by video phone or else some other way."

"Would you stay in New York? Or go somewhere else?" Eliza asked, keeping her voice neutral.

"Oh! I'd love to return to Kukundu, but for the moment this is my home. I want to stick around to see if we can get President Kundana before the International Criminal Court."

Augustina was back into action mode. The dark cloud had passed.

Eliza's face lit up in a smile.

"We can really use your help, as you well know! We need to encourage the NGOs, who are a part of the All-Win Network to stop our downhill slide!"

Augustina thought for a moment and said, "Perhaps, if I could show this video of Pierre during the series of talks you all are setting up for me, people could feel how easy it is to let things get out of hand. It was so easy to slide from being a happy, loving family into losing everything we had! I could end each talk with a discussion and we could explore ways both for the US and for Kukundu to do an about turn. It won't be easy, I know!"

The phone began to ring and Eliza motioned Augustina to go on.

"I have the answering machine on," she explained.

Augustina continued, "You know, I'm reminded so much of how things began back home when I see what is happening here: people from disenfranchised groups arrested willy-nilly, held without being charged, people arrested in police stations around the country and held against their will much longer than the 76-odd hours, permitted by international law. And then there are the prisons for terrorists, which have held people for years without them being brought to trial! If enough people become alarmed, we might be able to stop the US Administration from running rough shod over everyone's rights!"

"That's exactly what's needed!" Eliza realized how much she had dreaded Augustina leaving.

She added, "At the same time, I'll arrange for you and Pierre to meet by solar video phone. John said the dialogues between Mandus and Kukundus have started up.

57. Bertram At The Chicago Hilton

The wait at the Chicago Hilton on Michigan Avenue was longer than usual. It was a large and popular hotel and Bertram had arrived early. He had been told his room would be ready at 3 p.m. sharp. Bertram looked at his watch. Another two hours, at least! He signed to the bellman at the stand, close to where he was waiting.

"Could I store my suitcase with you until my room is ready?" he asked, and slipped him a couple of dollars.

Carrying just his briefcase and laptop, he hurried out to Michigan Avenue. What was the little restaurant called where they were always so friendly -- the 8th Street Bistro? Or was that in another city? He'd been travelling so much; he was getting tired. He looked around and there on the corner he recognized the restaurant where he normally lunched. They knew him and would give him the window table where he could use his sun-triggered laptop to download his messages.

While he was waiting for his tuna fish salad, he started up his computer and skimmed his incoming mail. Slightly disappointed, he noticed there was nothing from Eliza.

He scrolled back to the first message. It was from a Juanita.

He frowned. The name rang a distant bell.

For a moment he was back in his Las Vegas bedroom in Luxor, seeing the Egyptian columns reflected in the mirrors.

"Juanita... Juanita...he remembered the name. He glanced at the content

> *Urgent ... Snake ... Heads of State – 102 dictatorships mentioned. Teaching divide and rule skills. The policies of Kukundu... can't tell you his name... must protect my friend...but he's trying to stop me from acting. Can the All-Win Network help... urgent! Banging on the door ... Police outside to arrest me!*
> *Juanita Ciara*
> *Reporter for Global Trends (Student from Oxford)*

He reread the words. Then he remembered her congratulations on his book. Yes, she was the one who hung out with that guy from San Leon, the prince, or general or something ... She'd been okay, bright, involved with social issues, level headed.

Even so, her words refused to sink in.

He turned to the next message. It was from Mary with the latest update.

> *Things are moving!!! Our Peace Warrior friends have organized a Young People's letter writing campaign to all Governments (some 200). They're demonstrating how the all-win principle works by applying it to problems the Governments are dealing with at the U.N.*
>
> *They want to show what young people can do. Their aim: to be taken more seriously during governmental deliberations[57]. Also they want to get the all-win principle accepted as a worldwide standard.*
>
> *The oldest ones (Annette, Takeshi, Hugh, Winston and Sharifa, as well as Pat and Arturo, who have become very close) are heading for New York to lobby one of the U.N. Conferences, as representatives of the All-Win Network.*
>
> *Of course, I'm also teaching the all-win principle in all my ham radio classes. Every month we do a tally and more and more young people are being elected to school, library, and municipal boards and on their Governments' U.N. delegations.*
>
> *I'm surprised at how many people on line are now taking classes at All-Win Education Centers and some of these are actually tuning in to our hookups for the general public.*
>
> *Keeps me young, I hope, all these activities, although I must say that I am tired at the end of the day and have taken to going to bed at nine.*

I really need my eight hours and do what I will, I am awake at five o'clock sharp.

The newest thing: I have been contacted by a number of friends from UNICEF centers around the world. They are inviting young peace workers from Wealthy Countries to stay in private homes to get to know poorer countries from close by.

See you in Santa Cruz at Pim's workshop in a few days time!!!!

Bless Mary's heart. The world according to Mary was a hopeful, creative place, which filled him with courage. He felt happy they would be meeting soon. Every day he was more aware of how much practice he still needed to apply the all-win principle to everyday situations.

Carefully, he reread Juanita's e-mail.

Snake, divide and rule, 102 dictatorships…

He took out his cell phone, dialed international directory inquiries, requested the number of the *Global Times,* and got them on the phone.

"I'm looking for your reporter in San Leon, Juanita Ciara. We met in Oxford."

"Juanita Ciara? One moment, please" There was a muffled conversation, as the receptionist covered the mouthpiece with her hand. She seemed excited about something and had forgotten to place the phone on hold.

"Sorry to keep you waiting," the receptionist returned, "May I know what this is in reference to?"

Without going into detail, Bertram mentioned he had received an e-mail from her requesting he undertake some action.

Again the receptionist's voice disintegrated into a muffled conversation.

"Sorry she is on a leave of absence. I'm afraid I don't know for how long. We have no way of reaching her…."

Bertram thanked her and hung up.

The situation was serious. Yet somehow, the urgency refused to register. He stared out of the window.

Wealthy tourists leaving the Hilton for the brief walk to the Museum of Modern Art -- an *Impressionist Exhibition,* he had noticed as he had driven by in a taxi. Here on Michigan Avenue, a plot to take over the world seemed a crazed figment of the imagination. Everything looked so normal.

How far away, the long nights seemed in Maurice's library! How distant the mysterious documents! How unlikely unknown visitors listening in on their meetings! And now all of a sudden, the possibility of a conspiracy was attempting to force itself back into his world. Did the Holy Order of the Snake really exist? His mind balked at Juanita's message.

Mary might help. Thank Goodness! She was back. He dialed Mary's number in Santa Cruz.

She picked up at the first ring!

After a few comments on their young friends, he quickly outlined the situation: Juanita, an Oxford student he barely knew; her story about the Snake; and the fact that she seemed to have disappeared.

Mary listened quietly.

"It sounds serious, Bertram," she said as soon as he had finished, "She clearly needs our help!?"

"Huh! *Divide and rule!*" Mary pondered.

Bertram waited.

"Divide and rule is a way to rule by fear. If we oppose it, we increase fear and with it their power increases.

"But what can we do?"

Both were silent for a while.

"The only possible thing is to undermine what they are doing by showing up its limitations…" Mary mused, "For instance, show how win/lose policies tend to create opposition (which sometimes stays out of sight) and then when the pressure has built up, there is an explosion, a revolt, a revolution, which catapults the authorities out of their positions of power. We could then give examples of specific people being brought before the International Criminal Court and the U.N. Tribunals…"

Bertram saw what she meant, "Isn't that what the young people are doing: showing a problem first from a win/lose, *divide and rule* approach and then contrasting it with an all-win solution?" Bertram fell silent, trying to imagine the impact of such an action gradually building, as more and more groups participated and broadcast their findings.

"Exactly," Mary mused, "The young people's action could be expanded. It could target the win/lose-divide and rule policies actually being used by dictators. That would show up the limitations of what they are learning from Snake, and undermine Snake's credibility."

Bertram suddenly saw the beauty of Mary's idea. "Just expanding what they are already doing!" he repeated.

"Might even convert a dictator or two to the all-win approach," Mary laughed.

"But wouldn't such an action get people thrown into jail?" Bertram was suddenly serious.

"Yes, for their own safety, people living under a dictatorship couldn't criticize their own governments, but they can help one another out by showing up the limitations of one another's governments."

"I'll get them a list of addresses of dictators and give them some Internet sites to consult. I'm sure a number of young people will take the ball and run with the action."

"Brilliant, Mary!" Bertram beamed. "I suppose, I should write back to Juanita…? But I don't want to give away what we are planning…It's possible she is being watched."

" Why don't you write back and ask Juanita for more information?" Mary suggested. "In the meantime, I'll see what I can do and get back to you as soon as I can."

"Tuna fish salad?"

Bertram was suddenly jolted back to the 8th St. Café on Michigan Avenue in Chicago. Still on the phone, he smiled at the waitress, and moved his computer aside, as he said to Mary, "Okay. I'll send you a copy of her e-mail. You can write to her directly, if you like. That will save time. And… Mary, you're a champ!"

"Oh, just a minute, Mary!" he interrupted himself, "Any idea where Eliza is? We have been staying in touch sporadically, but I haven't heard from her recently."

"Oh, Eliza is off on a lecture tour lasting several weeks and then off to Europe for a break."

Bertram felt a pang of disappointment, not sure whether it was because she had not told him personally, or whether it was that she was out of reach.

"Love to you, Mary. And thanks for everything!"

"Thank you!"

He smiled at the waitress. "Could I have some more water? No ice, please."

58. Augustina And Pierre Meet By Videophone

The moment had arrived. Augustina and Pierre finally sat face to face, connected by videophone. Both were struggling with their emotions. Neither was able to speak.

For a long time Augustina and Pierre just stared at each other.

Finally, Pierre asked in a small voice, "How can I try to make up for what I have done?"

"Oh, Pierre! I barely recognize you! You're so thin! And your hair – it's white. Your face is full of wrinkles! You look like a very old man, a shadow of the person you were. How are you? … I mean how are you managing to survive?"

"I work for the Underground. We're trying to undo some of the horrors we have created here.

"But how are you, Augustina?"

With a pang, Augustina noticed that he was not using, Footsie, the term of endearment he used when they were alone. The chasm between them hurt.

"What will you do now that the U.N.'s Human Rights Committee didn't work out?"

She swallowed, trying to ease the pain that was threatening to strangle her voice. Gratefully, she clutched at the opportunity to talk about something less personal. She launched into an explanation of what the NGOs were doing at the United Nations.

"The NGOs have taken up our cause with the U.N.'s Security Council. They will be pushing for sanctions against Kukundu unless President Kundana calls a referendum. They are also using Kukundu as an example of how a government, which uses a win/lose approach, is automatically breaching its peoples human rights.

"It's all part of a much larger movement. They want to foster a global community based on all-win norms. Their actions with regard to Kukundu illustrate how the principle works. At the same time, they hope it will convince countries to use it at all phases of governance and to apply the all-win principle to all subjects taught in educational institutions, beginning in elementary schools along with reading, writing and arithmetic."

She then told how the NGOs were seeing their own Governments slipping out of control and the role, using his film, she was to play in persuading them to turn that around.

"I let things slide, Augustina. You fought me tooth and nail!"

"No, Pierre. I should have put my foot down. In the worst case, I should have simply left you before it could come to this!"

For a long time, they just sat again looking at each other, feeling what it was like to be back together.

"I've missed you!" Augustina said in a tiny voice.

Pierre's lip quivered. Desperately, he fought back his tears. He did not want his eyes to cloud over while he could still see and hear her.

"What do you do all day?" He managed to get out.

Augustina felt Pierre's pain. Trying to keep the tremor out of her own voice, she told him. Talking about their daily activities gave an air of normalcy to her first meeting with Pierre that helped to steady Augustina.

Then Pierre told how he moved between the jungle hideout and their village home. How he had forced himself to live in their little hut with the grave of their children, covered with her altar cloth; and how he spent every moment he could, helping friends, neighbors, whoever was open, to look at returning peace to Kukundu.

"But surely President Kundana and the militia don't tolerate that?"

"We talk quite openly about international tribunals and what has happened in other countries. We show our concern for whoever is maintaining the status quo, including Kundana and the militia, as well as for what we ourselves have done. You see, we are all guilty and realize that we have come to a dead-end. I think that President Kundana must know his time is limited. With the exception, perhaps, of a few of his followers, the militia are actually people much like you and me. They crave a normal existence. They are all aware that the resistance both inside and outside Kukundu is building and that there will come a time when they will have to confront what they have done. Kundana can no longer rely on them.

"All see that it is time to find a way to exist together while even criminals, like Kundana, are treated in a just way. Kundana realizes he can only benefit from a discussion about all-win solutions. That way, instead of coming to a gruesome end, he will be taken before the International Criminal Court. Here, even in the worst case scenario, he will be treated humanely. He and his militia tap ham radio discussions all the time. They know what their people are thinking.

"Just imagine, Augustina, sitting in the middle of the jungle with Josette, my teacher, and in the distance hearing the first drum speak. Then gradually, the beat swells as others join in. Finally, all of Kukundu seems to come alive, as if breathing new energy into its citizens!"

"What do the drums say exactly?" Augustina asked.

"Things like, '*Follow your hearts, allow others to do the same and together, we can create a just and peace-loving Kukundu!*'"

For the first time, Augustina smiled. As Pierre spoke, the sounds of the drums seemed to resonate in her heart.

"So, the new spirit of Kukundu is being drummed back to life!" Augustina's smile marked the turning point in their estrangement. The tiny seed was germinating – the beginning of a new love.

"Oh Augustina! I've missed you so!"

"I'm so happy that we shall be working together!" Augustina was close to tears.

They arranged their next meeting and some of the topics they had to work on. And so ended their first meeting.

59. Joaquim Studies How To Divide And Rule

Joaquim and his teacher met again in his private quarters.

Like a bird with long sharp talons, his teacher perched on the chair where recently Juanita had sat. Joaquim's thoughts flinched from her image. He had had to have her arrested, he told himself. She was much too impetuous. There was no telling what damage she, as a foreign journalist, could do. Joaquim focussed on his teacher.

"The Alliance to Rule the World!" his teacher announced with a perfunctory smile.

Joaquim's heart thrilled with anticipation. Each of you, who are my most distinguished students, will rule your nation and together we shall rule the whole world!

"You, like others of our clients, who are also Heads of State, daily confront groups and individuals, who would move heaven and hell to usurp some of your power. How to make these your servants?"

Was this really true? Joaquim was suddenly doubtful. Some, like the generals, were indeed out for power. Others were pretty decent people, only too glad to support him. He didn't really feel groups *confronted him.* It was his duty to listen to his people. After all, a successful country needed the input of its citizens and it was his pleasure to respond to their needs.

He was here to learn from his teacher. He decided not to argue.

"So what do you see as the most powerful emotion?" his teacher asked.

"Love, of course!" Joaquim responded without thinking.

"How about fear?" His teacher asked evenly. "Once people are afraid, they will do anything to ingratiate themselves with you. Instead that they demand favors of you, you can then demand favors of them. You see fear comes about when people feel they aren't in control of what gives them pleasure or pain. And once we know how to inflict pleasure and pain, they are like putty in our hands.

"Find out what gives people pleasure, dangle it in front of their noses, and people come running. Instant servility! Convince them you can hurt them in some way, and they will do anything to avert the pain. Either way, they gladly give you what you wish.

"To many do-gooders, duty is the greatest pleasure they know. So pleasure and duty can both be used as a carrot."

"If pleasure and duty are carrots, then pain is the stick?" Joaquim asked.

"That's right".

Despite his boyish head of white hair and potent, athletic appearance, Joaquim's teacher betrayed no feeling. He might have been talking about the weather.

"*A cool blooded individual!*" Joaquim decided. "*Not the sort of person I'd like to cross.*"

"There's just one way that control may elude you. That's when people identify with a group. Then the group mind takes over, and they can slip out of your control."

"Is that what is referred to as the morphogenetic field?"

His teacher looked at him sharply. "Ah, so you are in touch with that band of scientists meeting at the U.N.'s University of Peace?"

Joaquim looked blank. "No, this is a well-known scientific theory and many of us are fascinated by it."

His teacher continued, "So the second part of the golden principle is: '*Destroy all groups.*'"

Joaquim realized how little he had in common with this man. He protested, "But people are social beings. It's natural for them to want to do things together!"

"All the better," his teacher continued without interrupting his train of thought, "Then make the group experience one filled with fear. You kill two birds with one stone. Turn person against person so that the group fights, claw and jowl, among themselves. That way, people are kept busy defending themselves; they don't have eyes for you and don't meddle in your affairs."

"*Divide and rule?*" Joaquim held his breath. The phrase Juanita had mentioned!

"Good man! You're a bright student!"

For a moment, his teacher sat looking at his long, carefully manicured fingers, giving Joaquim time to absorb his teachings. Then he turned to Joaquim, commanding him with his eyes to listen, "Your job as leader is to keep each person and each group dancing to your strings. That is child's work once you find out what each individual's hooks are: money, status, power, dignity, health, attractiveness, importance, compulsion to feel that they are doing their duty and are a 'good' person, and so on, and so on.

"At the same time, you make it your duty to know what each fears most."

Joaquim tried to focus, but in the background he kept hearing Juanita's warning.

What sort of monster was this man that he could manipulate people by filling them with fear? Which strings had he pulled to get an appointment with him, King Joaquim, without first being placed on the waiting list? Were the generals beholden to him? Did he have them in his power? Was Juanita right after all? Was this "teacher" sent by the Holy Order of the Snake? Had the Snake's money enabled the generals to usurp his father's power and to now keep him, their King, a prisoner in his own country?

The Holy Order of the Snake – the name kept slithering through his thoughts. His revulsion grew. *"They must not know that I suspect!"* Joaquim thought. He needed time to size up the situation.

He swallowed.

To cover up his confusion, he decided to jump into the exercise. "Fear?" he said smoothly, "Well, there're all sorts of fears. I suppose it depends on the individual as to which one is most important."

"Good you've got the point. As a ruler, it is your job to know who's in a position to undermine your authority. Then, by using the pleasure and pain carrot and stick, see they are delivered into your hands. For each person, every experience weighs differently on the pleasure/pain scale.

"Now," his teacher continued, "How can you eliminate your inferiors?"

Joaquim swallowed again. "You mean *kill?*"

"Well, if need be, but chop them down to size is better. Kill their spirit first, and then when you are done with them relieve yourself of their physical presence. Killing everyone is, of course, an option, but then there's no one left to rule." His smile was mirthless.

Joaquim was aghast. But he was too deeply involved now to turn back. He forced himself to play the avid student. Gradually, he got into the act.

It occurred to him that the thought of ridding himself of his generals was not without appeal.

"Sanchez definitely enjoys prestige," he said.

"How to get him into a stranglehold?" His teacher intoned.

"He loves to give speeches before huge audiences on radio and television and he is always immaculately dressed. Deprive him of money, elegant clothes..." he stopped to think, while his teacher was making notes.

"Demoting him would probably be a fate worse than death to poor Sanchez," Joaquim admitted. He suddenly laughed, " I could imagine how he would deflate like a balloon, if he had a pie thrown in his face." Suddenly serious, Joaquim added, "Or worse still, if in public, he were stripped of his medals

"Yes, he would certainly commit suicide."

"That's the spirit." Joaquim watched the shadow of a smile snake around his teacher's lips without reaching his eyes. This was the first time his teacher had shown any emotion at all. What was he, Joaquim, doing making sport of the downfall of another human being, however much he disliked the general? And what did his teacher want from him? Why was he teaching him without being paid?

"Who's next?" His teacher spoke casually, pencil poised.

"General Mendoza is definitely into power. He loves to see people cringe." Joaquim had caught Mendoza beating one of the ladies in waiting. Joaquim had had to have her brought to hospital where, thank God, she had survived. He then got her out of the country without Mendoza knowing. Joaquim kept this to himself. His teacher must not suspect he was having second thoughts.

Mendoza -- how he disliked that man. He demanded blind obedience. His "respect" for Joaquim was but a veneer. His suggestions, thinly veiled threats Yes, he disliked and distrusted Mendoza. How he wished he could somehow get rid of him. Without Mendoza, Joaquim's life would be almost bearable.

"Mendoza's worst fear was almost certainly to be powerless and treated as such."

"Good! So when you are in a position of power, you could have him flogged in public until he begs forgiveness." Joaquim could not see such a thing happening. Mendoza was too powerful, backed by the whole army, navy and airforce. Joaquim nodded to move off the subject.

As his teacher was busy writing, Joaquim hesitated. Fernandez, he scarcely knew. Fernandez was totally absorbed in seeing that the armed forces worked well. The army was his pride and joy. If his army were degraded – that would be a huge blow. He said, "Fernandez would be afraid if his precious army didn't perform. Mutiny among his men, or getting beaten on the battlefield are almost certainly his two greatest fears."

"Good, that's the spirit!" His teacher underlined something he had just written down. "Now, what about groups? Like people, these each have their pleasure/pain sensitivities."

"Most importantly, we have the trade unions," Joaquim volunteered.

These were more a façade than anything else. They would politely ask for a favor here or there, but would never insist. They couldn't. They had no power at all. The generals would grant them their request every so often for the sake of appearances. That was what annoyed Joaquim most about this group. They were cowards. They did not do their job. Too scared of reprisals if they stuck their necks out.

"A death or two among the trade-union leadership where someone stood up for workers rights - that would do wonders to keep the whole workers' movement cowed," Joaquim was surprised to hear the words come out of his mouth.

While his teacher scribbled away, Joaquim allowed his thoughts to roam.

If only the professional associations would do their jobs, stand up for their rights, get their citizens to vote and to write letters to let the world know how they were being disempowered. If only they would alert the world press, ally themselves with associates in other countries, and get the U.N. to impose sanctions. Then the generals would not stand a chance, and he, Joaquim, would finally be able to run his country for his people.

With disgust, Joaquim realized he had sunk so low as to shirk the responsibility that was his to shoulder. Could he not have mobilized his social activist friends outside of San Leon?

"Okay, what other major groups do we have in your country?" his teacher said, putting down his pen.

"There are a number of professional associations…" Joaquim hesitated. These came to him with a desperate hope that there was something he could do for them. He could not think in terms of manipulating these. He felt suddenly revolted …and words refused to come.

"Come on, Your Majesty, you can plan your power strategy faster than this. What are each of these groups after? And what do they fear most?" There was the nasty edge in his teacher's voice of a man used to blind obedience.

Joaquim realized what a breach of protocol this was. He decided to let it pass until he had had the chance to fully assess the situation.

"Well, the professional associations are pretty decent people really," Joaquim said in an even tone. "They want the best for their members, they want to be able to perform their jobs. They are fed up of having no money and supplies and they want freedom to develop their expertise. Unfortunately, books and access to the Internet are often limited for lack of resources. This situation is maintained, I believe, to prevent them from using the force of world public opinion."

"What motivates them, Your Majesty? What hold do they give you over them?" His teacher's nasty tone had become menacing.

Joaquim willed himself to stay calm. Any flutter of emotion would give his teacher the upper hand. "I suppose they are honor bound to do their jobs and do them well!" he insisted.

"Good! Send your militia in, arrest their officers, and then destroy their quarters – that should deliver them into your hands!

"Okay, we're moving right along. You have quite some opposition, if I may be so bold. But if you continue in this way, you will soon be a proud member of the Alliance to Rule the World. But first, you must further master the pleasure/pain and divide and rule principles."

And so ended Joaquim's first lesson.

Joaquim had learned two important principles by playing a mere 'what if' game. He had also learned that these games were not for him. He was feeling his own impotence. He realized he would never be able to live his life as he had planned, and worse still, his people would never be able to clamber out of poverty. And yet he knew he could not go along with this teacher's devilish approach. At this moment, he had only one choice: to give up all that was dear to him and to do the right thing.

But how to extricate himself? To whom could he turn?

With a sinking feeling, he realized that the only one who he trusted enough to help him deal with the situation he had thrown into jail. Blinded by his obsession with his life's work and the "good of his people," he had betrayed the very standards he wanted to introduce in his land by arresting Juanita, his very best friend and the only ally he had.

60. Antonia

The ham radio meeting started without a hitch with Antonia in the chair. After some hesitation, Antonia had finally accepted. As soon as she had decided to meet the challenge, her shyness had disappeared.

Antonia had had her fair share of teasing. Her family spoke Spanish at home. She had immigrated when still a baby to California from San Leon via Mexico. Her father had been a wet back and now worked in the artichoke fields. Since being a part of Mrs. Gladstone's remedial class, Antonia had become an exceptional student.

When Antonia took the chair, she honored the period of silence that David had introduced. How easily she tapped out the Morse code. Mary was delighted.

Antonia, like so many young people, had taken the trouble to learn Morse so that she could talk to those children in other countries without access to the Internet or modern Ham Radio equipment. Antonia was always excited when she sensed someone was on the air from a Spanish speaking background. Once or twice, Mary had encouraged her to communicate in Spanish.

Powerlessness was the theme that dominated the ham radio that day.

"So many young people of 10 years-old already work as servants," one message said.

"Seven million in Bangladesh." This probably from a teacher.

"Children between 5 and 10 years old are hired to carry boxes."

Antonia took over, "Both in Watsonville where I live now in the United States and especially in San Leon, where my parents come from, lots of kids are on their own. No parents. Or else mothers who are too poor or too young to care for a family. These kids look for support in gangs, led by kids our own age. And in San Leon, the street kids are like terrorists. But you can't blame them. It's survival and there's nowhere else for them to go," Antonia ended her communication. The brain storming session continued.

Freddy who had attended each of the classes now put up his hand and asked, "What about teasing, Antonia?"

Antonia's eyes lit up as she spirited the information on Challenge Day out of her bag. "Thank you, Freddy! I wish people could read this." She looked at Mary for assistance.

Mary said, "Let me see whether I can send this story around by mail to all schools which participate in this hook-up.

"Antonia, why don't you describe briefly by ham radio what the Challenge Day is all about. Perhaps we, in Santa Cruz, can arrange a Challenge Day here."

As Antonia started tapping away, Mary turned to the class and admitted, "I was actually touched to tears when Antonia and I watched the video showing what a Challenge Day is. Imagine one hundred teachers, kids, bullies and victims after one day together actually sharing their innermost feelings and vulnerabilities. And that as total equals! And when they realize how similar their fears and longings are, then all barriers disappear!"

In the meantime, Antonia's message was evoking a spate of enthusiastic responses and many said they would like to organize a Challenge Day at their school.

"But after a Challenge Day, how to keep this caring alive?" Antonia tapped out her message.

There was a long silence, then Antonia remembered the hook-up in Costa Rica. She tapped out the answer to her own question, "The All-Win Education Centers teach people to live by the all-win principle, to develop what they love to do and to help others to do the same."

Mary nodded enthusiastically. "I'll send a list of Centers around by ordinary mail," she said.

Antonia tapped out Mary's offer.

"How can we afford to visit an All-Win Education Center?"

"But our families need the money we earn!"

"Our whole family has to work to put food on the table!"

"It is hard to find the time to take this hour free!"

The kept messages kept coming through the ham radio.

Antonia responded, "In these Centers you work in exchange for the classes you attend. Once you have a skill, you earn a salary. So that would be like having a job. Each Center has a number of chores and also several small businesses which the students help to run."

Before ending the hook-up, Mary made her plea, "We desperately need your help to show up how dictator's win/lose policies hurt everyone, even the dictators themselves, and to find all-win alternatives." And she summarized the action she and Bertram had discussed and which was already being implemented at the UN by a number of NGOs.

After some questions back and forth, Antonia closed the meeting.

"I'm really impressed by how many people are joining our hook-ups," Mary said, "For the first time, we actually have an opportunity to influence world affairs!

As Antonia made to leave, Mary held her back and said, "By the way, I've had a request from an acquaintance of mine, a Mrs. Serazzi. Every year, she invites a young girl, a Spanish-speaking American, to stay with her for the whole summer. I believe you are the very person she is looking for. She volunteers at the local UNICEF Center. She's a dressmaker who lives on her own. She would pay your trip and your keep for the summer. While you're there, you would be like her daughter and attend a regular school, Spanish speaking, of course."

Antonia's eyes opened so wide that they looked as if they might pop. Mary burst out in a long good-natured laugh.

"But ... but ...*me?*"

"Yes, you have done so very well. It would be a wonderful opportunity for you and one which I know you would use well. See what your parents say.

"Here's Mrs. Serazzi's letter."

61. The Underground Connects

The jungle clearing filled with the rich pungent smell of yam and pepper, braised in wild onion and stewing in an iron cauldron over a wooden fire. Quietly the community members gathered one by one to pick up their portion and to scatter either alone or in small groups to enjoy the main meal of the day.

All Kukundu members in the jungle hideout were dedicated to "reclaiming their lives" before returning to their villages. The Mandus, who were persecuted as an ethnic group, could of course not leave. They were left to run the camp and some were trained by Josette to lead the regular "Claim Your Life Back" sessions.

When the resonant drums had first carried the all-win principle to every part of the land, every one was hopeful that together they could build a strong new Kukundu. But putting the all-win principle into practice proved to be too difficult without prior training. Soon people became discouraged. Most gave up. A fundamentalist movement was now being fed by the air of disappointment. People were too scared to invest in a principle that did not yield results, and so more and more were giving in to the bullying of the militia.

Kukundus had come streaming back to undergo additional training. It had taken weeks before a method had been devised to communicate the all-win principle. Weeks of valuable time, weeks during which, day by day, Kundana and his henchmen's hold over Kukundu had grown by leaps and bounds.

Finally, under Josette's leadership a network was forming to coordinate nationwide discussions. These started as isolated groups and were now spanning most of the population. The network consisted of a heart of Mandus, which lived in jungle hideouts and formed all-win think tanks, and Kukundus. The Kukundus ferried back and forth to pass along new insights between think tanks in the villages and jungle hideouts. And so very slowly, a consensus was emerging on how, once it became a democracy, Kukundu would be governed.

John St. Clair who was staying in the refugee camps outside of Kukundu had introduced some of the leading Kukundu thinkers to the All-Win Network for Businesses and together these were now developing a zero waste approach to agriculture.

Mealtimes were patches of relaxation in an otherwise intense day. They tended to be lighthearted and playful.

But today was an exception.

A shadow had fallen on the group. One of their drummers had been captured. Fallu had been assigned the most dangerous position on the outskirts of the Capital City where the government and militia were based. He had been arrested as he drummed out his message and was being held for questioning. He would, of course, say that he had only picked up the drum message and was passing it along. Given the ingrained Kukundu drumming culture, there was not much they would be able to do. Unless he cracked under torture...

All of a sudden the communications hut came alive with the tap! tap! tapping of Morse. Jules jumped up to transcribe the message.

"It's Fallu, our lead drummer!" Jules called out.

Sudden silence.

Would they have to disperse, or...

"He says he is safe!"

"How do you know it was him?" Someone called out.

"He used our secret code!" Jules answered.

From all sides people poured into the clearing to hear the latest news.

"He has been picked up by the underground in Capital City and has attended one of their meetings. He will be returning with someone called Jean and asks one of our members to meet them (and he mentioned a secret place). You will be able to keep a watch on the area to make sure they're not being followed. Jean's group wants to strengthen the ties between us and the underground in Capital City.

"Their question: What to do with President Kundana. He's turned down a referendum. Our only choice: to arrest him and somehow bring him before the International Criminal Court in the Netherlands."

Jules was met with a clamor of exclamations.

"Arrest him?"

"That means all out war!"

"A bloodbath all over again!"

"We can't risk it!"

"Not without support from the outside."

"Apparently, governments *are* willing to deal with Kundana's crimes against humanity -- the NGOs have made Kukundu such an issue!" Jules interrupted the speculation.

"How do you know?" a lone voice called.

"Augustina sent word via John St. Clair," Jules answered, "But she says that no country is willing to invade Kukundu to capture him. Too afraid of setting a precedent."

"Arresting him won't be easy without taking on the whole militia!" someone called out. There was general agreement.

"But I think Jean has a plan," Jules said. "That's why he wants to meet us in person."

62. Can Juanita Help?

Juanita, eyes flashing, face of thunder, wrenched herself free from Carlos's grip and stormed toward Joaquim.

"It's okay, Carlos," Joaquim nodded firmly toward the door, jumping to his feet.

As the door closed behind Joaquim's trusted friend and secretary, Juanita was upon him, lashing out at his face.

Joaquim raised his arms in self-defense, just managing to shield himself in time.

Trying not to hurt her, he caught both her arms.

"Are you crazy?" She screamed. "What the Hell got into you? Do you think you can get away with this? I'm an international journalist! I shall see that this gets into every publication!"

Joaquim held her arms gently but firmly. He had never seen her this way. He knew she had plenty of spunk, yes! But such passion! And that directed at him!

Then, it struck him. This was more than fury at having been confined. After all, other than her freedom, she had had every luxury a king could provide. This had to do with something more basic: he had betrayed the love and trust that had existed between them and which had, from her side, never died -- and that despite knowing that she could never hope to see him again, at least not in private.

She could never have harmed him. And by not seeing that, he had negated her very essence. He realized all this in a flash. At the same time, he also knew that his love for her had remained in tact.

"You're right, Juanita!" he gasped, still trying to hold her at bay, "I sank so low. You would never have betrayed me! How can I ever make this up to you?"

Juanita tore herself loose and backed away from him. "You can't! You've blown it! You are totally untrustworthy! You have betrayed everything that's ever gone on between us! You and your generals – you're all the same!" She spat the word out, "Your ideals -- figments of your imagination! You're out of your mind! Crazy! You have no idea what it is to be a half way decent human being. I'll see you fry for this!"

Joaquim clasped his hands together in a plea for forgiveness and took a step in her direction.

"Get away! No closer! Do you hear?!" Her nostrils flared dangerously.

Joaquim held up both hands in a gesture of *"Alright, don't worry!"* and quickly took a few steps back.

Two red spots had appeared, one on each cheek. Her eyes flashed as if she were on fire. The betrayal hurt them both. How blinded he'd been, not to foresee the full extent of her hurt. To think they'd been so close and he'd never plumbed her true depths.

He stood watching her, feeling her fury, until very gradually the torrent subsided. Then he allowed her tongue-lashing time to sink in.

For a while, both stood looking at each other too emotional to speak. Finally, he said simply: "Is there any way I can make this up to you? To us? After all it was a betrayal of the feelings we have for each other." There seemed nothing else he could say.

"The damage has been done! I want to go home, leave this country and never return!"

She turned and made for the door, yet his acknowledgment of their deeper feelings had reestablished a connection, how ever tenuous. And the explosiveness was no longer there.

"Juanita, you were right! But I need your help! There's no one else I can turn to. No one I can trust... even though I have hurt you so deeply," he blurted out. "It is the Snake. And I'm in their stranglehold and so are my people."

She turned, door handle in her hand.

He didn't dare to approach. The slightest provocation and she would flee.

Quietly, he began telling her about his first lesson with the Royal Finishing School for Heads of State and Government, of the Golden Rules for wielding power, and the practice sessions, using a combination of the pleasure/fear prod and the divide and rule principle."

"So what made you change your mind about this teacher of yours?" Juanita stayed firmly where she was.

"All at once, I realized he was propounding *divide and rule.* I thought about what you said. After that I hated myself for doing his revolting exercises. I simply can't continue!"

"And so, you told one of the most unscrupulous men how to make use of the weaknesses of the key powers in your country... You must be out of you mind!" she cried, "What do you think I can do for you now? Things have gone far too far! You've given them a psychological stranglehold. They have you where they want you!"

"But they don't! That's the point, Juanita. He wants more. The lessons have only just begun...

"They're building an Alliance to Rule the World. St. Leon is peanuts to them."

Juanita let go of the door handle. But he did not dare to approach her, or suggest she sit down. Any movement from his side, he sensed, and she'd go storming out.

"It's not just me. It's not just the generals or even the major groups in my country. Somehow, they're using all 102 dictatorships to get to something bigger."

Juanita sank down on a chair right next to the door.

Joaquim moved toward the hearth and beckoned. "Won't you come here, please, Juanita. I promise I won't touch you. It would be more comfortable if we were closer together."

She hesitated, her nostril quivered, then she grudgingly walked over and sat down in one of the easy chairs.

For a moment, he allowed himself to feel her proximity. How dear she had always been. And even now her presence was like a mirror reflecting his distorted actions so clearly, he felt a deep sense of shame.

A great deal had to be set straight. His marriage with Esmerelda. The information he had given his teacher. He must prevent this unscrupulous man from using it against his people.

Juanita just stared into the hearth.

Finally Joaquim said, "Whatever they plan has to do with increasing the level of fear. That's their main weapon. The Snake will make short shrift of anything that endangers their plans."

"There's just one thing you can do," Juanita pointed out. She had finally calmed down, "Continue the course until you find out what they're after and how they plan to get it!"

"And manage to stay alive." Joaquim added tentatively. "I sense that there are many fish in the sea as far as they are concerned. I am but small fry. If I threaten their plans – well, an unfortunate accident would easily solve the problem."

"They're training you to be one of their puppets...?"

"That, yes. But the hold they think they have on me and the other 101 Heads of State is but a step, I'm sure of that. Their goal? I doubt it would be anything less than to gain supreme control of the world."

"This is so huge. I don't know how I can help..."

"Juanita, I'm at my wit's end. I don't know whom else to turn to. Isn't there anyone you know?"

"Well, when I realized that you were in danger, I contacted one man. Didn't mention your name. Both you and I knew him at Oxford. Bertram Morris. Remember him? Loner. Lecture on Business Ethics. I got to know him quite well. I was for ever writing articles on him hanging upside down from cliffs or off somewhere to some distant place no one ever visited."

"I know. Tall, athletic type. Never saw him with a woman."

"Exactly. He just wrote a book, a best seller. Mentioned the Holy Order of the Snake. Quite exciting! About a fear epidemic. Come to think of it, he might be able to help."

"You were that worried, huh?" he asked. "Thank you, Juanita."

For a long moment, the two held each other's gaze. Then, sensing that he was genuine, Juanita got up to go.

"I have a secret line." Joaquim said quickly and gave her his number. "Please stay in touch. I desperately need your help."

"Won't Esmerelda get upset?"

"It's possible. But it's high time that I stop living lies. I've been living in fear and you're right! I have sunk to the same level as the generals and my so-called 'teacher'. I have to come clean."

"Please be in touch, Juanita," he repeated, "Also anything I can do for you. Perhaps I can supply information for your magazine articles?"

"I have no idea what the *Global Times* will decide after my spate in jail!" Juanita pursed her lips. "I'm not promising anything!"

She strode to the door.

Joaquim watched, unable to stop her without losing her all together. He only hoped she would forgive him and stay where he could reach her.

63. Juanita writes to Bertram

Juanita locked the door, threw the second bolt, and heaved the heavy police lock into place. She flung herself onto the sofa and, heart pounding, just stared into space.

This was so big that it would not sink in. Turn the situation how she would, her thoughts were in a jumble. Finally, her eyes focussed on her desk where, across the top, like broken arms and legs, the jacks of her laptop straggled.

Then she remembered.

With sudden apprehension, she jumped up, ran to her closet. Placing her shoulder beneath the chest of draws she was able to lift it and pull it aside. A sigh of relief. Her laptop was still in the air vent!

"Good!" she thought, took it back to the sofa, plugged in the telephone jack and checked her e-mail.

Most were urgent messages from her work wondering how she had landed herself in jail and concerned that she was missing her deadlines.

She looked up the article she had had ready to send and quickly dispatched it. This would be late. She hoped that they would still go ahead with the series. That way, she could stay on in San Leon near Joaquim.

And yes! There was an e-mail from Bertram, asking for more information and sending her Mary's e-mail address.

Juanita dashed off a note telling him that it looked as if the Heads of State in all 102 dictatorships were being taught to master the *pleasure/pain* and *divide and rule* principles; that there were probably many others also being trained. And Snake was milking them for ways to eliminate all opposition. This would leave just a small bunch of people to contend with in each of the dictatorships. And these were already fully in Snake's power. The carrot was membership in their coveted *Alliance to Rule the World*. Burning question:

"Where did this small bunch of people in the 102 dictators fit into Snake's Plans and how were they going to consolidate their hold on the world?

That was it! They must find out what steps the Snake intended to take both with regard to the 102 dictatorships and beyond. She added something about the urgency of the present situation and asked Bertram to reply by return. Then she sent off the e-mail and copied it to Mary Duffield. There was nothing more she could do—at least not for now.

She closed her eyes.

Yes, she was hurt. Yes, she had never stopped loving Joaquim, even though she had known that eventually they would be separated and might never see each other again. She was not jealous of Esmerelda; she was just disappointed that the man she had respected so could marry out of convenience. But then, what did she expect? Marrying for love was a commodity Heads of State could seldom afford.

64. Antonia In St. Leon

Antonia had enjoyed every exciting moment of her trip from California to San Leon. The flight attendants had treated her like a princess and she had even visited the cockpit. She had told them all about her peace work. The moment they had landed, she knew, San Leon would become a true home away from home.

Today, Mrs. Serazzi had taken her to the market. The Farmer's Market in Santa Cruz was tiny by comparison. At this market in San Leon, you could get anything your heart desired, it seemed. On their way to the section where Mrs. Serazzi was going to buy her materials, Antonia had already seen: food, furniture, pots and pans, shoes and dresses.

Now, Antonia watched in wonder as Mrs. Serazzi's fingertips expertly explored their richly colored textures. The one Antonia liked best was the thin peacock blue silk with yellow, black and a hint here and there of deep wine red. To her, the pure exuberance of the colors and the soft, delicate textures reminded her of the bright laughs of the people in San Leon, which already she had come to love.

Despite the squalor and poverty and the grubby, homeless children that terrorized the streets, there was an aliveness and a gaiety she did not see in the Santa Cruz/ Watsonville area where people lived in the shadow of an economy sliding out of control. The rapid change was frightening the people in the USA. In San Leon, people had got used to the poverty. They were in survival mode and part of their means of surviving was to seek fun and joy among the tatters of their daily struggles.

Yes, she loved San Leon and felt totally at home.

For months, she had counted the days until her trip would begin. As soon as Mary had given her Mrs. Serazzi's invitation, she had enrolled in an advanced Spanish class for native speakers and won a prize—enough pocket money to last her for the summer. And now here she was for the whole long summer with Mrs. Serazzi excelling in her role as mother.

When Antonia was not in class, Mrs. Serazzi took her wherever she went. Antonia felt really grown up.

Mrs. Aliaga de Serazzi was a dressmaker who worked hard for her living. She loved young people but had no children of her own and so took in exchange students once a year.

Today, she had spent several hours carefully selecting materials. Antonia had listened breathlessly as Mrs. Serazzi had commented on the different ones, pointing out the peculiarities of each design and each texture. Yes, Antonia above all loved the colors - they were so bright!

Now Mrs. Aliaga de Serazzi turned to the salesman. The long bargaining stage was about to begin. Coffee was brought. The dealer motioned her to take a seat. This was a time when Mrs. Serazzi had to concentrate. Antonia decided to walk around.

Her nose twitched from the acrid smell of urine and dung. For a moment she was transported back to her vacations back home: The crisp morning air, the first rays of the sun, and the lowing of cattle on the farm where her uncle earned a meager keep for himself and his family, working in Texas for wealthy gentlemen farmers.

Grunting sounds, the plaintive bleating of goats.

"Do you mind if I just look over there?" Antonia asked.

Mrs. Serazzi looked up. "Well, of course, Antonia. Just don't get lost. Let me see the watch I gave you. Okay it is 11 o'clock now. Be back by 11.15. Remember this is not America. It's dangerous to walk around on your own. Just make sure you stay within sight! Stay in the animal section where I can see you."

Right at the end of the animal section where the bushes and brush began, a pen caught Antonia's eye, filled with giant angora rabbits. She meandered over.

Most of the rabbits were huddled in the shade; one was hopping toward the part of the wire which was closest to the bushes. It had red eyes and did not see very well. It rose up onto its back legs and with the tip of its nose moving up down, up down, up down as if in harmony with its heartbeat, it reached up, stretching, until it looked like a giant furry caterpillar. Its nose located a leaf, poking through the iron mesh of the fence.

Delicately, it began to nibble.

Very slowly Antonia inched over and with her index finger gingerly reached through to stroke its nose. Just as she touched it, the rabbit drew back, turned, and hopped away.

"Don't go!" Antonia cried out, trying to coax it back.

"How thoughtless of me!" she chided herself. "I interrupted your lunch."

She looked over. From where she was standing, she could see Mrs. Serazzi sitting. She was reaching into her handbag and pulling out her purse.

She'd better hurry back.

Just then, a hand was thrust over her mouth. Little hands grabbed her arms, her legs, and she was dragged off behind the bushes.

65. Bertram Replies.

From Chicago, Bertram had flown on to Los Angeles. In both places, his talks had been a resounding success. Fifteen large transnational corporations wanted to experiment with all-win think tanks, 25 were joining the U.N.'s Global Compact, and others had invited him to speak. He would have to train a number of professionals to take over some of his work.

Bertram checked his watch and leafed through an *In Flight* magazine. As the engines reached fever pitch, he was eased back in his seat as the plane shot forward. Then, all of a sudden, peace was restored and the plane was in the air. It was a short flight. He was wedged in a window seat, but he must write to Juanita. He eased his lap top up from under the seat, started it up and wrote:

> *Dear Juanita,*
>
> *Relieved that you have your freedom back! Tried to get hold of you, but failed. It is essential that nothing you/we undertake is traced back to specific people who can be easily silenced by Snake.*
>
> *Mary has a possible solution, which she has already suggested to each of her groups. Think tanks and chat groups are starting up and a whole slew of NGOs at the U.N. started implementing it on the same day.*
>
> *The idea: to contrast win/lose and all-win policies by dictators to show up the limitations of Snake. Here there is safety in numbers. Snake can't eradicate a network that embraces the world.*
>
> *Mary has arranged a workshop for a group of our friends. Peaceful conflict resolution, using the all-win principle. I'm on my way there now.*

> *Please let us know of any new developments!! W e can't be sure how much Snake knows, nor how far their influence reaches! We have to assume they know everything we do almost as soon as we act.*
> *Courage and good luck!*
> *Bertram*

He copied it to Mary, ending with a personal note.

> *It looks as if we are on the verge of something colossal. I try not to allow my fears to get the better of me. Mary, am I glad we are in this together! I shall be seeing you shortly but don't know how much time we can spend together after the workshop today. This plane was late leaving and I fly back early this evening.*
>
> *But, after that, we shall all be meeting again in the South of France. Perhaps there we can get even more NGOs involved in your various actions. I hear that the huge conference wing of the Castle will be filled to capacity with representatives from different organizations. And Pim will be there, too. Under the present circumstances, cooperation is where it is at!*
>
> *I hear from Pim that Maurice's brother, Percy, who is organizing the conference with him wants to ban all communications with the outside world for the duration of the conference. 'All the better to focus,' he says. I hope he will make some exceptions so that we can stay in touch with Juanita.*
>
> *Any news from Eliza yet? Since she left on her lecture tour, I haven't heard from her. I had hoped she would change her mind and join us in the South of France.*

66. The 'What If' Shivers

As soon as the door closed behind Juanita, Joaquim knew that whatever it took, he would stop this hellish project. He would use his position as 'student' to gather what information he could.

The next time he met with his teacher, he had had time to reflect.

The 'what-if' games continued for a number of sessions. This time, Joaquim withheld anything that might harm anyone at all. He went into detail about things Snake could not help but already know.

But his teacher gave no new information about *The Alliance to Rule the World*.

Then, just as Joaquim feared his teacher suspected he was no longer motivated, Juanita called his private line.

"Contact's been made. Actions underway. Updates required. I need to see you in person."

At the very next lesson, before he could meet Juanita, his teacher broached his next topic: the *"atmosphere of fear."* Steepled hands supporting his chin, his teacher continued, "This is the fertile environment in which any *divide and rule* policy is rooted. The main thing: keep each part of the population believing that the regime is on their side and they are safe *as long as they cooperate."*

"Isn't that the tactic used by Mao Tse Tung?" Joaquim asked, eager to show he was thinking along, "Once his revolutionary army had succeeded in driving out the Japanese, Mao realized he had millions of wronged and angry peasants whose energies he would have to harness or the country would fall into chaos... "

"Okay, go on!" his teacher prodded.

"First, he made the wealthy land and factory owners the target of wrath. Together with the army and the peasants, he appropriated all their property and exiled the majority of this wealthy upper class and bourgeoisie for "re-education" to labor camps, prison -- or to the grave.

"Then he focussed on the intellectuals, artists and teachers who might question his policies and they, too, suffered the same fate.

"Later it was middle management."

His teacher stirred. Joaquim noticed a smile, snaking around his lips.

"Well?" his teacher suddenly looked up. "Why are you stopping?"

Hurriedly Joaquim continued, "Peasants on the collective farms and factory workers were encouraged to criticize themselves and their coworkers. In the schools, children were encouraged to spy on their parents. No one was safe. A petty disagreement could trigger a denunciation with dire consequences for the accused."

"Brilliant!" His teacher breathed. "Brilliant strategy."

Joaquim felt suddenly sick. The man was enjoying the scene!

With an uncharacteristically wide smile, his teacher said, "At every step, Mao had the support and even adulation of the peasants, the workers and the young." With great relish he added, "And when Mao unleashed the Cultural Revolution no one, not even the peasants or factory workers were safe.

"The art was to do it step by step!" his teacher continued. "No step so large as to generate resistance. Brilliant strategy!" he said with increasing feeling, adding so quietly, that Joaquim wondered whether he had heard correctly, "Even there we were involved!"

Aloud, his teacher said, "So this is an excellent application of the *divide and rule* principle, perfectly suited to decimate a huge population." This time his smile broke through and turned into a mirthless chuckle. "It always works well. Just look at Kukundu. And the whole slew of dictatorships are poised to follow suit.

"In the democracies, there are no outright bloodbaths – yet! But minorities are being targeted and jailed. And because it is being done, small group by small group, a person here, a family there, there has been very little outcry! Again gradual change is the key!

"Now the art is to get rid of the nuisances and to keep sufficient people for a vibrant economy. How would you handle that?"

His teacher asked the question in a conversational tone. Again that chilling neutrality! Joaquim quickly assessed what he was about to say. The scenario he would give was already well known, especially, of course, to the Snake.

"Well, a case in point is what was done in South Africa, where they had three distinct classes. Each was needed for a part of the work to keep the economy functioning. The three groups were the Blacks, the Whites and the Coloreds.

"The Blacks were practically starved. Had to move to the cities to get work. These were often hundreds of miles away from the villages where they lived with their families.

"At night, the cities were inhabited exclusively by the whites, and because the villages where the Black workers lived were so very far away, the Blacks were unable to go back home. They lived in squatter settlements outside of the city limits. Their huts consisted of walls made of scraps of timber with roofs of corrugated iron. Some Blacks even lived in shelters made from plastic garbage bags. For the Blacks, daily life was so hard that no energy remained to rebel. On weekends, the government kept them from relaxing with their loved ones and feeling the joys of a normal life by giving them as much cheap alcoholic beverages as they wished. After a while, many just stayed in the camps and kept their pay packets for drink. The combination of dire poverty and the escape of booze kept most Blacks in their places and the whites in control."

Joaquim wondered how many had actually rebelled. Probably many more than was known on the outside. But no point mentioning his doubts here. He must seem to believe in Snake's tactics.

"Very good, Your Majesty, *Apartheid* means 'separateness,' the very essence of *divide and rule*. Acting against your own conscience creates guilt, and drink is the perfect tool to deaden such unwelcome feelings. And so people live in fear of themselves. The main point: your citizens remain disempowered.

"But how to keep them productive?" His teacher posed the question in a conversational tone, as if he were asking the way, instead of disposing of the lives and well-being of living, sentient beings."

Joaquim decided again not to mention all those South African friends who were deeply involved in trying to change the situation. "Well the Whites had it pretty good, economically at least. Many were acting against their consciences, too. But they were safe. Only condition: don't become too closely involved with 'Coloreds' or 'Blacks'."

"The Coloreds were used to supervise the Blacks and to ensure the economy was productive. Again an 'us against them', a 'divide and rule' situation was used."

"And how were these kept in check?" his teacher asked.

"The original Boers were *illiterate* farmers. Initially, they imported people from Malaysia and other Asian countries that were highly educated and could make up for the shortcomings the Boers had at that time. That is why under *Apartheid*, the Coloreds had a slightly higher status."

"And how were these kept in their place during *Apartheid*?" His teacher insisted.

"They used the element of surprise. For instance, at night police cars patrolled the streets where the Coloreds lived. At random, these would stop at a house and arrest inhabitants.

"One of my friends from Oxford told me how he would lie awake all night. He could detect the soft sound of the tires, creeping along and then stopping. Until the patrol cars had passed, he would be unable to relax and then every nerve would stand on end as he listened to hear which of his neighbors would have disappeared when he got up in the morning. Very soon, he learned he could drink himself to sleep.

"I must say that these tactics weaken the morale and thus must affect the economy," Joaquim added. The words simply slipped out.

"No problem. The art: keep people breeding and cow the young ones from a very young age!" His teacher smiled to himself. "Right to life policies plays into our hands, as long as we ensure that offspring are brought up in an atmosphere of fear."

Joaquim felt queasy.

"Of course, a plan to take over the world requires long-term planning. The Alliance to Rule the World has been going for several centuries and more and more are putty in our hands, pawns of the mass media."

"So to summarize," Joaquim's teacher concluded, "We have the following rules to keep your citizens in line." He tapped the table to the beat of his own words, as if to underline each one.

✓The pleasure/pain prod,

✓Divide and rule, and

✓Terror tactics which involve:

    ✓Maintaining a reign of fear

    ✓Giving every one hope that they will be spared as long as they do your bidding

    ✓Breaking their resistance by using alcohol, the element of surprise, and *terror*.

Joaquim had, of course, suspected the policies applied by his generals, but never before had he seen the full evil spelled out in this way.

Joaquim was plagued with a mix of doubt, fear, and self-chastisement coupled with a grim determination to carry on as student, until he got a handle on the Plan. Playing a role in which he despised himself, even though it was for a good end, divided him against himself and fundamentally weakened him. *Could he keep going* he asked himself, *acting against all he held dear?* His feelings vacillated during each lesson. Still, he had collected information, asked questions and played the avid student, never supplying any information his teacher did not already have.

67. Antonia Is Whisked Away

Antonia screamed. But the sound was muffled by determined little hands. She lashed out with her handbag and kicked at whoever was holding her from behind. No trace of her old shyness. Just angry indignation!

Kicking and struggling, she was dragged into the bushes, gagged and tied up. Her handbag was snatched away and a child, no older than six years, snatched her watch.

To her fury, she saw that she had been assaulted by five boys, one of her own age. The others much younger. The eldest now took out a knife with his left hand and held it to her throat. He looked clumsy. Antonia noticed that his right arm was roughly bandaged and hung limply at his side.

"Stop struggling or I'll kill you!"

Antonia, now completely helpless, still did not feel afraid. Feeling her own anger gave her a sense of power – a totally new experience. It brought out a side of her that she had always suppressed. One that, despite her present circumstances, she actually enjoyed. Unbeknown to her, she was in touch with her own natural power. The gag pinched her mouth, but intent on keeping her wits about her, she focussed on her surroundings.

The boy who was her own age had that hard look she had seen in so many of her brother's friends. They, like these scraggly ragamuffins, lived in gangs.

Because she was feeling her power instead of being afraid, her heart was able to open. This boy's harshness was born of hopelessness and a heart that had never known tender care. Like so many poor children, she'd been brought up in an environment where the adults had given up hope and just lived to survive day by day. Too often, these grown ups made babies to find the loving they themselves had never had; they abandoned their babies when these demanded the care which they craved for themselves.

An order from the eldest kid. And the four younger boys, carefully staying under cover of the bushes, dragged her at a brisk pace into a nearby cave.

After the glare of the hot midday sun, Antonia was suddenly engulfed by cool dry air and semidarkness and dropped like a sack of potatoes.

One of the younger boys lit a candle.

Then she was hoisted up by the four younger ones while the eldest, a small sack slung over his shoulder, led them through a warren of passageways to a safe hiding place.

Here she was once again plunked down as if she were a lifeless object.

The jolt and the cool air cleared Antonia's mind.

She heard the striking of a match. A candle was lit, and, like a specter, the cave emerged out of the pitch dark.

"And now what?" The four boys looked at their leader.

"She's American! We ask for money!" The oldest said matter-of-factly. "If they don't pay, we kill her!"

"But who do we ask?" the youngest inquired.

Antonia noticed the older boy casting round in his mind. "She was carrying a handbag," he said roughly, "Stupid!"

The contents of a small sack were deposited on the ground. Among cash, credit cards, purses, and objects snatched from market stalls lay the watch and the lovely white handbag - gifts from Mrs. Serazzi.

The contents from the handbag were emptied out and a letter with Mrs. Serazzi's address was found. They handed it to the larger boy who again after the merest hesitation said, "This is the address!" To her surprise, Antonia saw that the envelope was upside down.

"Here, you read it!" He motioned with his head and the ten-year old removed her gag.

The boy couldn't read himself!

Antonia realized that if they had her local address, they would use her to collect a ransom, so she only read out the address of the sender. The letter was from Duffield, the United States of America.

He thrust the letter into his pocket, as if what she read was no news to him.

"Come on!" he ordered, "Back to the market. We still have a days work ahead!"

She was once again bound and gagged. With a signal from the older boy, the 5 left.

She was alone in the pitch dark.

Trussed up and gagged, she wiggled into a sitting position. The wall of the cave was smooth and cool.

She considered her situation.

This was one of the kidnappings this country was famous for. They wanted money. Neither Mrs. Serazzi, nor her parents had any to spare. But to them, she looked like a wealthy person in the pretty white frock Mrs. Serazzi had made especially for her and which today she was wearing for the very first time.

A sound!

She strained to see, but it was too dark. She wrinkled her nose. A fetid odor. She had smelt it recently… That was it! The stench of the eldest boy's wound!

"I know who you are; I can smell you!" Antonia said in her perfect Spanish. Suddenly, she felt sad. She had been teased all her life for being poor and had felt that she had no one to turn to. She had also known so many young people like herself who had dropped out of school. They were nowhere near as destitute as these boys were, but they had the same hard expressions. It was a hardness which helped to shield that part that desperately wanted to be loved for what they were from a reality that had nothing worthwhile to offer.

68. Planning The First Step In A Fear Regime

"Congratulations, Joaquim. You stood out as one of the 102 Heads of State and Government because of your extraordinary potential. And you have certainly not disappointed us. To the contrary, you're an exceptional student." His teacher, immaculately dressed in a gray pinstriped suite with delicately tinted pink shirt, gave him a slight nod of approval with a perfunctory smile. Perching himself on his regular easy chair, he continued, consulting his long, slender fingers, "And so we can move on to the next step! You have mastered the golden rule of how to control individuals and groups. "Now for real life applications.

"If you could choose to have someone removed in your country, who would that be?" His teacher pulled out his pad.

Joaquim wondered what could be behind the question. Careful not to hesitate, he replied, "Mendoza, without a doubt!" Mendoza was so powerful; there would be no chance of harming him.

"Okay now we are going to play another 'what if' game. We'll apply the pleasure/fear and divide and rule principles as we devise a plan.

"How would you rid yourself of General Mendoza, if you were sure you could not be caught? Remember, this is only a what-if game. You will never have to carry it out. It's your ability to plan creatively that we are looking to develop. For instance, how could someone else set about doing it for you?"

"*That's an impossible task*," Joaquim thought.

"He doesn't allow people to get close to him, particularly not 'the ordinary man in the street'. He's too afraid of becoming a target. His cruelty is legendary and most people hate and fear him. He has ordered the killing of countless people, usually after gruesome torture and when he can, without people finding out, he will rape women and children who, through his doing, are left without defense. He seems to feel his own power when he is in complete control and surrounded by revulsion.

"But he is not one to take risks. He only attends exclusive events. Here, he wears all his ribbons and is seen as the powerful man that he is. He never exposes himself to the wrath of those he has tormented and bereaved. Parties given for Heads of State, other well-guarded events - those are about the only occasions where he appears in public. I suppose poison in his drink might work. (Joaquim knew that this was a lie, since all his food and drink was personally prepared by his trusted aid who, prior to serving it to him, tasted everything in his master's presence and never let his master's food out of his sight.)

He continued, "You see, it would have to be a slow acting poison that would take effect once he is in bed. His death must seem to be caused by a heart attack. Since the wrath of his personal guards is legend. They are veritable killing machines."

"*The more specific I make the poison, the more difficult it will be,*" Joaquim thought.

His teacher said, "In fact such a poison exists. Not even hard to come by. An excellent plan, Your Majesty. You certainly warrant the trust that we have placed in you so far! My superiors will be delighted." His teacher still perched on the edge of his easy chair, steepled his elegant fingers and announced, "We have finished the first part of our lessons. We're nearing the end of our course."

69. Fear-colored Glasses, All-win Conflict Resolution And General Mendoza

Finally, the day had arrived when Bertram, Mary and her former crew would be back together again with Pim. Together, they would be practicing three sets of skills: removing their fear-colored glasses, all-win conflict resolution and working as a think tank. All except Bertram were assembled in Mary's classroom when he came hurrying up.

"You made it!" Mary beamed.

"Sorry, my plane was late," he said, slightly out of breath and gave her a quick hug.

They took their seats in the circle of chairs, and the buzz of excited conversation died down.

"Great to be together again!" Mary said. "Unfortunately, Maurice is unable to join us. He's at his Castle in the South of France, discussing changes to the Conference Wing to make it completely self-contained."

"You mean we can't go exploring the Castle?" Jan looked disappointed.

"Of course, we can!" Jeff hissed.

"Apparently, they want to concentrate on the conference and don't want people wandering off!" Mary explained.

"Unfortunately, it would have been too risky to wait until Maurice could join us. You see, the *Action to Loosen the Hold of Dictatorships* began with a bang. Everyone started on the same day. The idea was that if there were enough of us, ringleaders would not be able to be singled out and the action would be unstoppable. Now people are dropping out by droves. The problem: there's an art to all-win thinking that's different from other approaches. Our task today is to provide them with some easy-to-use tools.

"Here's the action we launched:" (She pointed to the board.)

> ➢*Describe a situation in a dictatorship first in all-lose (or win/lose) terms and contrast this with your all-win solution.*
> ➢*Then* **on the agreed upon date**
> ➢ *send a copy of your examples to all dictators on the list; and*
> ➢**Send copies to the media.**

If we all begin at the same time, not even Snake will be able to stop the action from taking off, providing enough people participate, and finally,

➢*Invite whoever is interested to join in.*

Bertram could guess how worried Mary was. She was placing the lives of her kids on the line. And now it was too late to back out. Bertram shivered. Their only way of being successful and staying alive was to involve huge numbers of people. Should Snake then decide to liquidate any of them, it would elevate its victims to martyrs and draw unwanted attention to Snake itself. And knowing that Snake wouldn't want to do this was their only refuge.

Mary continued urgently, "We must stop even more from dropping out!"

Bertram looked around the room. How different everyone looked. Pim was dressed in his neat olive green outfit, only now it was complete with tie. The crew of the *Peace Warrior* had also changed. Gone the exotic tans, no more hanging around in various stages of undress. They had become city kids in T-shirts and jeans. Annette's long blond hair was done up neatly in a chignon. Arturo's golden medallion was barely visible around his neck, hidden beneath his T-shirt, with "Chicano Power" displayed on his chest. His arm was thrown protectively around Pat's shoulders. Pat was snuggled up against him, a picture of contentment.

"Pim, thank you for volunteering to teach us the all-win art of Ubuntu!"

"Ubuntu is the ancient African approach to all-win conflict resolution," Pim announced and pulled his chair to one side, changing the circle into a horseshoe so that all could see the board.

"The Ubuntu approach to reconciliation helped to transform the ravages of the Apartheid era, so that South Africa could become a country where Blacks, Coloreds and Whites can explore living together as equals. Put succinctly, Ubuntu acknowledges that all is one. So when one person gets hurt, so does every one else (and in the long run, so does Mother Earth). Ubuntu sets out to rekindle the sense of unity when that has been destroyed. Unity makes reconciliation possible.

"Unity is what it's all about. Once unity is established between the parties, they see and experience one another's views and the conflict is transformed into a mutual search for solutions. Once all the facts and feelings are on the table, solutions tend to emerge.

"Here are the steps Ubuntu prescribes. He walked over to the board, and wrote:

➢ Get all the *facts* on the table;
➢ Allow each to fully describe her or his *experiences* so that all parties can *feel* what each of the others went through and what prompted their actions;
➢ *Continue to share all facts and feelings, until there is nothing more to say*;
➢ Then, when the whole picture has been clarified, a*nswers tend to surface*, and *resolution can take place*;
➢ Finally, allow an agreement to emerge which will keep the all-win solution in place,

There was silence.

Bertram commented, "It is very close to how Josette described the process during our hook-up in Costa Rica. Are these the steps we take as a think tank for all-win conflict resolution?"

"Quite right," Pim agreed, "but groups are getting stuck on the second step: how to empathize with people you don't know and you probably don't like – in other words, how to experience another's point of view from the heart without *pre*judging them."

Pim brushed the chalk off his hands, walked back toward the group and stood looking down at them.

"In the past, conflict resolution has involved a *rational* examination of motivations. But the *experiential* understanding is to many of us the most challenging aspect and so it tends to get neglected. Result? There can be no meeting of the hearts and without empathy, parties feel misunderstood or judged, the win/lose situation is perpetuated, and reconciliation is blocked.

"Both rational and experiential aspects are equally important, but I suggest that we first focus on how to *experience* another's point of view, because heart and empathy are central to the all-win approach."

He pulled up his chair and sat down.

Jeff blurted out, "But why are feelings so important?"

"Feelings and emotions are an integral part of every relationship," Pim pointed out, "Let's look at the phases of an ordinary communication, taking the following example:

A person says something to me. For instance, *'Hey, come over here.'*

1. The sound vibrations hit my eardrums, the light waves hit the retina of my eye, and an image appears in my mind.

2. If I associate this image with something potentially *painful* (the man has a menacing tone, he looks sinister and is pointing a pistol at me) I

will feel an unpleasant feeling (discomfort, fear – for short I shall call it *pain)*. If he is smiling, and I see it is a good friend who has a twinkle in his eye, then I will feel a rush of *pleasure. Pleasure and pain are emotions and constitute the experiential level.*

3. And *these emotions determine my actions.* If I feel pleasure, I will welcome the situation and possibly cling to it so that it will last a long time. If I feel pain, I will try to make my escape or somehow keep the experience at bay.

"So the reason the feelings or emotions (as I prefer to call them[58]) are so important is that these determine my behavior. *Our emotions are the strong motivating force behind what we do. They tend to yank us around.* And if we are not sure of either what we are feeling, or what moves the other, then we are unable to understand *why* a person acts in a certain way and are unable to empathize with her or him. Without empathy, there's no heart and no all-win relationship.

"At the same time, if in a conflict, we feel only our own pleasure and pain, it is as if the other parties don't have feelings, that they are '*its, objects, things* that don't count', and so we also have a win/lose situation.

"Conflicts tend to keep going until all feel empathy from all others.

"So, to bring a conflict (or a win/lose situation) to an all-win conclusion, it is essential to *experience* what each side is feeling, *as accurately as possible.*

And that involves two steps:

1. take off your emotion-tinged glasses; and

2. experience the situation from their point of view."

"I don't have emotionally tinged glasses!" Jan pulled a face.

"Most of us do," Pim answered gravely, "but many of us are not aware we are looking at reality through a whole host of emotions."

"But how come we have all these emotions and not feel them?" Pat frowned.

"Especially when we are young our survival depends largely on others, our families, peers, teachers. These are constantly pressuring us to feel and act in specific ways: to be good, to be quiet, to be strong. And so in order to be "in" with a social group (parents, fellow students, teachers, later our bosses) we learn to feel (and therefore act) in specific ways. If I am in a gang, then acting tough might be the thing to do. If I am a young girl, I might be encouraged to smile all the time and be *nice.* We get so used to these patterns of feeling and behavior, we forget they are there.

"And so they become more or less fixed emotions and unconsciously influence our behavior!" Bertram said.

Pim explained, "You can envision it, as follows: Our unconscious emotions are like the background music in a film. Sometimes we are barely conscious we are hearing it. Yet the music provides an atmosphere and determines how we react. For instance in a film, there may be a scene of an empty room, but the ominous music in the background gives us an impression that a crime is about to happen. And so, we sit on the edge of our chairs, or tense up, even though there is no other trace, except the atmosphere created by the music, of anything bad to come.

"In the same way, the background *feel* of emotions in our lives tells us how to interpret things. If we are used to being *nice* we shall constantly feel the desire to pacify. In the same way, some of us are always feeling 'ripped off', others vengeful, others eager to achieve. These are the emotion-colored glasses with which we each individually meet our lives.

"So in conflict resolution, we must first take off our own emotionally tinged glasses, before we can empathize with others, or can *feel what they are experiencing.*[59]

Suddenly Bertram realized the full meaning of what Pim was saying. "Pim, are these connected to the orange-tinted glasses, you were going to teach us to remove?!" he exclaimed.

"Exactly!" Pim beamed. "Our orange and fear-tinted glasses make up a part of this emotional screen through which we view reality."

"Can you give us some idea how to uncover these feelings, fear and all?"[60] Bertram asked.

Pim replied, "We can free ourselves permanently from the distortions of our emotion colored glasses. It requires that we develop an ongoing awareness of when and how they are operating as a screen—a special mental capacity which is constantly aware of what is going on inside and outside of us at the same time. This takes considerable psychological insight and self-knowing[61].

"It is also possible to remove their influence temporarily using various forms of meditation, or the tools I wish to teach you today. Here, the secret lies in our muscles!" Pim explained.

"That's where our emotions nestle. When we are gripped by an emotion, we tense a certain combination of muscles. This changes our form slightly and this form resonates with similar forms in the *morphogenetic field*. When we relax deeply, our posture changes again and our emotions lose their hold.

"If I imagine that my body has the shape of another person, I am able to tap into her or his *morphogenetic field*. I am, as it were, creeping into her or his skin and am able to experience what life feels like from within their experience.[62] "

"Adopting the *form* of another person, does that help us enter their *inform*ation field, or morphogenetic field and therefore see the world through the fields which contain all their storehouse of information?" Takeshi asked.

"Well seen!" Pim beamed. "That is precisely how it works!"

"I still don't understand!" Jan sounded indignant.

"Right you are, Jan," Pim smiled, "Enough talk. These things can only be understood by doing. Let's practice working together as an all-win think tank. Does anyone have a problem that urgently needs solving?"

"I had a letter from a friend," Bertram hurried to volunteer, "She described a dictator she knew. His name is General Mendoza."

Bertram rummaged in his bag and pulled out an e-mail from Juanita. It was accompanied by a summary of what Joaquim had learned from his "teacher".

Bertram read,

> General Mendoza is so cruel and tyrannical that, sooner or later, he is bound to come to a nasty end, -- assassination, execution or, at best, life imprisonment.

"Good example, Bertram!" Mary exclaimed, recognizing his source. "This would be a good example to send around the network as well as to all the dictators on our list. By the way, I was reading a newspaper article this morning in which this general was described. He is one of the generals who wields the scepter in San Leon."

She rummaged in her bag and pulled out a paper. "Here, this is what he looks like."

As the paper went from hand to hand, Bertram continued:

> General Mendoza is in a position of supreme power in his own nation. He feels a strong need to make his power felt. He enjoys inflicting pain. He enjoys watching his underlings rape helpless women and children and when he thinks no one will find out he does so himself. He is known for his uproarious belly laugh whenever anyone is maimed. Yet fear seems to act on him like a red rag.
>
> Is there any possible all-win solution for a General Mendoza?

"This is a man you probably would want to avoid," Pim remarked, "That makes it a perfect challenge to learn how the process works. Now look carefully at his photo so that you can imagine his posture and better creep into his skin."

"Okay, Mary! Over to you!" Pim said. "Time to learn to relax."

Mary got up. "Any form of relaxation will do whereby we remain fully alert," she began, "Meditation is very effective, but today, let's try some stretching to get the kinks out of our muscles. So, let's move our chairs to the sides of the room…"

"Now, reach up as far as you can. Good! Stretch each of your fingers out, your elbows, your shoulders. Come on, see how high you can reach and every time you breathe out, allow your reach to extend just a fraction more. Then maintain the stretch as you breathe in!" She went on focussing on each part of the body.

As Bertram stretched his head up, he felt the back of his neck relax. "*I never knew I was carrying all that tension,*" he thought. As he began stretching his waist, his sides, his knees, his ankles, he felt them tingle with renewed life.

"And now come up on your toes so that all your toes are stretched against the floor."

Bertram tried not to topple.

"And now … let yourself flop forward onto your haunches and scrunch up into a little ball!" Mary called. "Hug your knees, clench your fists, close your eyes tightly. And now all of a sudden relax each of these muscles!"

And so she guided them through all sorts of movements, aimed at alternately stretching and contracting every muscle. Finally, she allowed them to sink down onto their chairs with sighs and groans of pleasure that they were finally allowed to relax.

Pim had put on soothing music, barely audible in the background. Bertram was too relaxed to want to place it. *It could be Mozart …*he mused.

"Okay," Pim took over. "Now you are relaxed and have let go of your own muscle tensions, your screen of habitual emotions is less dense. Imagine you are General Mendoza. *Feel* you are he."

Bertram imagined himself in the form of this bull of a man. Tall, haughty and domineering.

In the meantime, Pim was looking at Bertram's e-mail, and adlibbed.

> *You are in a position of supreme power in your own nation. You feel a strong need to make your power felt by inflicting pain. You enjoy intimidating people and watching helpless women and even children being brutalized and raped by your underlings. Seeing fear in people's eyes triggers even greater acts of sadism.*

"What does it feel like to be inside this person?" Pim asked and gave them time to determine what they were experiencing.

From his relaxed state, Bertram was easily able to experience General Mendoza without condemnation. In fact, without being yanked around by any of emotion at all. He knew what his emotion was telling him to do but it had no hold over him.

"Just *feel* what it's like," Pim spoke quietly and persuasively. "Now, as General Mendoza, imagine that, as their dictator, you are moving around among your people.

"How do you feel about them? What does it feel like to have the power of life and death over a whole nation and to make your power felt?"

Bertram felt a rush of pleasure and excitement at his supreme power.

"Now, how, as General Mendoza do you feel about *yourself*?"

Bertram changed his focus from being far bigger and stronger than other people -- a sort of puppeteer -- to himself as a person in relation to others. Suddenly, as General Mendoza, he no longer felt powerful. He felt totally alone and ill at ease.

"Now feel what it is like to want to maim helpless women and children."

Bertram realized that, as General Mendoza, he was angry, terribly angry at being so alone and without any real comfort and ...*impotent!* What was that impotence about?

Yes, ...he lacked the capacity to reach out to get the nurturing he needed. Seeing people happy only intensified his loneliness and he would punish them for that!

Suddenly, he felt a rush of sexual energy. He was so taken aback that he lost his ability to concentrate.

"Now see, not anger, but fear in the eyes of those you are hurting!" Pim continued. But Bertram was unable to continue. He was no longer relaxed.

"See what other feelings you can pinpoint and when nothing else comes, write down what you've experienced."

He waited.

"So what did you come up with?" Pim asked when every one had stopped writing.

"At first I felt all powerful when I saw myself as dictator, but when I got into his feelings, I felt so very small and lonely," Sharifa said.

"Me, too," said Ian in his Scottish accent, "Also afraid and angry."

"Yes, that's what I felt!" Arturo agreed, "As if every one was having a good time except for me! And I really wanted to hurt other people to get back at them. 'Cause every time anyone was happy, it reminded me of how miserable I was. And it hurt to feel this way."

"And what happened when you saw, instead of anger, fear in the eyes of those you were hurting?"

Arturo said, "I loved the feeling of having so much control over other people!"

"Strange," Sharifa said hesitantly, "I actually felt fear when I saw fear in the eyes of other people... I'm trying to pinpoint where that's coming from... Yes, when I feel alone and isolated, I get afraid. Almost as if I'm still a little kid wanting to be taken care of and yet scared of letting people in close, scared of being bullied. Seeing fear in the eyes of other people makes me remember my own weakness. And any sign of weakness in my present position could be the end if me!" She looked up triumphantly. "Yes, that feels right!"

"Well, that seems to give us a good idea of where he's coming from! It's very likely that he felt a mixture of both fear and anger," Pim said.

Annette laughed outright. "One thing I did not understand! I got this surge of sexual energy!"

"So did I!" exclaimed Bertram, "Almost as if I wanted to rape people to feel my power over them and at the same time to really hurt them, change them from a person into an 'it', an object that is without...without value or feelings!" The words were out before he knew it and suddenly it all made sense. No wonder men raped people in scary war situations! It was a terrifying compulsion to feel powerful at all costs when, in fact, these soldiers felt just the reverse. And what better way to feel powerful than to plant your seed even in the womb of those who hated and resisted you. It was a way of procreating in the face of overwhelming danger.

"This General is responsible for the deaths of thousands of people!" Bertram added. "How can there be any all-win solution?"

"How to bring about reconciliation and at the same time keep society safe?" Pim rephrased his question.

"Let's creep into the skin of the San Leoni people."

The group then each undertook the process again. This time they took the place of those who had been abused. Coming from that perspective, many agreed that only the death penalty could make the world safe from sadists like General Mendoza.

"No way you can risk letting him roam around free," Annette said, "but, when as General Mendoza I was feeling so alone, I realized that I, -- me, *Annette*-- have felt the same way. I, too, would get jealous of people who were having fun. Of course, I wasn't in a position to kill them, but every now and again, particularly when I was a child, I would say, '*I wish so and so were dead!*' Perhaps, we can give him life imprisonment and try some rehabilitation to improve the quality of his life. I feel sorry for him now. And the fact that he has become such a monster only shows me how much pain he must feel."

There were nods of agreement.

Hugh agreed, "I must say, I don't loathe him as much as when we first started out. I feel more compassion, although I can't condone what he does."

"So you see," Pim said, "by imagining we are in the shoes of another person, we can feel what they feel and that often means feeling their pain. At the same time, because we are one with the person, the unity between us is restored. And that is why we feel more compassionate toward him than before we started.

"So to summarize: To drop our emotional bias, and take off our fear-colored glasses, we must

1.   deeply relax or meditate until our personal emotions lose their hold; and,

2.   when we experience life through the eyes of another, have the courage to face whatever comes our way.

"This is a way to get from revulsion to empathy."

There was a buzz of conversation, as everyone wanted to share at once. For a few hours, they practiced other cases. This time they added the two other steps: getting all facts on the table and talking the issue through until an all-win approach emerged.

Then Pim summed up: "I'll write up the steps of the Ubuntu approach and illustrate them with the examples we have come up with. Then we can send them around. That way, those who dropped out of the *Action to Loosen the Hold of Dictatorships* may want to rejoin it.

"I sense you are not altogether satisfied with the prison sentence that we have bestowed on General Mendoza," Pim observed. He consulted his watch. "But I have to leave now to catch my plane." As he spoke, he picked up his briefcase and with a "See you all again in the South of France!" he waved and hurried away.

70. Back Home

Back home, Mary was delighted with what they had achieved. But she, too, was not wholly satisfied with the life-long jail sentence they were suggesting for General Mendoza. So when she passed Pim's summary of the process around via the hook-ups and mail, she added a request for other ideas for an all-win solution.

Then one day, she received a letter from a Spiritual Foundation. It was written by a group of prisoners.

It was marked with the name of a prison and some long number. She read:

> *We are white collar-felons, mostly incarcerated for violent crimes, who, after years behind bars, have been transferred to a low-level security facility where we have extra privileges. Some of us are taking classes. A few are even studying law.*
>
> *Together, we are taking a course offered by the Spiritual Foundation, where we learn to quiet our thoughts, locate our inner strength and empathize with others. The Spiritual Foundation presented us with the case of General Mendoza. Many of us feel a kinship with him. Here's our solution. Feel free to pass it around. Could someone forward this letter to him?*

> *Dear General,*
>
> *We are all offenders living behind bars. We have each been in a position to harm and be harmed by others. We have much in common with you.*
>
> *We started paying for our deeds while we were on the outside because we lived in constant fear for our lives. We were always watching our backs and wondering when our luck would run out. The more people we harmed, the more hated us and the more we were hounded down until now, we are all serving life-long prison sentences.*
>
> *You are being watched by the whole world. Amnesty International, global justice movements, powerful civic groups, and the International Criminal Court are out to bring you to justice.*
>
> *And yet, we can not condemn you. We have too much in common.*
>
> *As think tank, we were unable to find a solution that you would really relish. We came up with the following meager thought:*
>
> *When one day you land in jail (if you are not first assassinated), there is a project, in the United States where old buffalo herds are being taken care of by the most hardened criminals.[63]*
>
> *Each prisoner has one buffalo in his care.*
>
> *There is something that happens when you have power over life and death of a huge, powerful, dangerous beast, which has been too inbred, is too old and sick to take care of itself; and which depends for its survival on you. The first inkling of what it is like to be appreciated and cared for by a fellow creature is necessary before you can benefit from courses like those offered by the Spiritual Foundation. The feeling of caring makes life worthwhile. Ironically, most of us did not discover this until we ended up in jail.*
>
> *General, sir, we hope that you, too, will discover caring some day.*
>
> *Friends of the Spiritual Foundation.*

Next time she was in San Francisco, she sent copies of the letter, beside to General Mendoza, to all participating organizations, adding, "At least, this is better than just languishing in jail, learning to be a better criminal."

She also sent a copy to the All-Win Network web site. This listed all-win solutions to a gamut of global problems for everyone who so wished to consult and apply. It also listed organizations, think tanks and individual people who used the all-win principle so that all could network, build on one another's work and, in so doing, form the building blocks for a sustainable all-win world.

71. The Fear Barometer

The three cousins sat in their grassy enclave, overlooking the sea.

"It sounds, from your reports, as if fairly soon we can call a Meeting of the Whole?" the bald one inquired.

The man with the purple birthmark reached over and poured himself a vodka orange.

"If you don't mind," he replied, "I should like extra time to complete my human incubator experiment. We want to milk Maurice's crowd for all the information we can get, while they are at our mercy in the South of France. Then, we shall be totally ready to begin our Final Phase," he added with a gleeful smile."

"Chateaux des Miracles! Where our ancestors used to do their disappearing act!" The bald one reminisced, "I've never been sure whether to put it down to legend or whether there was some intricate rabbit warren of tunnels that we were never able to discover!"

"Quite," the man with the purple birthmark smiled, "but the reconstruction effort is complete. The wing has been sealed off, so that no one, *no one at all,* can escape. Only a couple of secret panels lead to the rest of the Castle. They will only know of one outside entrance, which can easily be blown away. No computers, no phones, no communications with the outside world. Of course, no one knows who I am. But I shall have everyone where we want them neatly telling me about themselves, how their organizations work and what they plan…" Suddenly he laughed. "Just give me a little more time!

"And this time it will not matter at all that they know me by sight!" he chuckled.

"Just one small hitch," his youngest cousin steepled his hands, "It seems there has been a leak… Nothing to worry about," he hurried to reassure his cousins, as each looked at him sharply. "Just a childish letter-writing campaign contrasting our divide and rule principle with some preposterous, so-called *all-win* approach. Too infantile for words, of course. But disturbing, only because it indicates that someone has been talking...It's connected to the All-Win Network. Nothing we can do about it now. It has already spread."

"A leak?" the bald one asked sternly, "Anyone you suspect?" he asked, a note of uncanny calm creeping into his voice.

"I can't think who would dare!" his youngest cousin hurried to reassure him. "Perhaps, it's just a coincidence. They're all too intent on being part of our Alliance. Not one would dare to jeopardize that!"

"I'd expected it to cost much more money than the amounts you have withdrawn so far!" his cousin with the purple birthmark eyed him suspiciously. "Are you sure you can count on their loyalty?"

"Yes, the Alliance to Rule the World is proving an inexpensive tool," his cousin forced himself to smile. "Once they have committed to our course, there's no turning back. Of course, the lure of power once they have proved themselves to us is the first trap. Once they have committed murder, it will be even harder to escape. By that time, they will realize the vast extent of our reach, that everything they have done has been documented and that the penalty of escape is a swift death or *worse*. Finally, of course, each will wear their own form of signet ring—*Perhaps Maurice knows more than he's telling*!?" he interrupted himself, anxious to change the subject.

"He's becoming too independent!" The bald-headed one agreed, turning to the cousin with the birthmark, "Get Slug to give him a work-over. They have never met face to face and Maurice won't suspect us!" he ordered.

"Right you are!" The cousin with the purple birthmark assuaged him, " I'll see Slug is instructed exactly what information to extract from my soft-hearted brother before the conference begins!"

The bald man pulled out two tiny boxes and passed one to each of his cousins. "This will be part of the signet ring," he announced.

Inside each box was a speck carefully mounted on a piece of plastic.

"It's no bigger than a pin head!" the youngest cousin exclaimed. Both cousins looked up with admiration. "This is much better than we dared to hope," breathed the Einstein look-alike.

"Not for nothing has our dynasty been synonymous with the weapon's industry for centuries!" their leader said not without a touch of pride. "This serves a number of purposes which now for the first time can be combined in such a tiny pin head. It is a tracking device that lets us know exactly where each of our stooges is; it can be used as a tiny bug; and...."

"You mean we can listen in to anything they are saying from a distance?" his youngest cousin inquired.

"Exactly. Then it can be made to emit different types of waves. These waves can change their moods: relax them, send them to sleep, even produce coma, or make them anxious. And so we control what they feel. Finally, it can be detonated from a distance. So they can be vaporized whenever necessary."

"But being a ring, it can always be removed…" the Einstein look-alike pondered.

"They won't remove it. If they attempt to do so, it will detonate automatically. You see, each will, by then, know beyond a shadow of a doubt that they can never leave the Alliance alive. That will be made clear when the time comes. I shall watch each on a one way-video screen, as they put on their signet rings; and be in contact with our supervising stooge by earphone as they do so.

"Finally, our last Phase comes into view." The oldest cousin clapped his hands and while his butler appeared with refreshments, the three cousins relaxed without speaking.

The bald cousin stared dreamily out to sea. In his mind's eye, he imagined the spate of murders that would initiate the Final Phase—a spate of murders, carefully selected, planned, and carried out by all those leaders which sought access to the Alliance. This included leaders in finance and industry and other areas too, plenty in each country of the world, and then—the lapdogs.

The lapdogs were gradually being whittled down to the minimum number of strong rulers required. Some were Heads of State, others longstanding bureaucrats that survived changes in government, and in the more democratic countries their lapdogs included key opposition leaders. Each would commit a murder as proof of both their loyalty and of their ability to act without fear. In exchange, they would achieve Membership of the coveted Alliance to Rule the World.

"*Lifetime membership,*" the bald cousin emphasized to himself, "*whether they like it or not!*" These murders, carefully documented and signed by each of the Members would eliminate some parts of their opposition, which were at present hampering their ability to rule their personal domains. These murders would also serve as a guarantee that when necessary, they would do Snake's bidding, "on pain of death". Of course, none knew they were in any way connected to the Holy Order of the Snake! But this spate of murders all taking place within the space of two weeks would be but a warm up to the panic phase that would follow.

With a nod, he dismissed his butler as he finished pouring the drinks.

When the butler had disappeared through the hedge, the bald man said, "Okay, the Simultaneous Launch. Objective: to breed panic and whip that up to a fever pitch. Means: to sow fear, uncertainty and doubt, using computer hackers and the newest generation of vaporizing bombs which have only just been developed and for which there are no effective screens! I want to stress it is panic and only panic that we're after!

"The list I sent each of you—the one with our young hackers." He waited until his cousins had taken them out of their folders. "I had mentioned that these could be trusted. I should add that these are all our own flesh and blood from various branches of the family; each has been suckled on a careful diet of family philosophy and are experts at applying the *divide and rule* principle; and each has been carefully checked out.

"Have you been able to study the computer systems each has already broken into?"

His younger cousins nodded.

"Good. So which actions can we best launch simultaneously to sow most panic?"

The Einstein look-alike began, "I must say I was impressed by the brilliance of our young hackers. A number had broken into the top-secret circuits of the Pentagon.

"In broad lines, it strikes me that to sow most fear, uncertainty and doubt, we must target whole systems and hit people and organizations in their pocket books and in their ability to communicate.

"There's a computer network, a bit like a mini Internet through which banks communicate internationally. This is the line through which monies, often huge sums, are transferred. There are, of course, also the computer networks which link people's accounts within the banks themselves. Breaking into these banking circuits has proved for most of our brilliant relatives like chickenfeed by comparison to Pentagon type establishments. All that is needed is to cast doubt on the accuracy of the data transferred.

"Together with a small select group, I am in the final phase of my research into which combination of actions would cast most doubt on the computer networks which connect banks internationally and at the same time affect the savings of the man in the street."

"A number of well publicized financial losses should do the trick. These should fire the imagination of the herds and indicate that all savings —and all banks—are being targeted and that none are exempt from data corruption and breaking and entering. The resulting panic will snowball, if simultaneously the computer systems connecting the Stock Markets of the world are also shown to have been corrupted.

"The flames of panic must be fuelled. And this is where our stooges in the media come in with sensational conjecture, which is repeated over and over again. The most useful stooges to use in this case are those who are nestled in key positions in the world's largest media conglomerates. I have already secured their cooperation."

"Excellent!" his elder cousin commented. "This could cause an attempted rush on the banks, instability on the major markets, and people would find that all systems would be shut down for checking and major overhauls. People would be prevented from access to their accounts, distrust would spiral and vital transactions would be stalled. Large numbers of transactions would collapse. Why! Businesses might even be afraid to use the Internet itself for fear that their correspondence would be corrupted. It's the corruption of data that totally invalidates all money transactions and all other communications by computer.

"A perfect tool to sow panic!" his younger cousin agreed.

He continued, "I was thinking much along the same lines: hit whole systems, fan the flames of fear, uncertainty and doubt, and seem to substantiate wild claims by means of a few spectacular calamities.

"My plan would compound your over all effect," he smiled at his cousin and continued, "My plan would strike major traffic nodes and busy city centers. I would combine a corruption of computer data with a spate of bomb scares, one on top of the other, and a few well-placed explosions targeting large concentrations of people. These would include: major international airport hubs, where huge numbers of international air passengers change planes; large train stations and bus depots and city centers of the most densely packed cities—these particularly in poor countries which are less vulnerable to failures of modern technology. I have this plan worked out to the point where I have decided who would be involved in carrying out each action.

"We'd only have to combine ongoing warnings of bomb scare after bomb scare via the media with a few huge, well publicized vaporizings..."

His eldest cousin interjected, "The beauty of this new generation of weapons is that we can target within a few yards the area to be hit, say one square mile precisely. And anyone just on the edge of that area would remain unscathed to report, with colorful pathos, the full magnitude of the calamity."

He continued, "Of course, here too, full-blown reporting, burgeoning conjecture, constantly hammering in how random the actions are and how all inclusive the scale of these disasters—all this combined with long lists of bomb scares and all the other simultaneous emergencies...*marvelous!*" he gloated.

As the bald cousin paused, his youngest cousin, who had been contemplating his nails, went on, "If people doubted the computer system in airports, used by traffic control, then all airport activity would cease. This, together with you targeting the banking and stock market systems would bring much of business to a halt. First the airlines would be affected, and then all businesses teetering on the verge of bankruptcy would be pushed over the edge. And the specter of a global economic crash would loom large in people's imaginations. And all the time the media will be fanning the flames of panic. Soon the panic, like a firestorm, will be feeding off itself..." For a moment, all three contemplated the gratifying scenario, oblivious of their spectacularly beautiful surroundings and the sea still winking at them.

The eldest cousin roused himself and completed his vision, "Then, at precisely the right moment, a network of people who have been known in finance, industry and government speak out. They each have plans that reassure the herd that they can solve the situation. Their programs are well thought out and promise people security above all and a number of other things they yearn for.

"Oh the relief they will feel!" he smiled, "They will be clamoring for these strong leaders to take over! And no one realizes that they are nothing but new and old puppets of ours, whose strings are pulled by (and he made the sign of the Snake in the air, thereby emphasizing his words and ending the conversation).

As he did so, he rose. His cousins followed suit and each, in turn, brushed his ring with a kiss.

The bald gentleman gave a signal. A helicopter engine burst into life and a moment later the machine appeared over the fence. For a moment, it poised in the air like a bird of prey about to swoop and then gently descended onto the lawn.

"Thank you!" the bald-headed man bowed to his companions. "It's hard to believe that the Final Phase is now clearly in sight."

The two elderly gentlemen walked briskly across the grass and, totally belying their age, agilely hopped on board of the craft.

Swiftly, the helicopter took off.

72. Pedro's Wound

"You're hurt," Antonia said, "Your arm is terribly infected. You might lose it if you don't take care. You need to clean it out and take tablets to cure the infection.

The sound of a match. A boy loomed over her.

"What do you know?" he asked huskily. He lit a candle and the light created a dance of grotesque shapes on the walls of the cave.

"I had an infection once and that is how they cured it."

"Well, how do I get hold of disinfectant and pills?"

"There's not much I can do while you keep me here. But you need to go to a doctor and he will prescribe what you need."

"A doctor! Pah!" The boy spat on the ground, "What do you think adults do when we fall into their hands?"

"Beat you?"

"They kill us and sell our organs. Why do you think we always go around in groups? Every one hates us. Some see us as thieves, others as a pest. But those who hunt us down, they're worst of all. They kill us, sell our eyes, hearts and other organs on the black market to the Wealthy Countries. These men become filthy rich."

Antonia searched the boy's face to see whether he was mocking her, but he was serious.

He's desperate, Antonia realized. Of course, with only one arm, he can't defend his position as leader for long. He will become a liability to the gang. Without an arm, they will banish him. Hampered by one arm, he'd be too much of a liability. And how long could he survive alone? This might be her way out...

"Well, I can't help you unless you set me free!" Antonia said with finality.

The boy looked at her speculatively. "I can kill you, if you refuse to help!"

"What good would that be? You would be no better than those adults that cut you up to sell your organs. Anyhow, what good would I be to you dead? There's nothing you have to gain by keeping me here. You might as well let me go."

"We can get money for you!"

"And how do you propose to do that? You can't even read. And, anyway, I don't come from this country!"

"Well, if you refuse to help me, we can leave you here to die."

"Then neither of us would be any better off."

He looked at her, his lips pressed together into two pale strips, warning her he was about to explode.

"I tell you what," Antonia said gently, "If you take me to a phone, I shall arrange pills and disinfectant for you if you promise to set me free!"

"Ha! You make a phone call, I set you free and we never see the pills!"

They had come to an impasse.

"Okay, you let me make a phone call. I'll see what I can arrange, and when you have the pills, disinfectant and the bandages, you let me go. Promise?"

Antonia saw his mind working.

"Well, you make the phone call and then we'll see."

Antonia realized that, for now, that was the most she could achieve.

"Do you have a place which you can use as a drop off point? One which you can oversee? That way, you have nothing to fear." She was surprised to hear herself make the offer. But she would never be able to live with herself if she got these boys into trouble. They had so little to live for, as it was.

Pedro looked at her quizzically. He could barely believe she was serious. Here she was thinking of his well-being, not just her own. He gave Antonia a description, which was clear enough for Mrs. Serazzi to find. Antonia was thinking clearly now. Together, they worked out the details.

Waiting for dark and the return of the others, Pedro (that was the 15-year-old's name) was clearly in pain. The outside heat, he said, made the throbbing unbearable.

She asked him about his life.

He had left his mother's care when he was 6 years old. His mother was a prostitute who worked the side of the road. Even though he had never known a secure family life, his mother had always been warm and loving to him, defending him from her rough visitors. Whenever his mother had a customer, Pedro was removed from the bed. One day, he heard terrible screams. His mother was lying on the floor. A man, face contorted with fury, was beating her. When he peeked around the door, she was lying quite still. She didn't seem to be breathing. The man turned on him. Terrified, Pedro had fled for his life. As he ran down the stairs, a furious neighbor had kicked him down the last flight. "Out you go and your filthy mother with you!" It had been a miracle that he had not broken a limb.

He ran away as fast as he could. A day later, he had heard that his mother was dead.

There was no home, no warmth, nowhere for this kid to go. Antonia felt her throat choke up. She didn't dare to show her feelings. The pain this kid carried around with him was so great that he could not afford to feel it. Pity, sympathy, even empathy would only cut into the quick and weaken him. To cope, she realized, he could only afford to feel aggression. To him, aggression was survival.

He had been found by a leader of one of the local gangs.

"They're always looking for new members. They know where you're at. Most of them have been on the streets since they were really young. They've all been through the same."

So Pedro had survived, as one of the youngest members of a gang. First, he had served as their decoy, and later, a pickpocket, always grateful for any scraps he was given. Finally, he had managed to gather a small gang of his own. He left the larger group.

Antonia sensed that, wounded as he was, his authority was about to be challenged.

She told Pedro how kids in other countries lived, about those in India who, from the age of 5, carried boxes almost the same weight as they, themselves. She told how in the area of the States where she lived, many came from broken homes and, like Pedro himself, ended up in gangs.

As she spoke, she thought of the All-Win Education Centers. Not wanting to give him false hope, she focussed only on those parts of her world, which he could relate to.

When evening came, the others returned and the spoils were examined and divided up. Among the spoils were scraps of food which, with Antonia being given a fair share, they greedily devoured.

"What are we going to do with her?" the ten year-old asked. Already the air of deference had eroded. Antonia sensed he could be the first to challenge Pedro's authority.

"She's okay. Just leave her to me.

"Come! I need your help."

Her heart soared and immediately she felt anxious, as she realized that she was going to be on the outside with a gang of very young street children. Would she be tempted to escape, she wondered. No! She would keep her promise to Pedro!

73. Joaquim At The Crossroads

A few lessons later, Joaquim had completed his two plans: one to have Mendoza eliminated and the other outlining what his approach would be to ruling San Leon. As the next lesson began, his teacher perched himself as usual on the edge of the easy chair, opened his briefcase, removed his usual leather-covered pad and slender golden pencil, but this time he also fished something else out of his bag: it was a leather-bound folder, secured with a small golden padlock.

"You have made great progress, Your Majesty," he began, as, searching in his wallet, he located a tiny golden key, undid the lock and carefully opened the case.

"Here are 'final solutions' thought up by other mostly Heads of State and Government to rid themselves of their opposition. See what you think!"

Joaquim held his breath as his teacher read through the whole list: Everything from laser-guided bombs to bacterial warfare, shooting someone during a hunting trip, slow poisoning, blowing someone up while asleep in bed, stabbing him with a razor-sharp icicle, and pushing someone off a cliff at the spot where she - it was a she-- would regularly watch the sunset.

"Just over one hundred plans in all," his teacher said with a smile of satisfaction. You belong to the group, consisting of our world's elite. Of course, we have many other groups of future world rulers, not just Heads of State. And these other groups have lists of their own. Everyone who wants to join the Alliance to Rule the World must go through a trial of fire, whatever their background and status.

Joaquim was shocked. *The sheer scale of their planning!*

"Well?" His teacher pressed, "What do you think?"

Joaquim was at a loss for words. Intuitively, he knew that they were now nearing the point, which his teacher had been waiting for. But what was their ultimate Plan?

"Could I take a look?" He held out his hand.

His teacher hesitated. And then, as if deciding that it could not hurt, said, "Okay. I'd expected you to be able to assess these examples faster than you are doing."

Joaquim looked long and hard at each of the pages, imprinting them on his mind. He did it so expertly that, to his teacher, it must have seemed that he was just getting an impression of the number of entries. Finally, he hurriedly skimmed the lists again, one entry at a time. His own plan to eliminate Mendoza sprang out immediately: there were no names or features that gave away who Mendoza was, where he was from, and who was plotting his death.

"Surely, there's enough to choose from, it can't be that difficult!" his teacher frowned. "Okay, that's enough!" Firmly he held out his hand.

Joaquim looked away, visualizing what he had seen. Then, quickly glanced again through the pages and handed the list to his teacher, who hurriedly locked them away.

"Who would want to eliminate a woman, watching the sunset?" Joaquim thought. Then he remembered how his nursemaid had got rid of her dog, Sobaca, because he had ravaged a herd of his father's sheep. She had fed him a delicious piece of bacon—Sobaca's favorite treat—and then had him shot by one of the guards.

Dying while you were enjoying the sunset reminded him of this dog's death. It had died suddenly and unexpectedly at a moment of great happiness. That idea was less abhorrent to him than the rest. He mentioned his first choice to his teacher.

"Good!" his teacher smiled.

"Okay, now for the final step. Prove you are a worthy Member of the *Alliance to Rule the World!*"

Joaquim's heart pounded so hard in his chest, he was afraid his teacher would hear it. Unconsciously, he realized that the big moment was here. This was where Snake wanted him!

"To become a part of the *Alliance to Rule the World*, each of you must prove your dedication and undertake a deed which will forge a bond between you and the Alliance – the sort of bond which you break *at your own peril*. Once each of you has completed this next step, you will have proved yourself to be worthy of entering the *Alliance*."

"How do we prove we are capable of helping to rule the Earth?" Joaquim asked.

"Each of you will help another Head of State to solve his individual problem."

"Solve?" Joaquim was suspicious.

"Eliminating obstacles to his rule!" his teacher said matter-of-factly, "And it is our intention that all of you will act simultaneously.

"You mean assassination?" Joaquim fought to hold his voice steady."

Ignoring the interruption, his teacher continued, "The deed of elimination will take place when the Head of State who has designed the plan has an iron clad alibi." He hurried on as he saw Joaquim about to raise an objection. "The risk involved is negligible, for no one, outside of those who themselves are committed, will suspect another Head of State of personally carrying out such a deed. After all, everyone will assume that people in your position have an army at their disposal, a Secret Service and henchmen who carry out such work. You will be above suspicion.

"But to all members of the Alliance, you will have proved your loyalty and ability to act without fear! These murders will take place within a period of two weeks."

Joaquim shivered. He moved toward the hearth.

"Now finally, the fear epidemic made sense!" Joaquim's mind raced.

Over one hundred murders within two weeks, his mind did an instant calculation: 7.14 murders a day – almost all murders of *national leaders* and then there would be the murders of each of the other groups. How many would there be? Twenty? Fifty? One Hundred groups? What else, beside murder, had they planned to destabilize the world? Even in a healthy world, could such an intensity of high level murders be survived without chaos breaking out? But this was no healthy world in which they lived. It was a world debilitated by fear.

Joaquim, of course, had no idea of the scale of what was planned, but he knew enough to see the danger.

The fear that had been whipped up to a fever pitch had created a monstrous society in which no one was safe. Such murders, together with other equally horrific actions Snake had, no doubt, planned, were geared to breed wide scale panic. And then, he, and other Members of the Alliance, would be expected to step in when every one would be looking for leaders who could establish some form of security. And he, Joaquim, would have been converted from a prisoner in his own palace to a slave at the beck and call of the Holy Order of the Snake.

Thank God for Juanita!

Joaquim took a deep breath and steadied himself. Any hesitation, and he would be eliminated along with the others on their list. Whatever he did, he must seem committed!

"Okay, you have chosen number 84: to throw someone over the cliff."

It happened that this was to take place just over the border at a location that, as a child, he had often secretly visited. In fact, he had gone there regularly as a boy in his four-wheel drive, before he was allowed to drive on the roads. He had discovered the spot by accident, not realizing that he had actually crossed the border into a neighboring country until he met Enzo, a boy of his own age, who, like himself, was now Head of State. They had become instant friends and with a fierce need for personal freedom in over-regulated lives, the two had, for years, relished their secret meetings. When both had been sent abroad to study, their meetings had become less frequent. For 5 years now, Joaquim had not seen Enzo, except at formal receptions.

Of course, Joaquim did not tell his teacher how close they had been or even that they knew each other.

His teacher carefully unlocked his briefcase again. This time he took out a roll of parchment, a vial of iodine, a needle and an old-fashioned quill pen made of a feather.

"Here give me your right thumb," his teacher bade him.

Before he realized what was happening, his teacher had swabbed it with the disinfectant, jabbed it with the needle and was allowing the drops of blood to fall onto the yellow parchment.

"Okay, dip your thumb in the blood, place your thumb print and then sign your name. This is your application to become a Member of the Alliance to Rule the World.

You get one-month preparation time. All executions will take place between 4 and 6 weeks from now."

In a daze, Joaquim signed the Pact with his own blood.

74. Joaquim's SOS To Juanita

As soon as his teacher had taken his leave, Joaquim ran into his study and carefully reconstructed the list: 102 murders, carefully outlined. Then he scanned it into his computer and sent it by e-mail to Juanita with an SOS to be in touch.

That night he heard nothing from her. She must have been out on a job. His next meeting with his teacher was planned for the very next morning!

75. Pedro Seems To Get His Way

Gagged with hands painfully secured behind her back, Antonia was led to the edge of town. There stood a phone booth. She dialed Mrs. Serazzi's number and inserted coins from her own purse.

The phone rang.

Nervously, Pedro dug his knife into her ribs close to her heart.

"Ouch!" she cried out angrily. "I can't concentrate when you're half killing me!"

Pedro tried to relax. But Antonia could feel his tension. The knife was shaking in his hand and she could tell he was barely breathing. His ability to control his gang was hanging in the balance. He desperately needed her help. He had to show her and the rest of the gang he was still in control.

The ten-year-old was holding her watch. Antonia had been given 3 minutes exactly to make her point. Then the call would be cut off.

Mrs. Serazzi picked up the phone, an edge of hysteria in her voice.

Her voice became expressionless and controlled as soon as she heard it was Antonia. Antonia sighed with relief. At least she stood a chance of getting her point across.

In a few words, Antonia sketched the situation, explaining she had exactly three minutes to make her point. She assured Mrs. Serazzi that she would be all right and begged her not to alarm her parents.

"What they want is large bandages, plenty of them, disinfectant and antibiotics to heal a large infected wound. Oh, perhaps you can get some disinfectant cream, too, so that the bandages don't stick to it, as the wound heals."

As she talked, Mrs. Serazzi began to relax. There was something so assertive and caring in Antonia's voice. She almost felt the situation was under Antonia's control.

"Once the wound is getting better, they have promised to set me free." It was vital for Antonia to reassure Mrs. Serazzi, if her plan was to work.

"But how can you trust what they say?"

"I have no alternative, Mrs. Serazzi, but I think I can. They really need my help. They know I have no access to money, but that I can help them in other ways."

Quickly, she made sure that Mrs. Serazzi had all the facts down.

The ten-year old was pointing at the watch.

"You gave me three minutes. One more to go!" Antonia hissed angrily at him. It was obvious that he couldn't tell time.

On the other end of the line, Mrs. Serazzi felt slightly reassured as Antonia asserted herself.

"Please, Mrs. Serazzi, if you have enough time, could you contact Mary Duffield, and ask if there are any All-Win World Citizens Centers near this town?" She gave her Mary's e-mail address, the description of the drop off point, and told her that her kidnappers had given her until noon the following day.

The boys were slightly more relaxed.

Antonia took whatever time she had left to sketch the kids' situation, why they refused to trust adults, and how, if all went well, she hoped to be able to help them and earn her freedom.

Pedro suddenly jabbed her with his knife. Antonia suppressed a cry of pain and managed to get the words out, "Please don't wor..."

The ten-year-old reached out and the line went dead.

Until Mrs. Serazzi was due to drop off the package the kids took turns keeping watch above the drop off point. Mrs. Serazzi kept to the agreement and dropped off the package at the agreed upon time. Antonia remained bound and gagged in the cave until triumphantly they brought her Mrs. Serazzi's package.

Her hands were untied. Antonia rubbed her hands, her wrists and her arms to get the circulation moving and then still rather stiffly, Antonia unpacked the parcel. She motioned for her captors to remove her gag.

Her mouth was dry and ached. Yet when she tried to speak, the boys understood easily, "We'll need firewood, three cooking pots and plenty of clean water – as clean as possible," she cautioned them.

Several hours later, all the supplies on the floor, they set to work, Antonia directing the team.

The younger boys made a small fire, scrubbed the pots and then boiled one large pot with water.

"We need it to come to a rolling boil to make sure that all the germs are dead. Otherwise we will infect the wound further."

Finally, Antonia decided the water was ready.

She divided the boiling water over the three pots and again brought each one to the boil. One would be for drinking. She carefully mixed disinfectant with the water in a second pot and poured extra disinfectant over her hands to thoroughly cleanse them.

She gently reached out for Pedro's arm and tenderly held it until he relaxed. Then, very slowly and carefully, she began unwrapping the rags. Where they were stuck to the wound, she swabbed the bandage with the disinfected water until the rags let loose.

By the light of the candle, the other four watched in hushed fascination, as if every gentle movement were a personal caress. The stench of the wound increased steadily. Antonia forced herself to focus on the task. It helped her not to throw up.

An eternity and then, the last inch of the rag let go. Now the painful red skin was exposed. It was oozing blood and puss.

Pedro had withstood the whole procedure with the same rapt attention as the others. He seemed to drink in the tender care he had craved for so long.

Antonia reached over and again washed her hands in pure disinfectant and then poured more in the water.

"This is going to prick badly," she looked up at Pedro, "I'll be as careful as I can."

She tested the heat of the water, dipped in a wad of clean bandage, then with the utmost care, she swabbed the angry wound. Bit by bit she cleaned out the wound until the puss had been removed. Then she carefully smeared the disinfectant cream over the whole painful area, bandaged the wound and after surveying her work with satisfaction, she placed his arm in a sling.

By now, the water she had set aside was cool enough to drink. Antonia read the instructions on the package.

Mrs. Serazzi had understood the problem and the medications ought to help. Antonia handed Pedro two tablets and told him to take them with the clean boiled water.

"Now you must take one every four hours and she pointed to the hands on her watch, which he was now wearing. You must wake up at this time. It is important if the pills are to work."

When she had finished, the boys remained seated, reluctant to break the spell.

After a while, Antonia reached out and took the letter that had been among the medical supplies. It was a letter from Mrs. Serazzi, begging her captors to set her free. At the end, was an e-mail from Mary. In it, the address of an All-Win Education Center on the outskirts of town.

Mary wrote,

> *Mrs. Serazzi is terribly worried. She told me you had been kidnapped. She believes that you have been captured by street children and that they are in need of help. I have phoned the closest All-Win Education Center in your area. They have been painfully aware of the street kids' plight and are anxious to help. This Center was established with the help of Joaquim, the King of San Leon. A wonderful man, I might add.*
>
> *If you can't escape, Antonia, the World Citizens Centers are your best bet. If your street children can be persuaded to see these can help them, they will no longer depend on you. You will be giving them a great opportunity and they are bound to spread the word. Perhaps this can change the fate of street children in other places, too. Even so, their situation will not change permanently until street children everywhere are given a helping hand. All-Win Education Centers can make the difference.*
>
> *I am proud of you, my dear. At the same time, I am afraid. Yet, I know if anyone can handle this, you can, Antonia. But I don't underestimate the danger you are in.*
>
> *I am with you with all my heart and am standing by to help. I shall not leave the phone, until I know you are free. Mrs. Serazzi has kept her promise and has not told your parents. So you have just a few days to free yourself.*
>
> *Love,*
> *Mary.*

Slowly she read the address out loud. "Do any of you know where this is?"

Reluctant to speak, Pedro finally answered, "It's not that far from here."

"May I tell you a story?" Antonia asked.

She told them about her father, a poor laborer from San Leon who had entered the States illegally and found work in the artichoke fields; how he had managed to put her and her brothers through school; and how, because she was so shy, she had always been teased.

As she described her life, she realized how fortunate she must appear. Then, she told how Mary Duffield had offered a class where for the first time she had felt she was worth something. She told them how this lady had sent them the address of what they called *an All-Win Education Center*. She explained that these All-Win Centers were there to help people build the sort of life they really wanted without hurting other people or being hurt themselves.

Through the tenderness with which she had treated Pedro's wound, something had shifted between them. They had caught a glimpse of gentle caring in action that spoke much louder than words. Had that created a chink of openness to the world of love and appreciation to which Antonia wanted to introduce them?

Before they went to sleep, Antonia was trussed up again, her head resting against a stone. She was not gagged this time and her bonds were looser. It was as if the atmosphere of caring was beginning to rub off on her little companions.

76. SOS From Mary To Bertram

Bertram was back in Costa Rica, getting his belongings together. He had been on the road for months, it seemed, and he was feeling weary. On Maurice's invitation, he had returned to Costa Rica to bask in the sun for a few more days. Tomorrow, he would fly to New York where, after one last public talk, he would fly via Paris to the South of France.

Maurice and Pim had left together a few days before; Pim for a few days in the Netherlands; Maurice straight to his Castle.

Bertram decided he would pack one suitcase for his trip and ship the rest of his belongings to the sumptuous apartment he had bought in New York and which overlooked Central Park South.

Toiletries, a couple of pairs of slacks, shirts, a sweater. Probably he should take a suit for formal occasions, swimsuit and underwear, his laptop computer...? Yes he would take it in case they would make an exception and let him use it during the Conference. Moreover, he wanted to work on the plane.

He downloaded his messages and then before answering them, he headed down to the beach for a sunbathe and a last leisurely swim. How wonderful to lie in the warm golden sand and to hear the soft sound of the waves. How he missed Maurice, Pim, Mary and his young friends.

Finally, he reluctantly headed back up to the library and routinely skimmed his mail. No! Still nothing from Eliza. After all these weeks of silence, the disappointment was if anything more bitter. They had had such a loving and intimate contact and now she had disappeared into thin air. Off licking her wounds, no doubt. *Nothing we can do but to give her her space!* Wasn't that what John St. Clair had said when he had mentioned the death of her husband so very long ago.

There was a note from Mary. Bertram frowned:

> *SOS. The following is confidential.*
>
> *Given the situation with Juanita, I had already half decided to stay put. Now, one of my students is facing a scary situation. I have no alternative, I can not leave. It all seems under control, but I need to be there to monitor every step in case there's anything I can do.*
>
> *I had an urgent message from John.*
>
> *Apparently, things in Kukundu are coming to a head. After the about turn, they will need all the good ideas they can get.*
>
> *John had asked me to make notes of any interesting projects during the conference in the South of France. After all, every one who is anyone in the all-win movement will be there. Would you mind sending me all relevant information as the conference progresses?*
>
> *From my side, I'll keep you posted. See if you can't persuade Percy to let you keep your computer. Have you met Percy yet? From Maurice I hear he's a nice enough fellow – not very adroit, though, at all-win thinking.*
>
> *And please no details, even to him, about why I'm not coming!*
>
> *Give my love to all our friends,*
>
> *Yours sadly,*
>
> *Mary*

77. Eliza Makes The Plane

Eliza entered her apartment. She desperately needed a break. Her lecture tour had been exhausting. Neatly piled on the floor of her bedroom, were large piles, each a separate project. No! She didn't want to be faced with any more work. She hurried to the phone and, on impulse, called a cab. Her bags still packed, she decided to return to the airport and head back home to Europe. Her family home would be empty. She might still make that evening's plane. If she missed the one to Amsterdam there would probably be one to Frankfurt or Paris.

Just as the ground hostess slammed the gate closed, Eliza came running up. Holding out passport and boarding card, she gasped, "I'm a passenger. Can I still get on?"

"Hold it, Jack," the ground hostess spoke into the mike. She processed Eliza's ticket, opened the door and Eliza dashed through. Dragging her case along the passageway, wheels squealing behind her, she was welcomed by a male flight attendant, eager to get her settled.

"This suitcase is too large to go into the overhead compartment. Here, place it behind this seat." He helped her to wedge her suitcase behind one of the first class chairs.

"There's just one seat left on the whole plane," he said. "You're awfully lucky." He pointed her in the right direction. The seat was in the center isle in the economy class. Her access to the isle was blocked by a man, immersed in his computer. He had barricaded himself in with piles of books on his lap and a pile on her seat.

Eliza decided to approach the fort from the other isle. It looked like the only route.

As she approached, the man kept working. She inched past legs and feet, trying to avoid stepping on the hand luggage, which was protruding from under the seats.

Without looking up at her directly, the man sensed her approach. He scooped up the books from her chair and eased them down onto the floor. Then, without paying her further attention, he continued typing away, an invisible sign flashing in all directions, "Disturb me if you dare!"

Eliza wormed herself into her seat, squeezed her hand luggage under the chair and, still trying to catch her breath, fastened her seat belt.

Eliza loved liftoff, the feeling of being glued into her chair, the engines revving, the speed picking up and then a few jiggles, as the wheels left the runway; the feeling that you were never quite sure whether the plane had actually made it. Takeoff helped her to relax. Somehow, when she was desperately tired, being poised on the edge of (imagined) calamity, her mind became crystal clear.

Then, engines at full power, the plane was rushing along the runway. It lifted off smoothly and they were gliding upward, finally on their way.

Onwards to her parental home. Too bad this plane to Paris had been the last one to Europe that night. She would have to find a way to get to the Netherlands from there where her parents had lived. For the first time, she would be alone in her family home since Brian and both of her parents had passed away. She wondered what it would be like being confronted with the memory of each of these deaths without any scheduled appointments to distract her. Was she doing the right thing? A house full of loving memories and she there all by herself. Suddenly she felt nauseous.

She tried to relax.

The hostesses came by with drinks and peanuts, which only aggravated the feeling. Then came hot napkins. Eliza took hers and wiped her face.

"Vegetarian meal?" The flight attendant appeared in the isle.

Eliza looked up. "Yes! But…"

The flight attendant squinted, "Mr. Morris…"

"That's me!" The dark-haired man looked up from his fort. He shut down his lap top computer and eased it onto his knees under the little table to make room for his dinner.

Eliza thought half-consciously, *"Strange, that name sounds familiar."* She gave the attendant her own name, quite forgetting she had been too late to order a special meal. And before Eliza could tell her that she wasn't feeling up to it, the flight attendant was back in the galley trying to locate her dinner.

Eliza was now thoroughly sorry she had got on the flight. But there was no way back and her nausea was increasing. She must get to a bathroom! It was nerves, she knew. She regretted the bag of chips she had devoured in the taxi on her way to the airport.

The man was grinning at her. She couldn't imagine why. Just then there was a surge of nausea. Hurriedly, she assessed the situation. No way of getting him dug out of his fort.

She clambered onto her chair and carefully balancing her foot on the armrest between their two seats, she gasped, "Excuse me." Precariously balancing, she aimed her free foot at the outer arm of his chair, which bordered on the isle, and gauged the distance, still trying to fight down her nausea. Yes, from there she ought to be able to jump down and run to the back of the plane.

"Hope the bathroom is free," she worried.

She aimed her free foot at the armrest. At that moment, her other foot slipped. She landed squarely in the man's lap. His computer jumped up off his knees and shattered on the floor along with the rest of his dinner.

Mortified, her nausea forgotten, Eliza looked at him. To her amazement he laughed. "Bertram Morris!" He held out his hand. "Finally, we meet."

Eliza looked at him, her mind reeling. This man must be out of his mind, laughing away like that. She hurried to extricate herself, mumbling, "I'm … I'm… terribly sorry. If you give me your card, I'll reimburse your computer… And you're welcome to my meal."

Bertram was still laughing.

The airhostess came running up and started cleaning up the mess.

Eliza was still trying to extricate herself from the man. The more he seemed delighted, the more desperate she became.

"Eliza, my name is Bertram Morris. Remember our e-mail correspondence? You know! I'm a friend of Mary Duffield's?" he managed to get out. "Finally, we meet in person! The Universe plunks you in my lap!"

78. The Dungeons

"Am I such a coward?" Eliza wondered, as she walked by Bertram's side, "Couldn't I face being on my own in my parent's home without anything to do? Here I've saddled myself with a man I barely know, come to a Conference I have little interest in, and am exploring an ancient Castle with him, somewhere in the South of France.

She smiled.

Actually, she was having fun – more fun than she had had in ages. She had found a person who loved adventure as much as she. They had got to the Castle a day ahead of the conference on the invitation of Count Maurice Le Sage, and now Bertram was giving her a tour. The intimacy they had established during their e-mail correspondence had deepened. They had talked without holding anything back during the long hours of the night on their way to Paris, then the following morning on the flight to Bordeaux, and finally in the tiny four-seater plane which landed on a makeshift airstrip just outside of the Castle walls. They'd been met by the housekeeper – Consuela was her name – and taken to their rooms. She had then presented them with a welcome note from the Count himself. Now, she had the peculiar feeling she'd known Bertram all of her life.

A door beckoned.

Mysterious and just ajar, it stood out, a dark gash in the dimly lit, sumptuously red carpeted hallway.

Eliza looked questioningly at Bertram.

"I dare you!" He teased her with his smile.

"I dare you to follow!" She said, peering around the door. By the flickering light of a naked bulb, she could make out a narrow stairway. Without touching the door despite her large unwieldy bag, she slipped through the opening and started down the stairs.

The first stairway led down, down to a small landing and then continued.

Eliza hesitated. Bertram was so close behind her, she plunged on, sure he would otherwise bump into her and send them both hurtling downward.

A second landing followed.

Again a stairway leading down. Bertram was still hot on her heals. This time she moved more quickly to put distance between them.

Down to a third landing, then a fourth. Here she hesitated again. As the echo of her footsteps died away, his voice reached her, "Go on! See how brave you are!"

Eliza continued her descent.

"I must be crazy, plunging into the bowels of the unknown!" The thought crossed her mind, then evaporated as she rushed on down.

Finally after the seventh set of stairs, she reached the bottom: A cellar hewn roughly from the rocks with a sandy floor. This, like the stairwell, was also dimly lit with a few naked light bulbs, swaying slightly. There must be a draft. At the far side, she could make out dim shapes. Something was dangling from the wall.

She moved closer.

Shackles! She frowned.

A shadowy object caught her eye: a bed of nails and a little farther on racks and stocks, covered in eons of cobwebs. "We're in the dungeons!" she cried.

"All-win relationships?" Bertram mocked her, "Even for the poor sods, who spent their lives wasting away in these tombs?" Bertram's voice issued from somewhere near the bottom of the stairs. She sensed he was grinning as he spoke – at her, rather than at their fate.

Eliza did not answer immediately. She pressed herself into the shadows away from the pools of light, focussing on the rough and tumble of thoughts and feelings that had surged into awareness once she had stopped hurtling down the stairs.

Here she was, alone with this man in a dungeon. She was suddenly besieged by doubt. What did she actually know about him? He was a friend of Mary's, but Mary had never mentioned him. Did Mary really know him or did they just have many interests in common? Nobody had any idea where she was. She had been so desperate to leave New York behind that she had not told anyone, except Mary, that she was returning to Europe. Not a soul could guess where she was!

This man, almost a stranger, had egged her on, knowing what they would find. And here she was, completely at his mercy! She allowed herself to focus on him, in her mind's eye seeking him out at the other end of the cellar somewhere at the foot of the stairs.

No, she was not afraid. Not of Bertram. In fact, she instinctively trusted him. She was not even afraid of the instruments of torture or the terror that must have been experienced here. They seemed harmless, quaint out of date objects. Gone all horrifying associations, eroded with time. All this was rather fun, a welcome relief from the serious business of saving the world for posterity. She grinned.

Then another thought struck her. *She* was not scared of him, but more prudent women would be. She felt suddenly vulnerable—vulnerable to the feelings of warmth she was beginning to feel for him.

"I was talking about all-win relationships as a possibility." Her words were more fiery than his comments deserved.

She took a deep breath and continued more civilly, "Okay! Dungeons have made way for concentration camps and genocide. Violence and conflict are totally out of hand, but the time has come that *all must win*. We have to stop fighting one another!" Oh! how she longed just for warmth and closeness, no more global problems.

Suddenly, she had had enough.

"If after 8 hours on three planes and several hours waiting in transit lounges, I still have not been able to explain what I mean, I... I.... Oh...!"

"The lady is right!" The voice came from the beyond. Eliza jumped. Every nerve stood on end, as with all her senses she searched the shadows of the dungeon for an explanation.

Something moved a few yards away. Eliza shrunk farther into the dark and tried to edge away. There was a sudden crash. She had bumped into the stocks! They keeled over and shattered as they hit the floor.

Eliza's heart beat so wildly that her whole body seemed to shake.

An elderly gentleman emerged out of one of the crevices. He was in a short satin evening jacket. He looked as if he were about to retire to the male-only smoking room for an after dinner chat.

Eliza forced herself to take deep breaths and to exhale slowly with control. Gradually, her heartbeat slowed to normal. She began to take in what she saw. This elegant gentleman bore himself with a natural authority with an air of genuine interest and concern. She could imagine that he came from a long lineage of people who had wielded considerable power.

"All that is has to win in the long run," the gentleman went on, "As a human race, we seek to control the world without a hope of succeeding. Our greatest power lies in what we can achieve in cooperation with the whole. That is the all-win principle, my dear, you were referring to, I believe?"

He stepped toward Eliza and kissed her hand: "Le Sage!" he introduced himself.

Bertram, now standing close beside Eliza, added, "Count Le Sage is our host. He owns the castle and like us will attend tomorrow's conference. "

"Please call me Maurice," the Count inclined his head in acknowledgment of Bertram.

"Thanks for meeting us, Maurice."

"I didn't want to wait to suppertime to meet you. While Bertram was staying with me last year, he first started corresponding with you. Every day he would let me know whether he had heard from you or not.

"Knowing Bertram, the man who is impervious to all advances from women, I knew you had to be something special. I just had to make your acquaintance."

"Did you know he carries a newspaper clipping about you gallivanting around Syria in a skin tight red-colored pantsuit, pursued by terrorists? I knew you liked excitement, so I thought I'd prepare a little adventure for you as a way of welcoming you here."

"Maurice, *please*, you are destroying my image! I've been so careful to play it cool!"

Maurice with a chuckle said, "Okay, okay.

"Here, I want to show you something, a family secret. Nobody, outside of my immediate family, knows of this place and I don't think even they have been down here before. The secrets of a by-gone age and here you two are -- finally a couple of people who can appreciate them.

"Just follow me!" Maurice turned and disappeared into the shadows.

Eliza, now over her surprise caught Bertram grinning at her. There was a wicked, mischievous quality to his smile, which despite her anger, she enjoyed.

"I'm sorry, Maurice's materialization was rather sudden. I didn't mean to scare you to death. I've been waiting to meet you for too long to have you die on me of heart failure!"

Eliza could not help laughing, as he took her hand and led her in pursuit of the Count. This man was indomitable. Life with Bertram was fun.

Bending low to avoid an outcropping of rock, he led her in the wake of the Count into a dimly lit passage.

Here and there was a pool of light from a gently swaying bulb while a slight breeze ruffled her hair. There was the tang of salt in the air. A few minutes and indeed, they heard waves dashing against the rocks, as the passageway suddenly grew brighter.

Then rounding a bend, Eliza instinctively shielded her eyes from the unexpected onslaught of the sun.

A secret escape from the Castle! Eliza thrilled. "Can you imagine if you could look back in history at the times this tunnel was used? Make a pretty exciting plot for a film!" she breathed.

They stepped out from under a long ledge, which nestled along the side of a meadow. A luminous carpet of wild flowers spread out before them, each flower vying for a position from where to bask in the light.

These forces make our Universe tick. With a smile, Maurice made a grandiose gesture, embracing the meadow, the sea and the sky. Everything is bursting with life and each part of Nature is doing its thing and thereby helping the rest to proceed, each through its own life cycles. I just love this spot and came here often when I was a kid. I managed to keep it to myself. It was my little hideaway. This is where I first understood the all-win principle!"

Eliza bent down, as her eye caught sight of a delicate mauve bloom. It looked like a dainty drinking vessel, fit for a fairy to drink from.

"Look at this beautiful flower," Maurice commented, "It has taken root in stone. But see this tiny bit of sand that has eroded from the rock? It draws its sustenance from this sand, while the rock gathers the drops of rain and helps to keep the plant alive. At the same time, its roots are wearing the rock down and creating more sand. And so, flower and rock help one another to change, each according to its own life's rhythms. And look here!" Maurice pointed to a plant that was encircling another plant and was straining for its place in the sun. If you can't get what you need in the most straightforward way, you grow in whatever way you must! This to me is the essence of all-win living."

He fell silent.

With a sigh, Eliza slipped the bulky bag from her shoulder and deposited it carefully on the ground, just keeping hold of her much smaller handbag.

They all marveled at the view.

Then as if talking to himself, Maurice went on, "And below this wealth of flowers is an intricate root system, which connects all these separate plants. While on one level each plant seems to be competing for space, their roots conspire in unison to hold the soil in place. And when it rains, this combined root system captures the water so that each plant can drink its fill."

The group stood admiring the view. The contrast between the warm sweetness of the meadow and the wild waves below excited Eliza. To her, diversity was the spice of life!

Just then a huge wave smashed against a rock and with a series of shrieks, a flock of seagulls rose up into the air. After raising a rumpus of cries, they settled on a next clump of rocks farther out to sea.

Eliza looked around. The Count had disappeared.

79. The Woman With The Strong Face

That night, Joaquim got very little sleep. His next lesson was scheduled for the following day. It was as if his teacher wanted to strike while the iron was hot. How he wished he and Juanita had been able to get together.

His teacher was already waiting when Joaquim entered. Joaquim's heart was beating so loudly that he feared his teacher would hear it. Without further ado, his teacher presented him with the details. As he suspected, he was to eliminate a woman for King Enzo, his childhood friend. In wonderment, Joaquim looked at the photo. "Dumpy" was the description that came to mind. She looked like an old woman, with a middle-aged figure, a black dress - the sort old grandmother's wore in San Leon. But with an upright bearing.

"I wonder why he wants this woman out of the way?" Joaquim asked his teacher.

"None of our business. The less we know about the situation, the better. Then we can't give ourselves away. It's a straightforward deed. No emotional involvement!"

"Any close up of her? Be useful to prepare myself for the act."

His teacher fished in the package and handed him a large photo.

"A strong face," he thought. The huge black eyes held his attention. They had a deep glow to them, an expression of deep love and compassion. The love and benevolence that spoke from this face was what he wanted his people to find among themselves. No wonder Enzo wanted this lady out of the way. She would be a constant reminder of the compromises he was being force to make to join the Association to Rule the World.

For the rest of the lesson, nauseous and in a daze, Joaquim developed a plan to do away with this woman with the strong, compassionate face.

Finally his teacher left.

Joaquim pleaded a headache. He requested Carlos, his true friend and aid, to read his speech to the National Organization of Teachers. Facing them and the work they were trying to do reminded him of his own desperate impotence.

"Please make a note of all requests they have without giving them any hope we can help. I'd like to do for them whatever lies in my power. Perhaps connect them to groups outside of San Leon with full discretion, of course."

Head in hands, he sat in his private study in front of the open hearth, his thoughts in a whirl. There was a thick fog in his head, as if the brain cells themselves were involved in hand to hand combat. He tried to will the dull, gnawing sensation to go away, but to no avail.

Then he remembered what his grandfather used to say, "Always know what you are feeling. The feeling of fear is tied to the urge to run away. But the more you run, the more your fear grows. So always face your fear."

"You mean you may never run away?" he had asked.

"Sometimes there is no alternative," his grandfather had laughed, "If you accidentally surprise a mother bear with cubs or a wild buffalo and they attack, it 's wise to run as fast as you can. But if you *can*, look carefully before you act. It is best to intimately know what you are afraid of and then run away later."

Joaquim did not understand what he meant until one day, on his way to Enzo's land, he had been about to cross the frontier when he heard voices.

Knowing he had no right to be there, he was about to run when he remembered his grandfather's words: *Know what you are afraid of. You can always run away later.* Heart pounding, he froze. With his breath coming in short gasps, he took cover behind a small bush.

He found that if he focussed on his breath and slowed his breathing down, he felt calmer inside and he could hear every word. They were planning to rob Sonia, one of his mother's ladies in waiting. They knew her schedule exactly and planned to rob her when she left the palace.

Joaquim saw then what his grandfather had meant. He took in every detail of what the robbers looked like, what they were wearing, and every step of their plan.

Then the robbers brought out food and bottles of the local wine, and Joaquim realized that they were settling in until it was time to attack.

He beat a retreat, choosing the path he had never taken before.

By now, armed with his knowledge of what they planned, he could retreat without giving himself away. He was able to find his way home, tell his father of the danger without letting on where he had been.

The robbers were captured.

He now remembered how he had faced his fear and the clarity that had ensued. Now, instead of the robbers, it was the fog in his head that was preventing him from getting in touch with his thoughts. Desperate for clarity, he was afraid of the fog. This only worsened his condition. With his head in his hands, his eyes closed, he focussed on the fog with full concentration. Every time he felt the urge to turn away, he would force his attention back. Then, very gradually, the fog thinned and lifted. Suddenly, his mind clear and once more, he could think.

His mind turned to his present predicament: He was trapped.

He replayed the day's lesson in his mind: preparations for his first murder. If he withdrew now, the *Alliance to Rule the World* would be forced to kill him, too.

He shuddered.

With photographic clarity, he saw the gruesome list of murderous options, people had at their disposal. Barely had he allowed the fear in, or the fog came flooding back.

Patiently, he went back to focussing on the fog until, once more, it lifted. With a clear mind, he decided a different approach: "*What is the most important thing in my life?* "*Where does my personal power lie? What makes my heart sing?"* he asked himself, for he realized that the answers to these questions placed him in his personal power.

His thoughts dwelled on the lady with the strong, compassionate face. He must foil this devilish plan. It was as if she represented goodness itself. And to salvage that quality, he realized, was now his immediate goal. He would pretend to push her off the cliff and then smuggle her back to his palace and somehow get her to safety.

With a sigh of relief, his next steps became clear. Now how to carry them out? The first challenge was to see that his teacher did not suspect him until the lady with the compassionate face had been brought to safety.

He looked at the situation from every possible angle. Then he reached over, picked up the phone and dialed the number he remembered from when he had been a boy. It was a wild card. Odds were that it would have been disconnected.

To his surprise, a voice answered, "Yes?"

"Enzo?"

"Yes?!" the voice exclaimed in surprise, recognizing his voice, "Am I glad to hear from you!"

"Can we meet in private? When it gets dark?"

"Same place?"

"Same place! Don't breathe a word".

"Agreed. See you at 7:30!"

80. In The Meadow

Puzzled, Eliza looked at Bertram. I wonder where the Count went?

Together they walked over to the ledge. Look as they would, they could not find the exit of the tunnel among the tortuous crags.

"Strange!" Eliza said, "I feel I'm in a dream."

"The Count is very real!"

"But what was he doing in that dungeon? I can't imagine anyone wanting to hang out there."

"Waiting for you!" Bertram said matter-of-factly. "There's a lift from his personal quarters. A sort of personal escape route. He asked me to bring you there!"

"He *what*?" Eliza's head reeled. "You mean when you suggested we come ahead of the conference and that we would go exploring this ancient castle, you were setting me up to meet the Count?"

"Well, in a way." For a moment, he looked very young and vulnerable.

"You refused when, several months ago, I first invited you to this conference. You needed time to yourself. Well, I decided to give you some adventure to help you to relax and provide a change of pace.

"Then…" he hesitated, "I must admit, I, myself, did not want to let you go that now we had finally met. So I decided to give you a memorable time and do the types of adventurous things I myself love to do.

"It's my way of luring you to me." This time his smile had the mischievous quality of a man who does what he loves to do, knows he is doing right by others, and is not ,afraid to take risks.

"So when I called Maurice to ask whether there was room for you to come, I was casting around for something to make your stay more interesting. Maurice thought a chance meeting in the dungeons would get your juices going. And so it did!"

Eliza laughed wholeheartedly. "I must admit it's fun to explore secrets from a bygone age! So when did all this scheming happen?"

"Fairly soon, after you positioned yourself in my arms. The plane has telephones on board, you know," he teased, stating the obvious.

"Lucky I called, because the conference was full. Every one has been stuffed into the Conference Wing. As a close friend, Maurice made an exception for me and put me up in his wing without telling Percy. When I phoned, he said you could sleep in his wing, too. And the dungeons are right there. He explained how I could get you there. We arranged a time. And you know the rest."

"But what if I had not gone for the half open door? After all, it was a crazy thing to do!"

"I really don't know," Bertram admitted, "I was mulling that over in my mind from the moment I spoke to him on the phone. I could see Maurice waiting down there in the dark, all by himself.

"In the end, I decided if you hesitated I would tell you the whole truth: that these were the dungeons, a part of my guided tour, and that the Lord of the Castle was waiting to make your acquaintance."

"But why the urgency to get me to come?"

"Well, after you had plunked yourself down on my knee!"

Eliza laughed a full, spontaneous laugh as she thought of the absurdity of what had happened and the miracle that had brought them together. Then, suddenly serious, she picked up her large bag and, changing the subject, said, "Bertram I'm most terribly sorry. I brought my laptop for you to make up for the one I smashed."

"Good! That was very considerate of you!" Bertram thought of the three urgent situations which were developing at the same time: There was the situation with Juanita and King Joaquim, then John's message that things in Kukundu were about to start moving. Finally, there was the situation with Mary's student – nothing much he could do about that, but he could let Mary know about developments here. "Good!" he repeated, "I'd love to borrow it from time to time".

" I have another at home. And I always make copies of my files. So I lost at most half an hour's work. But I should be very grateful if I could borrow it just while we are here.

"Hey, you shouldn't be carting this heavy bag. It's too hot! Here! …"

He took the bag from her and, walking over to the ledge, placed it carefully in a deep cool crag, sheltered from the sun and rain. It was impossible to see it from where she sat. She noted its approximate location. Bertram returned and let himself down beside her, also leaning against the rock.

"But your conclusions about me are all wrong!" Eliza confessed, "I'm anything but adventurous. It's one thing to be a part of a group, which founds a network of All-Win Education Centers and quite another to deal with your feelings. I'm feeling decidedly tender inside and am probably running away from confronting the deaths of the three people who were closest to me."

"I know!" his voice was gentle.

"Being afraid, like any emotion, is a part of life. It is how you deal with it that counts. You can run away or you can deal with it, but it's not possible to deal with everything at once!"

Eliza looked at him quizzically. "You've been researching me?" She was on guard again. She wasn't sure she wanted people poking around in her emotional life without her express permission. On the other hand, she loved his willingness to be frank.

"Well, I have to admit that what Maurice said is true. As soon as you were mentioned in Costa Rica, I remembered that newspaper article in my wallet. I hauled it out and reread it and realized how similar we are…"

Eliza frowned. Again his presumption to know her.

"To both of us, life is an adventure with horizons which are forever new. Also the work we do is very close, except I work with businesses, you with NGOs. Then, when we began to correspond, your e-mails became more and more important. In fact, I found myself sharing things with you about myself that before I had never dared to confront."

"And then the Universe dumped me in your lap!"

They both laughed and Eliza felt at ease again.

With satisfaction, she noticed he did not use the situation to make physical advances. She trusted him, was enjoying his closeness, and felt comfortable in his presence.

She smothered a yawn and allowed herself to sink into a lying-down position. With the warm sunlight on her skin, the soothing zooming of the bumblebees and, in the distance, the crashing of the waves, the dullness of jet lag took over and soon, eyelids heavy, she drifted off to sleep.

81. Enzo

Carlos was laughing and joking with the guards as Joaquim slipped by. Down the small staircase, through the servants quarters to the jeep, waiting outside. There he crept under a plaid in the back seat.

Two minutes later Carlos had started the engine and was waving to the policeman as the jeep passed through the gate. Another few minutes and Joaquim had taken the wheel, dropped Carlos off and was speeding as fast as he could over rough terrain until he was over the border.

Enzo was already waiting.

As he climbed in beside him, the two men greeted one another with broad grins as if nothing had changed and they were once again two naughty boys, playing truant.

"Well, here we are now, two Heads of State!" Enzo laughed. "So much has happened!" For a while they reminisced and then Joaquim said, "I asked to see you because a document has fallen into my hands."

He held his breath, as he carefully took a piece of paper out of a plastic folder and, with some trepidation, handed Enzo the list, detailing the 102 murders.

Enzo glanced at it and looked at him aghast.

"Where did you get it?" he asked, trying to sound casual, not realizing that his face had given him away.

"I fear there's been a leak! I'm involved in this project and I know you are too." He carefully avoided letting him know about Juanita, or that he, Joaquim, was "the informer."

"That means that all 102 of us are implicated!" Enzo stated

"And that the whole plan is off!" Joaquim rejoined.

"Oh thank God for that!" Enzo sighed. "I chose my victim in a fit of anger because she criticized my enrollment in the *Alliance*. Margarita practically brought me up. I always share everything with her. When she turned critical and threatened to expose me, unless I changed my mind, I realized that either I kill her, or else the Alliance would kill me. It was clear from the first lesson what a bunch of scoundrels they were, and powerful ones at that!"

"Rumor has it that it is the Holy Order of the Snake!" And Joaquim explained about the divide and rule policy and, without mentioning Juanita, things she had told him about the Snake.

"I suspected they existed," Enzo acknowledged, "Since aspiring to join the Alliance, I know it. "

" Joaquim thought. *"If Enzo sees through their tactics, there are bound to be others."*

"Well, I am scheduled to murder her!" he said aloud, "What a beautiful face, she has. I am planning a sham murder and shall get her out of the country. So you can rest assured she's safe.

"I've been looking for a way to save General Mendoza. He's a monster, agreed, but assassination – that won't do."

The moon moved behind a cloud and Enzo's face was shrouded in shadow. Still, Joaquim could feel his eyes boring into his head.

"We have to stop the *whole spate of murders,*" Enzo's voice came out of the dark. "Just imagine the chaos they will create! They will destabilize the whole world!"

"But how?" Joaquim asked.

Enzo reflected.

"What would you do, if you received this list with the question: 'Which of these murders did *you* plan?" he asked.

"That would certainly jam a spanner in the works! There would be no way that I would be able to act. I see what you mean..." Joaquim sounded doubtful.

"We could send the list around to all Heads of State with two questions: '*Which of these people do you want to get rid of?* and *Which of these murders did you plan?"* Enzo suggested, "That would be enough for all – both Members of the Alliance and Snake – to realize that the cat is out of the bag!"

"But isn't that rather dangerous? Supposing they suspect. Their revenge would be..." Joaquim shuddered. "But if..." he stopped to think.

"I've got it!" he cried, "Imagine we make it a worldwide guessing game. Send it out via the Internet:

> *Give your version of what would happen if all these murders took place at once; and*
> *Which Heads of State or Government official would profit from the following murders...?"*

Joaquim felt himself come alive. Just then the moon emerged from behind a cloud and Joaquim noticed his friend was frowning.

"But wouldn't the Alliance put out the word that it was a clever trick by whoever planned the murders to lead the scent away from himself?" Enzo cautioned.

"But don't you see, if they said that, they would be giving themselves away. And that's the last thing they would want! Then, once the first murders were committed, the element of surprise would be gone. People would be expecting the others to follow and would take precautions. By then, too much suspicion would have been cast on the Heads of State for any of them to dare to undertake the murders. If they carried on anyway, people would realize that some powerful organizers were behind the actions and people would suspect the Snake and begin to investigate...Enzo! This has to be the way forward! Snake will have to call off the action!" Joaquim concluded.

Now Enzo was smiling, "I'm in touch with a number of international pro-democracy movements. If each undertook the action at the same time..." Enzo reflected. "Joaquim, I think this could work!" His eyes began to sparkle.

"I have some useful global connections, too," Joaquim thought of Juanita. "We should start simultaneously; make sure the actions originate in the Wealthy Countries; and are spread around at top speed.

"Here take this list! I have a copy and anyway, they're imprinted on my mind."

They discussed exact timing, wording of their action, how to cover themselves and make sure that participants would be safe.

Joaquim emphasized, "Timing is essential. If enough start simultaneously, it will be untraceable to any one person!"

"That should do it!" Enzo agreed, "No way the Alliance can carry out their plan with such an action going on! As soon as things are transparent, evil loses its hold."

After working out their plan in the minutest details, the two friends parted.

Joaquim phoned Carlos on his solar phone and was smuggled back into his quarters.

Immediately he called Juanita.

She was in!

"I'll send Carlos to pick you up," he said.

But would their "*World Game*" (as they had dubbed their action) catch on before Snake found out? Joaquim wondered, as he waited for Juanita to arrive.

82. Antonia Gains The Children's Trust

It was 10 days since Antonia had first dressed Pedro's wound. With the help of antibiotics and regular changing of bandages, his wound was beginning to heal.

Every night, Antonia told them stories about the young people in other countries and how they were improving their lives.

There was something about the combination of the daily ritual of cleaning and rebandaging his wound and the story telling sessions that was beginning to win them over.

A couple of days later, Antonia was allowed to phone Mrs. Serazzi for fresh supplies. By requesting just a few bandages at a time, Antonia was able to give her adopted mother regular updates every few days and keep her from alarming her parents.

Very slowly, Antonia succeeded in gaining the boys' trust. With luck, she would be able to persuade them to meet someone at an All-Win Education Center at a safe place where they felt they could escape if need be. Antonia hoped fervently that they would give such a Center a chance and that it would make a difference in their lives.

83. Juanita's SOS

A whole spate of murders in the 102 dictatorships to annihilate their opposition will place Snake's puppets in control! They will take place within a period of two weeks, beginning in one month's time. No telling whether similar assassinations will take place in Wealthy Countries as well.

Mary stared at Juanita's e-mail. She barely breathed as she tried to comprehend the enormity of what was about to happen.

Everyone was incommunicado in the South of France! Snake was about to strike; and only Mary, Juanita, and perhaps one or two others were available to do anything about it. This would change the global hierarchy and decimate the world economy.

Admittedly, an outrageously unjust world economy would be brought down, but it would make way for an even greater evil: supreme control by Snake and that within the next six weeks.

Fear was at a fever pitch. Cutthroat competition ran rife. People were on the point of snapping. And a tiny elite in both Wealthy and Poor Nations had colluded with each other to siphon off the world's resources for their personal gain. With the wealthy elite in the poor countries eliminated and the puppets in control, the flow of resources from poor to rich would be held up and in many cases halted. Gone would be their easy access to essential natural resources; gone, their access to labor at rock bottom prices; and gone, places where their industries could flaunt environmental and human rights laws. In fact, gone would be the mainstay of the power and wealth of this tiny elite that had control of the world economy. And if these resources dried up from one day to the next, huge businesses would grind to a halt and millions would, all of a sudden, be out of work. Even if this were a temporary hitch, the destabilization of the world economy at a time like this would be the spark in the tinderbox that could start a conflagration.

This unjust system was already teetering, as more citizens had found out. With the cornerstone of the world's economy in tatters—however criminal it may have been—everyone's standard of living would plummet in the short run both in Wealthy and Poor Countries, and with emotions at a fever pitch through the fear epidemic, chaos would break out. People would scramble to survive. There would be a wild grasping for power and Armageddon would take over. And it was more than likely that similar murders had been planned in Wealthy Countries to maximize the intensity.

Mary didn't doubt that the Snake had set this up, over the centuries moving toward this climax, step by inexorable step, and now had their stooges in place, ready to take over. Whenever Armageddon was unleashed, it would be only natural that people would start to clamor for strong leadership to save them from social meltdown. At that moment, they would be delivered unto Snake's supreme control.

What a plan! But a plan that relied on secrecy for its success!

Would Juanita's suggestion for a World Game be sufficient to defeat this plan?

A World Game! It was their only hope! She would send out an SOS to all her Networks.

But even as she set to work rallying interest in the World Game, she knew it was but a stopgap measure as long as the all-win principle could not fully take hold. She was sure that even if the World Game succeeded, Snake would be waiting in the wings, ready to go for the jugular of world power at the very next opportunity.

Mary got up from her computer and began restlessly pacing to and fro.

Unless the all-win principle took root at every level, all they were working for would be built on quick sand. And without a level playing field in the Security Council, nothing much would be gained. In a world organized by nation states, democracy among nations was as important as democracy among individual people.

So much would, in the end, depend on Hugh, his team of fellow students, and the lobbyists of the All-Win Network. Would they succeed in persuading the five Permanent Members that their long-term influence would thrive to the degree they were motivated by the all-win principle in their relations with other Nations?

84. Finding Their Way Back To The Castle

As the sun moved behind the stark rock face, Eliza and Bertram lay fast asleep. The air was suddenly cold, but neither Eliza nor Bertram woke up.

As Eliza lay sleeping, the exhausting journey and her adventure in the dungeons melted away. In her dream, she and Brian were together again.

Eliza sighed, as the dank cold shadow of the cliffs crept across her sleeping form. In her dream, she moved closer to the warm comfort of Brian's arms and snuggling there she reached up with her lips and, feeling deluged with all the love she had so yearned to express, she kissed the crook of his neck. "How wonderful to be together again. Thank you for waiting for me!"

Brian seemed to start and then held her close. Eliza sensed something unfamiliar and opened her eyes. Instead of seeing Brian's dark aquiline features, she was looking into Bertram's smiling eyes.

Deeply shocked, she drew back extricating herself from his arms.

"I'm terribly sorry!" she stammered, "I was sound asleep! I was dreaming you were someone else." Embarrassed, she rolled over.

"I know," he said, "but there is no harm in keeping warm!" He was so relaxed about the incident, Eliza surprised herself by laughing outright.

The sun was now setting fast. It was high time to get back. Once more, they scoured the whole cliff face, which ran the full length of the field. But it was no good, because they could not even remember approximately where the entrance had been.

There had to be another way out. It would be impossible to scale the rocky crag, where the exit of the dungeons had to be. The far side of the field was blocked by a steep rock wall. No hope of scaling those sheer heights either. Then there was the moat of the castle with its steep walls.

That left the fourth side with a sheer drop of rocks all the way to the sea.

Hurriedly, they walked along the edge. The sea was much calmer than before. Still, the cold wind alternately dashed and frothed the waves over the rocks. A shiver ran up Eliza's spine.

She stepped away from the edge.

There had to be a way out! Eliza felt a flash of anger. What sort of a man was Maurice, leaving them here like that? Was he watching them from his Castle room? No, somehow, she still really liked the man. Probably, he had not realized they couldn't find their way back.

"Look here!" Bertram called from the far corner closest to the castle.

There was a tiny path, leading down.

In the last rays of the setting sun, they followed the track with their eyes to where it leveled off, creeping along the side of the cliff to the other side of the Castle.

There was no time to waste.

They hurried down. Exhausted, Eliza's knees nearly buckled under her. Bertram caught her arm and carefully they picked their way. The path disintegrated into a narrow ledge. Then the ledge disappeared.

"Careful here, Eliza! Can you reach that foothold?" And Bertram pointed to a foothold farther along where the narrow ledge resumed.

Eliza looked down. A sheer drop! Only the angry sea below.

She reeled.

"Steady!" Bertram cautioned her. "Try not to look down. Focus on where you are going." Eliza took a giant step and just managed to reach the foothold.

She was keenly aware that if she were to allow fear to flood her mind, she would miss her footing and be lost. She concentrated on the path and Bertram's heels carefully feeling their way ahead.

Finally, they rounded a bend.

Expectantly, their eyes scoured the side of the cliff. Surely it must take them back up? It had to lead to the Castle! Why else would the path exist?

Instead, a huge rock barred their way.

At that moment, the sun plunged into the sea and that part was cloaked in shadow.

Pressed against the rock face, Eliza didn't dare to look down. The wind whipped the thundering waves against the rocks, while up here in the protection of a huge outcropping, they barely felt the breeze.

Eliza breathed deeply into her stomach. Her mind became calm and clear.

They needed a light!

Lodging herself firmly against the cliff wall, she eased her handbag, which she had dangled around her neck, around to where she could open it and felt for her keys. On her key ring she had a small torch, surprisingly bright. She handed the light to Bertram. He took it gratefully and immediately began searching for a way around the rock. And there indeed was a small opening.

They squeezed through only to find another sheer drop. Eliza grabbed the rock, her head swimming, afraid of losing her balance.

"Look, Eliza," Bertram squeezed her hand, "Hold on to me." He pointed ahead where the path continued. "Whatever you do, don't look down!"

With one stride he was on the other side, still holding Eliza's hand. Half jumping, she made the stretch, hot on his heels and the two were on their way again. Soon, the path began zigzagging upward. The castle now loomed overhead. As they finally reached the top, Bertram let go of her hand.

With relief, they noticed the drawbridge was down. But the massive entryway was closed.

Eliza once more unwound her handbag from around her neck, took out her keys and, with a sigh of relief dropping her bag on the floor, scanned the huge doors with her tiny flashlight. In the center was a bronze lion's head with a ring through its nose. She twisted the ring and to their overwhelming relief the huge doors eased open.

They were home!

At the bottom of the grand staircase, Eliza held out her hand. "Thank you, Bertram, I can find my way from here." As he made to protest, she insisted, "Really, I prefer it this way!"

He spluttered as she turned quickly and despite her exhaustion ran up the stairs.

At the door of her suite, she stopped to listen. He had respected her wishes and not followed her up. She was still slightly uneasy that he might take her snuggling up to him the wrong way. Intimacy! She didn't want to deal with that tonight. While she was leaning against the door, the tears welled up inside. Any thoughts of intimacy only served to increase her feelings of confusion. Had she been snuggling up to Brian or was it Bertram in her dream?

Quickly Eliza reached for her bag to get out her room key.

"Oh no!" She exclaimed out loud. She had left her bag at the front door.

She was desperately tired! In a daze, she made her way back down the stairs. Fortunately, Bertram was gone. She managed to open the large door from the inside and stepped outside. There—Thank Goodness!—stood her bag, where she had dropped it to open the door.

She let out a loud sigh of relief.

For a long moment, she breathed in the scene.

There was no wind at all at this side of the Castle. The moat lay quiet far below. And beyond, gently rolling hills stretched as far as the eye could see by the light of the waxing moon. In the distance she heard a cow lowing, as if calling its calf.

Drawn by the deep peace she had yearned for so long, she strolled over the drawbridge, drinking in the scene. For the first time since she had fled New York, she felt in harmony with herself and at one with her natural surround.

But it was late.

Eliza turned and looked up. For a moment, she took in the sheer grandeur of the Castle, which soared up to the sky. It was shrouded in a here and there luminous cloak where the soft moonlight caricatured the rough stones, turrets and wings. Just one light shone bright, like a watchful eye, way up at the very top. As she looked, she thought she saw a person gesticulating at the window as if in animated conversation.

Eliza smothered a yawn, crossed the drawbridge, and hurried off to bed.

85. The Fear Epidemic

Quick steps behind her, a tap on the shoulder. Guessing it was Bertram, Eliza turned and smiled.

"Well, I bet you didn't have much difficulty sleeping last night after all we went through!" Bertram greeted her with a grin, "I can't believe we actually made it back up. I'm really sorry to have put you through all that!" And with a light hand in the small of her back, he led her forward.

"I didn't go straight to bed," Eliza admitted, "Left my bag outside the door and went downstairs to fetch it.

"Oh Bertram, it is so peaceful here. I'm so glad I came.

"Just standing outside looking around, everything completely still. And then the huge expanse of walls reaching up to the sky. I felt so deliciously small and ... and ... part of it all.

"Just one small light right up there in the turret, straight above the front door..."

"Wonder, who lives up there..." Bertram mused.

"I did see someone, looked like a man. He was waving his arms around... Can't think what he was doing..." she said. "Anyway, at that point, I realized how tired I was, it was the most I could do to fall into bed. Slept like a log until morning."

Together they made their way to the Conference Wing, which they reached through a long hallway with on either side at regular intervals large potted ferns.

"The Conference Wing has been rebuilt specially for this meeting. It's sealed off from the rest of the Castle by a hidden sliding panel.

"See here's the knob!" Bertram pointed to a stone in the potted plant. Twist this!"

Eliza did as he suggested, and the panel slid open.

"It's a secret entrance just for Maurice, me and you! On the inside, no one knows the panel is there. Maurice gave me detailed instructions over the phone in case I wanted to take you here on your guided tour of the Castle.

"The Conference Wing has its own entrance and garden: a small path leading along the moat.

"Now don't forget, this is the fifth potted plant on the right," he said, "You might have to come here alone!"

They squeezed through the opening and found themselves behind a thick wall of plants. At the end was a small opening. Here they could squeeze between the plants. They now found themselves in a large bright room. Participants from all corners of the Earth were standing around chatting. The registration table was off to the side. As they walked up, an elderly gentleman with a shock of bushy white hair rose, hand outstretched.

"Bertram!" The two men greeted each other warmly.

"Who have we here?"

"Didn't Maurice tell you?" Bertram asked, "Eliza, this is professor Perspicio. We call him Percy for short." Eliza warmly shook hands with the Einstein look-alike, suppressing a smile as she noticed what could have been a birthmark, but looked more like a smudge of purple ink peeking from under his hair. *"Perfect caricature of the absent-minded professor who carries a pen stuffed behind his ear, not realizing it is leaking,"* she smothered a smile.

"Maurice gave me this note for you." Bertram handed him a small business card with a few scribbled words, "Eliza's his personal guest."

Percy ushered them into the adjacent conference room; it was large, but intimately lit. An extra seat was tagged onto the front row. Eliza deposited her bag. Percy slipped away, and suddenly they were surrounded by a group of young people. She recognized them as Mary's friends. She had met them on their visit to the U.N. with Global Education Motivators and later, when Hugh and others had returned to lobby the U.N.

To her surprise, Bertram was laughing with delight and trying to hug them all at once.

"This is the trusty crew of Mary's Peace Warrior and my comrades in arms. Together, we have sworn to salvage the world from the fear epidemic," Bertram chortled at Eliza.

"We met in New York!" Eliza couldn't help grinning. Bertram was radiant. Annette, sweeping her long blond hair out of her eyes, began introducing her to the younger members of the team, who she had not yet met: Jeff and Jan the twins, Molly and Ian.

Catching the look of sadness on Bertram's face, Annette said to Eliza, "David, one of our youngest and quietest members, passed away recently, after he had inspired kids all over the world to plant and tend 2 million trees! Now we consider him our Guardian Angel!"

Eliza was serious for a moment and then she said, "You guys made quite an impression yourselves– the professional way you lobbied the U.N. 'All-win' is becoming a household concept. So we're off to a running start! Now we just have to get them to adopt it as an international standard! Can't believe how things get moving once you guys are on board!" Eliza felt a rush of warmth, as she spoke. "Really great seeing you guys here!"

As she stood pleasantly engulfed by the bubbly conversation, she allowed her eyes to roam the room.

There was Terry, the little fireball with her guitar and Luci, her song partner.

A young man caught her eye. He was personally greeting participants, looking at each, in turn, as if he or she was the one person he had been dying to meet all his life.

Someone waved.

It was Gaia standing around with a whole slew of her All-Win Network friends.

With a rush of pleasure, Eliza waved back. She was content to be back again in her work-a-day environment—to her surprise. "*Try to run away from something and you find yourself right smack bang in the middle of it!*" Wryly, she smiled to herself.

In the background, the young people were telling Bertram that one of Mary's students, Antonia, was visiting St. Leon.

Hugh turned to Bertram, "Did you get a message from Mary? She wrote she had not heard back from you about some emergency. She said it was confidential and didn't go into detail!" *Juanita?* Bertram kept his thought to himself.

"Anyway, there's some emergency," Annette chimed in, "Really sad that she won't be coming! Just won't be the same!"

Bertram felt a rush of anxiety, and, as Takeshi spirited Annette away, he turned to Eliza and whispered, "Do you still have your computer?"

Eliza frowned. "I wasn't carrying it when we scaled that path...We must have left it down in the meadow!"

At that moment Percy appeared. "May I introduce you to my nephew Geoffrey?" Eliza saw Bertram look up in surprise and then greet the young man with a wide grin.

"Did you get time to read my book?" Bertram asked after some initial catching up.

"I did!" Geoffrey replied. "Absolutely artful, the way you turn the life of the Hero in your book around. I'm not sure how realistic that is, though. I can't really believe in the power of the all-win principle-- not in the face of the powers that actually rule the Earth."

Bertram looked disappointed and slightly puzzled. Then, as if a thought had suddenly struck him, a look of apprehension crept over his face. "I'd so hoped that you of all people would get something out of it!" he said. He was looking at Geoffrey intently.

Eliza shifted her attention from Bertram to Geoffrey. Yes, there was something incongruous about the young man, Eliza felt. Playfully, she imagined she was he, head held high, looking as if he owned the world, a fixed smile that dazzled in its brilliance every time he caught anyone's eye. Yet behind all that outward show, she sensed an internal void. She felt a chill of apprehension. She only hoped she was mistaken.

She focussed again, banishing all other impressions. Again, there seemed to be an absence of all feeling… This had to be a temporary 'uptightness', nothing more.

Nevertheless, it flashed across her mind that it was just possible that Geoffrey had the predisposition of what, by some, was referred to as a *sociopath*. Someone without any conscience at all.

Eliza looked away. *I wonder what he is doing here,* she thought. *No feelings, no empathy. No wonder he couldn't conceive of how the all-win principle could work.*

Geoffrey turned to Eliza. Now *she* became the one person in the world he was dying to meet. Eliza noticed the smoothness of his behavior.

"You'll like Maurice!" he said, in a tone that insinuated Eliza and he knew each other well. "He has not arrived from the airport yet. Neither has he phoned. He was flying out of Kennedy, New York. Fear tactics to keep people in their place – wreaks havoc with people's schedules." The image caused him to smile.

"What do you mean?" Bertram interrupted, "How can Maurice be in the States? We were with him only yesterday. He must be here."

Without mentioning the dungeons or the meadow of the night before, Bertram recounted their meeting. "He gave me a note of introduction yesterday when we met!"

Geoffrey switched his attention to Bertram. "Perhaps he was tired and decided to sleep in. He has his own Wing. He's not staying in Conference area with the rest of us. He's been coming here since he was a boy and always inhabits the same quarters!"

Eliza looked away, unable to shake her unease.

"Why don't we start?" Percy called, waving them to their places.

252

Bertram and Eliza sat down in the front row. Geoffrey went to the back.

"Ladies and gentlemen, kindly be seated."

Percy paused.

"I should like to welcome each and every one of you again," he said as the fidgeting died down." This meeting has been given a great deal of forethought. Each one of you has been carefully chosen. The matter at hand is extremely urgent. We are dealing with a fear epidemic which you, each in your own way, are attempting to contain. You are using a variety of approaches. Once we have all pooled what we know and thoroughly understand one another's plans, we shall be able to coax humanity to accept one comprehensive world rule.

Eliza looked sharply at Bertram. His choice of words reminded her of the Holy Order of the Snake.

86. President Kundana

For the hundredth time, Jean mulled over the arrangements. Surreptitiously, he glanced first to the right, then to the left, then again behind him. Yes! Every one was in place.

Finally, the big day. President Kundana was scheduled to address the people in the Capital. The event would be guarded, as never before. He'd be surrounded by a carefully trained army of henchmen and guards. No one would be able to approach him. But Jacques and he, high-up members of the police force, had been placed in charge of the arrangements. This was their opportunity finally to prise him free from his throng of armed militia that guarded him day and night!

In the first rows of the hall were only members of the resistance movements, each one was armed with a plastic poison dart gun. Lining the walls and close to each door were other members of the resistance. Each of these was also armed with poison dart guns, just in case they were attacked from the rear.

Carefully, he went over in his mind's eye each of the people he had trusted. Yes, he had known each for a long time now. Each came from a bona fide resistance group. Each was being watched by others, so that no group could take others by surprise without risking being shot down themselves.

On the stage, young children had strewn rose petals that very morning with only him in the hall. The dais from which the President would speak was in exactly the right position.

There was a hush as a lone figure appeared on the stage.

It was Jacques.

"Ladies and gentlemen," Jacques spoke, "Welcome!

"Our President has bestowed a special honor on us today in response to the '*Reclaim your life. Go All-Win Movement*' which has taken our people by storm. He will outline his policies and will honor us by assuming complete leadership of the project. For this momentous occasion, we have chosen the largest auditorium in our Nation. Everything has been arranged with the greatest of care.

"Just some practical announcements.

"The exits are behind you in the rear of the room. There are also doors on either side. So in case of emergency, please use the door closest to you."

As he spoke, six large doorways lit up. Jacques paused to allow every one to get their bearings.

"Because of our crowded conditions, the generals have decreed that we greet our president, as follows." Jacques held up his right arm at a 60-degree angle and looked straight ahead. The salute used by the Nazis! How appropriate, Jean thought, the nazi salute in Kukundu.

Jean was still double-checking. He had had Jacques personal assurance that all was ready downstairs. The ambulance was waiting close by. And below the stage every one was in position.

"Thank you!" Jacques ended and hurried off the stage.

Loud cheering from outside. Then sharp commands and the sound of marching. A bugle rallied the troops. Then the notes of the national anthem. From both sides, militia smartly marched onto the stage. They took up positions around the dais, leaving a narrow corridor for the President to take his position at the lectern.

Jean counted: Yes, exactly 50, in careful rows. The members of the resistance would now each be taking their bearings, ready to act. Jacques was a meticulous organizer. This was a master plan, which Jacques himself had perfected.

...a master plan in which one hundred things could go wrong.

Each of the fifty on the stage could do something unexpected. So could each of their own people carefully positioned among the audience. Something could shake the crowd before they had time to carry out their plan. The ambulance might get stuck ...

Hurriedly, Jean brought his mind back to the immediate situation as, through the public address system, a voice announced, "His Excellency, the President of Kukundu!"

A cheer arose from the audience. Every one craned their necks. The auditorium was so crowded that they had taken out all chairs and people were pressed, one against the other. Jean cheered along with the crowd, as Kundana entered the stage.

Jean held his breath until Kundana had positioned himself behind the mike. Two of the top generals stood close behind him so as to appear on as many photos as possible, as the international press flashed away.

So far so good.

A sign from one of the generals which were positioned behind Kundana, and the press filed docilely from the stage. A spotlight went up lighting the face of the President.

The national anthem sounded and as the last tones died away, the command echoed throughout the room, "Salute your president!"

The whole auditorium was suddenly alive, as each person in the crowd moved to salute, despite the cramped conditions.

That was the sign.

As if swooning at the honor, almost all of the militia sank to the ground, leaving only five standing and one of the generals. For a moment, those who were still standing stood blinking as if not sure they were awake.

Hurriedly, Jean took aim and hit the general. He fell with the remaining five, as the trap door opened, and the President with the two top generals disappeared from view.

The trapdoor snapped back into place within half a minute. If he had not known what was about to happen, Jean would have thought he had been imagining things except for the ravage of all the militia lying helter-skelter on the stage.

"Fire!" Jean screamed at the top of his lungs. At that same moment, both the theatre's fake fire sprang into action and so did their misting device, filling the stage with a fog that made it difficult to see what was happening.

"Quick, the doors at the back of the room," Jean and the other underground members cried out.

All double doors were opened at once allowing everyone to pour out. The underground, which had been positioned there, were the first to get out into the open.

Jean, with the members of the underground that had been standing in the front, waited a moment until those behind them had turned and the auditorium was emptying, they then made their way out through the stage doors at the sides.

Outside everything was swarming with militia, who had been standing in position, eagerly awaiting the words of the president to come through the loudspeaker system.

The bottom stage door burst open. A man in general's uniform ran out. "Into the auditorium," he commanded, "Save the President from the fire!"

87. The Conference Opens

With an air of benevolent control, Percy looked around the room. All fidgeting stopped.

He began, "Count Maurice Le Sage has generously made these premises available. Unfortunately, he is unable to make the first session.

"My name is Professor Perspicio, please call me Percy. I am in charge of logistics. So if there are any problems whatever, I am the person to see. "He then gave the floor to Pim.

In his quiet way, Pim described the fear epidemic, the way power was landing in ever fewer hands, the reptilian brain and how, once the defunct reptilian brain was in control, human beings became unable to temper their aggression.

"Fear is Global Enemy Number One!" Pim pointed out, allowing his eyes gently to roam the audience.

Eliza felt suddenly restless. She glanced at Bertram. He was frowning, deep in thought.

In the background, Pim continued, "Fear tactics fuel terrorism and terrorism fuels fear.

When terror is used to combat terrorism, global war is not far away."

The fidgeting increased. People began talking among themselves as if to alleviate the tension. A voice wafted across the room, "This is the way the world works. We might as well accept it!"

Bertram whirled around. Eliza followed his gaze. It was Geoffrey who had spoken.

Bertram caught Eliza's eye and whispered, "Distant relative of Maurice's. I tried to convince him that there were other ways of looking at the world. Clearly, I failed!"

The uneasiness exploded into a wave of chatter.

At that moment, a man appeared in the isle next to Eliza's chair.

"Hello, Edward!" Bertram greeted him. But the butler didn't hear. He was too intent on signaling Percy...

"Maybe it's possible to heal the rift in our reptilian brains!" Terry's voice rang out clearly above the buzz. The feisty, pretty brunette was sitting on the front row at the opposite side of the hall.

"The Native Americans have a saying: 'You are another me.' When we teach ourselves and our children to remember this, that is where the healing can begin.

"May I tell you a story? It was told to me by a woman I met at a Peace Conference. She was a concentration camp survivor, and a woman of great warmth and compassion.

Here's what she told me:

"When the end of the war was proclaimed, the concentration camp victims were all skin and bones, starving skeletons, dying like flies around her. The guards had fled the scene. The gates were left open.

"At first, the survivors, herself among them, were too dazed to act. And then, like a pack of hungry wolves, howling and screaming, they surged toward the neighboring bakery shop. Day in day out, this shop had sent the smell of freshly baked bread wafting through the camp full of starving people. The bakers must have known about the atrocities that were taking place there.

"As she tore into the bakery, she looked around. There, under a table, cowered the baker with his family. She grabbed a knife, ready to strike. Their faces filled with naked terror.

"She stopped dead in her tracks.

"This was the exact expression, she had seen on the faces of so many concentration inmates, as they were herded toward the ovens. If she were to execute her tormentors, she would be doing to them what the Nazis had done to her. Until that moment, she had thought that the Nazis had been her enemies. Now, she knew her enemy was actually something much deeper that lurked in every human being: It was the willingness to lord it over another or the willingness to blindly submit to another's power.

"She stood there, knife poised. In the terrified faces of the baker and his family, she recognized herself. At that moment, she knew that if she were to execute them she would be no better than those who had decimated her life and were responsible for the atrocities against her friends and family, the gypsies, the intelligentsia, the Slavs and her fellow Jews.

She held back.

"If anyone was in the clutches of the defunct reptilian brain, it was this woman. She was totally in the fight or flight mode without any inhibitions. And at that moment, she rose above it[64].

"From that day on, her life was dedicated to helping people heal their wartime traumas. She spends her time learning and teaching the art of forgiveness and reconciliation.

Her fight and flight response had not gone away. It had become so large that it embraced the rest of humanity. The enemy was that part of herself that did not realize that we were all one. She had the choice to nurture that feeling of being an integral part of everything else, or to live in a nightmare where, at the slightest provocation, violence would once again erupt and take over her world.

"If a concentration camp survivor can overcome such trauma, then perhaps we all have that in us!"

"Thank you, Terry, this is the type of insight we were hoping to get from you all. Any other comments?" Pim asked.

The man, Bertram had called Edward was still trying to catch Percy's eye.

"Excuse me," Percy whispered to Pim "I am needed elsewhere." And he hurried to join Edward.

Just as Percy and Edward brushed passed her, Eliza heard Edward whisper, "Sir, it's about the Count. We're not sure what to do with him next."

In the background, Pim was saying, "This is our common goal: to create an all-win world in which reconciliation can take place. The objective of the conference is to share how we are doing this."

With a quick "Excuse me!" to Eliza, Bertram slipped out of his chair and, before Eliza could respond, hurried out of the room.

The image of the one lit up turret room surged into Eliza's mind and that lonesome figure waving. *"Could that have been Maurice?"* she wondered. Eliza tried to concentrate on the discussion, but without success.

Eventually, careful not to disturb anyone, she slipped into the reception room, entered the little passageway behind the wall of plants, found the button in the potted plant, slid the panel aside, and stepped into the hall.

"Where was Bertram?"

88. Where Is The Count?

Just minutes before, Bertram had hurried after Percy and Edward.

As the secret panel slid aside, he carefully peered out.

Quiet voices …He stepped through the opening and crept in their direction down the hall, around the corner, holding still at a half-open door.

"He's still our prisoner. Slug needs more time." It was Edward speaking.

"No idea at all where the leak is?" asked Percy

"No, none at all!"

"Maurice was a prisoner! *Leak?! What did they mean?*" Bertram felt a sense of foreboding, as memories flooded his mind: Maurice's wealthy family, houses all over the world, priceless first editions scattered among the books, that hideous school exercise, a child brought up to *divide and rule.* Then that figure hidden on the balcony. *Was Maurice an inadvertent informant about those people and activities which Snake feared could undermine its plans?*

Barely did the thought enter his mind, or Bertram pushed it aside. Too preposterous for words! But *'leak? leak? What could they possibly mean? Juanita was the only one with inside knowledge of Snake's business.*

Of course, there was the young peoples' action taking dictator's strategies and giving them an all-win twist. This, he had heard from Mary, had been gathering steam.

Was that making such a difference? Were they impacting the fear epidemic? Or was that, too, wishful thinking? It sounded as if Maurice was in trouble and Percy and Edward were in league.

Percy raised his voice in anger, "All-lose policies of foreign dictators! A lead article in the local scandal sheets. Surely no one else in this neck of the woods is going to be concerned, except my brother's friends! Damn it all! Is Slug losing his touch?"

Bertram's mind reeled, *Percy was a part of Snake!*

"Sir, Slug worked him over all yesterday evening and again this morning. When he made no headway, he decided to let him stew for a bit and try again later!"

"The Count doesn't suspect, does he, that Slug's in my employ?" Percy asked sharply.

"No, Sir. They've never met. Slug gathered the information at the Costa Rica abode without anyone knowing he was there. A close call once or twice, but Slug knows the consequences of being indiscreet. He's been with the family long enough!"

Bertram's thoughts were racing: *Maurice was unwittingly related to Snake and was being used to gather information on groups like the All-Win Network and Pim and his scientist friends. Edward was their spy, working for Percy and therefore also unwittingly for the highly secretive Holy Order of the Snake!* No wonder Edward had hung around in the library, on the terrace and in the auditorium. It had been Edward who had first suggested to Maurice to invite Percy to this conference!

"Once Slug has got the information, and we've administered the drug, the Count will fall asleep for a few days and at the end, sir, he'll believe he was delirious and not remember what happened," Edward reassured Percy.

"We don't have very long. As soon as we have the information, we must vaporize the wing. By that time, Maurice must be far away."

Vaporize? Bertram reached out to steady himself against the door. The bottom was dropping out of his reality. There was no end to the cruel lengths Snake would go to achieve its unscrupulous ends. They had gathered all the movers and shakers of those organizations which could frustrate their plans; they were milking them for every last drop of information and would then *vaporize them.* No wonder the wing had been rebuilt. Once they were finished, the Castle would still be standing as before but there would be no trace of those who had been there, even their clothes and papers would have disappeared!

Edward was continuing, "Pardon me, sir," he hesitated, "How do you suggest we explain his Lordship's absence?"

"So far, only two have seen him, Bertram and that girl! Tell them he suddenly had to leave. If we have to, we eliminate those two first!"

Bertram held his breath, straining to hear every word. His life and Eliza's were in immediate danger and only they could save everyone else!

As Percy paused, Bertram's thoughts began racing, trying to make sense of it all.

So Percy was Maurice's brother. He was one of those who "ran the family business", which was no other than the Holy Order of the Snake. No wonder Maurice considered *divide and rule* was an everyday concept. And while he, Mary, Pim and their young friends had been planning to neutralize fear, Snake's chief weapon, they had been smack bang in the middle of the worldwide communications center of the Holy Order of the Snake, their every word being faithfully passed on to Snake's Members all over the world!

Then that childish exercise. Generations of children had lived in that place, each carefully groomed to become loyal Snake supporters, unless, like Maurice they were considered inept.

That must have been Slug he saw on the day of the hook-up on the second floor balcony.

"I must phone," Percy's voice penetrated Bertram's jumble of thoughts.

Desperately Bertram looked for a place to hide.

An alcove. He slipped inside. Aghast, he saw the phone!

Out! Back into the hallway! The only cover was a potted fern. As the two came through the kitchen door, Bertram desperately tried to melt into the wall. The plant offered little cover. Luckily the lights were dim.

Percy entered the alcove and dialed a number. Edward made toward Bertram, who flattened himself against the wall, willing himself to disappear.

Edward suddenly stopped short, hesitated and then turned back.

With a sigh of relief, Bertram looked around. No! Nowhere else to hide. Had Edward spotted him? He must move. He had to find Maurice and set him free before Slug could get to him again. And no one may stop him! He must get away before Edward returned.

Percy was busy dialing the number.

Bertram slipped from behind the plant, ran quietly down the hall and turned off toward the Count's wing.

"The dungeons—Maurice has to be there!" he thought.

In the distance, he heard Percy exclaim, "No! They have published the list!?"

Bertram registered the edge of panic in Percy's voice, but was in too intent on reaching cover to give it a second thought.

Edward peered around the kitchen door, waiting until Bertram was out of sight, and then hurried in wily pursuit.

89. Eliza Follows

Eliza looked both ways. No one to be seen. Where could Bertram have got to?

Bertram had sat up and listened when Maurice's name had been mentioned. Perhaps, he was checking the dungeons to see whether he was still there. He had carefully avoided mentioning the dungeons to Percy, Geoffrey or any one else. "The Count's secret domain" wasn't that what he had said? Too bad, if she had thought of it earlier, she could have asked him to pick up her computer. She could hide it in her room without Percy knowing it was there.

She hesitated and then headed for the main stairs. She might as well check the turret. Perhaps it had been the Count she had seen. Perhaps he had accidentally locked himself in and had been trying to get her attention.

90. Chaos!

In the largest auditorium in Capital City, Kukundu, a tense group waited below stage, desperately trying to form a picture of what was happening around them from the sounds they were able to pick up. They could hear steps marching outside, some entering the building and then continuing, clearly audibly, right above their heads. Then the national anthem sounded. They waited with baited breath.

Finally, the command came, "Salute your President!"

A minute.

Then the trap door opened. Three bodies, arms and legs flailing, hurtled down onto the huge rubber trampoline, which was waiting to ease their fall—three limp forms, temporarily unconscious, poisoned by the darts.

Above them, there were shouts. "Fire!" Screams from all sides. Then the order, "Quick! the doors at the back of the room!"

Three of the men dressed as orderlies rescued the bouncing forms and took off their uniforms.

Three other men were standing by. These now donned the uniforms, while the "orderlies" pulled tightly fitting masks over the faces of the president and the two generals and then strapped them onto the stretchers, which had been prepared for that purpose.

Above bullhorns roared, "Okay, keep your heads. Everything's under control. Just remain calm and we shall get you all to safety."

Fallu's voice came through the walkie-talkie, "Three ambulances are waiting."

One of those now disguised as a general threw the doors open and ran outside shouting, "Wounded! Make way for the ambulances!" as he motioned the ambulances to approach.

Another, dressed as a general, followed hot on his heels and shouted through a bullhorn, "Attention! A fire has broken out in the auditorium. Rescue the President!"

The waiting militia looked confused.

Then all doubts dissolved as the side doors disgorged hordes of people, all civilians, crying and shouting with relief as they found themselves in the open. Anxious confusion followed, as, finally out in the open, friends and loved ones tried to locate one another.

In the confusion, the ambulances moved into position.

The below-stage doors were now flung open wide and the stretchers were rushed out and placed in the ambulances. Then the "orderlies" and "generals" jumped on board and before anyone had realized what had happened, they were on their way.

At the same time, the rest of the underground dispersed in all directions, away from Capital City and into the safety of the jungle.

The whole operation had lasted under 10 minutes and completely taken the militia by surprise.

91. The Turret

Eliza wound her way up the grand central staircase to the next floor. Then up another two flights. The stairs were much smaller than those leading to Eliza's floor, but elegantly carpeted. At the top was another hallway. Bedroom doors on either side.

Halfway down, a much smaller arched doorway. She hurried over and tried the handle. The door was unlocked. She pushed it and peered through.

A dark stairwell led upward.

Hesitantly she entered. Afraid it might fall into the lock, she left the door ajar. Up and up, she went until, leaving the light from the door behind her, she was forced to feel her way, step by step, in the pitch darkness until she came to a small landing.

She felt her way along the walls. No other exit, just another flight of stairs, leading upwards.

Again a landing! Her foot hit something heavy, which skidded over the floor and then clanged against the stone wall. Eliza got down on her knees and with her hand explored the floor. Clouds of dust engulfed her.

"Hachooo!" she sneezed. At the same time her hand closed around the key.

A sudden movement caught her attention.

Quickly she rose to her feet and headed in the direction of the sound. A door! She felt the handle. There was a large keyhole. She inserted the key! It turned! She twisted the handle and pushed.

The door was wrenched open. The force yanked Eliza forward, hurtling her headlong into a room and skidding across the floor.

A figure darted past her. Eliza caught a glimpse of a face, eyes bulging, mouth distorted by a grin of fear.

The figure dashed through the door, slammed it, and turned the key.

It was the Count, barely recognizable, beside himself with terror.

Footsteps pelted down the stairs, seeming to take them two, three at a time.

A wail, followed by staccato cries, as if the air was being knocked out of him. Scuttling sounds! He had slipped and was falling down the stairs!

Then silence.

Was he unconscious? Eliza lay where she had fallen, gasping for breath, trying to make out what had befallen the Count.

Deathly silence!

Ouch! Her hand hurt. Carefully she moved her fingers. Nothing broken. Only her elbow and knees were grazed.

She looked around.

The stark room was lit by the single window. Slowly she rose to her feet and crept to the door. Trying the handle she realized it was solidly locked. She threw herself against it. She rattled the door handle. The door was massive and so was the lock. Her thumping fists could barely be heard.

In a sudden frenzy she called out at the top of her lungs, "Help! Open that door! Help! Help! Help …" until she was hoarse. Then she sank down, exhausted, on a pile of sacks, allowing her mind to clear.

Finally, she painfully hoisted herself up and looked around. The room was bare. There was a stench of urine and defecation, a bucket of dirty water, a cattle prod. She frowned. What was a cattle prod doing here?

Then it hit her: instruments of torture, the thought sent her heart pounding, her head reeling and again, she was gasping for breath.

Eliza willed herself to breathe deeply into her stomach to counter her fear. Gradually the panic abated, and her inner strength started to return. She must focus on the matter at hand. But as her mind pictured the terrifying possibilities, adrenaline was propelled through her body, sending her heart pounding and clouding her thoughts. Whatever happened, she must remain calm!

Breathing deeply into her stomach again, she steadied herself. Then making sure to focus on what she was doing so that her imagination would not take off, she gingerly picked up the cattle prod and inspected it. There was no cord. The thing ran on batteries. It still smelled of seared flesh. For a moment, the panic attack threatened to come back. Again Eliza focussed on her breath until the feelings subsided and her head cleared.

Concentrating on the items in the room, rather than her own thoughts, she clinically inspected her surroundings. The room had only one door, roughly hewn stone walls, and a pile of sacks. Beside what she had already seen and smelled, the room was empty.

Again she tried the door and carefully inspected the walls.

There was no way out.

Looking out of the window, her head swam, as her eyes followed the awesome drop down to the drawbridge where the night before she had stood, looking up at the Count.

Slowly, the situation sank in.

She was locked in a turret where as early as the night before, the Count had been held prisoner and tortured. That was clear from the terror on Maurice's face, the mad dash he had made for the door, and his fall down the stairs. Was he alive? His torturers had no idea that he had been found and would probably return to finish the job.

Her only hope of staying alive was to remain clear-headed and keep her fear at bay.

In her mind she ran over all she knew about fear and how to contain it.

Fear was a natural part of life, a healthy and necessary response: it gave the body a boost of adrenaline, narrowing the arteries and sending the oxygen-rich blood fuelling the body, eyes bulging open, ears straining to hear, all senses on alert. Shallow breathing served to pump oxygen to all the muscles, poised for fight or to flee. This was the response to fear humans shared with the rest of the animal kingdom and which was generated by what Pim had called the "reptilian brain". This state of preparation to fight or flight was usually of short duration, in response to an emergency. In humans it need not last for long. You could counteract it by focussing on pleasant, non-fear-producing thoughts, and breathing deeply.

Eliza allowed her gaze to wander farther afield, absorbing the soft contours of the gently rolling hills. She allowed the images of the field, the bees, and the flowers to suffuse her mind. Gradually, her sense of inner and outer connection returned. With this, her strength came surging back. Finally, sure that for the time being she had her fear in check, she allowed her mind to turn to the problem at hand.

There was a second fear response which could endanger her in this situation. This was fuelled by imagination. This too had a function. By imagining what could happen, she could plan to avoid future threats.

The real complication arose when a person held fear-provoking images in their mind (or in their subconscious) for long stretches of time. The body then remained in a fight and flight state of alert. At the slightest provocation, the fear response would surface in full force. Not in response to what was actually happening but to some imagined situation. A sort of Don Quixote response that missed its mark and would then result in a panic attack. This she must avoid at all costs. It would deliver her straight into the hands of Maurice's torturers.

Again she focussed on the peaceful scene, the hills, the drawbridge, the sun winking at her from the moat as if to say, "remember last night? You were not alone. Help can still reach you in time!"

Quickly, she banned the thoughts out of her mind. Hope was as dangerous as fear. Both jerked her away from what was actually happening and could cloud her mind.

She looked at her watch. It was just 12 o'clock. There was no alternative but to wait. Every one would soon be heading to lunch.

Gradually the heat wore her down.

Her concentration slipped and her thoughts began to meander. Where was Bertram? Had he been down to the dungeons? Was Bertram himself safe?

It was clear that the conference had been infiltrated. What information did the torturers seek? If they discovered her here, could she bluff her way out?

In the afternoon sun, the stench from the bucket permeated the room. A dull ache gnawed at her temples. Eventually, Eliza began to nod.

She struggled to her feet and walked over to the window and then started pacing up and down the room.

92. Escape

The ambulances sped through Capital City. From there out toward the large hospital, which lay at the edge of town.

Just before the hospital compound they turned off. Out of sight of the hospital itself, they made for a subsidiary road, heading to the river. A mile farther they veered off onto a dirt path. Here after several hundred yards on the left, long lianas formed a curtain.

The first ambulance pulled over. An orderly jumped out and pulled the liana's aside. One by one the ambulances pulled into the hiding place behind. Hurriedly, the lianas were rearranged to hide their frantic activity.

Two "orderlies" uncovered a truck and a jeep carefully hidden in the undergrowth. Then together the six transferred the three stretchers with their unconscious loads. The 'orderlies' changed into the farmer's clothing, which was waiting for them in the jeep.

Within ten minutes the three inert bodies were hidden beneath what looked like a truckload of wood. The ambulances were hidden where before the truck and jeep had been, and the truck with three farmers eased onto the road.

A few minutes later the army jeep pulled out. The liana's had been carefully replaced. At a leisurely pace, the jeep followed the truck, ready to foil any possible pursuit.

93. Bertram In A Tight Spot

Bertram crept around the rocks, moving as fast as he could, oblivious of the large waves, pounding the cliffs below. He tried to focus on the path, but his mind was in a whirl. Surely the wind could have slammed the door? It did not have to be a person? But who then had switched off the lights?

Edward must have seen him behind the plant, bided his time, and followed him when he had made his move. So Edward did not know there was a way out of the dungeons, or he would have followed him down and put him out of commission.

Bertram jumped the few feet where the track was missing, and reached the outcropping which seemed to block the path. Without problem, he located the crevice and wormed his way through, jumped over the place where the path had fallen away and then scurried along the track until the path split.

He stopped.

If Percy, Edward, and whoever else was involved were planning to 'vaporize' the Conference Wing, this path along the cliffs might be the group's only escape. The drawbridge was the only other exit from the Castle. And if they were bent on killing them all, they would certainly guard the bridge to prevent anyone from slipping away. If the whole group were to take the path he had taken with Eliza back up the cliff, they would exit at the Castle entrance and walk straight into Percy's arms, and Percy wouldn't hesitate to kill them all. Easy to do with vaporizing guns!

But if they couldn't go up the path to the Castle, whereto from here?

His eye followed the faint track that continued straight ahead, Gingerly, Bertram picked his way between the boulders. Gradually, the track ascended, almost reaching the top of the cliff. Then it evened out and continued just below the edge. An adult could walk the path without being seen from the top.

Bertram continued further along the uneven track. After a while, he noticed trees above him. Then the path came to an abrupt end.

Ahead of him six, giant steps. These would be hard for anyone to scale without strong knees. He thought of Pim on his straight back chair and his slight stiffness whenever he rose. Then there was Nannette. She had difficulty walking. If the whole group would have to be evacuated, the stronger, more athletic members must assist the others.

Bertram mounted the stairs.

Nearing the top, he stooped down low, so as not to be seen from above. Then, he carefully peered over the edge of the cliff. Above him was a dense forest. For a moment, he scanned the surroundings, searching the forest for he knew not what.

No one to be seen.

Two last steps and he was over the top. Here the group could congregate without being spotted from the Castle. It would be a long trek on foot from here to the next village, but the hardship was negligible in comparison to the fate which awaited them if they stayed put.

Quickly, Bertram turned around and hurried back to the junction with the old familiar path he had taken with Eliza. He reached the top.

Fortunately, no one was around and he was able to get over the drawbridge, through the front door, through the hidden panel and into the conference room without being seen.

There was a friendly buzz of conversation. Everyone was seated in circles.

Bertram scoured the room before entering.

Percy had not returned, neither had Edward. He looked around for Eliza. He must find her now.

But Eliza was nowhere to be seen. If only she had not done something reckless and followed him!

Again he searched the room, this time more desperately, but Eliza was not there.

Participants were assembled in large circles with Pim wandering between them listening to now one then to another of the projects being discussed.

Everything was being recorded.

Annette was closest to where Bertram was standing, sitting with her back to the door. Bertram crept up behind her without being noticed. No one who knew him was facing his way.

"Seen Eliza?" he whispered in her ear.

Annette turned with a wide smile to Bertram.

"Hi!" Where did the two of you get to? We thought you were together.

Eliza followed you out about five minutes after you left. She was neither here during the coffee break, nor for the rest of Pim's lecture.

She turned to Takeshi. "Did you see Eliza at lunch?"

Pat saw Bertram and nudged Arturo. The two leaned across. "Looking for Eliza? We were looking for her, too. Nowhere to be seen. We thought she was with you!"

"Thanks!" Bertram tried to smile reassuringly. "Must be resting. I should go and find out if there's anything she needs!"

Followed by the grins of his friends, Bertram crept away, hurried through the deserted reception area, then through the sliding panel, through the hall and up the stairs.

He knocked on her door but there was no reply.

Carefully, he tried the handle. The door opened easily, but Eliza's room was empty.

Bertram ran up the next flight of stairs, taking the steps, two, three at a time, his steps muffled by the luxurious red-pile carpets.

Just as he neared the top, he held back. That smell...

He was catapulted back to Costa Rica to the balconies above the auditorium. That had to be Slug! He crept up the next flight of stairs, the smell intensifying as he went.

Voices!

He crept up the last few steps and peeped around the corner.

There stood Percy, Edward and a crude looking fellow. Tattoos on his huge bare arms, which stretched his T-shirt to maximum. Slug! He thought of the broad back he'd seen on the balcony. Yes, that could be the guy...

In a crumpled heap on the floor, lay Maurice.

"He's dead!" Edward looked badly shaken. With deference, he closed Maurice's eyes and stiffly got up off his knees.

"Been with him all his life!" Edward's voice wavered. "Always tried to protect him from himself."

"You protected him, but forgot your duty to the family!" Slug grunted.

Bertram felt a lump in his throat. "What could have happened to poor, dear Maurice?"

"I had nothing to do with this! Edward pointed accusingly at Slug. "You never could follow orders!"

"Stop this, you two!" Percy glared from one to the other. "We must get my brother out of here without anyone knowing. There is no minute to lose!

"Okay, take my brother's body down through the kitchen area. The freezer's the best place. No one ever looks there, except of course Consuela. Where's she now?"

"She has gone to the village. All's set for supper. It's a cold buffet. She's off until after dinner.

Bertram recoiled down the stairs and hid in Eliza's room. He sank down on a chair, his heart heavy. "Poor, kind Maurice with his endearing French ways. Always so generous, so deeply involved with the beauty of Nature and people..."

In the distance, he heard the voices of Percy, Edward and Slug approaching and then recede as they lugged Maurice's body further down the stairs, step by careful step. They had the run of the place what with Consuela safely outside the Castle and the others secured in the wing. Outside of Eliza and Bertram, himself, no one knew about the secret panel.

He waited, feelings reeling.

As their voices receded, he got up and listened at the door. With great care, he inched it open and looked both ways.

Good! No one to be seen.

He dashed along the corridor, up the stairs and through the hall to where the body had lain. Slowly, he opened the little arched doorway, which Percy had carefully closed.

In the dark, he could faintly make out a stairwell leading up.

This had to be the way to the turret. Eliza must to be there. She had indeed seen Maurice the night before and guessing that he, Bertram, had gone searching for Maurice, she had thought she would find him here.

He paused and took a few deep breaths, trying to steady his anxiety. If only she was all right! Barely had they met, or the lives of a whole conference gathering depended on their ability to work together in complete harmony.

94. To The Border

"A trill, three times repeated.

"They're here!" The crew came alive on the police sloop, temporarily borrowed by the Underground from their friends in the police.

"How's the ferry man? Still asleep?"

"Yes, he'll be out for a while! The poison knocks you completely out for a couple of hours and you wake up without knowing what hit you. No ill effects. We use it on animals whenever we need to tranquilize them."

As the truck with the three "farmers" appeared, followed by the "generals" in the jeep, the engines sprang to life and the police boat pulled out of its hiding place. The three unconscious forms were transferred. Their uniforms hurriedly returned and as the three that had temporarily assumed their uniforms changed clothes, the "farmers" turned the truck around and were on their way back to town.

"Hope you make the border by nightfall."

"Thanks and good luck!" The small crew waved as first the "farmers" then the three militia, no longer in disguise, got into the jeep. Soon both the truck and the jeep were out of sight and the police boat had pulled away.

The sounds of the jungle took over.

Fifteen minutes later, the ferryman stirred and rubbed his head. Strange, he thought as he sat up. I must have fallen asleep.

95. Escalation!

Eliza paced back and forth. Her feet creaked on the dusty floor.

A sound! She froze.

Footsteps?

Quietly, she retreated to one side of the door, so that if anyone entered she would be shielded from view.

The key turned in the lock. Very slowly the door budged. Eliza was ready. She tugged the door open, just as the Count had done.

It was held firm. A man stepped into the room.

"Bertram!", she exclaimed.

"Oh Eliza, I'm so glad I found you." For a brief moment, they just held each other, too relieved to speak. Then Eliza extricated herself. "Let's get out of here. They can return at any moment! We can talk in my room!"

They crept down the stairway as fast as they could.

Eliza was still unsure on her feet. Twice she stumbled on the narrow steps. *"The Count must have slipped and fallen all the way to the bottom," she thought.*

Bertram carefully opened the door. The hallway was empty. No one had heard them. They slipped through the hallway, down the stairs, into her bedroom and locked the door.

"Are you really okay?" he asked. "If ever you needed to be firm on your feet, now's the time!"

Eliza was stiff, her grazed knees still hurt, but, other than her self-confidence, everything was in tact.

Urgently she turned to Bertram, "That man who fell down the stairs? It was the Count. I'm sure he had been tortured. Did you smell the cattle prod? It smelled of burned flesh!"

"I believe you! Quickly, tell me exactly what happened." Bertram pulled her over to the bed and they both sat down. "We need to conserve our energy!"

Eliza took a deep breath and began, sticking to the main points, so as not to waste time. "His death had to be an accident!" she concluded.

"That places them in an awkward position!" Bertram nodded. "He's Percy's brother and Percy's a Member of Snake. In Costa Rica, Maurice joked that his brothers used him to keep tabs on movements like the All-Win Network."

He then told Eliza of how he had overheard Percy and Edward plotting to vaporize the group.

Eliza took a deep breath. Forcing her voice to stay calm, she said, "I wonder whether Maurice's death means that they will act sooner than planned..."

"I think they first want to get as much information as they can. Their strategy seems to be to milk us for all the information they can get. If Edward sees I've escaped ..." "Escaped?" Eliza asked.

"That's a long story, but you need to know the details," he said. "I went down to the dungeons! Thought Maurice must be there. Just as I reached the first landing, I heard the door close and all the lights went out!"

"You mean Edward locked you in?"

"It had to be him.

"I ran back up, but the door can't be opened from the inside. Moreover, it was padded. And bang as I would, no one could possibly hear. Anyway, every one's isolated in the Conference Wing. So there was nowhere to go, but down."

"In the pitch black?" Eliza gasped.

"It was slow going, but in the end, I got to the bottom."

"I called out, but Maurice didn't answer. Then I searched every inch of the dungeons, afraid he was lying somewhere, unconscious."

"How did you get out?"

"Well, I inched my way around the walls and found the door to the lift. Then I located the button. It was on the right near the ground—a stone knob. But the door of the lift refused to open."

"So the lift to Maurice's quarters was no longer working? What about that passageway?"

Bertram noted that unconsciously Eliza was asking for the precise details she would need, if she were to be the one to help the group escape.

"I found the entrance to the tunnel, but it came to a dead- end—a tight-fitting rock wall!"

"Bertram, you must have been beside yourself!"

"I was.

"At that point, I can tell you, Eliza, I had visions of being marooned down there. Only Maurice knew the entrance to the dungeons and he was no-where to be found. And then of course you had been there once. But not even you knew how to find the door. I cursed myself: I had been so careful to disorient you, by leading you around in circles."

"Oh, Bertram, I'm so relieved you're alright!" she exclaimed. Reaching out, she took his hand and caressed it with her cheek.

As their eyes met, he could see the concern mixed with relief in her eyes. Gently, she placed his hand back onto his lap, allowing her hand to linger on his.

"But how did you get out?"

"For a moment, Bertram was lost for words. A barrier between Eliza and himself had suddenly dissolved, which, he now realized, had separated them from the beginning. A barrier, he knew, came from her fear of being truly intimate and his own fear that they would never be able to explore the depths he sensed could develop between them—a fear that had prompted him to obsess about her and most probably gave her a sense of being stifled. Now that he knew that she genuinely cared, he felt relaxed! He was no longer alone. Together with Eliza, he felt ready to meet whatever lay in store.

His old confident self, Bertram continued with a new vibrancy in his voice, "At first I was desperate! But then I began to examine the rock, inch by inch, until, after what seemed an eternity, I did locate the knob.

"Now this is important, Eliza. The knob is located where the tunnel wall meets the rock face. Again, it's at the bottom near the ground on the right. A smoothish outcropping of stone."

It hit Eliza, she was being prepared for coming events. She held her breath, listening attentively without interrupting.

"I sensed the different texture, grabbed it firmly and jiggled it, until the stone wall rolled outwards. I tell you!" He sighed and his face told the rest.

"Oh Bertram!" She closed her eyes, imagining what his close shave with death must have been like. "You *have* been through the mill!" A wave of tenderness washed over her. "It's funny all the things that go through your mind, when you think you might be about to die. I realized that I would be the cause of *your* death, Eliza. That really bothered me!

"It was just a flash, mind you," he added, "I did not really have time to think until I was out in the open. And then I did sit down and think things through.

"I'm terribly sorry to have brought you here. I was so happy when we finally met, I didn't want to let you go. And now your life is in danger!" The words tumbled out, the feelings for her he had pent up for so long. For a moment, all he wanted was to savor his relief that now things had shifted between them.

Eliza allowed his words to hit home. This time she did not run away. And then, the urgency of the situation penetrated the moment of quiet togetherness they were sharing.

Eliza took a deep breath. At the same moment, Bertram blurted out, "It's worse than you can possibly imagine! Snake's plan to vaporize us, once they have got the information they need, is part of something much greater." And he told her of how they were grooming the 102 Heads of State and other key leaders to perfect their ability to *divide and rule.* He continued, "As I sat there against the rock, *our rock*, trying to sort out my thoughts, I remembered how Annette said something about Mary and urgent developments. Thank God for solar technology and that your computer was right there! I was able to read my e-mail. Eliza, we're facing Armageddon!

There was a message from Mary with a list of murders commissioned by a batch of puppets of Snake in the 102 dictatorships. Snake's plan: to get Heads of State and other key individuals in the dictatorships to commit one another's murders. The plan is to be executed over a period of 2 weeks, starting a month from now!"

"But that's horrendous!" Eliza exclaimed. "Once they have committed the murders, the murderers will think they are in control of their countries, but in reality Snake will be in supreme control!

"Just imagine a spate of high-level murders! People will freak! Gone the last vestiges of order! People will lose confidence in their leadership and take the law into their own hands!" In a flash, Eliza saw the political volatility this would create, the instability in the Wealthy Countries, as those regimes they had counted on in the Poor Countries economically, disintegrated into political and economic mayhem.

"The Anti Terrorist Acts will be nothing in comparison to what is to come! Before we know it, Snake's power will be absolute, particularly if all the leaders of the most influential NGOs are vaporized. Then only Mary and her young people will know what is happening and be left to calm a panic-driven humankind with the all-win principle! No way that they can succeed!

She fell silent.

"Bertram this requires action on every front, or it will be too late!"

"Mary and Juanita are publicizing the list!" And he told her about the "World Game" Mary had described in her e-mail. "Apparently, everyone she has contacted today senses the urgency, and the World Game is taking off like wild fire. People liked the idea of puzzling over who will benefit from whose murder and how it would affect the world. There are a number who know it is no mere game and they see the urgency.

"I wonder..." his voice trailed off... He remembered hearing Percy on the phone, while he was escaping down the hall, and the panic in his voice as he exclaimed, *"No! You mean they have actually published the lists!!!?"* Now he saw the connection. "That's what Percy's was so upset about! He knows their plan has been leaked!"

Urgently, he turned to Eliza, "You know we might have to use that escape route sooner than I had thought! He knows about the World Game. He can't afford to let any of us get away! And he told Eliza what he had heard.

"We'll have to take the same path you and I took. It was quite something, walking it alone today. And we walked it as night was falling!

"Eliza, the dungeons are our only way out. They're bound to have the drawbridge covered.

"Let me tell you about the escape route I discovered. You and I may have to split up to get the group away from the surroundings of this Castle..." Bertram looked at her intently.

"Once I was outside, I marked the tunnel exit with three stones and scoured the area around the door to see whether there was another knob. And there was! It opens and closes the passageway. As I sat there, the door closed of its own accord. It must be on a timer. After all, in the olden days, they didn't want it to be accidentally discovered if the family was forced to leave in a hurry and forgot to close it behind them.

From where she sat, Eliza could see out of the window. In the distance, meadows alternating with wooded hills. How peaceful these looked. So different from what was happening within the Castle walls.

Soft voices outside in the courtyard.

She walked over to the window and peeked out, shielded by the curtain.

With an urgent gesture, she beckoned to Bertram. "I wonder what they are doing!?" she whispered.

"My God!" he exclaimed, "It looks as if Percy, Edward and Slug are preparing to move out already... "

Eliza caught his arm and pointed.

Geoffrey strolled out from just below their window, where the main entrance was located.

Percy swung around at Slug. "How did young Geoffrey get out?"

"I destroyed the pathway! I did! Honest, sir!" Slug flinched, as if expecting to get slapped.

Geoffrey swaggered toward them.

"How did you get out?" Percy demanded.

"I sensed something was going on, so I went outside to the Conference Wing garden, saw the path was gone. Figured you might be up to something, so I came through the sliding panel!"

Seeing his uncle's furious look, he grinned. "Well, you don't think I spend all this time with you and don't pick up a trick, or two. I watch you all the time, uncle dear. I'm the best student you've ever had. I saw you exit through the panel when you thought no one was around!"

"Well, we can use an extra pair of hands. I don't want to waste any time!" Percy turned to Slug.

"We have to move a very heavy instrument from my wing." He pointed to the opposite side of the Castle to where the Conference was being held. "To that point over there! You take care of that with Master Geoffrey!"

"That's exactly where the path comes up over the cliff!" Bertram whispered.

Eliza nodded without taking her eyes off the scene.

"Be extremely careful!" Percy was cautioning them, "It's on hair-trigger alert. The slightest vibration and it will go off, before it is patched with the bomb in the freezer. And that could mean the end of you! Not that you wouldn't deserve it. Fools, each one of you!"

"My God!" Eliza said under her breath. They plan to vaporize us all now. There's no time to lose! We've got to get the others out."

"Bomb in the freezer?" Bertram frowned.

As they turned to go, Percy's voice wafted through the window. Eliza held back.

"Edward! I must get our ancient family documents out. We don't want those decimated and we won't be able to return for a while. I'll need your help!

"Edward, you come with me.

"Slug, Geoffrey, once the vaporizer's in position, come up to my office and help Edward with the boxes I'll have packed by then. There will be quite a few! We'll load Maurice's car. Slug, see his Rolls is waiting outside the main entrance!"

"Can I detonate the bomb?" Geoffrey asked, his voice trembling with excitement.

"We'll see!"

"Quick, Eliza! We must warn the others!" Bertram whispered in her ear and drew her toward the door.

96. M'bwene Arrives

Josette paced to and fro at the edge of the clearing.

Behind her, the whole camp was gathered.

Had they succeeded to smuggle M'Bwene and John from the refugee camp over the border into Kukundu? Had they been able to time their action to coincide with the chaos in Capital City? Would the kidnapping of Kundana go so smoothly that Jean could make the rendezvous with 'Daddy' M'Bwene? And most important: Would the kidnapping of Kundana succeed?

Three trills!

Josette's heart started pounding. The moment she had worked for for so long had arrived.

"Marcel! I think they're here!" she whispered, always aware of the danger of intruders happening upon their hideout.

Marcel ran out of the communications hut where he had been waiting in case emergencies arose.

Respectfully, they stood at the edge of the clearing as two armed men appeared, dressed in fatigues. They were followed by John St. Claire, Jean and—yes!—President "Daddy" M'Bwene!

There was a soft drum roll and then in two-voice harmony the Kukundu national anthem emanated from the tiny crowd, gathered in the clearing. *May Kukundu shine in peace!* All eyes were moist, here and there a voice broke under the emotional strain.

Finally, a new era was dawning and their next step could begin.

M'Bwene turned to the peace builders. His voice was deep and rich, "Thank you all for the courageous role each of you is playing. Jean tells us Kundana, together with two of his top generals, have been successfully captured. They were driven away safely in three ambulances and transported over the border in one of the police boats which is in the hands of the resistance."

"Three cheers for our beloved President!" The cheers were accompanied by a choir of excitement as birds and monkeys joined in.

"Thank you," M'Bwene laughed. "Just one caution! I'm not your President yet. That's for a referendum to decide!"

But to the freedom fighters "Daddy" M'Bwene was their rightful leader. They thronged around him, each one eager to shake his hand.

Josette standing close to her leader for the very first time saw that beneath his smile, he looked pallid. He must be tired after the trek. But beyond that, she suspected a deep emotional fatigue.

"We'll hold our planning meeting over dinner," Marcel announced, "I hate to rush you, but would you be ready to join us in 30 minutes, Your Excellency? We must get you over the border in time for the police boat to be back on duty by daybreak."

97. The Whole Gathering Attempts To Escape

Bertram grabbed Eliza's hand. Together they ran down the stairs.

At the panel, which sealed the conference area from the rest of the Castle, Bertram stopped short and carefully scrutinized the knob. There didn't seem to be any wiring attached. Heart in mouth, Bertram gave it a nudge.

Thank God! The panel moved aside. They were probably planning to vaporize the interior of the Conference Wing and leave the rest of the Castle in tact.

"Just a minute, Bertram, we can't just go bursting in – what are we to say?" Eliza grabbed his arm.

Bertram hesitated. "Better keep it as simple as possible," he said, "We could say that almost all the global coordinators of the all-win movement are gathered in this room. And if anyone wanted to sabotage our work, this would be the chance of a lifetime."

"Okay, then we can tell them about Maurice…but do you think they will believe us?" Eliza's hand was still resting gently on Bertram's arm. "People who know you or me will, of course. But what about those who know neither of us?"

"Let's talk to Pim first. By now, every knows him," Bertram suggested. Hurriedly, both stepped through the doorway into the room, shielded by the row of potted plants.

When they entered the conference hall, the large circles were still in deep discussion. Annette nudged Takeshi, and they both smiled at Bertram as he entered with Eliza. Bertram scanned the room. Pim was at the far end.

Bertram winked at his young friends. Then Eliza and he walked over to Pim and led him to the kitchen area.

"Snake's about to strike!" Eliza burst out, as quietly as she could.

Pim looked slightly taken aback.

Bertram looked around

In the far corner of the kitchen, he located the door to the large walk-in fridge. He walked over, opened the door, and turned on the light. There lay poor Maurice.

Bertram's eyes filled with tears.

Pim hurried over.

"Oh, no!" he whispered.

"Remember what Maurice told us about being the son of a fabulously rich family who was not allowed to meddle in the family business? Remember those scraps of paper, we found in Maurice's library? Maurice is related to the Holy Order of the Snake! Percy is his brother!"

Bertram then told Pim about how Eliza had discovered Maurice, the instruments of torture in the turret room, how Percy, Edward and Slug had discovered Maurice's body at the foot of the stairs, and their plans to vaporize them all.

"You know, those devices that can be triggered from a long distance? Could this be one?" Eliza asked. While Bertram had been talking to Pim, she had been checking the freezer. Now she was pointing to a small square box, a cube, six inches each side. Pim signaled urgently to the others to leave the fridge. He then hurriedly closed the door.

"It's the newest generation of mini bombs! Extremely powerful!" he said urgently. "They vaporize flesh and bones and materials of all kinds. They leave all else in tact. No way of dismantling it without special equipment. It can be patched with a vaporizer. When they pull the trigger, the bomb's power increases hundred fold. "

"How far is its reach?"

"Hard to tell. The vaporization of living matter and material will probably be limited to this wing. But the shock waves are a different matter. I'm not sure how far the vibrations will travel. It could be that they will affect us, when we're outside of the Castle."

"What if there are other members of Snake who we don't know about among the participants? They might decide to detonate the small bomb, if they knew it is there."

"Best not to let anyone know," Pim answered Bertram, "How shall we tell the group?"

"Let's talk to our closest friends first—those who already know about Snake," Eliza replied, "They can help to break the news to the rest. No time to do any convincing!"

"All three of us can select our friends," Pim suggested and led the way back into the hall. Speaking through the microphone, he said, "There is a new development. Eliza, Bertram and I shall be asking a group of you to help us. We shall be back with an explanation as soon as we can."

Eliza and Bertram walked around the room, gathering those they knew they could count on into the kitchen area.

Eliza hadn't seen any of her friends for a number of weeks.

She kept their questions at bay with a smile. "I got kidnapped by Bertram when we met on the plane and now here I am. We'll have time to catch up later."

The huge kitchen was packed. Most of them she knew personally, each representing networks of organizations which belonged to the All-Win Network. Many of her closest friends were there, Gaia, Nanette, who was walking with a stick, Robin, Dana, Henry, Emile. Then there were Terry and Luci and the crew of the Peace Warrior and a whole slew of people she knew from All-Win Network meetings.

"An emergency has developed and we need your urgent help," Pim addressed the group. "Time is of the essence. It is vital we work as a team. Please just listen to the situation before asking questions. It is important that we don't make the rest anxious, so that we can get them to safety. The others are mostly people you yourselves invited. We wonder whether you can help us by vouching that what we have to say is indeed the truth.

"Eliza, please begin!"

Eliza looked around the group. Thank God for the long history she had of working with most of those present. Together several years ago, they had faced the threat of the Holy Order of the Snake and to foil one of their plots to take over the Earth, these very friends had formed the All-Win Network. She knew most, but not all of Bertram's young friends. There was just one young lad, who looked familiar, but whom she could not place.

She began, "This Conference was called to gather together leaders in the all-win field. So that we could share the details of our work and then, together with Pim's fellow scientists, develop joint strategies to bring the fear epidemic to a halt.

"For anyone invested in keeping the fear epidemic going as an instrument for harnessing political power, this gathering is an excellent opportunity to find out what we, the opposition, are doing and then while we're gathered in the same confined space to get rid of us all in one fell swoop.

"Bertram?"

Bertram told of his experiences in Costa Rica and what he had overheard that day, and how Percy, Edward Slug and Geoffrey were getting ready to blow up the Conference Wing with everyone in it and then leave.

"I think that they believed that Maurice knew something that was going to sabotage their plans. He didn't. And so he was tortured in vain. Finally, in his haste to escape he fell down the stairs and broke his neck."

Eliza watched the faces of her friends. They were barely breathing. There was no doubt that they believed what they were hearing. They'd all experienced the havoc wreaked by Snake when Snake had tried to isolate the U.N. by blocking the telephone lines in New York City.

Her eyes fell on Nanette. Dear Nanette, one of her very closest co-workers and founders of the Network. She had recently taken ill and been in a wheelchair for months. Walking with a stick, would she be able to make the path? Would her knees hold up?

"The Snake!" a young boy exclaimed with a thick Scottish accent. "That's right, Ian!" Eliza finally recognized the boy. He was the ham radio expert who had saved the day, helping them to get around Snake's blockade and, with the help of his little friends and their ham radios, reconnected the All-Win Network to the outside world.

"The only exit out of here has been blocked," Bertram remarked.

"Are you sure?" Hugh asked, "I came along the path just this morning. Everything was alright then."

"Perhaps you could quickly check it, Hugh!" Bertram suggested.

Within minutes Hugh was back. He looked shaken.

"Part of the path has fallen away. There's a huge drop, straight into the moat."

"Is there any proof of what you are saying?" Another young man asked. I know Pim, but I have never met either of you. Before I go off on a wild goose chase, I would like a little more proof. After all, the fact that the path has caved in doesn't prove anything."

Pim opened the door of the walk-in fridge.

Eliza helped Bertram to lift Maurice's body out and then quickly closed the door before anyone would see the bomb. Bertram knelt down next to him and gently positioned his head in a more natural position. His eyes had been closed. His hands had been crossed across his breast. Edward, gruesome as he was, must have cared for him deeply.

The group huddled around.

Bertram looked up. He was close to tears. "I have known many good people but no one kinder than Maurice. It is shocking that he of all people should come to such a tragic end."

Pim knelt down and for a moment laid his hand over Maurice's. "Goodbye, dear friend." he said tenderly.

One by one, the young people knelt by his side and took their leave.

"But they can't hope to get away with this!" Pat said indignantly. Arturo placed his hand on her shoulder and gave her a reassuring squeeze."

"They'll probably put it down to terrorism. A very convenient excuse!" Hugh exploded.

"So just one push of the button and they vaporize the whole Wing—can all these people get out in time?" Jan asked.

"And how do we get out if the draw bridge has been wired?" another voice piped up.

"The only way is through the dungeons!" Bertram briefly explained how Eliza and he had been down there and of the path he himself had found. He carefully described how the path forked and that the track they must take went straight on over the boulders, leading up to a wooded glade.

He added, "We can wait there for the whole group to assemble and then make our way to the village, as soon as the coast is clear."

"Eliza you and I are the only ones who know the way. You lead with Pim and I'll bring up the rear," he ended.

"What about those who have difficulty walking?" Eliza asked. "Nanette, you can probably use a hand."

Hugh walked over to Nanette. May I walk with you, Nanette?" Nanette looked relieved. She had met Hugh when he had come to New York with Global Education Motivators and again when he had returned to lobby.

"We have to let the rest of the group know now," Pim said urgently.

"Perhaps we should let them see Maurice," Eliza suggested. "That should help to convince them!"

"I'll stay in here with Maurice to stop people freaking out! Some may never have seen a dead person before," Gaia volunteered.

"I'll join you, as soon as we have told the rest of the group," Bertram called over his shoulder as he hurried after Pim.

Pim took the mike. Again the three of them went over their story. As Bertram finished, a voice shouted.

"Excuse me! You can not be serious. With all due respect."

"We have proof! Perhaps you would like to take a look," Pim suggested.

Hugh accompanied the man into the kitchen where Gaia was standing respectfully next to Maurice's body. The young man walked over and gingerly poked Maurice's hand, hurriedly withdrawing as he felt the chill. Hugh then led him outside to see the path.

A number of others streamed into the kitchen. Soon the others were thronging in first to see Maurice, then the path that had caved in.

Pim stood by the door and ushered them back through, as fast as he could.

"Time is of the essence. We must get going now! Bertram can you and Eliza lead the way through the registration area to the hidden door?"

Bertram took Eliza's hand as a way of prolonging their contact. "It's lucky that Percy and his gang are in the wing at the opposite side of the Castle and won't be able to see us make our great escape," Bertram whispered. "Oh, how I hate to leave you. Will you be okay, Eliza?" he asked.

98. Changes In The *Field*.

The dessert -- fresh fruit, honey and sour cream—had been especially brought in for the occasion. This was an unheard of delicacy in Kukundu, a country largely covered by jungle.

Josette allowed her eyes to roam around the hut. There were three concentric circles of around thirty people each. Everyone was sitting cross-legged on the floor. Each a leader in the reconciliation and reconstruction efforts of her beloved Kukundu.

"Mr. M'Bwene, may I ask you to address the gathering?" She looked at her neighbor, the man she had admired for so long. "Thank you, Josette, although I have come mainly to listen to *your* needs." He remained seated. "I have, like so many of our countrymen, been living in a Mandu refugee camp, attempting to encourage those inside and outside of the country to start the reconciliation process. What happens in Kukundu must however be seen in the context of what is happening elsewhere. Whether we can succeed in creating a durable peace in Kukundu will depend on in how far the rest of our world is stable.

"John, would you mind giving a run down of what is happening there?"

"Thanks Guillaume.

"We owe a great deal to Mary Duffield and her Young People's Network. When no one heeded our cries for help, they came through!" John began.

Josette stole a glance at "Daddy" M'Bwene. She could almost feel him listening, so intent was he on what was being shared. From a distance, he had seemed younger than his 45 years. From close by, she noticed his hair was graying and without his ready smile, there was a slight droop at the corners of his mouth. He must be exhausted, she concluded.

John continued, "For the first time in history young and old are working together. Young people have got themselves elected to all levels of governance on civic boards of every description: museums, postal and telephone systems, schools, city and county councils, and U.N. delegations. Their platform: full implementation of the all-win principle and the *Universal Declaration of Human Rights.* Both are intimately intertwined. We can't have one without the other.

As he spoke, John's large gray eyes assessed the group. *Would these brave freedom fighters understand the urgency of working closely with the rest of the world without him having to convince them of the existence of the Snake?*

He continued, "National governments have been sluggish in giving young people a voice. We suspect that there are powerful commercial forces, the arms industry in particular, which stop at nothing to prevent the majority of government officials from responding to the will of their people." He looked around, wondering whether anyone knew he was referring obliquely to the Snake. "So at the national level, the *Universal Declaration of Human Rights* is being blocked. In many cases, peoples' rights have been suspended. This is a breach of both traditional and constitutional international law.[65]

"Here, young people are on the offensive!" For a moment, he surveyed the group, a huge smile lighting up his face. "During a Young People's hook-up an e-mail working group on human rights was started, consisting of young people as well as adults. Here's what they decided to do:

"They made a list of the worst offending countries and researched which export products were key to their economic viability. Then they organized a boycott of those nations' products where they knew they could have most success. By focussing the boycott, they are meeting with a measure of success."

"Kukundu is one of those being targeted!" Josette said. "We get daily reports from person after person, who has been persuaded by the sanctions to look critically at the Kundana regime. These are now increasingly joining our resistance groups."

"Yes, I hear the Young People's boycott is having success in other countries, too," John continued, "and the beauty of this action is that it is fear of being targeted that is getting other Governments to respond."

"Fear tactics in service of the all-win principle?" Jules grinned. For a moment, it looked as if he were winking, as the sun filtering through the trees caught his thick glasses.

"It's not really contradictory," John said, "You see, when we seek all-win solutions, it makes sense *not* to buy products that have been made using *win/lose* means."

"Fascinating!" Jules smiled, "So by breaching human rights, governments are toying with young people? But how can the Young People's Network stop products from being bought?" he asked.

"They are in weekly contact through hook-ups with their peers and also with adults worldwide. These go home and talk to their friends and relatives, who then join the boycott.

"Wherever possible, they take a two-pronged approach. Outside the targeted country, the export products they have singled out are boycotted while inside, their production and marketing are, whenever possible, zapped by go-slow actions. There are plenty of points where communications can be held up through go-slow actions without anyone acting illegally—during the manufacturing process, and while they are being warehoused and shipped. A regular go-slow can wreak havoc. These boycotts and go-slow actions serve as a warning for other nations who are breaching human rights. And here the impact of "socially aware consumerism" is also bringing about changes."

There was a sudden thrashing in the jungle nearby.

Every one held their breath. Had they been discovered?

But it was only a large animal jumping its prey. It was accompanied by shrieks and jabbering as the monkeys made for the highest reaches of the trees.

John's eyes darted from one to another and continued, "And now, a number of large international corporations, out of fear of being targeted, are joining the U.N. Secretary General's Global Compact and vociferously lobbying their governments to honor both the all-win principle and their people's rights. Here, our friend, Bertram Morris, is playing a pivotal role.

"We aren't there yet, but judging from reports I get from around the world, breaches of human rights are gradually decreasing. No-where is this happening as much as here in Kukundu.

"Over to you, Daddy M'Bwene."

99. Leading The Group To Safety

Bertram waited as Eliza stepped through the secret panel and entered the hall. Hurriedly he gave her instructions how to reach the door to the dungeons.

"Eliza, keep Pim close. He has natural authority over the group. You can leave him in charge, in case any problems arise. But I have the impression his knees are stiff. Remember there are two places where the path has fallen away. One is behind the outcropping. He might need a helping hand there. Do you think you can manage?"

Not waiting for a reply, he hurried on, "And don't forget, the path splits, where it heads back up the cliff. At that point, there is a very faint track that leads over some boulders. Take that, or you'll end back at the Castle, exactly where Percy will be standing.

"Please be careful! The Universe dumped you in my lap. And we don't want to get separated again!" He gave her a wink and suddenly with a mischievous grin, he bent over and tenderly kissed her lips. "Good luck and see you soon."

Eliza stood blinking uncertainly, fighting her feelings. "Bertram, you're in a great deal of danger, bringing up the rear. Please don't take any unnecessary risks!"

She hesitated. Then reached into her pocket, pulled out a tiny black and white toy panda, its body was covered in fur. It looked as if it had been around for a while.

"Here, take this. I've had it forever. It is so soft. I always carry it with me. I want you to have it. That way, a small part of me will stay behind with you.

"Take care!" she said, and with a wan smile, she turned and hurried away.

Eliza walked down the passageway at a brisk pace, Pim following close behind. Turning left at the end, she then took the first hallway to the right. Every so often, she glanced over her shoulder to make sure that the others were keeping up. One, two, three, four, she counted and stopped behind the fourth potted palm.

The door to the dungeons was closed.

She felt around in the pot and located a knob. She pushed it, pulled it. The door didn't budge.

Oh, dear Lord! Please don't let the door be locked! she begged.

"Mind trying the handle when I say so?" she asked Pim.

Dutifully, Pim held the handle.

Eliza pushed the knob. "Okay!"

Pim pushed the handle down, then pulled, but nothing gave.

Eliza pulled the knob with Pim pushing and pulling. Still the door did not open. By now, some fifty people were anxiously waiting, and more were approaching.

Eliza tried turning the knob to the right. Still no success.

Heart pounding, Eliza turned the knob to the left. To no avail. Frantic, she rattled at it and suddenly the door gave.

"Would anyone mind staying out here in the hall to hold the door and make sure that no one gets lost?"

"I'll do it!" Winston volunteered.

Eliza felt around for the lights, but could not find any. "Would someone locate the light switch. There are lights for sure. They were on when I was here last. I'll lead people on down.

"I'll do it. That way Winston and I can stay together!" While Sharifa scanned the walls with her hands, Eliza carefully felt her way down, step by step, at first very slowly until gradually she was able to pick up speed. "*Seven sets of stairs,*" she remembered.

It seemed like an eternity. Finally, she was at the bottom.

"Okay, give me a moment," she whispered to Pim. Carefully she felt for the wall off to her left and then sliding her hands along its rough surface, she moved slowly forward until it suddenly stopped. "Yes!" I've got it!" she said.

At that moment the lights went on and she saw that she had been right. She was standing at the entrance of the passageway that would lead them to the exit.

"Would one or two of you mind staying down here to guide people to this passage? I'll continue on. We'll need to keep every one moving."

"I'll wait here!" It was Dana, her U.N. lobbyist friend from Ghana volunteering.

"Thanks, Dana!" Eliza smiled. For years he had been her right hand.

"Mind your heads!" Eliza ducked under the outcropping and made her way through the passage. Slowly, she led the way forward, until she came to the end.

Right bottom! Bertram had said. She kneeled down and felt around. There was the knob! Again she moved it around until all of a sudden the rock face swung out, and she was out in the open.

Dusk was falling.

"Quick, there's no time to lose," she called over her shoulder. Outside in the fresh air, she felt around and located the outside knob. "Would anyone mind waiting until the whole group is through? This door is on a timer. Every time it closes, you twiddle this knob.

As she spoke, the door suddenly started moving. The huge slab of stone inexorably closing while she watched. There were muffled cries on the inside. One person tried to creep through but was forced to withdraw and just avoided being squashed, as the rock face slammed closed.

"I'll help!" It was Terry. She had her guitar strapped to her back.

"My God, Terry. You might not be able to make the path, lugging that along…"

Eliza thought of Bertram bringing up the rear. How could such a tiny woman negotiate the path with such an unwieldy instrument on her back?

"But if I succeed, we'll have music!" Terry beamed. "Let me stay here 'til last. That way I won't hold up the others."

Eliza really needed Terry's help and if she thought she could make it all the more power to her! They must not be noticed from the Castle. She felt she could trust Terry to see people stayed out of sight as they hurried across the pasture to the edge of the cliff.

"Well, thank you, Terry! Are you sure you'll be alright?" She explained the need for people to stay out of sight, and with an "All the very best!" she hurriedly made for the edge of the cliff and located the path. Gaia agreed to stand there just out of sight from the Castle to make sure the others found their way.

Gaia hoisted a broken branch to the point where the path started, just below the edge of the cliff. Then she signaled to Terry who pointed the first people in the direction of the branch, while Gaia in her white sari, slipped back just out of sight.

Meanwhile, with Pim close behind her, Eliza plunged on down.

Suddenly she realized Pim's footsteps had stopped.

He had slippery leather soles and was inching his way down the incline. Reaching out, Eliza gave him a hand and together they felt their way down the steep path.

Walking half backward, she could keep an eye on the rest of the group.

"Thank God for Pim!" Eliza thought. This way the others were not tempted to hurry. If anyone lost their footing, they would go hurtling down to their death.

And so the group snaked forward.

Then came the chasm. Here a yard or so of path had fallen away. To her relief, Pim with his long legs easily scaled the distance.

"Let me see what I can do!" Takeshi said and scrutinized the rock face. Soon he was chipping away first with his sturdy looking penknife, then with a sharp edged stone, he had managed to locate. "I learned to read cliffs and create footholds in my rock climbing days," he explained and gingerly placing his foot in the ledge he had just sculpted, he gradually placed his weight on it. Finally, sure it would hold, he scaled the gap.

Eliza located Robin another of her U.N. teammates. "Mind staying here to help people negotiate this foothold?" she asked, "Takeshi, we'll need you again a little farther on," she called softly and then moved on as fast as she could with the others following along.

There was the rock outcropping!

"We'll need one person to stay here and show people how to get through," Eliza said.

Emile, her colleague from Switzerland volunteered. If anyone was trustworthy, it was he.

With people piling up behind her again, she wormed her way past the outcropping. There was a tiny ledge and then the spot where the path had once again fallen away.

She looked down. Her head started spinning. "I can't!" she panicked, hearing the crash of the waves and seeing the foam shooting up as they dashed the cliffs.

She steeled herself and took the leap. She made it. "But can Pim make it!" She looked around. Then jumped back, as Pim scaled the distance in one long stride.

Right behind him came Nanette with Hugh. Hugh jumped across. He held out his hand, but Nanette's knees were beginning to buckle.

People were piling up behind the rock in a long line. Finally, Takeshi appeared.

"Here, let me help," he said. He knelt down and carefully scoured the cliff. Then pulling the fist-sized stone with the sharp edge out of his pocket, he created another foothold with a few adroit taps.

While Nanette reached for the foothold with her right toe, Takeshi gently supported her until she could grasp Hugh's hand. Together they almost carried Nanette over the chasm. As Nanette at the other side of the gap inched forward, Pim reached out and gave her a hand.

Takeshi stayed put to help the others to scale the chasm, while Pim, Nanette and Takeshi, followed directly on her heels.

At the point where the path headed up to the Castle, Eliza paused. It was quite dark now. Where was the track? *Had she understood Bertram correctly?*

She scoured the boulders until she noticed a foot print. It was pointing straight ahead toward a cluster of boulders, behind which the track continued. The track gradually mounted toward the rim, turning away from the Castle just below the top, where they could not be seen from above. In the distance, Eliza finally saw the roughly hewn six steps which led to the forest glade.

With a few strides, she had mounted the steps and was standing in a clearing among the trees. Then, Pim and Nanette with Takeshi's aid were standing next to her.

Eliza breathed a deep sigh of relief.

"I'll stay here!" Pim volunteered, "I'll be able to hold the group together. You need to go back to sort out any hitches."

She turned and went back the way she had come. She passed the throngs of conference participants, among which some of her very best friends. She had not realized how many they were, until right at the end she saw Winston and Sharifa and behind them Terry. She had actually crossed both chasms, guitar and all!

"Are there any others?" Eliza asked softly.

"Just Bertram!" Terry whispered. "He said we should all wait for him under the trees. He was just in the middle of sending an e-mail. He's not sure how the blast might affect the computer and doesn't want to take any risks."

"I'll see you guys a little later," Eliza said. "The challenge now is to keep the morale up!"

"I'll do my best," Terry smiled, as Eliza sped away.

100. Reconstruction And Reconciliation

Josette blew her nose loudly, Jules wiped his glasses. "Daddy" M'Bwene was finally in their midst and for the first time about to address them.

Gently, M'Bwene absorbed the depth of feeling with which he was enveloped. He must avoid the adulation of his people. The all-win principle demanded that, as leader, he would keep his citizens actively involved in governance and remain open to their input.

He began speaking slowly, "All over Kukundu and in the refugee camps, reconciliation talks are a daily affair: Kukundus and Mandus share by any means of communication they can until all facts and feelings have been aired. Now, solutions are emerging, and rifts are beginning to heal. We have no alternative. For Kukundu, it is up or under."

He turned to John St. Clair. "John, it was a brilliant idea to consult Macek of All-Win Business, International[66].

While M'Bwene eased a letter out of one of the side pockets of his rucksack, Josette took another helping of cheese. For a few moments, she savored the soft creamy texture and its contrasting tang. Such delicacy! She had not tasted anything like it since being in this jungle hideout.

M'Bwene continued, "I had mentioned to Macek that from the reports I had been getting, most of our people favored basing our economy on our natural wealth, beginning with native livestock, crops and medicinal plants. Once our own needs are covered, we can export the rest.

Macek suggested that we aim for a *zero-waste* economy, using effective microorganisms (EMs[67], for short) to enhance the vitality of our soils and to promote the recycling process. These have been kept inexpensive in price and are freely available. With these microbes our products would be fully organic and be popular in surrounding countries.

"Microbes?" someone asked, doubtfully. A buzz of concerned remarks.

"Here's an excerpt from Macek's letter in which he explains the process."

M'Bwene donned a pair of glasses and began to read:

> *Agricultural scientists have been interested for decades to create a more favorable environment for plant growth, using beneficial microorganisms. Now, finally the technology has been developed.*
>
> *Microorganisms have been discovered which can coexist in mixed cultures and are physiologically compatible with one another. When these cultures are introduced into the natural environment, their individual beneficial effects are greatly magnified in a synergistic fashion.*
>
> *Kukundu has always been good at using all parts of its crops with minimal waste. The beauty of these effective microorganisms is that they both enhance life and can also be used to convert any remaining plant waste into high-grade animal fodder and nutrient-enriched compost. They can even clean polluted bodies of water and be used for maintaining and operating septic systems, municipal wastewater treatment plants, landfills and dumpsites. A wonderful recycling tool!*[68]

"Are these synthesized chemically, these effective micro-organisms? Or genetically engineered? That would really make their use rather questionable," A young man pointed out.

"No these microbes are totally natural and not harmful in any way," M'Bwene answered.

"In fact, if Kukundu is successful in using this technology, we might even be able to help other nations to solve a number of their environmental and food production problems."

He went on, "That way, instead of exporting *products* for foreign income, we would provide mainly services to other countries and keep most of our production for use by our own people.

"Here, Macek continues,

> *A zero-waste approach is seldom used. Industrial firms seldom think of producing a product without also producing waste. Imagine the increases in efficiency and profit if there is no waste at all! No health risks and no clean-up costs!*
>
> *"The transition to a zero waste economy can be made by a radically new form of taxation, whereby taxes would zap only those products which are not zero waste or, worse still, pollute the environment.*

"Nothing else would be taxed?" Josette asked.

"No, nothing at all, only those products and practices which harm the environment," M'Bwene stressed. He continued to read,

> *This way, initially, work would not be taxed at all. This, too, would stimulate the economy.*
>
> *Further information and expert support is available whenever you request it!*

"This is where you all come in," M'Bwene added, "If Kukundu is to be built on the all-win principle, we must all rekindle the economy together. Even though the government is responsible to coordinate its citizen's efforts, the economy consists of the sum total of our peoples' labor and exists to meet the needs of *every one* of us. So if we are to have a flourishing economy, each person must help to inform our government of how it can best serve them. We have begun to make a start through the network of think tanks, which have quite naturally sprung up to, come to grips with our crises.

There was a buzz of excited conversation.

One woman pointed out that somehow women's labor, whether in bringing up children or running the home (often besides holding down a full time job) should be seen as a vital part of the Kukundu economy and credited as such.

A young man suggested that, beside think tanks, which tended to attract a more educated type of person, regular use could be made of town hall meetings in which important matters could be discussed at the local level; and local recommendations passed periodically on to the national government.

Jules jumped up and started lighting the lamps. Outside night was falling. Birds were saying their last goodnights. Listening to the others sorting out the details, Josette plucked a few more grapes and savoring the subtle range of flavors, allowed herself to relax.

"So Kukundu is to remain largely an agricultural state?" a young woman asked.

"Actually, I discussed our people's preferences with Macek. He, as indeed do most of us, sees this as a first step within our long-range plans. He suggests we take a look at Taiwan." M'Bwene held the letter to the light and squinting to make out the letters, read,

> *In Taiwan, the government took a carefully worked out, long-term approach. First they focussed on food self-sufficiency. Then once the population's basic nutritional needs were met, they first developed the clothing industry and then moved into electronics.*

Developing in steps made it possible for the educational system to keep pace. First they developed a strong elementary education system, which covered most of the needs of the agrarian economy. Then High Schools were improved and finally, in preparation for the development of their electronics industry, they expanded their Higher Education facilities.

Kukundu can possibly become a part of the new university networking idea, where students can spread their studies over universities in different countries. This promotes language proficiency and will be a necessary preparation for today's global world. Where necessary, carefully selected students can go abroad to learn subjects Kukundu can not yet offer. That way, Kukundu would not have to develop every field of study and its system of universities can develop as its economy grows.

As M'Bwene fell silent, and for a moment the stillness of the jungle by night was almost tangible in the room. Just a few were still eating away, while the rest allowed his words to sink in.

"But a burning question remains: How can all this be financed?" Jean asked at last.

"He gets to that!" M'Bwene smiled. "Perhaps I should read on.

While recovering from the ravages of civil war, cash flow can be a constant problem. Here are some ideas:

Start with barter. Here you are already experts.

That way local economies can be regenerated without delay. There are a number of forms this can take. People can exchange services based on the time they put in: so one hour cooking for one hour of gardening, or teaching. Some barter systems create local currencies and even pay taxes. Taxes are, of course, essential for the country as a whole. The LETSystem[69] is one of the best known and is used all over the world.

The most incisive in terms of the all-win principle is the World Marshall Plan, designed by Dutchman, Pieter Kooistra. Here, each child, woman and man is given a basic income from which only sustainable products and services may be purchased. It starts with $250 for each woman, man and child and grows annually as this supplementary economy expands. This Marshall Plan is self-financing and focuses on the full development of each individual person. In other words, Article 26 of the Universal Declaration of Human Rights. To implement, it will take about 10 years.[70] Since this Marshall Plan is based on an economy which embraces all nations, it can best be developed under auspices of the U.N.

M'Bwene looked up. "I have brought copies of this self-financing world Marshall Plan for each of you to take back to your individual resistance groups. In the refugee camp, we have a study group of experts looking into how it would work. These are in regular discussion with an international network of thinkers. Although it is considered brilliant, it functions according to everyday economic principles. Its ingenuity rests on its ability to apply these to a global world. Kukundu has the opportunity to be at the forefront of economic innovation," he concluded.

The rest of the evening was spent reporting to him what the various groups were doing. Then shortly before midnight, M'Bwene, John and their following took their leave.

101. Annihilation

Eliza scaled the gap with a flying leap, aiming for the narrow ledge behind the outcropping of rock. Clamoring for the rock face, her hands began to slip. Just at that moment, from the other side, Bertram wormed his way past the rock, just in time to steady her until she could regain her balance

"Thank God you're okay!" Bertram sighed as, for a brief minute, he allowed himself to realize that they were together again.

"Quick! We must hurry!" He turned her around. This time, Eliza remembered Takeshi's foothold. And they both scaled the chasm with ease.

In silence, they reached the fork in the path. Then, with the briefest of exchanges, they headed toward the Castle where they assumed Percy would be standing. Before reaching the top, they veered off staying out of view of anyone standing on the rim.

Soon two boulders loomed overhead. No one could see them from there! In a moment, they were on top of the cliff and peering around the great bulk of rock.

No one was in sight.

Then suddenly, a voice just a few feet away said, "Okay, here're Edward and Slug now."

Eliza and Bertram froze, hearts pounding.

Geoffrey and Percy, shielded by the boulders, were standing just at the other side of the boulders. Geoffrey's voice shook with excitement. Eliza could just make out his hand. It was resting on a fairly large device.

Bertram gradually eased himself back, so that they were hidden by the rocks, pulling Eliza with him. Neither dared to breathe, let alone drop back over the edge. The smallest loose pebble would give them away.

"This'll be my first elimination!" Geoffrey said proudly. "Finally, I'm in a position of power! Soon, the family heritage will be mine."

"Not yet, my boy!" Percy cautioned. "You have a long way to go!"

"That's where you're wrong. I have watched you carefully. I am able to perform at least some of your duties, as well as you, uncle!" he said.

They heard the soft purring of an engine. Very carefully they inched around the rock, as Maurice's Mercedes pulled up, with in it Edward and Slug and loaded with boxes. Fortunately, Bertram and Eliza were shielded from their view.

"Okay, turn off the engine!" Percy ordered. And get out of the car. Did you place mine safely in the garage, as well as your own automobiles?"

"Yes, sir, exactly as you ordered!" Slug replied.

"You can detonate the bomb now!" Percy said to Geoffrey.

"Now!" Geoffrey's voice was still trembling. He laughed suddenly, "I hereby send a hall packed full of do-gooders to their Maker!" and with a whoop of joy, he detonated the bomb. There was a strong vibration and a loud rumbling noise as loose rocks and sand, propelled by the tremor, went cascading down the cliffs and plunged into the sea.

Under cover of the sound, Eliza and Bertram, in one accord, jumped over the edge, hurriedly slithering out of sight. A part of the path had been torn away. One of the huge boulders teetered precariously, then toppled over, missing them by inches. With a roar, it gashed the cliffs as it hurtled downward, hitting the sea in an explosion of white foam.

Eliza and Bertram pressed against the cliff face were now safer than before. Urgently wanting to know what had happened, they peeked over the edge.

Three loud whooshing sounds! Deathly silence followed. Geoffrey, then Slug and Edward disappeared before their eyes. Percy nonchalantly strode toward the waiting car, hurling a small device onto the front seat. Then he hauled the vaporizer over and hoisted into the car, jumped in, gunned the engine and went speeding away over the rough country road.

"My God! Percy's vaporized Geoffrey, Slug and Edward! He was armed!" Bertram was deeply shaken. Unsteadily, they got to their feet. In silence, they watched the Mercedes disappear in a cloud of dust as it skimmed over the unpaved road.

"Percy got away alone!" Bertram, ashen, was trembling.

Eliza took his hand and for a while they just stared after the car. She felt light-headed. She had been holding her breath. She now forced herself to breathe deeply into her diaphragm, as she tried to take in what she had just seen.

Then slowly, they made their way down to the fork in the path. Clambering over the boulders, they approached the steps. They were both still unsure on their feet. They needed all their energy to keep from stumbling.

Suddenly, placing her hand to her ear, Eliza held him back.

They listened.

Very softly, almost as if gossamer threads of fantasy were wafting toward them, they heard the strumming of a guitar and the sound of voices singing. The singing was barely more than an atmosphere. Eliza recognized the tune. "It's Terry," she breathed.

They crept up the steps to where they could distinguish the words. Here, so as not to disturb the group, they sank down and listened.

The whole group was singing:

> *Where there are no roads,*
> *we will open roads,*
> *Where there is no light,*
> *we will shine our light,*
> *Where there is no love,*
> *we will fiercely love,*
> *Where there is no peace,*
> *we will be that peace.*

Then Terry and Luci took over and sang in a lilting duet:

> *My brother and my sister,*
> *the torch has been passed to us,*
> *There is no more time for doubting:*
> *we must live what we believe.*
> *Take up your sword of truth*
> *that others might be free.*
> *And live every moment,*
> *aware that we choose*
> *for all that is to be.*

The others joined the refrain with Terry and Luci lending it a choral quality as they sang second voice.

And where there are no roads,
we will open roads.
Where there is no light,
We will shine our light.
Where there is no love,
We will fiercely love.
Where there is no peace,
We will be that peace.[71]

As their musical statement wound to a close, Eliza felt as if, in the silence that followed, the song danced around them in ever growing circles, spreading the message far beyond where they had gathered in the clearing.

Eliza and Bertram mounted the last steps and joined their friends.

The group was sitting on the ground, facing Luci and Terry with her guitar. They exuded an inner purpose, an unexpected strength. They must have witnessed what had happened from the woods and were now allowing the music to transform the terrifying experience into a shared higher purpose.

As their friends greeted them with a show of relief, Eliza and Bertram sat down and told them what they had witnessed from close by.

To Eliza's amazement their tale was met with grief, rather than shock or fear.

"How deeply depraved can we people become...!" Gaia remarked gently.

Eliza noticed a togetherness that could only have grown as with unrehearsed coordination and split second timing each had contributed to their great escape, stood by one another as the vaporization took place, and now were uniting through their singing.

Eliza wondered whether the strength each had derived from this would link them, even when they were apart. Would each be able to draw on this energy? And, would the *field* still connect them?

102. A Year Later

Bertram flung the door open as he heard Eliza arrive.

"Happy Birthday! Welcome back from your sabbatical!" he cried. "Come in and make yourself at home!"

Eliza found herself on the huge marble terrace that encircled the penthouse. Behind her a view of Central Park as far as the eye could reach.

She gasped as she peered over his shoulder into the apartment behind him.

"So this is the nest you described in your letters to me? I must say, you didn't do it justice. It's so ... so ... spacious, so sumptuous! What a wonderful place!"

A huge expanse of white marble floors extended to all sides, transforming the apartment into one single space.

With a flourish he waved her through the door: "Welcome home!" he repeated, chuckling.

She entered a large hall in the center from which each of the rooms fanned out. Bertram led her around. He had opened all the doors wide, so that she could admire the view, a spectacular 360-degrees! There were three bedrooms, each with an adjacent study and bathroom. The master bathroom had a bath, shower and Jacuzzi. Then there was a large live-in kitchen with a cozy eating nook for two, a huge sitting and dining room. It was bright, clean and sparsely furnished with white overstuffed chairs and sofas.

Eliza laughed, "If I sat down in one of those, I doubt I'd want to leave!"

"That's the idea," he said with a mischievous grin. "Welcome, Eliza. This place is where I rest my head when I'm not on the road giving talks. I should like nothing more than to share it with you. It's around 20 minutes with the 107 bus from here to the U.N., instead of the hour it takes you from your place Jamaica Estates in Queens. I'd feel honored if you would consider it your own. I promise not to bother you, unless, of course, you get down on your knees and beg!"

Again, Eliza burst out laughing.

"Watch out! You never know when the time will come! Bertram, what an amazing invitation! How very welcome after a late meeting not to have to go back to Queens! I'm not sure that I can actually accept your generous offer, though, to live here with you! But I'm very much enjoying our friendship!"

He had been leading her around. She now started to explore on her own.

A large ficus tree in the hallway had welcomed her, as she came in. It spoke of care and comfort, which made her feel instantly at ease. The sitting/dining room was dotted with flourishing green plants and orchids. Each added its particular color and scent to the atmosphere of welcome she felt. And on the table a huge bunch of pink roses. "These are for your birthday!" Bertram beamed.

In the bathroom, Eliza noticed that the Jacuzzi was heart-shaped and had room for two.

"A regular love nest!" she giggled. "I must be crazy to feel so safe with you!"

He reached out and taking her hand led her into the kitchen.

On the table was a candle, it's flame flickered as they approached. Around it, as on an altar, she noticed a number of objects: Her little toy panda caught her eye.

"Remember you gave that to me to keep me safe, during our escape from the Castle? Ever since that day, I have carried it with me!" Bertram grinned.

Next to the conference nametags, a leather-bound file lay open. She peeked at the text. Then flipped over the pages.

"Are these all the e-mails I've ever sent you?" she asked, sinking down on one of the chairs.

"Every last one. I've read and reread them again and again on my long, lonely nights on the road. Our correspondence was a constant companion. You inspired me to follow my heart. In fact, the first time I consciously followed my heart was when in an irrational moment in Costa Rica, I reached out to you!

"Then writing to you helped me to sort out what was really important. And all the while you egged me on, encouraging me not to give up.

As he spoke, he sank down on a chair, tenderly watching her face. She looked more radiant than he had ever seen her, as she waited for him to continue.

He paused and savored the moment.

Then with a half-smile, he admitted, "Of course, I didn't dare send you everything I wrote, it might have bowled you over."

With a sense of wonder, Eliza looked at him. His dark hair, his passionate eyes, the mischievous smile that, every time their eyes met, lit up his face ... She felt both excited and peaceful. With a sense of adventure, she allowed herself to be transported by her symphony of feelings.

"Your e-mails were very precious," she said softly, "After losing those closest to me, I could not help but wonder, whether I would ever allow myself to feel true intimacy again. And then, day after day, your e-mails would come. You were so bravely clambering through all your self-doubts, giving yourself to your new life's purpose and being so touchingly honest with me. I felt humbled by the way you trusted me. Finally, I screwed up the courage to feel my growing feelings for you."

"And what is it that you feel?" he whispered, hardly daring to breathe.

"Oh, Bertram! It's...it's that thrill of excitement, that heightened awareness, a spark! The sense of a great adventure when I am with you!" He reached up and took both her hands, torn between wanting to hold her close and not wanting to take his eyes off her face.

"My word, you're gorgeous when you look so happy!" he laughed, unable to turn away.

The musical chimes of a clock wafted in from the sitting room. "Oh no! There is more I want to show you!" he added. "I lost all sense of time and this can't wait!"

Hurriedly, he led her out through the front door and down to the apartment below. That, although slightly smaller, was also surrounded by a terrace.

"You own this too!" Eliza looked at him impressed.

"Yes. I have bought the two top apartments in this block of flats, the annex and the garden on the roof, all with splendid views The roof annex is for entertaining guests and contains my housekeeper's apartment.

"And this one is for any of our friends who want to stay over in the City."

103. Kukundu And The *Field*

Eliza thought she heard someone giggle. But the terrace was empty. There were no lights in the windows of the apartment. She must have been hearing things.

Bertram opened the door, turned on the lights, and there in the large white marble sitting area, Eliza saw a huge crowd. She blinked. For a moment, she could not place them. Then it sank in: they were Mary's young friends! And there were Gaia, Nanette, Robin, Dana and her other friends from the U.N. Even Emil had come over from Switzerland!"

"Happy Birthday!" Terry and Luci sang and everyone joined in. They all sang in three-part harmony and ended with resounding cheers.

As they sang, Eliza realized that almost all of their closest friends were there with whom they had escaped from Maurice's Castle in the South of France. When the cheers died away, she was so touched, she could barely speak.

"I feel, I feel..." she stammered, "Thank you!!!"

Someone reached out and gave her a hug. "And Mary, you're here too!" she beamed.

"Yes it's Mary and her whole crew! And look here's Pim!" Bertram said.

"It's just under a year ago that we had our great escape!" Bertram gave Eliza a squeeze. "Many of us have been working together at a distance, each doing our own thing. We decided that your birthday would be an excellent occasion to catch up!"

As if he had uncorked a bottle of champagne, every one bubbled over and greeted one another at once"

"Bertram told us we had to keep quiet. And so we haven't had a chance to talk yet!" Jan laughed. Her coal-black eyes sparkled. "Jeff kept trying to tickle me!"

"You're just looking for excuses for giggling!" her twin grinned and gave her a soft poke in the ribs.

There, too, was Consuela. She came walking out of the kitchen, bearing a large tray.

"Consuela's been at it again!" Bertram's nose wrinkled as she offered him a large slab of quiche. She has the rooftop apartment! Whoever of us is staying at this address will be in Consuela's care!"

Someone tapped Eliza on the shoulder. "Augustina!" Eliza exclaimed. "You're here, too! Last thing I heard you were in Kukundu! My word, you look so happy! And that after being nabbed by the Reconciliation Commission! How did it go?"

Augustina grimaced. "Pierre and I were called up together and they accused him of armed robbery and me of being his accessory!"

"Accessory!?" Eliza tried to hear her above the din.

"Yes. You see, I confessed to them that I stayed with him even after I noticed he had changed."

Eliza took her friend by the arm and the two strolled out onto the terrace. Leaning on the railing, they looked out over Central Park South.

"But can you still live with him, after all that's happened?"

"You know, hearing him confess, acknowledging my own guilt, hearing all the terrible things others have committed – it somehow makes me realize, I am no better than anyone else. How easily we are swayed by an atmosphere that says *such and such is the norm! We're all doing it, so it's okay!*"

Down below, like dinky toys, traffic moved around Columbus circle, people walked like armies of ants at either side of the street. How normal everything seemed.

Eliza reached out and gave her friend's arm an affectionate squeeze.

Augustina continued, "Now the atmosphere has changed, reconciliation's in the air. Suddenly, we all want to come clean. It's almost as if we're puppets, our thoughts and feelings being determined by something that's in the air. Just allowing the *field* to take over without being conscious of what's happening – that's dangerous. We saw what that did to Kukundu. We must take responsibility for the atmosphere, we are creating, and then *use* it consciously!"

For a while they looked out over the park. The sun playing through the trees.

"The Reconciliation Commission gave me a choice to stay with Pierre or not and to exact some retribution. You know," Augustina admitted, "… I still love Pierre. I've known him all my life! I think he has suffered enough. I can't think of being parted from him again."

Eliza felt deeply moved. After a while, she asked, "So what was the verdict?"

"We are going to have to work for free for the families, Pierre has wronged. Both he and I. They have lost everything: their social standing, their possessions. They have also lost face. There is some U.N. assistance to help them get their land back and build up their farm again.

"Pierre and I have two tasks: to help on the land and to help their children adjust. Of course, they are all severely traumatized. We have been forbidden to have children of our own!"

"For ever!?" Eliza exclaimed.

"No, just for the next four years!"

She turned and faced Eliza. "It's a miracle! Working with these families is one of the best things I've ever done. We have been completely adopted. We are forced to act, bearing in mind, what is good for them, ourselves and the community as a whole. The good all-win principle!"

"How long will this last?"

"For two years. But, I sense life-long friendships are in the making!"

"But what happens if people can't or don't want to do as the Reconciliation Commission says?"

"Then there is jail, hard labor, and group therapy – group therapy is quite an effective way to deal with resistance!"

"But, you know, most of us are so relieved to leave all the atrocities behind us. And the adventure of building a brand new society along all-win lines with this new zero-waste economy – it's as if there's a whole new life ahead.

"Then, we're getting the hang of what it means to 'do as you would be done by', cooperate and do things that work out for everyone. Goodwill's increasing in leaps and bounds. Life is so different. I mean, even different from what it was before Kundana's coup! When you're there, you feel it. All-win relationships simply flow! The whole *field* around Kukundu has shifted"

Eliza looked at Augustina in wonder. "So in Kukundu, the Reconciliation Commission has become judge and jury! Blame is replaced by understanding. No more wasting away in jail at the community's expense! Instead, you are allowed to put your heart and soul into improving your own life while helping those you have wronged!

"It's all too idyllic! It's hard to believe!"

"No alternative, when a whole nation is guilty!" Augusta said simply. "You can't put a whole nation in jail!

"I only hope that the rest of the world can make the change without going through what we went through!" she added.

In the late afternoon light, traffic was picking up. As from a different world, the hooting of taxis wafted up to where they were standing.

"Even harder to believe!!!" Augustina turned to look at Eliza again, a huge grin on her face. She hesitated for a few moments, heightening the drama of what she was about to say. "San Leon and several other dictatorships have sent delegations to Kukundu! They want to follow our example!"

Behind them, the excited buzz had abated. Pim's voice could be heard above the rest, "The energy is definitely shifting! You each have such good news."

So as not to miss even more of the updates, Augustina and Eliza hurried back.

104. Together

"Oh, there you are, Augustina!" Gaia called out, "Tell us about Kukundu!"

Augustina needed no encouragement. She poured out what she had told Eliza.

"Any news from John?" Mary asked.

"John St. Clair and Josette, my husband's mentor, are heading the National Reconciliation Commission. They travel from one village tribunal to the other, helping in any way they can."

With Augustina giving her update, Eliza looked around the room. Almost all of the seats were taken, and so were the dozens of pillows, dotted around the floor. All those faces, which were dear to her, friends she hadn't seen for so long, everything had a far off, hazy quality, as if she were in a half-lit room. Exhausted, Eliza leaned against the wall. Her jetlag was making itself felt.

"As systems' scientists, we're now all the rage!" She heard Pim say. "Everyone wants to find out about systems thinking, the *field*, the all-win principle and their human rights! Last week alone, my colleagues and I were interviewed on three prime-time shows!"

"It's a huge step forward, but the adventure continues. Living in all-win relationships is quite a challenge, people will need a helping hand. And that's where we all come in.

"So there's plenty more for us all to do!" he repeated.

"Do you and your colleagues still meet regularly at the University for Peace?" Winston asked, his arm draped around Sharifa.

"Yes, I now rent a room near Maurice's villa."

"Any sign of Percy?" Pat and Arturo asked in unison and, looking at each other, burst out laughing,

"Since our adventure in the South of France, no one has seen any one there, except an old caretaker and his wife. At least that's what I hear in the village. Percy and the rest of the family've disappeared. It has happened regularly over the ages—these disappearing acts—, it seems. They always tend to return in time—but no telling when ..."

Then it was the turn of Mary's crew to share their activities.

Eliza shifted from one leg to the other. Her jet lag was taking over. As she scoured the room for a seat, the students from Corps Elite discussed Golden Haven School, tours for adults around the garden, and how the Corps Elite School Council was now in full swing, their ideas even welcomed by the Board.

"Annette and Takeshi had both been accepted at Harvard. Their aim: to apply the all-win principle to business...

Eliza had difficulty concentrating. Vaguely she registered that someone was waving at her. It was Bertram motioning her to join him on the sofa.

Hurriedly, Eliza clambered over and around her friends, until she sank down into his arms. All she wanted was to close her eyes and drift off to sleep.

Hugh was speaking. He had got into Columbia University to be close to the U.N. Together with a group of students, he was persuading governments to reform the decision-making process in the Security Council.

Suddenly, Eliza was wide-awake. This was the issue on which all their work hinged!

Hugh continued, "And when the Security Council was considering whether to lift the sanctions against Kukundu, all Members of the Security Council, including the Permanent Five, invited the views of *all* Member Nations of the U.N. Because the request came from the Council as a whole, the Permanent Five didn't lose face."

"Brilliant!" Eliza said. "Each country had the chance of a lifetime to give their views, even though they weren't on the Council.

"What a huge step, Hugh!" she cheered him on. "If you guys can keep up the pressure, it is bound to pay off. They actually heard you!!! And what a relief it must be for the five Permanent Members not to constantly be battling opposition, feeling the full measure of goodwill from each of their colleagues!"

"Didn't it take an eternity, before all the answers were in?" Winston asked. "After all, the ambassador of each country has to consult her or his whole government."

"No! Just a day! You should have seen the ambassadors rally around. The phones in the delegate's lounge were buzzing all day. No, they realized the importance of the gesture!"

"And it worked out for all concerned!" Hugh raced on, excited by Eliza's enthusiasm. "In the end, the Security Council passed the resolution. I had been hoping that it would be backed by countries together representing 2/3 of the world's population, owning 2/3 of the wealth of the world, and who contributed 2/3 to the UN budget. In the end, they had full backing of *all* UN Member Nations. Not a single nation was opposed!"

He laughed.

"And then we spent days publicizing what had happened and the importance to the rest of the world!"

Everyone clapped and cheered and Takeshi reached over and shook Hugh's hand. "Next step is our evolutionary leap!" he grinned.

Mary waited until the excitement and joking had died down. Then she said conversationally, "And this year I'm heading out to San Leon with my next crew of ham radio operators. We'll be guests of no one less than King Joaquim himself!"

"How on Earth did you manage that, Mary?" Sister Gaia gasped.

"You remember Juanita suggested the *World Game* and how our Young People's Network took the ball and ran, broadcasting the plan and getting people guessing whom the list of murders were targeting and who the beneficiaries would be? Well, King Joaquim and King Enzo are convinced that that **saved them from the Snake**. Because their teachers suddenly disappeared. All communication stopped. No explanations, nothing for almost a year! So it does indeed look as if we have put a halt to Snake's grab for power— *for now, at least.*

"Anyway, they were so delighted they invited a delegation from the World Game to receive the royal treatment.

"King Joaquim was so grateful, he actually contacted me personally!"

There was an excited buzz of conversation. As the exclamations stopped, Mary held her breath, wondering whether to continue.

"Come on, Mary, what's on your mind!" Pim egged her on.

"Okay!" she suddenly laughed. "Here's a bit of gossip!

"Remember that think tank we started, focussing on General Mendoza, Pim? The irony is that Mendoza seduced Esmerelda, Joaquim's wife. Just before he was deposed, she divorced Joaquim and married Mendoza instead. And now Joaquim's getting married again."

"Surely, not to Juanita?" Bertram sat bolt upright, "I met them both at Oxford when I was lecturing there. Great couple!" He beamed. "I bet you they'll be really happy!"

Eliza was fully awake now as the energy sparked in the room.

"San Leon is the place where the first street children joined an All-Win Center," Gaia commented.

"Yes!" Mary jumped in. "Antonia, one of my students, helped to bring that about! And the U.N.'s helping the street children to build simple brick houses for themselves and other shantytown dwellers[72]. Can you imagine what a change that will be for these young street kids! Finally, a place of their own and a small basic income!

"You remember how shy Antonia was when she first came to class, and here she has unleashed a whole social revolution!" Mary laughed wholeheartedly.

"She'll be joining the crew of the Peace Warrior again– she'll fly over to California and, of course, she'll be one of the group who will be presented to King Joaquim in person!" "Weird and wonderful how things have changed!" Pim mused. "A couple of years ago, everyone was too afraid to think about more than what was going on in their backyards. And now people are reveling in working together; think tanks are springing up all over the place; every one and their brother wants to master the all-win principle, at home, at work, and are clamoring to support the U.N."

"Pim, is this the shift in *the field?*" Mary asked the question that was on everyone's mind.

Pim beamed. "As far as I can tell, we are fast approaching the shift, even if it has not quite taken place yet! But we're certainly on the right track. As I see it, we are consciously pushing it along in four powerful ways:

"Firstly, we are improving our two-way communication with the field. This gives us access to vast amounts of information and energy. And the more information and energy we absorb, the wiser and more potent we become. And this, in turn, increases the range of our access to and our influence on the field. And so, as each of us becomes ever wiser and more powerful, the process escalates at ever greater speeds.

Secondly, we are constantly improving our ability to work in harmony with the forces which propel evolution itself—the forces which are operating in all systems of the universe. Of these, the all-win waltz is the most relevant and therefore by far the most powerful, due to the phase of evolution humanity is in.

Thirdly, human evolution involves all of humanity. Cooperation is therefore where it is at! And we are infusing the *lifeblood of humanity as a whole* with the wisdom and power of our insights regarding humanity's next evolutionary leap. Here it is vital to work with people and networks that themselves are plugged into the field and that are consciously working with all three levels of the all-win waltz. With each of these we connect with, our combined influence burgeons. For each one's strength and wisdom is spiraling in a process of ever-greater escalation. In this process, the U.N. is the most powerful tool we have. It enables us to tap into networks of people and governments, which encompass the Planet as a whole. The U.N. is also increasingly the coordinator and motor of evolution of humankind..

And finally, the more completely each of us embodies the all-win principle in our lives, the more compelling it becomes both to ourselves and our surroundings. After all, working with the all-win principle *feels good*, and what is a greater incentive than doing things simply because the are fun?

"Now that people are beginning to see how the *all-win principle* works and are willing to give it a try, it is likely to continue, unless..." his voice trailed off.

There was an expectant silence.

"Unless, what?" Jan prompted.

"People cede to their old ways. Remember, old habits die hard!?"

"But if they don't, things will be alright?" Jan asked.

"For a while, yes! Until ..." He hesitated.

Again, everyone held their breath.

"Until, what?" Jan couldn't contain herself.

"Until the next challenge comes along: an energy change, chaos, and then the long slow process of rebuilding a new all-win situation. Who knows, perhaps our next step will be to expand our borders into Space."

"Oh no! Not another challenge! That's even huger than what we're facing now!!!" Jan groaned.

Every one laughed.

And so with banter back and forth, the evening came to a close. For those from out of town, there was ample room to spend the night. A few others decided to linger on before going home. Eliza and Bertram took their leave and together headed upstairs.

105. The Dancer

The sitting room clock chimed midnight, as Bertram unlocked the door. A pitcher of fresh mango juice greeted them with a welcome note from Consuela.

Just then, the doors must have opened in the apartment downstairs, because a hum of voices drifted up from the terrace below. Then they heard the strumming of Terry's guitar. A strange rhythm, Eliza couldn't place. Eliza felt Bertram's arm encircling her waist. Forgetting how tired she was, she relaxed into the music, as the pure, yet warm coloring of the notes brought the words to life

> *Oh, do I dare be a dancer?*
> *Oh, do I dare to be all I can be?*
> *Oh, do I dare let the world know I care*
> *in the light that I bear as a dancer?*
> *All of my life I've been choosing this moment,*
> *not knowing how it would feel.*
> *Now I dare to be radiant and free,*
> *graceful, and always a dancer.*

The seductive Latin American rhythms pulsed through her when all of a sudden she realized that Terry and Luci, blending perfectly with the accompaniment, were not singing to the Latin beat, but to the tempo of a waltz. She was filled with wonder that *such* contrasting rhythms and moods were blending so consummately. Together, they and their music were a hymn of praise to the rhythms of Life itself.

At that moment, Bertram gently whirled her around, and before she knew it, they were dancing. Their torsos swaying to the fiery music, their hips swinging in sensual abandon. Their bodies just inches apart, and yet never actually touching. Neither was leading the other. And yet they danced as one.

Through the open doors wafted the voices of their friends, with Terry calling out the words. Their voices responded flawlessly to her cues, as they gave themselves over to the music.

> *Come take my hand and dance with me.*
> *Join in the joy of the rhythm, the melody.*
> *Let yourself loose in this moment of truth*
> *in the magic, the wonder, the ecstasy.*
> *Have you not noticed that when you are dancing*
> *all of the world dances, too?*
> *Oh dare to be radiant and free,*
> *graceful, and always a dancer.*

Then Bertram gently took Eliza in his arms and barely skimming the floor, they were suddenly dancing a waltz. The voices, the music, Bertram's body and her own were one intricate flow of sound, movement and sensation.

Oh, that we dare be The Dancer.
Oh, that we dare to be all we can be.
Oh, that we dare let the world know we care
in the light that we bear as The Dancer.
All of our lives, we've been watching and waiting
and hoping;
and now it's come true!
We dare to be
radiant and free,
graceful and always The Dancer.
We dare to be
radiant and free,
graceful, and always The Dancer.[73]

The couple felt so completely at ease, so joyously ecstatic, moved by the singing of their friends that when Eliza looked up and their eyes met, the radiance with which each engulfed the other transported them beyond all fear to a world where *all that is* thrives.

ADDENDUM I

The Universal Declaration of Human Rights
(Adopted unanimously by the General Assembly of the United Nations in 1948)

Preamble

Whereas recognition of the inherent dignity and of the equal and inalienable rights of all members of the human family is the foundation of freedom, justice and peace in the world,

Whereas disregard and contempt for human rights have resulted in barbarous acts which have outraged the conscience of mankind, and the advent of a world in which human beings shall enjoy freedom of speech and belief and freedom from fear and want has been proclaimed as the highest aspiration of the common people,

Whereas it is essential, if man is not to be compelled to have recourse, as a last resort, to rebellion against tyranny and oppression, that human rights should be protected by the rule of law,

Whereas it is essential to promote the development of friendly relations between nations,

Whereas the peoples of the United Nations have in the Charter reaffirmed their faith in fundamental human rights, in the dignity and worth of the human person and in the equal rights of men and women and have determined to promote social progress and better standards of life in larger freedom,

Whereas Member States have pledged themselves to achieve, in cooperation with the United Nations, the promotion of universal respect for and observance of human rights and fundamental freedoms,

Whereas a common understanding of these rights and freedoms is of the greatest importance for the full realization of this pledge,

Now, therefore,
The General Assembly,

Proclaims this _Universal Declaration of Human Rights_ as a common standard of achievement for all peoples and all nations, to the end that every individual and every organ of society, keeping this Declaration constantly in mind, shall strive by teaching and education to promote respect for these rights and freedoms and by progressive measures, national and international, to secure their universal and effective recognition and observance, both among the peoples of Member States themselves and among the peoples of territories under their jurisdiction.

Article I

All human beings are born free and equal in dignity and rights. They are endowed with reason and conscience and should act towards one another in a spirit of brotherhood.

Article 2

Everyone is entitled to all the rights and freedoms set forth in this Declaration, without distinction of any kind, such as race, colour, sex, language, religion, political or other opinion, national or social origin, property, birth or other status. Furthermore, no distinction shall be made on the basis of the political, jurisdictional or international status of the country or territory to which a person belongs, whether it be independent, trust, non-self-governing or under any other limitation of sovereignty.

Article 3

Everyone has the right to life, liberty and security of person.

Article 4

No one shall be held in slavery or servitude; slavery and the slave trade shall be prohibited in all their forms.

Article 5

No one shall be subjected to torture or to cruel, inhuman or degrading treatment or punishment.

Article 6

Everyone has the right to recognition everywhere as a person before the law.

Article 7

All are equal before the law and are entitled without any discrimination to equal protection of the law. All are entitled to equal protection against any discrimination in violation of this Declaration and against any incitement to such discrimination.

Article 8

Everyone has the right to an effective remedy by the competent national tribunals for acts violating the fundamental rights granted him by the constitution or by law.

Article 9

No one shall be subjected to arbitrary arrest, detention or exile.

Article 10

Everyone is entitled in full equality to a fair and public hearing by an independent and impartial tribunal, in the determination of his rights and

obligations and of any criminal charge against him.

Article 11

1. Everyone charged with a penal offence has the right to be presumed innocent until proved guilty according to law in a public trial at which he has had all the guarantees necessary for his defense.

2. No one shall be held guilty of any penal offence on account of any act or omission which did not constitute a penal offence, under national or international law, at the time when it was committed. Nor shall a heavier penalty be imposed than the one that was applicable at the time the penal offence was committed.

Article 12

No one shall be subjected to arbitrary interference with his privacy, family, home or correspondence, nor to attacks upon his honour and reputation. Everyone has the right to the protection of the law against such interference or attacks.

Article 13

1. Everyone has the right to freedom of movement and residence within the borders of each State.

2. Everyone has the right to leave any country, including his own, and to return to his country.

Article 14

1. Everyone has the right to seek and to enjoy in other countries asylum from persecution.

2. This right may not be invoked in the case of prosecutions genuinely arising from non-political crimes or from acts contrary to the purposes and principles of the United Nations.

Article 15

1. Everyone has the right to a nationality.

2. No one shall be arbitrarily deprived of his nationality nor denied the right to change his nationality.

Article 16

1. Men and women of full age, without any limitation due to race, nationality or religion, have the right to marry and to found a family. They are entitled to equal rights as to marriage, during marriage and at its dissolution.

2. Marriage shall be entered into only with the free and full consent of the intending spouses.

3. The family is the natural and fundamental group unit of society and is entitled to protection by society and the State.

Article 17

1. Everyone has the right to own property alone as well as in association with others.

2. No one shall be arbitrarily deprived of his property.

Article 18

Everyone has the right to freedom of thought, conscience and religion; this right includes freedom to change his religion or belief, and freedom, either alone or in community with others and in public or private, to manifest his religion or belief in teaching, practice, worship and observance.

Article 19

Everyone has the right to freedom of opinion and expression; this right includes freedom to hold opinions without interference and to seek, receive and impart information and ideas through any media and regardless of frontiers.

Article 20

1. Everyone has the right to freedom of peaceful assembly and association.

2. No one may be compelled to belong to an association.

Article 21

1. Everyone has the right to take part in the government of his country, directly or through freely chosen representatives.

2. Everyone has the right to equal access to public service in his country.

3. The will of the people shall be the basis of the authority of government; this will shall be expressed in periodic and genuine elections which shall be by universal and equal suffrage and shall be held by secret vote or by equivalent free voting procedures.

Article 22

Everyone, as a member of society, has the right to social security and is entitled to realization, through national effort and international co-operation and in accordance with the organization and resources of each State, of the economic, social and cultural rights indispensable for his dignity and the free development of his personality.

Article 23

1. Everyone has the right to work, to free choice of employment, to just and favourable conditions of work and to protection against unemployment.

2. Everyone, without any discrimination, has the right to equal pay for equal work.

3. Everyone who works has the right to just and favourable remuneration ensuring for himself and his family an existence worthy of human dignity, and supplemented, if necessary, by other means of social protection.

4. Everyone has the right to form and to join trade unions for the protection of his interests.

Article 24

Everyone has the right to rest and leisure, including reasonable limitation of working hours and periodic holidays with pay.

Article 25

1. Everyone has the right to a standard of living adequate for the health and well-being of himself and of his family, including food, clothing, housing and medical care and necessary social services, and the right to security in the event of unemployment, sickness, disability, widowhood, old age or other lack of livelihood in circumstances beyond his control.

2. Motherhood and childhood are entitled to special care and assistance. All children, whether born in or out of wedlock, shall enjoy the same social protection.

Article 26

1. Everyone has the right to education. Education shall be free, at least in the elementary and fundamental stages. Elementary education shall be compulsory. Technical and professional education shall be made generally available and higher education shall be equally accessible to all on the basis of merit.

2. Education shall be directed to the full development of the human personality and to the strengthening of respect for human rights and

fundamental freedoms. It shall promote understanding, tolerance and friendship among all nations, racial or religious groups, and shall further the activities of the United Nations for the maintenance of peace.

3.Parents have a prior right to choose the kind of education that shall be given to their children.

Article 27

1.Everyone has the right freely to participate in the cultural life of the community, to enjoy the arts and to share in scientific advancement and its benefits.

2.Everyone has the right to the protection of the moral and material interests resulting from any scientific, literary or artistic production of which he is the author.

Article 28

Everyone is entitled to a social and international order in which the rights

and freedoms set forth in this Declaration can be fully realized.

Article 29

1.Everyone has duties to the community in which alone the free and full development of his personality is possible.

2.In the exercise of his rights and freedoms, everyone shall be subject only to such limitations as are determined by law solely for the purpose of securing due recognition and respect for the rights and freedoms of others and of meeting the just requirements of morality, public order and the general welfare in a democratic society.

3.These rights and freedoms may in no case be exercised contrary to the purposes and principles of the United Nations.

Article 30

Nothing in this Declaration may be interpreted as implying for any State, group or person any right to engage in any activity or to perform any act aimed at the destruction of any of the rights and freedoms set forth herein.

© The Office of the High Commissioner for Human Rights, Geneva, Switzerland
Send e-mail with comments and suggestions to: webadmin.hchr@unog.ch

ADDENDUM II

A SELF-FINANCING WORLD MARSHALL PLAN
A SUPPLEMENTARY INCOME FOR EACH WOMAN, MAN
AND CHILD

Poverty, disintegration of societies and unemployment are challenging us all to take responsibility for our world in new ways. The following self-financing World Marshall Plan would provide every person with a means to regenerate their own lives while helping to build a healthy environmentally-sound world economy in which all people are able to develop in their unique ways. This Plan is described in several books, including two sponsored by the Dutch Foreign Ministry.

The Effects of a Life-Enhancing Supplementary Economy

If every man, woman and child were given $250 (compounded by 7% p.a.) every year to be spent exclusively on his or her wholesome development, poverty and pollution would fade away. In poor areas, where a person earns $400 annually, $250 for each member of the family is a fortune. It could be spent on seeds or instruction on soil regeneration. Villagers could contribute to a water pump or sewage system for their region. Soon poverty and disease could make way for flourishing cottage industries and international markets would expand into poorer areas. In richer countries $250 could be spent on personal growth or the development of mind or spirit. Attitudes would change as every year again each person would be asked to choose environmentally friendly goods and services for personal development. All would be encouraged to consider such questions as: "What is health?" "What adds depth and meaning to life?" and "How can an individual develop personally without harming others or the environment?"

The world economy could change without lay-offs. As world markets for life enhancing and environmentally sound goods and services expanded, arms industries, drug, energy and electronic companies and others could gradually redirect research and development to qualify for these new markets. Business would adopt more life enhancing values. Attitudes would change as individuals, industry and governments experienced the benefits of serving the well being of people and Planet and saw poverty, unemployment, social disintegration, and pollution decrease.

The Supplementary Economy Is Similar to a Mail Order Barter System

Every year, a census in taken in every country to establish which wholesome, life enhancing goods and/or services every person wishes to order for the year. In the Technical and Evaluation Division of the U.N. Population Fund, it was suggested that countries could agree to attach a questionnaire to the ongoing census programme of each country. This questionnaire could be tabulated separately. This would be particularly useful while the infrastructure for the Marshall Plan is being put into place.

Each person is given a credit of the equivalent of US$250. Once a year each person is asked to order goods and services for up to the amount of this supplementary income for her or his personal development. Nothing harmful to anyone or the Planet may be ordered. The credit of those not wishing to participate is cancelled for that year.

These "orders" are entered on a computer banking system, which links all countries and people. Existing commercial banks are connected to this system both for the benefit of the consumers and of the producers. People who can supply the life enhancing goods and services requested also make this known to development workers and are matched with the demand. Once supply and demand are exactly matched, marketable goods and services have come into being and the exchange can take place.

How is this Supplementary Economy Financed?

In the past, a country's currency was considered "hard" to the degree it was covered by gold reserves. Today, a country's currency is considered "hard" to the degree it is covered by "marketable goods and services". In essence, money can be seen as a point system that is allocated to each product and service to facilitate barter.

In today's world both rich and poor limit currency production for opposing reasons. The rich have the potential to produce the goods and services, but lack the markets. The poor are in need of goods and services, but lack the ability to produce the necessary goods and services; and so neither is in a position to create hard currency as long as the currency is created on a national or regional basis. As soon as the world is seen as an economic whole, additional currency can be created to meet the WORLD situation of supply and demand. The additional currency can be divided among the world's population and can then be used to facilitate the exchange of goods and services as previously arranged via the computer system.

If the whole world were combined in one market, economists estimated that the world economy would be able to grow by 5%-10%. Let us say conservatively by 7%, if the production capacity would be matched by people's needs. This amount can then be used for several aims, including the building of the infrastructure and the implementation of this Plan. Once these costs have been deducted and the rest is divided equally among the world's population, each person would receive the equivalent of about US $ 250.

Each year more people will become contributors to this supplementary economy and so growth will continue. Each year by, say 7% and each person's part of the new economy will increase. (Because the whole world is in constant flux, these figures change constantly and these calculations would have to be done to meet the situation. The 7% is therefore just a means to illustrate how the financing would work.

The Supplementary Economy has two characteristics, not shared with any economy elsewhere in the world, made possible by modern computer technology and census taking infrastructures being developed with the support of the U.N. They are:

1. Every woman, man, and child has an account and is connected through this banking system;

2. It would be known from the outset, each year, exactly what is needed and what can be supplied through the U.N. Economy.

This makes it possible to create a hard international currency for this Supplementary Economy and to determine the goods and services that will promote wholesome human development.

How Do People Determine Which Goods and Services May Be Offered through this Supplementary Economy?

Decision making in connection with this Supplementary Economy should involve all people. One way proposed uses the *sociocratic method*, by which people must grant their consent to each decision for it to be taken. If consent is withheld, the decision must be reformulated.

To determine which goods and services are to be made available and which to be withheld, each community is divided into groups of approximately 25 persons who make community decisions regarding goods and services considered harmful and thus not permitted. Each of these small groups sends 2 members with the outcome of their decision making to the next level of decision making, say for the local regions. Here, too, people meet in groups of approximately 25 people. Again consent is sought. And then 2 of each group go to the next level, say the country level, and so the process continues. It was estimated that if all 6 billion people were involved in this form of decision making just 8 or 9 levels of decision making would be involved. This type of decision making is already used by some world organizations. The advantage that community is formed as such topics are discussed regarding what is wholesome and what harmful to individual or planetary health.

What is Required?

The proposed World Marshall Plan provides a supplementary income for all people in every nation. It will take about 10 years to build the necessary infrastructure.

The infrastructure will consist of:

1. an electronic communication system, such as the Internet, connected to a

2. Bank, which works exclusively with money transfers, rather than actual currency and is built on the model of the Dutch Giro System, run by a branch of a world institution, like the U.N.; with

3. accounts for every man, woman and child in the world; and

4. two U.N. development experts for every one thousand people, each with access to this fully computerized banking system both for informational and data entry purposes.

It Would Be Impossible To Achieve the Same Through World Taxes.

Organizationally, it would be very complicated and financially impossible to levy any form of world taxes in order to generate income for a worldwide development income for all people to be administered by the U.N. Nobel prize winner, Jan Tinbergen, calculated that the U.S.A. would have to provide 2/3 and the EC one-half of their means if every citizen in the world were to receive a reasonable income. He quite rightly considers this impossible. Rich countries would collapse through a lack of funds, money would become too expensive, and the poor countries would only be helped in an ad hoc fashion. Soon there would be a lack of purchasing power.

Great Advantages for Existing Economies.

Because the Supplementary Economy creates a constant upward pressure on existing economies, there are many advantages. After all, the same producers deliver to both economies.

Because of their extra income from the new economic circuit and the higher demands in terms of quality and environmental friendliness, producers will be able to manufacture better quality products in the original economies. There is, as it were, a wholesome interaction between all private businesses and those activities performed for the Supplementary Economy. This produces profit, spent differently in each economic circuit.

In this way both economic systems can be transformed, enabling the development of body and mind of the individual citizen. The Supplementary Economy constitutes a synthesis between market and planned economic approaches and the resulting balance benefits all people in every aspect of their existence. Every consumer is encouraged to function as both a national and a world citizen through the use of his or her supplementary income. As world citizen, he or she is directly connected to the U.N., if it is chosen as administrating agency (i.e. humanity). No national government or organization can take away these human rights and at the same time the increased individual well-being provides the stability which governments require to carry out their mandate.

We would be able to refer to the Supplementary Income as the much-needed Human Rights Economy, or a psychological and spiritual economy in which the development of body, mind and spirit are in balance. In this way, we can respond for the first time in history to our spiritual and political calling to produce a more loving and more reasonable world community, in which every individual can be a full-fledged partner in all situations.

Additional Characteristics of the Supplementary Economy

Decisions regarding which goods and services may be offered through the Supplementary Economy are made by all people in small community meetings. There are numerous precedents for this. Decisions will be made by consent, that is, people would have to agree on which products and services do not harm other people or the environment. This form of decision making builds community, raises consciousness and fosters responsibility with regard to the quality of life.

➢ **It Does Not Affect The Sovereignty Of Any Nation**

Instead it enables each person to choose ways of contributing to the regeneration of their own economic and social environment in ways that benefit all people and the nation as a whole.

➢ **It Finances Itself And Is of No Cost To Any Nation.**

On the contrary every individual, every business and consequently every country benefits.

➢ **No Interest Payments or Inflation, No Speculation. Less Likelihood of Fraud.**

There is a direct link between production and consumption and there are no interest payments. There is therefore no inflation and can be no speculation. The rules of this Marshall Plan are monitored by the development workers and by all individual people who so wish. There is therefore less likelihood that there would be fraud using U.N. dollars, than there is in today's less transparent economies.

➢ **Decrease In Pollution, Safeguarding Non-Renewable Resources**

Production will be pollution-free and selective, and based on the prior consent of all people. There would be one type of goods and services for those who are physically poor and other types for those who are financially well off and would benefit from mental or spiritual enrichment and the full range between these two extremes. Those receiving material goods are subject to regulation, because pollution and the depletion of natural resources through this Supplementary Economy is not permitted. In the long run these problems would significantly decrease.

➢ Less Unemployment

Unemployment will decrease drastically, as the supplementary economy expands and provides increased opportunities for new producers. As standards of living rise, the focus of the economy will shift from material goods (which often deplete the earth's resources) to services which refine personal and spiritual education, interpersonal and community relationships, and artistic and cultural expression. It will result in a constructive shift in the relationship between people and their planet.

For Contact information, please see ADDENDUM III

ADDENDUM III

Contact With The Author

How to purchase *Fearless*. *Ordinary People Doing Extraordinary Things in a World Gripped by Fear*

➤ **at a discount** via www.authorhouse.co.uk.

➤ In Europe and the Pacific region: AuthorHouse UK Ltd, 500 Avebury Boulevard, Milton Keynes, MK9 2BE, UK. Tel. +44 (0)8450 753456; Fax +44 (0)800 1974151, www.authorhouse.co.uk

➤ From the US: AuthorHouseTM, 1663 Liberty Drive, Suite 200, Bloomington, IN 47403, USA. Tel. +1 (888) 519.5121

➤ **via** www.amazon.com www.amazon.co.uk;; www.Barnes&nobel.com;

   www.Borders.com.

available for order at retail outlets and bookstores:

➤ throughout the UK, the rest of Europe, and the Asia Pacific marketplace via Bertrams, Gardners and Nielson BookData; and

➤ throughout North America via Ingram.

Other works by the Author

➤ *A World Citizens Manual*, available in English, Dutch, German and Chinese.

➤ *Crossroad. The Year 2000.* A basic income for every woman, man and child and the. Implementation of a Self-Financing World Marshall Plan for the Earth. (available in English and Dutch ISBN 90 391 0673 8)

➤ *Samenzwering Samenspel.* Naar spiritueel wereldburgerschap, ISBN 90 202 82581

> *A Listing of Financing Mechanisms* can be downloaded from www.worldcitizensaction.com.

For lectures/discussions, workshops, think tanks and books by Dr. Lisinka Ulatowska, author, educator, public speaker and UN NGO representative. (Languages: English, Dutch, German and French): info@worldcitizensaction.com; info@allwinnetwork.org; www.worldcitizensaction; www.allwinnetwork.org ;

Other Useful Contacts And Organizations

Prof. Dr. Ralph Abraham is an expert in Chaos Theory.

At a conference I helped to organize, Ralph set up an exercise, which gave me a first hand impression of how chaos theory can operate within groups of people: a life-changing experience for me!

For writings and appearances: homepage: www.ralph-abraham.org

with links to several other sites created and maintained by Ralph Abraham.

The All-Win Network is a network of individuals and organizations, that are applying the all-win principle to life and work, including to the content and process of education; and as a standard for human relations.

Activities: Talks/discussions, seminars, workshops, think tanks, educational programs for schools, and an all-win lobby of the United Nations.

Pim van Monsjou, Secretary General, Zweerslaan 31, NL 3723 HN Bilthoven, the Netherlands; www.allwinnetwork.org; E-mail info@allwinnetwork.nl.

The Association of World Citizens's goal is to work with people, progressive governments and international institutions to create a Global Village of lasting peace, social and economic jstice, and the foundation for a new civilizatin based on respect for life and the environment. President: Doug Mattern. Office, 55 New Montgommery St., Suite 224, San Francisco, CA 94105, USA. Tel. +1 415 541 9610. Fax 650 745 0640; E-mail info@worldcitizens.org

The Baha'i Community. The aim of the Baha'i Faith is the unification of humankind; its five million members are engaged worldwide in activities, open to all, designed to achieve that eventual goal. www.bahai.org

The BBC World Service provides international news, analysis and information in English and 42 other languages. Also programs on business, health, the environment, and high-quality entertainment. Most of their programs encourage input from the general public. Their global network of correspondents provide impartial news and reports on location. BBC World Service, Bush House, London, U.K; www.bbc.co.uk/worldservice/

The Self-financing World Marshall Plan (See Addendum II).

This plan was developed by the late Pieter Kooistra. Books on the self-financing World Marshall Plan by Pieter Kooistra and Lisinka Ulatowska can be ordered from:

Foundation for a Supplementary Income For All People, Waalbamdijk 8, 4664 CB Varik, the Netherlands. Tel. +31 (0)344 651 953; Fax +31 (0)344 651 2536. E-mail uno-inkomen@gmx.net. As this book goes to print, their web site is being overhauled.

The Challenge Day vision is that every child lives in a world where they feel safe, loved and celebrated. Its mission is to demonstrate the possibility of love and connection through the celebration of diversity, truth and full expression. Address: 3237 Alhambra Ave., Suite 2, Martinez CA 94553, USA. Phone: +1 925-957 0234; Fax +1 925-957-9425; Email: office@challengeday.org (a non-profit organisation)

The Club of Budapest's mission is to be a catalyst in the transition to a sustainable world through fostering a global consciousness and building bridges between generations and cultures, The President and Founder, Prof. Dr. Laszlo, is a prolific writer and, as speaker, much in demand. His most recent book, *Science and the Re-enchantment of the Cosmos: The New Vision of Reality,* by Inner Traditions International, Rochester, VT., USA. is due to appear in March 2006.

The Club of Budapest, International, Planet Plaza Heinbroich, D 141472, Neuss, Germany.

Phone: +39 0586 650 217; Fax: +39 0586 650 395; www.clubofbudapest. org.

EM Corporation and EM Research Organization. EM stands for Effective Micro-organisms. The term EM was coined by Dr. Teruo Higa, Ph.D. (" by himself.")

4-1-15, Yamauchi, Okinawa-City, Okinawa, 904-0034, JAPAN, Phone: +81-98-930-7100;

Fax: +81-98-930-7101, (HP http://www.emro.co.jp/english/)

Emissaries of Divine Light believe that people are responsible for the quality of their lives and experience. They offer seminars, workshops, conferences and writings which foster spiritual awakening and develop leadership skills. Through their classes, I have gained skills which are useful in working with the *field*. Sunrise Ranch, 5569 County Road 29, Loveland, Colorado 80538, USA. They have communities all over the world.

Global Education Motivators, Inc., educating a second generation to global awareness and responsibility in an interdependent world. Wayne Jacobi, 112 Woodland Drove, Landsdale, PA 19466, USA. www.gem.ngo. org

The Hunger Site. Once every day you can ensure one hungry person is given a free meal by visiting www.thehungersite.com and clicking on the *Enter* button.

The Institute for Planetary Synthesis. Goals: To awaken an awareness of spiritual values in daily life; to promote planetary awareness, which leads to planetary citizenship; to analyze and help solve world problems on the basis of spiritual values. IPS Geneva, Secretary General, Rudolf Schneider, P.O. Box 128, CH-12 Geneva 20, Switzerland. Tel. +41 (0)22 733 88 76;

Fax 733 66 49; E-mail ipsbox@ipsgeneva.com; www.ipsgeneva.com.

The Rainbow Bird: To order CDs by the Rainbow Bird, write to Freddy Narewski, Petkumerstr. 169. 26725 Emden, Germany. Tel. +49 (0) 4921 22418; e-mail lucina@rainbowbird.nl

Rupert Sheldrake, renouned author of many books, including on morphogenetic fields, www.sheldrake.org

World Women's Summit Foundation (WWSF) is an international, non-profit, non-confessional empowerment NGO (U.N. consultative status ECOSOC, U.N.FPA and DPI) serves to help implement women's and children's rights and the U.N. Millennium Development Goals MDGs. Every year it gives prizes to 35 rural women.

Elly Pradervand, WWSF Executive Director, 11 Avenue de la Paix, CH-1202 Geneva, Switzerland, Tel:+41 (0) 22 738 66 19 Fax +41 (0) 22 738 82 48,

E-mail wwsf@wwsf.ch, www.woman.ch

Social Venture Network, General Secretariat, Members of the Social Venture Network are businesses who are concerned with sustainable and ethical development. P.O. Box 29221, San Francisco, CA 94129-0221, USA. Tel +1 415 561 6501, E-mail, svn@svn.org.

The United Nations was founded to build, make and keep the peace.

U.N. Plaza, New York, NY 10017, USA. Tel. +1 212 967 1234. www. un.org

The United Nations Global Compact is a global platform which convenes companies together with United Nations Agencies and civil society in support of fundamental principles. Director, Georg Kell +1 212 963 1234; E-mail: global compact@un.org; .www.globalcompact.org

ENDNOTES

[1] Copyright Terry Burke, Little Bear Music (ASCAP). See Addendum III.

[2] The book by Ervin Laszlo is entitled, Science and the Re-enchantment of the Cosmos: The New Vision of Reality. Inner Traditions International, Rochester, VT. It is scheduled to appear in March 2006.

[3] Lynne McTaggart, the Field, ISBN 0 00 714510 1.

[4] This is an accurate description of the real Mary Duffield who is as active as ever, now almost ninety. Of course, the role she plays in this book is totally fictitious, although she actually works with young people much like these described here.

[5] Mary herself refers to this as *Planetary* Citizenship.

[6] The character, Pim, is also based on a true person—an engineer who specialized in artificial fertilizers (not bombs), and has spent the latter part of his life exploring and promoting new, inclusive paradigms. He founded and is Secretary General of the All-Win Network (See Addendum III). Pim's role in this novel is also fictitious.

[7] The role played by the U.N. University for Peace in this novel, as well as the meetings held there are fictitious. The U.N.'s University for Peace is indeed situated in Costa Rica.

[8] The role of the BBC World Service is fictitious in this novel. For more information on the BBC World Service, see Addendum III.

[9] The story told about St. Lawrence's experiences with Wayne Jacoby's Global Educational Motivators (See Addendum III) is true. Phoebe actually exists as a person but with a different name.

[10] For more information on Global Education Motivators, Inc. , see Addendum III.

[11] The school garden program is inspired by Fritjov Capra's Ecoliteracy Program. To receive his newsletter: Fritjof Capra PO Box 9066 Berkeley, CA 94709, USA.

¹²"The Saturday Morning Talkies" airs 9-10 a.m. on KPFA on Saturdays in the San Francisco Greater Bay Area. Kris also has another show LIVING ROOM", which airs noon to one Thursdays and Fridays.

¹³ Some of these shows do exist, but their role in this story is fictitious.

¹⁴This broadcast by the BBC World Service is fictitious. For more information on the BBC World Service, see Addendum III.

¹⁵ NGOs don't have offices inside the U.N. In the sequel to this novel, the All-Win Network is given a special office space to help governments at the U.N. introduce the all-win standard into human relations. This office does not, in fact, exist. To contact the All-Win Network Secretariat, see Addendum III

¹⁶ Prof. Dr. Erwin Laszlo, founder and president of the Club of Budapest (For more information, see Addendum III) writes in Chapter IV of his new book, *Science and the Re-enchantment of the Cosmos: The New Vision of Reality* (to be published in March 2006 by Inner Traditions International, Rochester, VT., USA):

> *"...according to the new physics, the particles and atoms – and the molecules, cells, and organisms – that arise and evolve in space and time emerge from the virtual energy sea that goes by the name of quantum vacuum [called in Fearless the morphogenetic or energy/information/ communication field] These things not only originate in the vacuum's energy sea; they continually interact with it. They are dynamic entities that read their traces into the Akasha or A-field-- the holograms they create are not evanescent. They persist and inform all things, most immediately the same kind of things that created them.*
>
> *"This holds true for our body and brain as well. All we experience in our lifetime, all our perceptions, feelings, and thought processes have cerebral functions associated with them. These functions have wave-form equivalents, since our brain, like other things in space and time, creates information-carrying vortices; it 'makes waves.' The waves propagate in the vacuum and interfere with the waves created by the bodies and brains of other people, producing complex holograms..*
>
> *The two-way transformation from brain to field and back again removes the limitation on information storage by the brain alone. This would be a major limitation, for the brain alone does not have sufficient information-processing capacity to produce and store the perceptions,*

sensations, volitions and emotions we experience in our lifetime. Computer scientist Simon Berkovitch calculated that to produce and store a lifetime's experiences the brain would have to carry out 10 to the 24th power operations per second. [...]

Even if normally our A-field [information field] recall is limited to what we ourselves have read into it —that is, to our own long-term memory-store — there are instances in which we can access other people's holograms. These holograms are primarily those of people with whom we are physically or emotionally bonded for example, our sibling, parents, children, spouses, and lovers. In near-death experiences, out-of-body experiences, past-life experiences, some varieties of mystical and religious experiences, and the experience of communication with the deceased it is their holograms we access, and not only ours. This broader access endows our mind with an element of universality, even of immortality.

[17] Copyright Terry Burke, Little Bear Music (ASCAP). Terry Burke and Luci Narewski together form a duo, called the Rainbow Bird. They have a large repertoire of international songs and others which they, themselves, compose. Their role in this novel is totally fictitious.(For more information, see Addendum III)

[18] The legislation described here is inspired by the US Patriot Act which was passed soon after the September 11th attacks within the US and, as I complete the last draft of this novel in July 2005, is still in tact. The Patriot Act has much in common with similar legislation passed in other countries, including the UK and Australia. More and more countries are, step by step, following the US's example.

[19] See the book, *Tranen van de Krokodil* by Dutchman, Piet Vroon, ISBN 9041405534.

[20] Prof. Dr. Ervin Laszlo, an authority on systems theory, helps us to visualize how an atmosphere (be it of fear or of anything else), which he refers to as the A-field or Akasha field (and in this book is called energy/ information field or simply *the field*) can permeate everything. He points out that Physicist, Kamerling Onnes won the Nobel Prize in 1913 for being the first to liquefy helium by cooling it until its density had increased 800 times. Under 4 degrees on the Kelvin scale the density effects become manifest--and when further cooled, the superfluid effect. When superfluid: it could flow through almost anything, because it produces practically no friction. Consequently, we can be permeated by a superfluid substance, or an

"atmosphere" for that matter without knowing it is there. And yet, it would have an effect. This can also explain why fear tends to be "infectious."

[21] Prof. Dr. Erwin Laszlo points out that in the case of the information field, the effect would be to "in-form matter" or "provide the information which will determine the form matter will adopt." Genes absorb information from the information field which permeates them, and so do our brains. So it is the field and not the genes or the brain that stores information. Our brains simply don't have the necessary capacity. Genes and brains are receivers and transmitters of information and energy.

To substantiate this point, Laszlo goes to quantum mechanics where it has been established that two electrons which have been in contact with one another constantly stay in touch. When one is made to spin in a different direction, the other will follow suit, despite separation across time and space. The information would be instantly available to the second electron via the information field.

A similar experiment was done with humans. They were divided into two groups. One group was hooked up to EEG machines and asked to synchronize their brain hemispheres. (These are normally not synchronous while we're awake). All people in this group had been trained in meditation. In the other room, they had gathered a group of close friends of each of the first group members. These were also hooked up to EEG machines so that the brain waves in their hemispheres could be monitored, too. Two seconds after the EEG machine of a person in the first room registered that her or his brain hemispheres were synchronized, the brain hemispheres of the person he or she was close to in the other room became synchronized, too. This experiment seems to substantiate the existence of the all-permeating information field (also, as we have seen, called by Laszlo the *A- or Akasha field* and by Rupert Sheldrake *morphogenetic fields*). These two experiments also support the phenomenon of telepathy and explain why fear tends to be "infectious."

[22] Prof. Dr. Ralph Abraham, mathematician and expert in the field of chaos systems' theory, points out that this field has been modeled mathematically. It is also generally agreed that there is an immaterial information field and an energy field. The two are related, but scientists do not agree on how.

[23] The Seth books by Jane Roberts provide an interesting perspective which has much in common with the scientific theories presented here.

[24] See endnote 16.

[25] See endnote 20.

[26] Prof. Dr. Erwin Laszlo, (For more information, see Addendum III) writes in Chapter IV of his new book, *Science and the Re-enchantment of the Cosmos: The New Vision of Reality* (See footnote 14):

[The interactions with the field create complex holograms]. Generations after generations of humans have left their holographic traces in the A-field [information field].

These individual holograms integrate in a superhologram, which is the encompassing hologram of a tribe, community, or culture. The collective holograms interface and integrate in turn with the super-superhologram of an entire species. This is the 'collective unconscious' of humanity: our shared memory bank.

To some extent we can read the holograms created by other humans as well. On the principle of 'like meshes with like,' we can first of all read the hologram we ourselves have created. Reading out what we have read into the A-field [information field] *is like reading out the materials we have placed on the Internet. If we have the right key, we can retrieve all the things we have placed there, at any time.*

Reading out what we have read into the A-field is the basis for long-term memory. The key to this extrasomatic memory store is the structure of our brain and body: this is what has created the vacuum-waves that make up our hologram, and this is also the code that selects this hologram and allows us to retrieve the information it contains

[27] Professor Ralph Abraham is an expert on chaos theory. He showed this film at a conference in the Netherlands, *Seeds of Wholeness, Science, Systems, Spirit (2001)*. In this conference, we employed systems theory to inspire conference participants to work together cross-culturally and inter-disciplinarily. Ralph Abraham ended his lecture with an experiment in which he divided up the Conference participants completely randomly into groups of 3 and then asked each group to come up with a fully designed project, accompanied by a financing plan. At the end of one and a half days, it turned out that all 50 participants had created integral parts of one overarching project.

[28] Ralph Abraham stresses that chaotic signals operate according to precise formulas and are not the same as random signals. The important point here is that the computers are out of sync with one another and at the end of the experiment they are *in sync with one another.*

²⁹ As I was correcting this part, I suddenly realized I have, quite unconsciously, taken over the phrase "Evolutionary Leap" from Peter Russell's book with the same title.

³⁰ The U.N. invites groups of so-called 'Eminent Personalities' to advise them on important issues. Eleanor Roosevelt played a central role in the development of the Universal Declaration of Human Rights.

³¹ The sequel to this novel, *Samenzwering Samenspel. Naar spiritueel wereldburgerschap* (ISBN 90 202 82581) tells how Recluse came by this knowledge. It also shows in more detail how this (fictitious) organization works to maintain a hold on our world. *Samenzwering Samenspel* is available in Dutch.

³² The broadcast by the BBC World Service is fiction.

³³ *The World Corruption Watch* does not exist in this form. There are a number of organizations (NGOs) which monitor businesses, including some which are associated with the U.N.'s Global Compact.

³⁴ The statistics on the Baha'is are accurate and so is the possibility of carrying out such an action. The role of everyone in this part of the narrative is however fiction.

³⁵ See Addendum I for a copy of the Universal Declaration of Human Rights.

³⁶ The Universal Declaration of Human Rights, 1948, is available from the U.N. in its six official languages: Arabic, Chinese, French, English, Russian and Spanish and probably in many other languages and from regional U.N. Informational Centers. The U.N.'s address: U.N., U.N. Department for Public Information, New York, NY 10017 USA, Tel. +1 212 963 1234, E-mail: www.un.org.

³⁷ Eugenie Nouale Nkoro was awarded a prize by the Women's World Summit Foundation in 2003 for women's creativity in rural life. Each year, five of the 35 prize winners are invited to the U.N. where, usually with the help of an interpreter, they are allowed to speak before NGOs. They are also treated to a dinner. It is moving and humbling to meet such women. Many have never been outside of their country. Some live in huts with dirt floors and have just one spoon to their name. So many women have been able to achieve so much with so little! Many of them have inspired 1000s of other

women in their areas. Elly Pradervand, Executive Director of WWSF points out that women do 2/3 of the world's work, earn 10% of the world's income; and own less than 1%of the world's property. For more information about WWSF, See Addendum III.

[38] As this book goes to print, this network is being developed.

[39] Also called *Emissaries of Divine Light*. See Addendum III.

[40] The Emissaries call this 'generating substance'. In their classes, they teach how this is done.

[41] The Baha'i Office of Public Information, opi@bwc.org. See Addendum III.

[42] For more information, see **www.unglobalcompact.org**. See Addendum III.

[43] All-Win Business, International is mentioned in the sequel to this novel. It does not exist yet, as far as I know. The Social Venture Network bears some similarity.

[44] The *Global Compact* consists of three aspects: a letter of intent to keep to nine international agreements and only to do business with firms that honor these, too; the commitment to regularly join in discussions with other Global Compact member businesses to explore how best to comply; and every year to hold an audit for the whole world to read describing in how far the company has made progress in abiding by the nine agreements. The Global Compact is monitored by NGOs

[45] The Global Compact addresses three fields: 1. *human rights*. 2. *labor laws*: your employees have the right to collective bargaining, no forced or compulsory labor, abolition of child labor, and elimination of discrimination in respect of employment. 3. the *environment*: err on the side of precaution, be responsible at all times and support environmentally friendly technologies. In all cases your firm undertakes to respect the nine laws and not tolerate abuses in any firm you do business with.

[46] For more information on the Social Venture Network, see Addendum III.

[47] For more information on the Global Compact, see Addendum III.

[48] Although all three organizations exist and each one provides valuable trainings, their role in this novel is fictitious.

[49] Although this story is set in 2010, it is true, that Rajiv and his wife did a great deal in the past to encourage young people to communicate internationally, using ham radio.

[50] Freddy inspired a program in the Santa Cruz area for young non-English speaking offenders, who were deemed to have taken to criminality out of frustration with the language. They were unable to get a foothold without the necessary English language skills. Mary and her friends organized English classes in Juvenile Halls, using tape recorders. The young offenders would complete a lesson and then speak it into a tape recorder. The thought that they have something to say that is worth recording improves the way they feel about themselves and increases their self-confidence. I hear that when we focus our full loving attention on people with Altzheimer's, and take them fully seriously, this can also have a beneficial effect.

[51] NGOs are *Non*-Governmental Organizations in contrast to the U.N., which is referred to as a Governmental Organization, because its Members are Governments.

[52] The World Federalists have proposed a variety of mechanisms for making the UN more democratic. To extend the U.N.'s General Assembly to make 'binding' decisions, they have proposed various 'weighted and qualified voting' proposals. The above proposal is called the "*binding triad*"Its author is Richard Hudson of the Center for War and Peace.. Here I have taken the liberty to apply the binding triad idea to Security Council resolutions to ensure they carry the necessary support to be fully implemented.

[53] One of Mary Duffield's networks of ham radio operators did indeed plant two million trees. In reality, the young man who led this project was also suffering from a terminal disease, but his circumstances and character have been changed. He, too, passed away soon after the project had been completed.

[54] The Universal Declaration of Human Rights has been translated into The Covenant of Economic and Social Rights, the Covenant of Civil and Political Rights and the Optional Protocol. In this form, it can easily be inserted into Nations' and regional Constitutions.

[55] All these programs exist.

[56] For more information on The Challenge Day program, see Addendum III.

[57] The U.N. has a blue book, listing all the addresses of its Ambassadors.

[58] A distinction can be made between feelings and emotions. *Feeling* is often used interchangeably with *sensing*, or *intuiting*. *Emotion* comes from the Latin root *emovere*- to move away from. In fact, when you are responding to your association with something you perceive, you either *move away* from it (if you feel a painful feeling) or try to hold on to the situation, thus, by your action, *moving away* from the natural flow of reality.

[59]Emotions are deeply connected to the musculature of the human body.
This can be perceived from within:
Pull a sad face and if you pay close attention, you will notice that you *feel sad*.
To envision how this works, think of the human body as a guitar. The muscles are like its strings. When you shorten one combination of strings on a guitar, you might get a minor chord and you will feel a sense of melancholy. Shorten a different combination, and you get a jarring impression. So, too, with your muscles, when you tense different combinations, you change the emotional "tune". In other words, how you feel emotionally, and the hue of your emotionally-tinged glasses.
This 'emotional tune' (or the emotionally-colored glasses) through which you experience reality can be likened to the background music in a film, as mentioned above.
It is often difficult to be aware of our emotions from the inside (to know the full extent of what we are feeling)., since we have become habituated to them and barely know what it is like to be without them. And so they can color everything we experience and, because we don't know they are influencing us, we can't do anything about it.

Emotions can also to some extent be seen from the outside (by others)
In some cases, the connection between musculature and emotion is easy to see. When a person frowns with mouth corners turned down, stands with hunched shoulders and clenched fists, you think, 'That person looks angry!"

When they smile, they are tensing a different combination of muscles and give a happier impression.

But most of us experience life through complex sets of emotions. We may feel angry and cover it up with sadness because, unconsciously, we fear arousing aggression in others and prefer to arouse pity. These complex combinations of emotions are much harder to read from the outside.

To resolve a conflict durably, it is important to make each party's emotion-colored glasses conscious for all parties to see.

We can experience another persons emotional screen by adopting their body posture and facial expression. (This is connected with the information field which in-forms and connects people and things with similar forms.)

. **To become aware of our own emotion-tinted glasses**, we can use the approach used by Pim or certain types of meditation (for temporary removal) or to become conscious of them all the time, I have found a combination of the teachings of J. Krishnamurti with a variety of therapeutic and spiritual approaches helpful.

We can become aware of other people's emotions. The approach used by Pim (In chapter 69) is to free oneself from one's own emotional bias through relaxation (and/or meditation) and then to "read" another's experience by adopting their "form": body posture and facial expression. The similarity in form connects us to their morphogenetic field.

[60] This process is gone into in more detail in the sequel to this book, *Samenzwering Samenspel. Naar spiritueel wereldburgerschap.* (See Addendum III)

[61] The teachings of Krishnamurti used in conjunction with a wide range of psychological and spiritual tools can be helpful in developing this capacity.

[62]Ervin Laszlo in his book, *Science and the Reenchantment of the Cosmos: The New Vision of Reality* (See endnote 14) describes the process as follows:

"Experiences that testify to consciousness extending beyond the physical brain are also reported by psychotherapists who place their patients in an altered state of consciousness and record the impressions that surface in their minds. Stanislav Grof notes that in the 'experience of dual unity,' a person in an altered state of consciousness can experience a loosening and melting of the boundaries of the body ego and a sense of merging with another person in a state of unity and oneness. In the experience of 'identification with other persons,' merging can be total and complex, involving body image, physical sensations, emotional reactions and attitudes, thought processes, memories, facial expressions, typical gestures and mannerisms, postures, movement, and even the inflection of the voice. In 'group identification and group consciousness' one can have a sense of becoming an entire group of people with shared racial, cultural, national, ideological, political, or professional characteristics. In deeply altered states, it is possible to expand one's consciousness to the point where it encompasses the totality of life on the planet. It can also extend to the inorganic domains of nature.

Analogous experiences are reported by astronauts. Apollo X captain Edgar Mitchell said that in higher states of awareness every cell of the body coherently resonates with 'the holographically embedded information in the quantum zero-point energy field.' In Science and the Reenchantment of the Cosmos: The New Vision of Reality, such resonance is logical and understandable. It is conveyed by the Akashic A-field [information field] that underlies and connects all things, from particles to galaxies.

[63] One such project works with buffalo that used to live in San Francisco's Golden Gate Park.

[64] A similar story was told on US television in the early 1980s. I'm afraid I neither remember the name of the person who told this story, nor the television channel that broadcast the interview.

[65] The Universal Declaration belongs to the body of *traditional* human rights, because these rights have been generally accepted as a standard for so long; they therefore apply to every person, no matter where he or she lives. Moreover, most countries in the world have also adopted the *Universal Declaration* as a part of their Constitutions via the so-called "*International Covenants on Economic, Social, and Cultural,* and of *Civil and Political Rights and the Optional Protocol.* This means that all governments of this large majority of nations, besides being bound by traditional international law, are also legally bound to implement laws which are derived from the Universal Declaration by their own constitutions.

[66] All-Win Business, International is a fictitious organization.

[67] For more information on EM Research Corporation, see Addendum III above.

[68] For more information on this technology, http://www.rakuten.co.jp/goemco. (In Japanese and English)

[69] For more information: http://www.letsystem.org/

⁷⁰ See Addendum II for a synopsis of the self-financing World Marshall Plan . E-mail uno-inkomen@gmx.net. The following books provide more information: *The Ideal Self-Interest, An extra World basic income for all people* by Pieter Kooistra, ISBN 90 7084 1011; and *The Year 2000—Crosroad of Mankind* by Lisinka Ulatowska available from The Foundation UN-Income for All People, Waalbamdijk 8, 4064 CBVarik, the Netherlands. Or from www.worldcitizensaction.com; or www.allwinnetwork.org.

A copy of: *A Listing of Financing Mechanisms* can be downloaded from www.worldcitizensaction.com.

⁷¹ Copyright Terry Burke, Little Bear Music (ASCAP).

⁷² The United Nations Development Programme has had a number of such projects whereby slum dwellers were given the means to replace their shacks with brick houses. A condition: that they tear down their old habitations to make sure no one else would take them over. A delight to see these houses five years later, covered in colorful Bourgainvilla.

⁷³ Copyright Terry Burke, Little Bear Music (ASCAP)

About The Author

Lisinka Ulatowska has a Ph.D. in Psychology. Since 1969, she has been associated with the U.N., first working for its Department of Public Information (formerly OPI), now as an NGO representative of the Association of World Citizens and the Institute for Planetary Synthesis. At the U.N., she co-founded and chaired an NGO Task Force on Financing. She has written among others: A World Citizens Manual (available in English, Dutch, German and Chinese); and the Year 2000 on the implementation of a self-financing World Marshall Plan. Fearless is her second novel, a sequel to Samenzwering Samenspel which has inspired an international All-Win Network, consisting of organizations and activists "with heart" who are helping humanity to transform into a durable global community in which all can flourish in their own ways.

Printed in the United States
37660LVS00005B/16-78